VINDICE

BY

2

Jerry Baker

Special thanks to Sheriff Darrel Bobbitt

For your friendship and encouragement

in the writing of this book.

4

Chapter 1

Fury poured down Jake Powell's face like sweat as he scanned the remains of the city he loved, Atlanta. He had heard the stories from troops he'd met on the roads as he made his way back home through the beaten South, after a war he knew could have been victorious for the Confederacy if only they had two more sacks of flour and another shotgun. In reality, Jake knew the war was senseless and totally unnecessary. The North and South could have lived in harmony as good neighbors, but Lincoln wanted the South's money. After all, who was going to pay for the government to run like Lincoln wanted it to.

He had heard of the devastation left by Sherman in his "March to the Sea". The stories left behind by Sherman and his men traveled down the roads of the south while weary southern soldiers, brave men who stood and fought for a freedom worth dying for, made their way back to their homes.

Some found their homes destroyed, families and possessions taken away by murdering thieves hiding behind what they boasted to be a righteous cause, preserving the Union. Some of those wounds would never heal.

Jake thought of a town he passed through in North Carolina as he made his way back to Georgia. He didn't remember the name of the town but he did remember it was under Union authority and the Union Army was out in force patrolling the streets, hopeful that a still angry southern boy would step out of line. He remembered hearing a man dressed in a fancy suit talking to some black folks that had gathered around him in front of a general store. The man in the suit spoke false words to those people about the atrocity of slavery and how they should hate the southern man for what they had done to them and their people before them. Jake wanted to drag the man by his fancy jacket collar out in the street and beat him until he changed his mind to the truth. Jake knew doing that would have gotten him locked up and brought before a harsh military court ran by the north. He never owned a slave and he knew many a man that fought who didn't as well. He knew the truth and he lived it. He had no idea at the time how much this war and its carnage would forever affect his life.

Jake Powell, a broad shouldered six foot four sandy brown haired Georgian entered the war a cavalry boy eighteen years of age. His right shoulder was scarred by an angry musket ball from a union rifle, a scar still tender from a bayonet on his right side and many reminders on his bearded face showed the effects of growing up in just a few years fighting for his life. He was tough, and strong as a bull.

As he walked down a dirt street in Atlanta, his sharp green eyes surveyed the damage left by the Union forces. He shook his head in disbelief. His long sandy brown hair caught the breeze that traveled through this once beautiful place. The muscles in his strong arms hardened, filling with hot southern blood, as he clinched his fist in anger from what he saw. It made him wish the war was still going so he could attempt to satisfy the thirst for revenge that welled inside of him. He knew he had to calm down or he would get himself in trouble. He stopped and closed his eyes and thought of the one he had left behind. He thought of his sweetheart, Sarah.

Sarah Tunstall was the most beautiful girl Jake had ever known. They met at church but still a passion raged inside the both of them they had at times failed to hold back. He thought of the night before he left to join the Confederate Cavalry. It was a wonderful night. He could not imagine a more meaningful send off as Sarah gave him. That night he held her in his arms after they made love. Her long golden hair blanketed his rock like shoulder as Sarah rested her head on his muscular chest. Her sky blue eyes filled with tears as she lay there thinking that the next day could be the last time she might see Jake. She wanted to make the most of it so she gave in to her desires and made love with him.

Jake allowed the thoughts of Sarah to calm him down from the rage he felt after seeing the leftovers from the war. He quickened his pace and his stride extended as he set his goal of getting to the house Sarah shared with her parents. He couldn't remember the name of the street but he knew how to get there. Jake thought of breaking out into a run but his tired legs talked him out of it.

While away, Jake remembered getting letters from Sarah. He carried them, twelve in all, in an inside pocket of his jacket. He figured when the letters stopped the Union had halted any movement of mail to the Confederate forces, so his hopes and memories of Sarah kept him going along with the determination of forcing the Union Army from his beloved Southland.

As Jake covered the streets that separated the homes in this once thriving city, he ran into a family he remembered. It was the Garrett family and they were gathered together in the front yard of a house that had been burned down completely. There was a haggard looking man in what was left of a gray uniform with the folks. The man was holding on to the shoulder of an elderly gentleman who appeared to be praying with the family. Sorrow covered the face of an elderly lady there as her weathered wrinkled hands held a Bible to her heart. He recognized her as Theodore Garrett's mother. Her husband, weeping as well stood by her side. All Jake remembered them by was Mr. and Mrs. Garrett. No doubt they had just received news of their son Theodore being killed in battle. The man in the gray uniform, the one assigned with the task of bringing the story of the tragedy home to a brave fallen soldier's family, appeared weak from his journey. He had trouble standing as the elderly gentleman praying caught the battle worn soldier by the arm to steady him.

"Father, in the name of Jesus, cover this sweet family with your peace and reassurance that their dear boy Theodore rests in your gracious and merciful arms", the elderly gentleman prayed. "May he see your glory for all of eternity. I pray in your Holy Name, Amen."

Jake stopped and faced the grief stricken family and saluted as he remembered Theodore was the only child of this family. He thought, as he brought his saluting right hand slowly to his side of the many other families feeling the same terrible grief as this one. He continued on and turned his mind back to Sarah and how joyful he will be once he wraps his arms around her and to absorb the love from her heart for him.

Block after city block went by as Jake remembered the buildings, shops and homes that once stood. Houses full of laughing children with hearts full of excitement once decorated these neighborhoods where life was sweet to those that lived here. Now despair occupies these places. Despair not felt by the people who make up the families of the north. They weren't treated with such evil disregard. General Lee would not have stood for it. Still, it's done and the rebuilding must commence.

Jake held a dirty hand up in front of him shading his vision from an afternoon sun that stared him in the face. He squinted his eyes trying to let in just enough light to see into the brightness of the day. He caught a glimpse of a stately wood frame house still standing. It's the house Sarah lives in with her parents. Its white paint showed signs of soot from smoke of the fires that burned out of control from a northern attack on the city. The homes proud face now tarnished by a war brought on by a government filled with hate and disrespect for the people they call fellow Americans. He quickened his pace, never taking his eyes off the house where the eyes of his sweetheart waited to look upon his face.

Jakes heart was racing, not from the pace he maintained in the distance he covered when he recognized Sarah's house, but from the anticipation he felt in the long awaited reunion of the woman whom he adored. He stopped just for a second at the gate that stood between the street and her front door. Jake took a deep breath before pushing the gate open and then rushing to the steps that lead up to the porch that wrapped around the entire house. He saw the swing was gone that hung from the rafters of the porch cover. He was confused because he knew Sarah loved it and how she loved swinging on it with him while laughing and stealing glances at one another. Jake knocked on the door, his heart pounding expecting to see Sarah. He heard footsteps inside approach the door. Suddenly the door opened and there stood an elderly black lady that Jake recognized as Miss Peachy, the lady who worked for Mr. and Mrs. Tunstall, Sarah's parents. She stood slightly stooped over from the years but she was able to look Jake in the face with big brown eyes that looked as if they could see right into Jakes soul.

"Miss Peachy?", Jake asked taking his old gray cavalry cap off of his head revealing a scar on his hair line left there by a Union bayonet.

Miss Peachy as she was called, was in the employ of the Tunstall's. They abhorred slavery and paid their help well. Miss Peachy was one of the family to the Tunstall's. She had worked as their house keeper and cook for as long as Jake could remember. As far as Jake knew Peachy was all the name she had. He had no recollection of a last name for her.

Peachy looked up and said with a heavy black southern accent, "Yes, I Miss Peachy and who is you?"

Jake swallowed hard and took a deep breath. He looked down at his boots as a shy boy before saying. "I'm Jake, Jake Powell, Sarah's caller. Is she here?" He asked looking up and over Miss Peachy's slumped shoulders to see if he could catch a glimpse of her. Peachy stood about five feet tall so Jake, at six foot two inches had no problem seeing over the elderly lady.

Jake felt his heart trying to beat right out of his chest. He looked down into Miss Peachy's eyes and saw tears. They rolled down her dark wrinkled cheeks as her bottom lip began to quiver. She stood in silence trying to think of the words to say to Jake. She knew he had been through a lot while he was gone but so had this little family Peachy was a part of and loved dearly. She took her kerchief from the sleeve of her black and white maids dress and wiped her eyes. Jake could tell all was not well.

Peachy opened the door to the house all the way welcoming Jake into the home that she so diligently took care of all these years. Jake stepped in still holding his cavalry cap in front of him. He looked around what part of the house he could see trying to take in any sign or evidence of Sarah. There was a sick feeling in Jake's gut that told him Sarah was not there. He remained silent, his eyes still moving through every inch of the rooms he could see trying to see Sarah or anything that could put his heart at ease. Miss Peachy walked by him still silently weeping over what she was about to tell Jake.

"I spect you betta come in heah and take a sit. I's got the awfulest story to tell you," Miss Peachy said as she walked into the sitting room of the house.

The sitting room was where the Tunstalls received their guests through the years. There had been gatherings for an assortment of occasions from Mr. Tunstall's nephew's wedding reception to Sarah's piano recital. Still, every picture on the walls hung perfectly in place and there was not a speck of dust to be seen. Peachy went out of her way to make this house a home for the Tunstalls.

Jake brushed the seat of his gray Confederate uniform pants before he sat down. He chose the same dark green cloth chair he had sat in the few times the Tunstalls welcomed him in to their home. The fabric covering the cushion was soft and fancy. The arms and legs of the chair were stained a dark brown. He had a concerned look on his face that showed the dread he had for the news he was about receive from Miss Peachy. He put his cap on the floor by is feet and looked up at her with pleading eyes, bracing himself for what he was afraid to hear.

Miss Peachy shook her head from side to side as she searched her heart for the right words to say to Jake. She knew how Sarah felt about Jake from all the nights she talked to Peachy about the plans they had made when he came calling. Sarah never would accept the fact that Jake was bound to go to war as soon as he reached the legal age to step up and volunteer. Sure as the world he made that decision the day he turned eighteen. His Pa gave his permission and Jake headed to Athens Georgia to muster up with the 3rd Georgia Calvary.

She took a deep breath and said, "I guess dey ain't but one way to tell you than jist to come out wit it. Sarah is dead. So is Mr. Tunstall and the Misses. Dem Union devils come up in here and went to tearing up evathang. Miss Sarah was a walkin back from the chuch and them Union soldiers grabbed her up right out in fronta da house. It was awful, jist plum awful. Mr. Tunstall took off afta dem no good fa nuttin wreaches and dey shot him dead rat out chonder in the skreet. Oh Mister Jake it was terrible, awful terrible."

Miss Peachy began to cry out load. Jake reached out and touched her frail shoulder to give her support. He had to know so he came out and asked.

"What happened to Sarah?" Jake asked not wanting to hear the answer.

Miss Peachy looked up at Jake and through tear filled eyes and said, "Dem Northern devils took her down and dey had dey way wit her. She screamed and fought but dey wa too skrong. Afta dey done dey deed dey just shot her as dey walked away justa laughin. I hope dey in hell fer it."

Miss Peachy hated to tell Jake but she knew he wanted to know. She wiped tears away again and looked up at Jake and said. "I wa in the back room wif da babies but when I heard the ruckus I came out to see. It wa awful, jist plain awful. It was dat

General Sherman's men what done all this..I hear bout his men kilt an had dey way with slave girls too. Tant no doubt with all da mixed babies runnin round Georgia now. Dey say dat Lincoln up in Washington knew how all the foke down heah was gettin treated. He jist let it go. Dat man didn't care bout peoples down heah, black nor white, free nor slave. Lawd hep us." She just shook her head and got quiet.

Jake and Miss Peachy sat in silence. Jake wiped away tears from his eyes. His heart broke from hearing this terrible story. He loved Sarah more than words could describe. The dream of being with her for the rest of his life gave him strength to carry on through the war many times. They had talked about a little horse farm. They talked about growing cotton and a few head of cattle. Dreams that many young couples had and cultivated by talking and planning on porch swings and picnics all over the country. The dreams and plans he and Sarah made were destroyed. Destroyed by a government led by a man who just wanted the south back in the union for its money. He could let his hate grow to such a rage he could turn to a life of crime against those that could have made the decision to allow the Confederate States of America to be a neighboring country, but he knew it would get him nowhere and he knew Sarah would not approve.

Suddenly Jake stopped his thoughts and looked over at Peachy as she put her kerchief back under her sleeve. The white cotton kerchief with its lace around the edges got a lot of use over the last few years. He sat back in his chair and cleared his throat.

"You said you were in the back room with the babies. Were you keeping them for somebody?" Jake asked out of curiosity not knowing what to expect in an answer to his question.

Miss Peachy put her fingers to her lips as if she regretted saying anything about the babies. She held her hand there and her eyes to Jake's. Miss Peachy always told the truth in all things. She however wasn't sure what the truth might bring. She closed her eyes and sighed out loud.

"You needs to know Mr. Jake. Dems yo babies. Miss Sarah say you da onlyest man she evah be wif. She wa proud you be dey daddy. She talked awful lot bout you and her would rearum up proper once you got back." Peachy watched for Jakes reaction to what she had just told him.

Jake closed his eyes and rubbed his temples trying to make sense of all he had just been told. He held his head down thinking, wishing that he would just wake up from this terrible nightmare to find out that none of this ever happened. That he and Sarah were asleep side by side in the Tunstall's porch swing. He had to accept the fact that this was all very real. Sarah was gone and now he is left with the responsibility of raising children.

"You said babies. How many are there?" Jake asked.

Miss Peachy smiled and said, "Sarah brought you twins, frayternal twins, dey callem. A boy and a girl. Dey just precious. Dey wa bone Febuwary fourteen of sixty three makin dem two and haf. Dey down fa dey nap rat now but it'll be time to gitum up drectly."

She got up and started toward the back of the house. The babies stayed close to Miss Peachy all the day long. She took care of them as well as if she herself was their mother. Peachy never thought of them as being any trouble or a burden. She loved them like her own but she always knew there was a possibility of Jake returning from the war and she hated the thought of ever having to let them go.

Miss Peachy stayed gone a good ten minutes. Then suddenly she appeared with the children. The two toddled in behind her holding each other's hand as they entered the sitting room.

"Come on in heah babies. Time to meet cho daddy. Mister Jake, this is Flora and Jacob." Miss Peachy smiled big showing her pearly white teeth. She thought how joyous this day would be if Miss Sarah was here to see it.

The little girl, Flora had big blue eyes like her mother. Her hair was like gold and it hung straight down just like her mother's hair. She looked at Jake with eyes that showed complete confusion. She wore a white cotton dress that went to her ankles with white lace socks. She smiled big as she looked at her father for the very first time in her life.

The little boy, Jacob, took a seat on the floor as he looked up curiously at this strange man. His little teeth shone as he gave his father a grin. Every time his and his father's eyes met, he grinned big. Little Jacob had golden blonde hair like his sister that was growing out. Jake thought, it won't be long until he took him for his first haircut. He had fat little arms like most little boys and Jake hoped he would grow up strong and lean just like him.

"Hey little Jacob." Jake said to the toddler. He got more grins from him.

Jake knew it would take time for the littles ones to get used to being around him. He wanted to spend as much time with them as he could but he knew he had to find work. He had no idea what was available since everything was in such devastation. He walked into the lives of his children and Miss Peachy with nothing but the clothes on his back. He pondered the thought of asking Miss Peachy if he could stay here at the

Tunstall house with her and the babies in spite of him still feeling out of place in a way.

Jake reached out to Little Flora and opened both hands to see if she would come to him. Her big blue eyes got even bigger as she looked with puzzlement at the two dirty hands of her father. She backed away not out of being scared but rather not being quite sure of the situation. Jake thought, this might take a little time'. He knew the love from the children Sarah brought in to this world by him would be the only replacement for her. A different kind of love of course but a product of the love he and Sarah shared in their very short time together.

"Come on Sweet Flora, I won't hurt you." Jake gave her a smile and she smiled back but still kept her distance.

Jake thought to himself, maybe I smell bad. He knew he had to since it had been quite a while since he had been under some hot bath water. Quick baths in just any old creek or stock pond they ran across during the war just didn't get you clean.

"Miss Peachy, can I stay here with you and the babies?" he asked. "I promise I won't be any trouble." He spoke without ever taking his eyes off of his children. He was feeling the love of a father at the birth of a child, yet these were two years old. He just wished he would have been here when they were born.

Miss Peachy looked up from the babies and smiled big and said, "I was sho hopin you'd ast me dat. You gots a awful lots a catchin up ta do. Let's gits you started wif a baf."

Miss Peachy went to Mr. Tunstall's closet and found pants and shirts suitable for Jake to wear. Mr. Tunstall was an attorney so he didn't have much use for clothes worn by hard men like Jake. He mainly had suits and formal clothes. Mr. Tunstall did however keep a pair or two of work-around-the-house pants and shirts. He was a big man like Jake, tall and relatively broad through the shoulders, just not muscular as Jake. The boots Jake had on would have to do. They were a high cavalry boot. They fit him well and they were well broke in.

That was the best bath Jake had had in some time. It felt good to be clean once again. The faded cotton trousers and tan cotton work shirt Miss Peachy found for Jake to wear fit just fine. He was ready to get a good meal in his belly and lay down in a clean comfortable bed.

After a hot supper of Pork bone and collard greens and cornbread Jake sat down in the same green chair he had sat in earlier. The two toddlers, Jacob and Flora played in the floor in front of Jake. Miss Peachy after finishing with the kitchen chores walked in and saw Jake had taken the same chair he was in when he first got there.

Mr. Jake, git ova in dat big comfy chair of Mr. Tunstall's since you da man around heah now. Dats where you needs to be," she said as she wiped her hands on her apron.

Jake did as she insisted. He found it to be comfortable enough that he was afraid he would go right to sleep. It was made of fine cow leather and the cushions were firm. The huge back of the chair wrapped completely around his broad shoulders. He knew he could sleep here for a week but he wanted to stay up and watch his children play until they were put to bed.

Jake continued to watch his children through tear filled eyes. He could see Sarah in both of these precious babies. He missed her so much. His mind drifted away to the last night they spent time together. He figured that night was when Sarah conceived his children. He could still see the love from Sarah's eyes and the warmth of her touch as their bodies came together that night. He made the conscious decision right then that he would honor Sarah and raise these two children up to be the best they could be. He would start by getting a job, first thing tomorrow.

Jake and Peachy sat and talked as the children played at their feet. He asked her how she was able to make it with just her and the babies.

"Well, Mista Hornsby, Mr. Tunstall's law potna come by from time to time and brings me groceries and thangs fa da babies. His misses do as well. He been good to me an da babies since all dat happened wi da Tunstalls and Miss Sarah." Peachy explained. She was very grateful for what all the Hornsby's had done to help her and the little ones.

"I remember him and I remember going to their home with Sarah once after church. I will stop by and see them and give them my thanks. It will be good to see them again. Maybe he will know where I can find a job if there is any at all to be had." Jake said still not taking his eyes off of his children as they watched him watch them.

"Dat be good. Now, I thinks it time to put dem babies to bed. Come on now babies." Miss Peachy commanded as she got up from her chair. They both obeyed and got up from the floor and hurried along toddling behind her. They both stopped and looked back at their father and smiled.

"Good night". Jake said to them both with a wink. They both tried to wink back at him by closing their eyes at him. Jake smiled a happy smile.

Peachy had again insisted that Jake take his place as man of the house by sleeping in the Tunstall's bedroom. The huge bed with its four post was soft and comfortable. He could just imagine himself sinking down to the floor as he lay in it. The clean crisp sheets felt like nothing he had ever experienced against his naked back. The farm house he grew up in, just east of town, offered nothing the likes of this. He can't remember being so relaxed even though in his sleep he could still hear the cannons and gun shots. He had taught himself to sleep right through them even though the sounds haunted his nights. In time he knew the sounds of war would dissipate.

Jake thought for just a moment of the need to go out to his old home place to check on it. He had been caught up in the events of the evening with his children that he forgot all about checking on his father's farm. Jake would walk out there first light and check on things before coming back to Atlanta to see about work.

He thought about his father and how he took care of him after his mother passed away. Jake always knew that void in his father's life was deep and it weighed on his father. He often found him on his knees at the foot of his mother's grave. It was evident that his father was moved to tears.

Jonah Powell was a broad shouldered man like Jake. The farm work made his body lean and hard as he toiled to make a living working the dirt to bring the very much in demand cotton to the markets in Atlanta. The farm Jonah Powell worked lay only a mile outside of Atlanta on the road going to Athens. The house was a small two bedroom dwelling most folks would call a shack but it kept Jonas and his son Jake out of the wind and rain. A log barn kept the tools and animals as well as their feed out of the weather. It was all Jonah Powell needed to pound out a living. It would be good to see the old home place again even though he knew his father had died during the war.

Jake turned over and tried to shut off his mind. The images and sounds of war still flashed and roared in his head. He figured it would take years to erase the things he had seen and the things he had to do out of his brain. He hoped it would come sooner than later. He was proud to have served, however he wasn't proud of the lives he had taken while serving. He was especially proud that he made it back and met the children he made with Sarah. He knew where Sarah was now and that nobody would ever hurt her again. For that he was truly thankful. It would have been better if she were here with him safe and sound so they could have started that life together they had both so much wanted. He made a vow in his heart that he would raise his and Sarah's children to be good and respectful.

Jake closed his eyes and whispered before drifting off to sleep, "Sarah, what do I do"?

Chapter 2

When Jake opened his eyes it was morning and the Georgia sun shone bright through the perfectly white curtains that covered the east windows of the Tunstall house. His dreams were filled with the face of the young woman he had left behind when he went off to war. His eyes were wet with tears as he recounted the story Miss Peachy told him of the night Sarah was viciously raped and murdered on the street where she lived with her parents and two lovely babies...his babies.

As Jakes feet hit the floor, he went to find water to wash the sleep from his face. He thought of the places he needed to go today. He wanted to go and look at the farm he lived on with his father. Most likely it was destroyed by Sherman's troops who were known to kill, steal and destroy like the devil himself and he didn't expect to see much there. After a year of being gone Jake received a letter informing him of the death of his father. Jake was too far away to even think of coming back and he knew his father would get a proper burial.

He remembered the nights his father came home smelling like the shine he and his friends made on one of their farms back in a holler away from the house...just in case a fire got out of hand and blew the still up. Jake knew if his mother was still living she would be able to smell the scent of the women that frequented the drunken gatherings around a barrel of hooch. Yet Jake's father took care of them in spite of his shortcomings up until the death of his mother. That's when his drinking and carousing got worse.

Jake stepped into the dining room of the Tunstall house and saw two precious little kids sitting at the table in high chairs having their breakfast. Miss Peachy feeding both of them. They all three looked up and saw Jake standing in the door leading into the room and all gave Jake a grin. Peachy knew it was a good thing having their father home to influence their raising.

"Good moanin Mr. Jake," Miss Peachy said, her big beautiful white teeth shining behind her thick dark lips. "I knowed you had you some good sleep."

Jake stepped up and pulled out a chair from the side of the big dining room table and said, "Yes Ma'am, I sure did, thank you."

It never went unnoticed how well Miss Peachy kept the Tunstall home. She always went out of her way to see that the place was spotless at all times. Mrs. Tunstall received the praises of every visitor in her home that either stopped by for a cup of tea or coffee or during the dinner parties the Tunstalls would host for their clients and friends. Their beautiful home never failed to sparkle and shine, the atmosphere always accented with gracious hospitality showed to one and all. It was always top shelf thanks to Miss Peachy.

Miss Peachy jumped up and said, "No suh. You sit at da head ah dis table Mista."

Jake stopped and pushed the chair back under the table just how he found it and like a timid and humble school lad took the chair at the head of the table just as Miss Peachy insisted. As he sat down his eyes never left the two children still looking at him and still grinning. Jake couldn't help but grin back. He knew he had to put his mind on doing right by his two children. Taking care of them was now the most important thing in his life.

"Whatchu wantin for yo breakfast this moanin Mr. Jake?" Miss Peachy asked as she got up wiping the faces of both Little Flora and Jacob. "I gitchu anathang you be a wantin.

Jake thought a second and said, "I reckon just whatever you feel like fixin me will do. I ain't picky when it comes to eatin."

"Okay den. I be back wif you some eggs, bacon and biscuits." Miss Peachy said taking the children's dishes with her as she headed out to the kitchen house that set just off the back of the main house. It was separate just in case it caught fire. There was a greater chance of keeping it from burning the main part of the house down by it being separate.

Jake just stared at the children. He couldn't help but smile back at them. They both seemed very content just sitting there watching him, neither fussing at all when Miss Peachy got up and left the dining room. It was though they both could sense they were safely in the presence of their father.

Flora laughed and said, "Papa", in a baby voice with her head leaned over toward Jake. He couldn't help it. He leaned over letting their heads touch. Her little hand reached up and touched his face as she whispered, "Papa".

Jake said, "Yes, I am and I'm awful proud to be yall's Papa." He then held his hands out to her. She reached her little arms out and went to him. As she crawled into the arms of her father he looked over at Little Jacob and winked at him. Jacob grinned big and said, "Papa." He held his hands out to come to Jake. He got up holding Little Flora like a watermelon and took Jacob up with his right arm and sat back down with a child on each side of his lap. Jake hugged both of his children to his chest with tears rolling down both cheeks. Thoughts of Sarah pounded away in his heart. He missed her so. This was a special moment in Jake's life. The bond that was just made will in his heart last a life time.

The two children sat peacefully there on the lap of their father until Miss Peachy returned with a plate stacked with four eggs over easy, four thick slices of fried bacon and another plate stacked high with her famous cat head biscuits. Miss Peachy's biscuits should be called two cat heads since they were about the size of two cat heads instead of one. Jake had been by in days past and had breakfast with Sarah before he went off to war, so she knew how he liked his eggs cooked. She knew he liked to sop that yolk up with her biscuits. Miss Peachy was quite the cook and loved to fill a man's stomach with good grub, especially at the start of a day.

"Heuh, let me take dem babies," Miss Peachy said as she set his plate down in front of him. She took them both, one on each hip and sat down herself. She closed her eyes as Jake closed his and bowed his head to pray over his food. Both kids did the same. They had been taught well.

Jake dug into his breakfast. It brought back the memories of being here with Sarah enjoying Miss Peachy's cooking. He found himself thinking, 'we move forward'. He had to think that way because the children needed him to. The past is the past and the future lies ahead. He had to make it happen for him and his two children. He was young but still had to set his goals to evolve around Jacob and Flora. They would depend on him to make a way through this world.

Miss Peachy sighed and said, "Well Mista Jake, whatchu got planned for da day?"

Jake stopped and wiped his mouth on a cloth napkin Miss Peachy brought with his meal. "Well, I think I'll go out to the old place and see if there's anything left of it. While I was away I received a letter that said my father had died so I'm thinking I'll go up there and give it a look over. Then I need to go find work. I have to make a living for my two young'uns." Jake said as he gave them both a wink. Little Jacob blinked his eyes in an attempt to imitate his father. That made both Jake and Peachy laugh with joy.

Miss Peachy put the children down allowing them to move freely. They were never bad about getting into things, especially after finding out Miss Peachy would spank their little hands. Peachy got up and rushed out of the dining room. In a moment she returned with a bag made of deer hide. Jake could tell by the sound of the jingle coming from the rawhide bag there were coins inside.

"I wantchu to take dis and go git you a good hoss. Now don't chu be a tellin me no, you heuh me. I means it. Mr. Tunstall showed me how ta fine dis and told me don't be a scared to use it if I seen fit and I sees fit now," She demanded as she set the bag down in front of Jake. "Deys fifty or sixty pieces in dat bag and you use it. It oughta gitchu a decent hoss and tack and don't chu even say no. You need it to git around."

Jake sat and looked at the bag for a few seconds before he picked up. It was heavy with silver coins. He felt the weight of it before he agreed. "Okay, but you've got to let me replace it."

"Deys time for dat after you gets you a hoss and a job." Miss Peachy took her chair again with a satisfied look on her face.

Jake thought as he took the pouch in his hand how amazed he was at the generous love Miss Peachy just showed him. He knew in his heart that this sweet lady that called the Tunstall house her home was full of love in heart for he and his two children. She didn't have to be but yet she was…good as gold. He knew that so many other black folks in the South didn't have the heart of Miss Peachy because they weren't thought of like Peachy was by the people she served. They loved her like family and gave her the option to be here or send her north with black folks that managed to escape slavery although they didn't look to her nor treat her as a slave. Miss Peachy would not have it. Her place was here and here was where she would stay. Miss Peachy knew that she was needed here especially after Sarah showed to be with child...or in her case, children. The people that lived around the Tunstall's knew as well and they had nothing but respect for Miss Peachy.

Jake said, "Okay, I'll light out here in a bit and go in to Atlanta and find me a good mount and tack."

He thought to himself that as soon as he could he would replace the money with money he made. The money Mr. Tunstall left in the bag was for Miss Peachy and not him. Jake had nothing but respect for the sweet old black lady and he would help take care of her as well. The truth is that he needed Miss Peachy to help him with Jacob and Flora so everything he could do to help Miss Peachy was what he was going to do. He knew and kept in mind that she was pretty much all the mother his two kids have known and for that itself warranted his complete and total devotion to the well-being of this precious lady.

After a shave and spit bath Jake dressed in some of the work clothes that belonged to Mr. Tunstall Miss Peachy laid out for him. The boots Jake had been wearing in spite of the holes in their sole would have to do for now until he could acquire another pair suitable for whatever work he was able to find. He had no idea what work was even available since that devil Sherman and his troops tried to destroy as much as they could find to tear up. He didn't want to think about that anymore since he knew himself. It would be real easy for him to get in trouble from kicking the crap out of a smart mouth union low life or an uppity carpetbagger so it was just best to not think of such things.

Jake kissed his children and gave Miss Peachy a hug and left the house and headed toward town with his bag of coins shoved deep down inside his right pants pocket. He remembered a blacksmith shop and livery he would stop by first before going on. He hoped he would find luck and not have to spend too much time looking for work. Work was work and he was not particular as long as it was honest.   Dirt and sweat didn't bother Jake none.   Jake thought back to the days when he hung out at one the few blacksmith shops around Atlanta. He could still hear the sound of the hammer as it fell upon the forged steel anvil that the men with large muscular arms covered with grime and sweat used to shape glowing pieces of metal in to useful tools and such.   He even managed to get a job as a kid being a helper so he knew what to expect. He even knew how to form the caulk of a horseshoe and what color the metal should glow from the heat of the forge. In his heart he kept his fingers crossed as he approached the shop he had in mind. It also had a livery as well with horses to sell. The sign above the shop read "The Red Scotsman's Blacksmith and Livery". Jake heard work going on inside as he walked up.

   "Hello in the shop", Jake yelled out not to surprise the big redheaded man inside with what looked like a four pounder raised over his head and about to bring down on a bright yellow glowing hot piece of steel.

   The man stood about six feet six inches tall. His shoulders were ever bit of a yard wide and his arms were like large branches from a white oak tree that had a diameter of about six feet around. His pale skin was covered with dirt and sweat and coarse red hair like that of a Duroc boar hog. His hair was long and it hung down to his broad shoulders. The red hair and long beard on his face was naturally decorated with streaks of gray that made the man look to be in his late forties. He wore bib overalls with no shirt on under them. His belly was not big from fat but muscle and his hips were proportion with his powerful torso. His hands were bare and looked like they could wrap around a watermelon and strong enough to choke down a mule in short order. He looked up from his work when he heard Jake call out.

"Howdy", the redhead blacksmith called out. "What can I do far ye? Oliver Currie's me name."

The big Scot laid down his hammer and approached Jake extending his hand for a shake. Jake felt the grip of a man used to hard work. His grip was like a vice and his hand felt like sand paper. This was definitely a man that could put a hurt on an enemy that would most likely be lethal.

Jake cleared his throat as he withdrew his right hand from the big Scotsman's steel grip and said. "Well, I'd like to talk to you about a job."

"A job ye say lad. Well what kind of work are ye used to doin?" Oliver Currie asked in a hearty voice that made Jake feel like he was in the presence of a friend.

Jake looked around the shop and found that every tool was in place and this place of work was well kept and organized. Just by this and the feeling he gets from the big Scot, The Red Scotsman's Blacksmith and Livery would be a good place to work.

"Yes sir. I just got back from the war and I need to work to take care of my young'uns I had born while I was away." Jake said still looking around the shop.

Big Oliver Currie put a fist on each of his hips and leaned back and looked down at Jake and said.   "So, you went off and fought the yanks did ye?

Jake full of pride looked Currie straight in the eye and said, "yes, I sure did". He was wondering if he may have stumbled into a northern sympathizer but was again surprised when the big blacksmith stepped closer and put his large right hand on

29

Jakes left shoulder. The weight and strength of this man was very noticeable in the grip Jake felt from Oliver's mighty hand. He patted Jakes shoulder and stepped back.

"I'm glad to meet ye lad. What's ye name?" Oliver Currie asked and then said, "Ye call me Red like the rest of me friends do."

"I'm Jake Powell and glad to meet you too Red".

Red nodded agreement and turned to the forge where a pot of coffee set, its steam billowing from its spout bringing with it the aroma of coffee ready to drink. He walked over to where two cups hung from a nail drove into a cross member that run the width of the shop. He took both cups and filled them with boiling hot coffee and handed one to Jake and gave him a motion toward a stool that indicated to Jake that Red wanted to sit and talk...hopefully about a job. Red pulled up another stool close to where Jake sat.

"I'm glad ye did lad. Those yankee bastards needed their arses handed to 'em, especially that sorry ass Sherman bringing his men through here like he did. I couldn't go fight. They wouldn't take me. My limp was too bad they said. I couldn't keep up with the march I guess was their thinking. I never could stay saddled to a horse for very long. Of course I was a little old too I think," regret a definite show on Red's face.

Jake looked at Red and thought if Red could have gone it would had been hell for them yanks. Yet, why would he want to wish that on anyone. The war was hell as they say. It's probably best he didn't go. Jake thought if he hadn't he could have been here to protect Sarah and she might still be here to raise their sweet children. He closed those thoughts out and hurried his mind back to the task at hand.

The coffee was good and it warmed his belly as the brew poured through him. He set his cup down on a work table and looked up at Red waiting to hear him say that he needed a hand here in his shop.

"So, do you think you could use a hand around your shop?" Jake asked hoping to get a quick answer.

Red took another sip of his coffee and looked up and took a deep breath to speak. He stopped and studied Jake some more before he finally asked.

"Six dollars a week okay with you, lad?" Red asked as his cup came to his bearded face.

Jake didn't hesitate in saying, "Six bucks a week is good for me. When can I start?"

Red smacked his lips from the taste of the coffee rubbed his long red and gray beard stomped his right foot against the dirt floor of his shop and said "Right away lad right away".

Jake jumped to his feet and gladly extended his right hand out for another excruciating hand shake from Red. He was glad to endure another moment of pain for the opportunity to work for Red.

Jake walked to a side door of the shop to where there were horses munching hay in a corral. He saw some that were good looking horse flesh and some that were not. During his time in the war he learned from some the best horsemen in the Confederate Military how to pick out a good mount. Jake stepped out to the corral and was giving the horses a once over. He wanted to get inside and put his hands on them. He wanted to run his hands along their legs and feel their muscle structure to make sure one could hold up to a long hard ride. He heard Red step out of the shop behind him.

"Looking for a horse are ye lad?" Red asked as he took a place against the corral next to Jake.

"Yes, I reckon I need one to get around. I got money to buy one. Can I get in there with them and pick me one out? If they's for sale I mean." Jake said still leaning against the corral.

Red smiled and said, "I got a better idea. Why don't ye find the best in there and I will give him to ye. I don't need one any longer lad. I've taken a likin to ye and just want to bless you. I know you will be a good hand for me and I trust you'll be a man of his word." Red slapped Jake on the shoulder and opened the gate to the corral to let him inside to mingle with the horses.

Jake walked in slowly to not spook the horses and to see if he could quickly gain their trust. He slowly made his way straight to a buckskin gelding that caught his eye right off. Its mane was a deep dark brown color and his shoulders and rump were wide and muscular. He met Jake half way across the lot as if he too was drawn. Jake could tell right off the buckskin trusted him and he felt like he could trust the buckskin. Jake bent down and ran his right hand down the front left leg of the horse. The horses muscle tone was good and firm...hard like a rock just what Jake liked in a horse. He felt nothing that would make him think any bones had ever been broken or ligaments torn. The horse was a brute that stood a good fifteen hands high. He walked around the horse and the horse never moved a step but stood still and remained looking forward as Jake slid his hand around the back and hind quarters of the horse checking every leg.

"I like this one. What's the story on him?" Jake asked as he stood up straight and looked at Red from over the back of the buckskin.

"He was one Sherman's men missed because I hid him in the tack room when they come demanding mounts for the sorry

32

arses to steal. I was sure glad they missed him too. I would've felt like slitting my throat if I let one of those yankee bastards ride off on such a beautiful mount. I still scratch me head at the thought of the original owner making a gelding out of him. His sire must have been a sight to behold," Red said shaking his head.

"Do you have a saddle, blanket and bridle for him?" Jake asked still stroking the buckskin's back.

"I sure do and I'll throw them in with the gift to ye laddie and it's a good saddle...will fit you well." Red stated as he turned and headed for the tack room. He added, "I'll get it and you can take him up the street a bit so you and this fine animal can get more acquainted".

Jake looked up and said, "yes and then it's time to get to work"

After a few laps up and down the street in front of the blacksmith's shop Jake worked up a good sweat being Red's assistant. He did a lot of the heavy lifting and even took his turn at heating and pounding steal. Three customers came by with their horses for shoeing. One old farmer brought in a mule that needed shoeing. The mule was ornery but Jake got it done just the same. He thought to himself that he could be ornery as a mule any day.

Jake was pounding out the delicate job of making a new set of rings for a wagon's pole hooks when a well-dressed gentleman walked into the shop. He was bearded like most gentlemen were and wore a business suit that was dark. On his feet he had on shining dress quarter boots. His dark fedora set with a slight tilt on his head which was covered in thin gray hair. He had thin wire spectacles on his face and he spoke with a sophisticated tone.

33

"Can you tell me if Jake Powell is here by chance?" The man sounded very nice and that sophisticated speech had a southern draw to it.

Jake raised up from his work and with a suspicious look on his face said, "I'm Jake Powell. What can do for you?"

The gentleman extended his hand and introduced himself. "I'm Richard Longhorn of what was previously known as Hornsby, Tunstall and Longhorn Attorneys at Law. May I have a moment of your time for there is something of great importance we need to discuss concerning the Tunstal estate that may be of some interest to you."

Jake said, "I don't mind a bit I just want to know how you knew to find me here?"

Longhorn cleared his throat and said, "Well Miss Peachy told me you were back and that you were out looking for a place of employment and, as I passed by, I thought I'd try my hand with investigating possibilities and stop and ask. So here I am."

Jake scratched his head and said, "Well I guess you're pretty good at it or lucky one or the other. Yes, let's step outside it's hotter than crap here in this shop."

The two walked outside where it was a lot cooler. It refreshed Jake. He just let the breeze cool him from the coat of sweat he was wearing. He was feeling like himself again. He stopped at the carriage Mr. Longhorn drove up on. It was fancy and even had shiny metal and glass boxes on the front of it where the driver sat for candles Jake guessed so you could see where you were going at night.

Jake wondering asked, "How is Mr. Hornsby? It's been a few years since I've seen him. I guess it was just before I went off to war."

Mr. Longhorn stopped and said, "He is quite well...gone on business to Macon at the moment. He should be returning in a few days. He asked me to try and seek you out while he is away. He wasn't sure if you had returned but asked me to check. I'll tell him you asked about him."

Jake stopped and said, "I speck this will do for a place to talk. What can I do for you, Longhorn did you say?"

"Yes as I said, I was one of the partners with the late Mr. Tunstall in the law firm. He had a document that he saved to be given to you and Sarah upon you and her being married. It is officially going to the first born child of you and Sarah, which I think is young Jacob. I would like to meet with you at my office to make it official since you are now the legal guardian to the children. Could you come by after you are done today and take possession of the document? I will make arrangements to stay late if necessary, I do not mind." Longhorn stated with a trusting voice. He sounded more like a pastor of a church instead of a lawyer.

Jake was amazed at what he was hearing. He figured this man would be more interested in beating him out of something. He must have been a good friend to Mr. Tunstall to go through such great lengths to do the right thing. He knew he could trust Mr. Hornsby but He wasn't so sure about this man that he had never met until now.

"Yes, I will be there, Jake said looking back at the blacksmith shop giving a quick thought to the work he still had to do. "I'll be there as soon I get finished with my work."

"Splendid Mr. Powell, I'm three blocks down this street. Turn left and find the third door on the right. You'll see my shingle", Longhorn said.

"Just call me Jake and yes I remember where the office is located, I'll see you soon."

"Fine, Jake it is then. I'll look forward to seeing you again. Mr. Tunstall was a very dear friend and partner to Hornsby and myself and we miss him and the wife and Sarah. Our hearts were broken at the news of that awful incident." Longhorn had tears in his eyes which told Jake this man is sincere.

Jake started to pat him on the back but thought better of it seeing the dirt all over his hands. He nodded to Longhorn and stepped back to give the attorney space to climb into the carriage. He waved as Mr. Longhorn Attorney at Law drove away.

Jake didn't have a bit of problem finding Longhorn's office since he had been there a time or two with Sarah visiting her father. It was clearly marked with a finely painted shingle that still read 'Hornsby, Tunstall and Longhorn Attorneys'. He walked in after wiping the bottoms of his worn out boots which reminded him he needed to go and buy another pair, maybe two, one pair for Sundays. As he entered the office he noticed how clean and fancy it was, although fancy never impressed Jake in the least, it still caught his eye. The wood work in the office was richly stained making its beauty stand out. The furniture was what Jake called high dollar furniture much like what is in the Tunstall house where he lived with his children and Miss Peachy. There was a young man dressed in a business suit much like Mr. Longhorn seated behind an oak desk that was probably worth more than Jake would make in a year of hard work at the blacksmith's shop. He walked up to the young man who was reading what looked to be legal papers when he looked up and spoke.

"Yes, I bet you are Mr. Powell here to see Mr. Longhorn," the young man spoke, his hair greased back and a tiny mustache that didn't move when he talked.

"Yep, I'm Jake Powell." Jake said looking down at his boots hoping he got all the dirt off of them before walking onto this fancy paisley carpet.

"Good, I'll let Mr. Longhorn know you are here," the young man spoke very properly. "Would you like to have a seat, maybe a cup of tea or something?"

"Nope, I'm good". Jake said thinking a cold beer would sure hit the spot.

The young man disappeared behind a set of double oak doors that matched the rest of the wood in this office and quickly returned saying, "Mr. Longhorn will see you now. You may come this way."

A hallway led a short way to two offices which were decorated like the rest of the office in fine oak wood and paisley rugs. It had a sweet smell in the air like spring flowers. Jake knew that he was ruining the sweet smell with his stinking self from a hard day's work but thought again that this might be what such a place like this needed since folks who work here had never enjoyed a hard earned sweat in their lives.

The young man stopped at the second door on the left side of the hallway and opened the door. He stepped back to allow Jake room to enter and then closed the door as he left. Mr. Longhorn Attorney at Law was seated behind an oak desk that was stained dark just like the rest of the wood in this office building. There were books on tall shelves behind his desk as well as tall shelves on one whole side of the room, from floor to ceiling. Jake figured them all to be law books.

Longhorn stood and greeted Jake just like he was his friend. His hand extended and Jake took it and gave it a friendly shake. Longhorn spoke and said. "Please Jake sit down".

Jake sat down hoping the chair would not have to be thrown out or sent off to be cleaned after he got up. Still, Jake made himself as comfortable as possible.

"Jake would you like some sort of refreshment while we talk. How about a glass of cool water"? Mr. Longhorn asked getting up and walking over to a large crock with a spout for dispensing water which set on a table in the corner of the office. He took a clean glass filled it for Jake who was sure glad to get it because he was mighty dry.

"There you go Jake, good and cool." Longhorn said starting around his desk to take his seat. "I know you are quite concerned with what I have to talk to you about but I assure you it is very simple and doesn't come with any type of binding legal mumbo jumbo so please don't worry. Arrangements have been made to take care of the taxes that come due annually, at least for several more years. Then of course you will need to make your own arrangements and I'm quite sure you will be on your feet and capable of taking care of it."

Jake was concerned. Anything that involves taxes always concerns Jake. It means that whatever this is has some form of government involved so that in itself makes for a depressing situation. Jake took a deep breath and prepared his burning question.

"Okay, what is it." Jake asked hoping for a simple answer.

"It's a clear deed to property in Augusta Texas which from what I understand is cotton and cattle country. Mr. Tunstall acquired it and was going to give it to you and Sarah at your wedding, but tragedy prevented that." Longhorn said hoping not to tear up again.

Jake said, "I wonder why Mr. Tunstall would want me and Sarah to move to Texas," This concerned Jake. He figured the Tunstalls would want him and Sarah to stay close to him and his wife, to watch their grandchildren grow up. "Why would he want us to move to Texas?"

"I know it sounds crude but let me explain. Mr. Tunstall was dying and he knew it. His wife was as well. Their hearts were both weak and he and the Mrs. had so many attacks. He also knew what the war did to this part of the south, and especially after Sherman got through with his awful march to the sea, and just knew it would be best for you and Sarah to take the children to Texas. I totally agreed with him." Longhorn said through tearing eyes.

"You must have really been good friends you and Mr. Tunstall." Jake said after taking another sip of water.

"Yes, we were. He was my best friend and Hornsby's as well. We could tell each anything under the strictest of confidence. We prayed together every day. We kept each other in check, not allowing each other to fall or fall too hard and even be there for each other when we did. So yes, he was the best friend I ever had. I know I'm speaking for Hornsby as well." Longhorn claimed while wiping away the tears in his eyes.

Jake's heart was touched by what Longhorn said. He left the office with the clear deed to five hundred and fifty acres in Augusta, Texas not knowing what to do with it. Mr. Longhorn told him it was in the eastern part of Texas just west of the Neches River. Jake didn't know if he would ever see it, ever lay his eyes on it.

After leaving Longhorns office Jake rode to the old home place. He climbed down from the saddle and sat down under the large oak tree that shaded the front yard of the house. The wood was starting to show signs of rot, and the paint was cracked and fading away. Life was gone from this old place. Like so many houses Jake has seen in his life, once life is gone, the house dies from its lose. He saddle up and rode to his new home and his children.

The setting sun found Jake staring at three head stones. Buried there, three people he loved and lost. Of course he missed Sarah the most...his true love. He wanted nothing more than to return and live out their lives together. While he stood there he wondered about the men that took her life after they took advantage of her. He knew God would judge them and repay them for what they had done. He made a promise to himself standing there that day looking at her grave that he would not let hate get the better of him. He still hoped one day those men who did that awful thing to her, would meet him.

"I love you, Sarah."

Chapter 3

"Bring out that flat stock lad...we need to make a set a special shoes for a customer's mule. Mr. Shepherd has a mule with hooves bigger than most so we'll have to fit him." The big scot yelled from the back lot where the big mule stood munching hay. The animal had hoofs the size of a hungry man's dinner plate and stood eighteen hands tall. No doubt he was bred from a draft horse and built for work. This mule was one that could pull stumps plum out of the ground. Mr. Shepherd, a farmer and breeder of draft stock knew the right combination to produce a first rate work horse.

Jake was in a storage room locating a proper stock of steel to make the shoes for the mule. There were round pieces of different lengths and diameters as well as flat pieces of different widths all in various longs and shorts. If a piece he picked wasn't suitable he placed it back where he got it. He was thinking that one day he would know right where to go to get the perfect piece of steel for any job that was placed before him, but right at the present, he just wasn't acquainted with the big Scots storage system but he was getting there.

"Jake me lad...what's takin ye so long?" the big red headed scot asked as he walked in to the storage room. "Another year could come and go wantin fir ye."

Jake was stuck on a piece of flat stock looking at it with confusion on his face trying to figure out if the piece was what the scot had in mind for a proper mule shoe. The scot walked up beside him and took the metal from Jake's hand. He tapped it a few times with a hammer he had in his hand. Jake looked up at him even more perplexed.

"You hear that lad? Does that sound like a mule's shoe? The scot asked with a grin.

"Sure does to me." Jake replied.

"Then it's good." The big scot handed it back to Jake and laughed and slapped him on the back. The big scot had to admit that he didn't know if tapping the steel with a hammer was a proper test or not...he was just giving Jake a hard time.

After the two men finished the mule shoes and fitted them all on the animal, it was just about time to quit for the day. Oliver Currie retired to his cabin next to the blacksmith's shop while Jake saddled his buckskin and rode toward the roomy white framed house where his two children Flora and Jake, always awaited his arrival home. They had come attached to the papa and their papa had become attached to them. He loved them just like a father should love his children. He even had to give a spanking or two to them both when they misbehaved... of course, Miss Peachy took care of any disciplinary issues that came up while Jake was off to work. Jake didn't mind, though, for he trusted Miss Peachy.

Jake rode the buckskin around the big Tunstall house and pulled up in front of the barn which still stood from when Mr. Tunstall kept his carriage horses stabled in them. He dismounted and took the saddle and bridle off and placed them in the tack room. Then Jake brought the horse to his stall where the buckskin received cool water from the well with oats and hay. While the buckskin munched on its feed Jake gave him good brushing all the while gently talking to the horse. Jake wanted the horse to know his voice. Every morning when Jake walked out to saddle up for the ride to the blacksmith shop he always whistled the same "tweet tweet tweet" letting the horse know that his friend and master was there and he was ready to take a ride. Jake used the same whistle just to summons the horse just to get a pet and a rub. It was the buckskin's signal to come to Jake. The buckskin was a better horse than Jake first thought and they were friends for life.

Jake looked over to the back door of the house and noticed that neither of his children came running out when he rode up. This was unusual because every day since he started working at the blacksmith's shop, and that was a good six months ago, both children ran out to greet their papa when he arrived home. Today was different, for neither appeared. Jake hurried his task and started toward the house.

As Jake walked in the house through the back door he expected to hear and see his two little ones run to him making a fuss about him being home, but he didn't see nor hear neither child nor Miss Peachy. He looked through the house starting with the big dining room and parlor then on in to the formal living room and Mr. Tunstall's study room he used as an office when he worked from home. Jake stopped and wondered where they could be. He thought maybe it was bath time after an early supper but he didn't smell the aroma of food cooked or being cooked. When Jake reached the children's bathing room he stopped and saw two tubs of water and droplets of water on the floor but no children. He proceeded to their bedroom and found them both and Miss Peachy.

Miss Peachy was on the floor on her knees and she was praying quietly. Both Jacob and Flora were tucked in their beds and both were rumbling as they breathed. Jake could hear a wheeze in both of the children's breathing. Both of his babies were shivering even though they were both covered up in blankets. Jacob coughed deep and smacked his lips as he tried to relieve himself of the dark phlegm that come up when his little body coughed again and again. It broke Jake's heart to stand there watching his children he loved so much to suffer with a sickness.

Miss Peachy looked up with tears in her eyes and said, "Mista Jake, dees babies is sick. I heard dem coughing and gagging last night. I sent for the doctor dis moanin and he came right away. He said it's da feva and he say it stauted in dey noses and den winded up in dey lungs. It ain't good Mista Jake. I'z scared for dees babies."

Jake knelt down between the two little beds where his two sick babies laid. He reached his hands to both of their foreheads and felt a fever coming from both of them. He closed his eyes and prayed the Lord would heal his children. He pleaded for the Lord to spare them both. He lived his whole life believing God could do anything and he lived his whole life knowing that what God decided was what God decided. Again, in his heart Jake asked that the Lord spare them both and heal them.

There was a bowl of cool water there on the floor between the two beds. In the water were two little towels to make compresses that Miss Peachy had been placing on the children's sweet little foreheads to help bring down the fever. Jake took the little towels and squeezed the cool water from them and laid them on each of the children's heads just above their eyebrows. He stroked their hair as his tears flowed down his cheeks. He felt the fear that came with the possibility of losing his children. He had seen what was known as "winter fever", kill grown men so he knew it would take true providence from a loving God to bring wellness back to their small bodies.

Jake stayed by his children's side all night. His eyes never closed. As the sun shone through the clean white curtains in the children's bedroom, Jake looked up and saw that Miss Peachy had never left the bedroom as well, both watching over the children just in case one woke during the night. Neither child moved during the night. The only sounds from them came from the wheezing sounds each made as they breathed and

44

coughed in their sleep. Jake reached and touched them both on their warm foreheads...both still with fever.

He wondered if the doctor, Doctor Cyrus Clay would stop by today and check on them. He decided not to go to work at the blacksmith shop. His place is with his children. Jake got up and walked outside and saw people moving about. He stopped Henry Jones as he walked by on his way toward the heart of the city.

"Henry...would you stick your head in Red's blacksmith's shop and tell him I'm staying home today to help Miss Peachy with the children. They are both bad sick and will you ask Doc Clay to stop by as well.

Henry Jones raised a skinning hand and said, "I sure will Jake. Let me know if you need anything else. I'll be passing by again this evening. I'll stop to check."

Jake raised a hand and told the little statured man how much he appreciated him. Henry Jones was a little man that stands about five foot three inches tall. He wore little overalls every time Jake had seen him and as long as Jake has known Henry he worked at the local feed store and leather shop that sits on the left side of the street on toward downtown Atlanta from the blacksmith shop where Jake worked. There's no telling how long he has worked there. Jake guessed he worked there even through the war.

As Jake walked back in to the children's room Miss Peachy was just finishing placing another pillow under each of the children's heads hoping it would help them breath better. She didn't want to see either of them choke as they coughed up the mucus that had filled their little lungs. As she labored over them she continuously thanked the Lord Jesus for being here with the children and touching their sick little bodies. She turned and faced Jake as he walked in the room. She had the look of concern on her face so that it scared Jake.

"Lawd Mista Jake, I ain't a bit surprised that both of these babies come down sick at da same time. Mercy Lawd how they do everythin at the same time. One would fill they diaper and de otherd do the same." She said as the tears began to streak her dark aged face.

"I just needs the Lawd Jesus to come up in heah and do some healin now. He know I's scared for dez babies I iz. Mista Jake I don't know what I'd ifn...", Peachy caught herself before she said anything about these two children dying. She shook her head from side to side to fight off the thought of it. She had to stay positive and trust in God.

A little before noon there was a knock on the down of the Tunstall house. Jake shot straight up from where he was sitting on the floor between the two beds where his children laid sick with a cough and fever. He headed to the front door of the house and was relieved to see Doctor Cyrus Clay standing on the porch with his medical bag. Jake opened the door and stood back to give the doctor room to pass through.

Doctor Cyrus Clay was a short round man with no hair on his head but a full beard on his face. His beard was dark but speckled with gray. He wore a white cotton shirt with a silk vest that hardly covered his big belly. His sleeves were rolled up and he looked like he just left someone in need of a doctor's treatment. He moved as hurriedly as he could, considering his rotund physique. He spoke with a slow and heavy southern accent.

"Jake, I'm sorry it took me so long to get back over to check on the children. I've been so busy delivering babies since I'm without a mid-wife these days. Please forgive me." Doctor Clay pleaded as he rushed passed Jake on his way to the children's room.

Jake was in a daze and said nothing as he slowly followed the doctor back in to the bedroom of his two sick children. Miss Peachy was just putting a cold compress on Flora's forehead. Neither of the children had moved...just slept wheezing and rattling in their breathing. Doctor Clay bent down on one knee next to Jacob and removed a wooden monaural stethoscope from his doctor's bag. He gently set the larger beveled end to the boy's chest and his right ear to the smaller beveled end. Doctor Clay listened to little Jacob breath for several breaths. He raised his head, turned and looked at Jake.

"I think the boy is getting worse. His lungs are full of fluid. If he were awake I would say to make him drink a lot of water. It may help him get rid of some of the mucus build up that he is trying to breathe through. If we can't get it to break up it will likely take his life." Doctor Clay explained as he moved over and listened to Little Flora breath. He stood up when he finished and gave the same prognosis.

Doctor Clay continued by saying, "I've seen these cases before with twins. One gets sick and at the same time the other does as well. One gets worse and the other does too...It's a terrible thing. Let them rest for now but when they wake up start making them drink as much water as they will drink. Not too much but plenty for little ones. I wish there was more that I could do."

After the doctor left, Jake returned to his place on the floor between his children's beds to keep an eye on them through the night. He insisted that Miss Peachy return to her bed to get a nights rest so she could take over for him in the morning. He knew he would have to return to work at the blacksmith's shop to fulfill is obligation as the bread winner for his children and Miss Peachy. He knew he would be dragging through the day, but he had to keep going for his kids. Jake had to have the money to pay Doctor Clay for his services. He was not going to be known as a freeloader.

Through the night both children woke up, neither saying a word, just looking at their papa with glassy eyes that spoke out loud that they felt awful in their little bodies. Both coughed what seemed to Jake to be every other breath. He kept water and chicken broth handy ready to give them both, a sip or two if they would take it at all. Neither would use the bucket their Poppa kept at the side of their beds so they would not have to go to the privy. Jake kept cool compresses for both of their tender foreheads handy as well as trying to bring down their fever.

As morning arrived Peachy was up and stirring. She had trusted the children all night to the care of their father. She knew he would watch over them and doctor them the best he could. She walked in to the children's room and Jake raised his head up to greet her with a worried look on his face. She could tell he was troubled and heartbroken over the condition of his children. She was proud of Jake for being such a father that would watch over his two babies the whole night while they laid in their beds wheezing with every breathe they took. Most men would have left it to the woman of the house to take care of the little ones in a time such as this.

Miss Peachy looked down at Jake and said, "Mista Jake, let me fix you a bite of breakfast before you goes to work. You knows you can't work on a empty belly."

Jake just shook his head and responded, "No Ma'am...I'll be fine. I ain't in much mood to eat anyhow. I'll just take one of your biscuits and go on to work."

"Mista Jake, iz you sho...I don't mind none atall."

"No Ma'am, I'm good for now. Hopefully Jake and Flora will be better when I get back and we'll have a good supper." Jake said with hopefulness in his voice.

"Dats what we gonna be spectin Mista Jake." Miss Peachy proclaimed as she wrapped two of her biscuits up in a towel for Jake to stick in a pocket of his work pants.

He didn't bother changing from what he had on the day before. He intended to have a good bath when he got back home in the evening. He knew he could make the day with no sleep. He had gone without a lot of rest while he was away at war with the Union. He thought that he would rather stay awake all night listening to cannon and rifle fire than to listen to his two children laboring to breathe.

Jakes heart was breaking. Every time he looked or even thought about his two children he saw Sarah's face in his mind. He lost her...he didn't want to lose Jacob and Flora too. Even though he hadn't known them long they were a part of him...a part of he and Sarah and they were both very precious to him. He thought about how Sarah's heart would be crushed if she knew how her two precious babies were suffering the way they were with this awful sickness.

Jake saddled his buckskin and somberly rode toward the blacksmith's shop to start his day. He kept his head down every bit of the way with the thoughts of his children never leaving his mind. As the buckskin made its way down the quiet street Jake's head relaxed and fell forward. Suddenly he felt someone grab the horse's bits and force him to a stop.

"What's this, a Johnny Reb ridin a fine lookin buckskin? Did you steal it Reb?" asked a man wearing a blue Union uniform. There was another soldier with him dressed the same way.

They both had sorry attitudes and it was evident to Jake they were trying to get a rise out of him. The one doing the talking was a hulk of a man that stood about six feet four inches tall. He had long straight nose that became wide at the nostrils. His face had a five day growth of beard on it and his chin was dimpled. Coal black hair stuck out from under a black flop hat and he spoke with a deep voice that sounded as if he was from up north and of Italian descent. The man had strong arms and he wore a Colt Army model 1860 .44 caliber revolver in a cross draw black leather holster. It hung to the left side of his flat stomach. He still had a hold of the buckskin's bridle. The other stood about the same height and had blonde hair and shaved thin face that looked to be about eighteen years old. This soldier looked like he was scared of Jake. He held a rifle, a trap door 45-70 on Jake while the one holding the horse did the talking.

"Where you headed on this fine horse Reb?" the soldier asked obviously trying to show the younger soldier how tough he was. He kept jerking the horse's head back and forth while looking up at Jake to see if Jake would take the bait. Jake wanted to take the bait and beat this man's ass with it. If the man knew what Jake was thinking at this very moment he would have turned the bridle of the buckskin loose and head for the hills.

Jake held his tongue and restrained his rage and calmly said, "Just headed to the blacksmith shop up here where I work. I'm not trying to bother nobody."

"You trying to give me lip Reb?" the soldier chided while he continued to jerk the buckskin's bridle back and forth being a bully not only to Jake but his horse too.

"No sir, I'm telling you the truth. I'm just headed right up here to the blacksmith's shop." Jake replied still thinking how he would like to plant his right boot in this jackass' face and ride on. He could tell by looking at the young one that he would drop his rifle and high tail it if he just farted at him. This mouthy soldier though...needed his butt stomped.

"Why don't I just drag you off that fine horse there Reb and take it for myself? The soldier kept on with his mouthing.

"What's going on here? Soldier, why do you have the man detained? Has he broken a law? asked another man in uniform that silently rode up to where the soldier had Jake stopped. He was dressed in a crisp blue uniform with First Lieutenant Bar's on the shoulders. He wore a black hat with a gold colored roped hat band. His leather belt and holster shone like a new penny right along with his high top cavalry boots. He had long dark hair and a full beard covered his slender face. He looked to be in his late twenties. The Lieutenant set upon a tall sorrel colored mare in a shining leather cavalry saddle and tanned leather gloves covered his hands that held the horse's reins.

"I asked you a question soldier" the Lieutenant said a little louder.

The jackass answered the question. "Ah yes sir I heard you sir. We were on patrol and noticed this man riding this fine horse and figured we'd just stop him and make sure everything is in order sir is all."

"Did you find everything in order soldier?" the Lieutenant asked with even more force in his voice. It was obvious to the Superior Officer that the soldier was harassing the man, after all, he saw as he rode up how the soldier was treating the man and his horse.

"Yes sir. Everything appears to be in order" replied the jackass Union soldier showing signs of embarrassment that could not hide the rage in his eyes as he glared at Jake. He turned the horse's bridle loose and stepped back two steps allowing Jake to ride on. He turned to his partner who remained quiet and said, "Let's go."

The other soldier like an obedient dog snapped to and in agreement, "Okay Sal."

As Jake rode by, the Lieutenant tipped his hat toward Jake. Jake took it as a show of respect. In another place and time...all three would have died in their tracks. He hoped he never ran across them again in any situation. The wrong situation for that jackass soldier will not turn out well...for the jackass.

Jake rubbed his buckskin gelding down and gave him hay and oats to munch. He entered the shop and immediately Red could tell something terrible was wrong. The big Scot had come to love Jake like a son. He could tell when Jake was not his usual self.

"What's wrong lad" the Scot asked in his heavy Scot accent.

Jake just stopped and looked down at his feet. He wanted to just let his tears go and puddle around his boots but he held them back. He searched his heart for the words to say that would give Oliver Currie the true picture of how his heart was breaking over his two sick children he had to leave at home. He knew though, that they were in the caring hands of Miss Peachy, yet he still wanted to be there to see them getting better in their breathing and see them take food and get their strength back so that they could rip and play like little kids are supposed to.

"It's my children Red...they are awful sick. They can't breathe without coughing and their fever just will not break. They were like that all night." Jake said having to turn his head away from Red to keep his emotions from being detected.

Red stepped up and placed a mighty hand on Jake's shoulder and said, "I know you're worried lad, but we trust the Lord above on things like this. It's all we can do. Come have some coffee. I know it won't help the situation but it will do ye belly good to warm up a bit."

The two men sat and drank coffee for a good hour. Red tried to get Jake to go on home but he refused. He wanted to work so he could draw an honest pay. Jake got to moving and found orders that needed to be filled as well as building several sets of tongs for the shop. His mind stayed occupied with his work. Jake still stopped from time to time and thought of the children. He hoped they were doing better.

When the sun reached its place in the sky that said it was around four o'clock Oliver Currie put down his hammer and used a filthy rag to wipe dirty sweat from his face. He figured he and Jake had just about done all they could do for one day considering the state of mind Jake was in with his children being deathly ill. The big Scot walked over to a bucket half full of well water and pulled up the dipper and took a long draw from it into his bearded mouth. The drops that clung to the course hair on his face wound up spotting the bib of his overalls. The next dipper full went over his head and ran down the collar of his work shirt he wore under the gritty denim bib. The feeling refreshed him until he could get a tub of water drawn and heated on his stove for his evening bath. Once all the tools were put back to their proper place, the big Scot, Oliver Currie, sat down on a stump cut for an anvil stand and took a deep breath and blew it out hard.

"Me lad, go home and see about ye little ones," commanded Currie, still breathing hard from the hammering he was doing on a horse shoe he had been forming.

Jake was just putting back the last set of tongs when he looked over to his boss and just shook his head. He was too tired to talk because of the sleep he missed the night before. He was too tired even to consider the hours he had been awake. He just wanted to go home and see Jacob and Flora. He saddled up the buckskin and headed that way.

Jake gave the buckskin his neck and booted him against the gelding's sides telling the horse to take it to a gallop. The buckskin lunged forward and stretched out to full speed. If not for the children being in the sad state they were in Jake would have enjoyed the hard ride. In no time he was pulling the buckskin up to slow down to make the turn around the house to the barn. Doctor Clay's carriage was there telling Jake that Miss Peachy had sent out for him. Suddenly Henry Jones rushed out of the front door. He saw Jake and stopped.

"Oh Jake you're home" Henry said in as he gasped to breathe. "I had to run get the Doc. Miss Peachy just sent me after you and…well you better go on inside and talk to the Doc."

Jake ran up the few steps of the front porch and into the front door of the house. His heart was racing from fear of what he might find once inside. He noticed Henry catch himself as he was telling Jake that Miss Peachy had him come to get him. He just didn't want to think the worse. As Jake went inside Henry proceeded with his next errand in a rush.

Jake hurried into the children's room where Doctor Clay stood with Miss Peachy. Miss Peachy was crying hard. She turned to see Jake walk in the room. He saw Jacob and then Flora still lying in their beds, not moving, not wheezing, nor coughing. His knees buckled in the spot between the beds where he sat on the floor watching over his ailing kids. He went to his knees. There was no sound from either child. There was no movement from either. Jake reached out with both of his hands placing them on the foreheads of Flora and Jacob. Their little heads were not warm with fever any longer. Jake didn't want to believe the worst possible thing had just happened.

"No...no...no...this can't be...I can't lose them too. I...I just can't. Doc, please tell me they are better. Tell me they stopped coughing and wheezing because they are better and just sleeping. Please tell me that." Jake pleaded through tears in his eyes. He closed them hoping when he opened them again he would find that he was simply dreaming an awful nightmare and that his children were well and happy, but...

"Jake, I wish I could tell you that. I wish I could tell you that they are well...but I can't. I am so sorry Jake. I am so sorry." Doctor Clay spoke through his own tears. He never wanted to lose a patient, especially precious little children that he himself delivered into this cruel world. He sobbed openly.

Neighbors from both sides of the little dirt street rushed over to see if they could be of any assistance. The Justice of the Peace had been by to pronounce the children deceased and the local funeral director had been called for. Jake still knelt between both beds as the undertaker entered the bedroom. Jake was told by him to take as much time as he needed. Miss Peachy sat on the side of the bed where little Flora lay lifeless. Jake, rose up to his feet and then sat down next to his dead son Jacob. He looked up at the undertaker.

"I'll bring them out. I know you have your job to do. I just need to feel mine and Sarah's babies in my arms one last time. I won't be long." Jake's face was covered with his sorrow and grief. Miss Peachy had cried until she was out of tears. Her heart was completely broken. She thought to herself that she has no reason for being here on this earth any longer. She prayed to herself that God would bring her home very soon.

Jake had the heart breaking chore of meeting with the undertaker to make arrangements for the burial of Flora and Jacob. His orders were to put the children on each side of Sarah in their family plot...Jacob on her right and Flora on her left. Their names were too be added to Sarah's headstone on their respective sides as well. The service was a simple graveside ceremony. There were people from the church Sarah and her parents attended before the Union army led by Sherman burned it down. Only about half of its congregation returned once it was rebuilt. Some didn't return because they lost their lives during that Union march to the sea but, the people that did, knew what it meant to love their fellow man and they were back to growing in numbers again. After one of the ladies from the church finished her rendition of 'Rock of Ages' the preacher, Parson Jonathan Patrick, closed with a prayer. Finally, Jake through his tears, filled in both the graves. He took comfort in knowing that both Jacob and Little Flora were with their momma and the Lord Jesus.

Less than a week later, Jake filled in the grave of Miss Peachy. What she wanted in her heart, a, Loving and Merciful God granted her. Jake buried her beside Sarah and his children. There was very little protest over Miss Peachy being buried in a white cemetery. The little protest was there as Jake finished covering over MissPeachy's grave. There was one man that did the talking when he and six other prominent gentlemen approached Jake as he dressed her grave with his shovel.

"Jake, I really don't think it's right for her to be put with white people" said Theodore Gentry of one of the local banks. Theodore Gentry, a large man who worked his way to the top position in the First Bank and Trust of Atlanta Georgia, by being ruthless and conniving, stood with his big hands on his hips as he looked over the job Jake was completing. He stood over six feet tall and had broad shoulders. His face was shaved and his brown waving hair was well groomed. He wore a pin striped gray suit that was tailored for him. He had never had to put in a day of hard work of any kind. Theodore Gentry evaded the war because of a rich daddy that pulled the strings necessary to see that his precious son was not made to go. He was from a well-to-do family and they were all known to be just like Theodore.

After Jake was done at Miss Peachy's resting place he walked over to the buckskin tied to a carriage post in front of the cemetery. Gentry followed and the other men followed him.

"Now Jake you listen to me. If we have to get a court order to have her dug up and placed in a colored cemetery we will do it. Now Jake you listen to the voice of reason" Gentry said trying to be forceful with his tone.

"Well now" Jake said stepping up close to the face of Theodore Gentry, "If you get a court order and have her removed I'm gonna find you and give you the whuppin your pa never gave you."

"Do you mean you would attack me even if a judge orders it?" Gentry, was trying to sound tough but merely managed to sound like the worm he is.

"I mean I'm gonna find you and give you a spanking. Now do I make myself clear...Mr. Gentry? Jake asked, with a voice strong and confident and not mincing words. He meant what he said. Miss Peachy was better than most...especially those like Theodore Gentry.

57

The banker spun on his heels with a huff, turned toward the men behind him and said, "Gentlemen, let's leave this ruffian. He hasn't heard the last about this." All the men followed Gentry away and climbed into two horse driven buggies.

Jake stood by the buckskin still fuming over the conversation with Theodore Gentry about Miss Peachy being buried next the family who loved her like she was one of the family. He would contact Hornsby or Buckhorn to see to it that nobody is allowed to touch Miss Peachy's grave. He also knew the promise he made to Gentry stood.

Jake met with Mr. Longhorn at his law office the next day. Jake was given assurance that Miss Peachy's grave would never be touched by these men or any other men.

Chapter 4

Four years passed since Jake lost Miss Peachy and his children, Flora and Jacob. Their faces never left his mind and the memories of the short time he spend together with them will never leave his heart. The devastation he felt in his life will forever be bound to his soul. He spent time in the bedroom of his children everyday with the hope that he would just catch a hint of their scent from the bath soap that Miss Peachy used to wash them. He sat on the floor between their beds where they laid struggling to breathe the days and nights leading up to their last labored breath, two precious children born together, died together. He would close his eyes and see them playing on the floor and how their eyes would shine when he looked at each of them. He remembered the happy greetings he would get when he arrived home in the evening from the blacksmith shop. How they ran out the back door of the Tunstall house to meet him at the barn as he tended to the buckskin brought a smile to Jake's face. He would never forget his precious children, or his sweetheart that carried them in her womb nor the night before he went away to war. The night his and Sarah's bodies came together in love would always be a memory precious and dear to him.

The Barkley family from across the street from the Tunstall house checked on him as regular as clockwork, at least the daughter did...every day. Martha, every evening, interrupted his thoughts as she gently knocked on the front door of the house Jake lived in now alone, to make sure he had supper to eat and a lunch to take with him when he went off to work the next day. She was a twenty year old maiden with long brown hair that fell in waves down to the middle of her back. She had emerald green eyes and a soft slender face that would light up a dark night. Martha Barkley was just a beautiful Georgia girl with the accent that made it obvious she was from Georgia. She kept a look out for Jake every day through the big window on the front of the two story white house with sweet anticipation that today Jake would invite himself for a little front porch sitting on a star filled night. She handled the disappointment like any girl whose heart longed to be loved by a man like Jake Powell.

It was the end of the week and Jake had ridden up on the buckskin and performed his usual duties in the care and grooming of his mount. He was in his usual place in his children's bedroom when he heard the knock on the front door. He knew who it was and he had to admit Martha Barkley was a good cook and he always looked forward to a home cooked meal from her. He would give her back the plate or pot she left from the day before and he never failed to tell Martha how good it was. He did enjoy seeing her smile at his compliments. As he walked to the door he could see it was Martha Barkley. He opened it and was greeted by her pretty face smiling as always. She was holding a silver metal pot with the handle of a ladle sticking out from under a silver lid. Jake immediately smelled a pleasant aroma that spoke of delicious beef stew.

"Hello Jake. I hope you are hungry. I brought you my beef stew you said you liked and some of momma's cornbread." The smile on Martha Barkley's face was a pretty as a kitten and Jake knew she had feelings for him.

Jake opened the door wide so Martha could walk in and make her way to the dining room. She knew right where it was and she also knew where all of the eating tools were in the Tunstall house since she had been there so many times with food for Jake.

As she walked by Jake he caught the fragrance of her hair. It was the smell of honeysuckle. Jake had had that smell in his nose on many afternoon stroll with Sarah. He was sure Sarah had told Martha how well Jake liked the smell of honeysuckle since the two were close friends. The news of Sarah being brutally murdered by Sherman's men left a break in Martha's heart that may never mend but she knew she wanted to be here for Jake. She also knew that is what Sarah would have wanted.

"Thank you so much Martha, "Jake said as he fell in behind her on the way to the dining room. He really did feel the appreciation he expressed. He also knew Martha was very interested in being with him but he just wasn't ready to be with anyone. He would never hurt Martha so he always kept his distance from her or any other woman. He thought that in time his heart would be ready to love again.

Jake said, "The stew smells delicious and I don't mind telling you that I'm pretty hungry. Thank you for bringing me some of your stew. I know I will enjoy it as always."

"I'm so glad Jake...I do so enjoy cooking for you." Martha said not caring if Jake took her statement as a hint of her intentions. She gave him a deep look into his eyes as she said it hoping to get the response she so desperately longed for.

Jake looked away and said, "Martha you are quite the cook. Would you like to share it with me?"

Martha's heart jumped at his invite. She was stunned that he asked her to join him. In the past he pretty well took the food at the front door, said thank you with a bit of small talk, turned and walked away...closing the door as he retreated. Jake had to admit that he did need some company and he did enjoy talking to Martha. He just didn't want her to get the wrong idea thinking he had intentions of courting.

"I've already had my dinner meal Jake but I will certainly set with you and chat a bit while you eat." She flashed a pretty smile at Jake as she agreed to join him. She was serious in her heart toward Jake and wanted to do things to please him. Martha kept herself for the man she would one day fall in love with. When she began to bring Jake meals and do little mending jobs for him when he tore a shirt or pants she began to think he needed her which moved her heart to do more and be there for Jake in all things.

After Jake finished the entire pot of beef stew and pan of cornbread Martha washed them and got them ready to take back home. Her heart almost leapt right out of her chest and over her rather large breasts when Jake asked her if she would like to sit out on the porch and visit before she returned home. It was obvious Jake wanted to get something off of his chest.

"Martha, I just wanted you to know that I really do appreciate all the things you do for me. I know that you would never let me pay you because you've been such a good friend. I do wish there was some way I could pay you." Jake said as he looked toward the clear Georgia sky at the stars that were out.

"Jake, you know Sarah was my friend and I know yall loved each other tremendously and I know I could never replace her, but you've just got to come to a point where you are ready to court again." Martha said in her sweet Georgia voice. She couldn't believe she all but told him she wanted him to court her.

Jake took a deep breath trying to gear his mind to put an answer into words that would not hurt her feelings. He had been giving a lot of thought to going away and starting over again. He often looked at the land deed he had gotten from Mr. Longhorn the attorney and how Mr. Tunstall wanted him and Sarah to have to make a start. Jake cared for Martha as a friend. He had nothing but respect and honor for her and he would never want to hurt her in any way. Just like most men he never knew what to say in this situation that would not cause her heart to break. Jake kept looking at the stars hoping the words would come.

"I knew I shouldn't have shared my feelings Jake. Please forgive me." Martha said almost in tears. She could tell he didn't know what to say. She knew and trusted Jake enough to know he respected her feelings and would never want to make her sad.

Jake looked at her and then reached over and took her left hand into his strong, calloused right hand and said, "Martha, don't feel that way. I just don't know if I want to stay here. There is so much here that haunts my mind and I feel like I've got to get away."

63

She moved over closer to him and rested her head on his shoulder and said, "Jake, I understand."

Later that night as Martha lie awake in her bed, she thought about what Jake had told her. Tears moved down her soft cheeks as she mentally thrashed herself for saying anything that might have caused Jake to think of moving away…away from her. She knew the memories of Sarah and the children must be hard to live with but she knew she was willing to love him through it, if he would only allow her to. Martha made up her mind that until Jake moved on she would be here for him. She would continue as always to bring him meals and do whatever he needed her to do until that day comes. She also prayed it never would.

Across the dirt street in the Tunstall house Jake laid awake in his bed, with his mind racing between Sarah and the children, their graves and the land deed and the prospects of a new start in a new state. Thoughts of Martha and the talk they had earlier rushed through his mind as well. She is such a precious lady and Jake had nothing but respect, admiration and gratitude for her and all she had done for him since Miss Peachy died. Yet, he had the rest of his life to think about.

Jake drifted off to sleep dreaming, seeing an image of Sarah, Jacob and Flora walking hand in hand. He could see them walking away, into a setting sun.

The buckskin had finished his morning oats and hay as Jake threw his saddle over the horse's back. He spoke to his four legged friend as he tightened the girth around the gelding. Jake sprung into the saddle with ease and reined him away from the bar and walked him around the Tunstall house to the street that would lead him to the blacksmith shop. As he started to rein left, he saw Martha standing on the front porch of the big white house where she lives with her parents. She was dressed in a white cotton dress...her brushed hair lay over her delicate shoulders. She gave him a smile and waved as the buckskin turned and trotted off with Jake waving her way. He found himself thinking about the previous evening and how he had shared with Martha his feelings of restlessness. He hoped she took it well and that she would understand how he felt.

After Jake unsaddled the buckskin behind the blacksmith shop in the corral Oliver Currie maintained for customer's horses and mules that needed to be fitted and shod, he went inside the shop and met with the big redheaded scot as he sat by a hot pot of coffee. Jake helped himself and planted himself down on an anvil stump to take a sip of hot coffee before he and Oliver even spoke. Once the steaming brew hit his belly he took in the sight of the big scot and gave thought to what he was about to say. Oliver Currie knew by what he saw on Jakes face that something was on his mind.

"Okay lad, out with it...what's got ye mind a'goin this fine marnin." The big scot asked as he set his coffee cup down on a nearby work table.

Jake's eyes cut up toward Oliver but he didn't say a word. That being because he didn't really know how to put into words what he was thinking. He found talking to Oliver Currie, his big redhaired Scotsman boss, was harder to talk to than talking to Martha last night. Even though Jake knew that he wasn't going to break Oliver's heart by what was on his mind, he still hated to say it.

Oliver Currie was there for him when he needed a job and through the past four or so years the big scot has dropped hints of giving the blacksmith's shop over to him. Jake always looked at the shop as just a place of employment. He never was sure if he wanted to bang on steel for the rest of his life anyway, all though he had pretty well made up his mind...he didn't.

"Go ahead and tell me you've got a restless spirit walkin around in ye head. Am I right dear lad?" Oliver Currie said sounding more like a father than a boss as he got up from the anvil stump he was sitting on. He approached Jake and put a hammer like hand on his shoulder.

Jake raised his face and looked Oliver Currie directly in the eyes and said, "Yes, I need to go. Just get away."

The big scot gave Jake a pat or two on the shoulder and stepped back to say, "Jake me boy…I understand more than anyone. I understand how ye feel and I don't blame ye none. I wonder how ye stayed this long. I figure ye felt somewhat obligated to me but ye don't have to."

Jake didn't know what else to say. He was surprised to find the big scot so understanding. He guessed Oliver Currie did look at him as a son and for that he was truly thankful. It meant more than words could tell to find his boss felt this way.

"I know ye will be making preparations to go soon and I want ye to know that I will help ye all I can. Will ye be going by wagon or will ye be takin a pack horse or mule?" Oliver asked figuring he would be traveling as light as possible.

Jake had to admit that he hadn't really considered everything he would need for a long journey but now is the time to start giving it thought. He found a piece of a paper sack and a three inch portion of a pencil and put it to the side.

"After I give you a day's work I'll make a list. Would you help me?" Jake asked still scratching his head over Currie's reaction to what he had shared with him.

"With the list or the day's work," The big scot laughed and grabbed his belly like it might fall off for laughing to hard. "Lad, that is simple…the bare essentials, ye travel light just like ye did in the war. Ye won't be burdened down and ye'll get to where ye go quicker. So put away ye paper and pencil and get t'work."

Through the work day Jake caught up on all of the orders Oliver had received from customers for horse and mule shoes as well as wagon tongues and wheels. One wagon needed six spokes and a hound brace replaced. Once he was done he headed down the street and around the corner to the office of Hornsby, Tunstall and Longhorn Attorneys at Law to see if Mr. Longhorn or Mr. Hornsby were in the office. Jake again felt bad about walking into the nice plush law office in dirty clothes but he needed the help of one of Mr. Tustall's partners. The well-dressed young secretary that greeted Jake before was at his desk when Jake walked into the office.

"Are either of the attorneys in today". Jake asked the young man seated behind the beautifully stained desk. "I would like to visit with one of them just for a minute, if possible."

The young man looked up and gave a very professional smile and stood to his feet. His business suit was gray and tailored especially for him. His dark hair was plastered down to his head and parted in the middle. Jake thought how awful it would be to have to dress like this every day, but for what the firm paid the young man he might consider it...but then again...probable not.

"Why yes, Mr. Powell, I remember you. I'm sure Mr. Longhorn will see you. I'll be just a moment. Would you like refreshment like water, or perhaps coffee would be more to your taste?"

Jake thought about the cool water he had the first time he was here and how well he liked it. He gave the coffee consideration but settled for the more satisfying of the two. "Maybe a glass of water, thanks."

"Very well I shall return promptly with your water and a word from Mr. Longhorn." The spry young man stated as he quickly left the front office and entered the hallway, which lead to Mr. Longhorn's office. In less than a minute the young man returned holding a glass of crystal clear water.

"Mr. Longhorn will see you now, Mr. Powell."

"Thanks for the water." Jake stated as he walked through the doorway to the hall and on into Mr. Longhorn's office.

Jake was immediately greeted by a warm hand shake from Mr. Longhorn who spoke up and asked. "Jake, how have been? Please have a seat. Catch me up on everything...it's been so long."

Jake took a seat in one of the cushioned leather chairs that sat in front of the big stained oak desk where Mr. Longhorn did his legal work. Longhorn wore a white cotton shirt with the sleeves rolled up to his elbows, black dress pants, black leather shoes and no jacket. He had the appearance of one who had come dressed for court but once court was over went into a relaxed mode. He took a seat behind the desk and moved some papers around to get more organized in case he had to make notes concerning Jakes visit. He figured Jake had a simple legal question about the estate of Mr. Tunstall, which was all settled. The house and everything belonging to the Tunstalls was left to little Jacob but upon his death went to the control of the closest kin which in this case was Jake. The issue of Miss Peachy's burial was settled as well and it was ordered by a court that Miss Peachy's remains were to stay in the Tunstall family plot. So Longhorn could at this point only imagine what Jake had on his mind.

"So Jake...what can I do for you? Is everything okay with you?" Longhorn asked with true sincerity.

Jake collected his thoughts and then spoke up. "I've made up my mind to take the deed to that land to Texas and settle there to start a cattle ranch."

Longhorn's eye brows rose and he gave an impressed look as if Jake had been studying the subject for quite some time, which Longhorn admired in a man...never to be one to jump without thinking himself. Texas is from what Longhorn had read, is a place where a man could grow and really make something of his life. Not saying that Georgia is not, but over the last few years a lot of men found their way to Texas to start over. Most men, however, went there because the Union Army pretty well destroyed everything they had in Georgia.

"It seems to me that you've thought about this venture for quite some time." Longhorn said as he leaned back in his big leather office chair.

"Yes, I've been thinking about it ever since the children and Miss Peachy died. What I was wondering is if you would help put the house on the market to sell." Jake didn't know how that idea would go over since it belonged to his good friend Mr. Tunstall.

"I think you should sell it. As a matter of fact I will buy it from you immediately if you'd like with the understanding that you stay there until you get ready to leave for Texas." Longhorn said leaning forward to set Jake's full attention.

Jake was amazed at how quickly Mr. Longhorn jumped on the notion of purchasing the Tunstall house. He trusted there were no evil intentions from Longhorn. He had to ask him why he was interested.

"I figured you had a house here in town." Jake said, not trying to pry yet he was still interested.

69

Longhorn smiled again and said, "Well I did, but it was one that sustained quite a bit of smoke damage in the attack on Atlanta. We patched it up but my wife never felt at home anymore. It was like we were personally invaded, if you know what I mean."

"Oh believe me...I know exactly what you mean." Jake returned, remembering the Tunstall family being brutally murdered during the occupation of Atlanta.

"I tell you what Jake...I've seen the Tunstall house on many occasion and my wife and I have always loved it. I am prepared to give five thousand dollars for it. That will give you all the money you need to get started in Texas. How's that." Longhorn said as he began making notes. I will draw up the papers for the sale and bring them to you tomorrow, if that's all right with you.

Jake stared at Longhorn for a few seconds and then said, "That works with me. I'll be leaving for Texas first thing next week as long as I have Oliver Currie at the blacksmith's shop caught up. I don't want to leave him piled up with work."

Mr. Longhorn and Jake stood up together and shook hands on the deal. The Tunstall house will make a good home for the Longhorn family. They will be delighted in how clean the house is kept since Martha comes over and cleans it while Jake is away at work. Many days he has returned home to the scent of honeysuckle lingered throughout the house.

"I'll pay you cash so you will not be burdened with the exchange. Just keep it safe on your journey. I know you are quite capable." Longhorn stated as again he shook Jake's hand and gave him a few pats on the back. "Jake, those of us who know and love you will miss you, yet no one would ever blame you for seeking a change of scenery."

Jake looked down at his boots and replied, "I really do thank you a lot and you're right, I need to go and find my way."

Two nights later, when the hour reached one o'clock, a shadow stretched over Oliver Currie's blacksmith shop. A break in was being committed. A lone individual with evil intent pried open the back door that leads from the corral on the back side of the building and into the shop. It was opened very slowly to keep the hinges from squeaking to loudly. An average sized man wearing ragged clothes that stunk to high heaven slowly made his way through the blacksmith shop and into the living area occupied by the big scot. For a long while he had lived there alone.

Before the man carefully entered the small apartment that is connected to the shop he reached and took a hammer from a rafter where it hung between two square nails that had been driven there for tools to hang. It was a four pound cross peen hammer and his burly calloused hand held it to do harm. The man's arm muscles were like steel and the hammer caused him no strain.

The lone burglar was seeking valuables but first he had to eliminate the occupant of the quarters. He had been keeping his eyes on the shop for the last few weeks and knew Oliver Currie very seldom left the site. He also knew that his helper left promptly at the same time every day the shop was open.

The man crept silently through the sitting room of the small dwelling and into a room where the sound of a man snoring in his sleep was coming from. He took his steps very slowly making sure that no noise came from his boots touching the wood floor of the apartment.

He reached the doorway of the room. The snoring was getting louder and the man slowly leaned over to look into the room. He saw a beam of moonlight shining through an open window to the left of where the man laid sleeping. The light shined across the face of Oliver Currie who breathed heavily in his slumber completely oblivious of an intruder in his room.

An empty whisky bottle set on the floor next to the small bed Currie slept on. The man touched it with the toe of his boot as he inched his way toward the sleeping Oliver Currie. He stopped and looked down just before his boot came down. Had he not stopped himself the man lying on the bunk would have surely heard the sound made by the bottle and come awake. The burglar did not want a fight instead he wanted an easy elimination of his threat so he could take his time with his task of plunder.

The man raised his right hand that was clenched around the wood handle of the hammer and brought it down with extreme force. The four pound hammer of steel came down between the eyes of Oliver Currie. The flat part of the head of the hammer broke skull and embedded into the forehead of the big scot all the way to wood handle. Blood rushed from the wound and created a large dark spot that quickly grew on the dingy fabric of the victim's pillow. The pillow quickly turned to black with the life blood of the big redheaded scot, his eyes opened at the impact of the blow but they saw nothing.

The murderer dropped the hammer onto the big barrel chest of Oliver Currie and turned to walk out of the room. As he turned his boot caught the empty whisky bottle knocking it over. It rolled between the feet of the killer and stopped. He looked down with regret that it was not full of drink. He didn't need it to calm his nerves but just because he liked drinking whisky.

After searching through the whole apartment of Currie, the killer yielded a measly twelve dollars in paper money and seventy three cents in coins and a pocket watch made of silver that was inscribed "OC" in fancy cursive. He held it up to his ear and found that it was working. The time on its face read one forty three.

In the shop the killer found a metal can full of coal oil for the lamps the big scot kept but hardly ever used. He preferred candles and always kept several of them lying about along with wooden matches to light them. The murderer found the matches and after pouring the coal oil throughout the shop and apartment he struck a match and threw it down. He had even poured coal oil over the dead body of Oliver Currie. He wanted the whole place destroyed to cover up anything that might give away his identity.

The flames quickly grew until the whole building was engulfed in fire. The murderer escaped through the same door at the back of the blacksmith's shop that he entered. As he fled the scene he turned every so often to see that the building was completely ablaze. He rounded a building several blocks away when he finally heard the ding of the fire bell alerting the people of this end of town who had slept through his evil deed.

Jake mounted on the buckskin rode in to make sure all of the orders at the blacksmith's shop were filled before leaving Atlanta for good. He saw from a distance the burned building that was Oliver Currie's Blacksmith's Shop. He approached with his heart beating out of his chest. He didn't see his friend and boss anywhere. All he saw was a lone Constable standing by the hitching post that set in front of where the shop once stood. The Constable looked at Jake as he rode closer with a stern look on his face.

"What happened here?" Jake asked getting down from his horse. He mentally prepared himself for the worst not seeing Oliver standing by.

The Constable, a tall slender man with a huge brown mustache and close cropped hair that didn't make it from under his black hat spoke and said, "As you can see, there was fire here. One man was killed, the proprietor of the place...a Mr. Currie I do believe."

Jake's head went down and he closed his eyes wondering how many more people that he care about were going to die. His mind was quickly filled with Sarah, her mother and father...Jacob and Flora...Miss Peachy and now Oliver Currie. He turned and leaned against the saddle of the buckskin and just held his eyes closed which filled with tears but he quickly wiped them away. The Constable placed his hand on Jake's Shoulder and spoke to him in a calm voice.

"I'm sorry son...I take it that Mr. Currie was dear to you."

Jake looked up at the man and asked. "Did the fire take him?"

The Constable, an older man, old enough to be Jake's father looked down into Jake's eyes. He slowly shook his head as to answer him, no. He took a deep breath to speak.

"Mr. Currie was murdered. I found the body completely burned yet I could tell he had received a severe blow to the forehead. The burned hammer was found still lying on his chest when I discovered his body. I have no other information regarding the crime," Explained the Constable as Jake listened to every word.

"He had no family that I know of". Jake said as he turned toward the buckskin. "What will you do with his remains?"

"I'm sure a place will be found for Mr. Currie in the town cemetery." The Constable stated as he walked over to an undertaker's wagon that had just pulled up in front of the burned remains of the blacksmith's shop. Two old gray bearded black men who basically looked like brothers climbed down. One carried a thick quilt that was to be the burial shroud for Oliver Currie. There was no doubt in Jake's mind that Oliver would be placed in a simple wood coffin and buried, probably by the end of the day since the big scot had no one to claim his body.

Jake tipped his hat toward the Constable as he turned the buckskin and rode toward the heart of the city. He knew that he had to just let it go. He knew it was better for him to get out of the way and let the Constable do his job. There were no known witnesses to the crime so finding him would be next to impossible. Jake had no idea what Oliver Currie owned outside of what was in the blacksmith's shop. He would check with the Constable before he left to see if anything was found out about who killed his friend and boss.

The next day sod was laid over Oliver Currie. The simple wooden box that held his remains had been lowered into the ground by men employed by the funeral parlor. A Catholic Priest that knew Oliver stood by and read from the Bible Psalms twenty three. There was no choir and no one there to mourn for Oliver Currie no family and his only friend, Jake Powell stood with the Priest and the four helpers to bid goodbye to the burly blacksmith.

As Jake stood watching the dirt being placed into the grave of his friend he wondered who would do such an awful thing to a man like Oliver. He knew it had to be someone who killed out of the sheer pleasure of killing. A person like this had no sympathy for anyone... feelings for his fellow man was non-existent. Just like the man that took Sarah's life. They were evil men with no conscience, only a rotten soul full of violence and destruction, with no regard for anyone but themselves. The face of sweet Sarah and the faces of her loving parents came to his mind and how they were treated, slain in the street like their lives meant nothing. How Sarah was violated in the most brutal way a woman can be violated tore at his heart to the point he wanted to scream out to God and ask why He let such a thing happen to someone so precious. Jake made a promise to himself then and there, that if evil men such as this come against him...they will die.

Jake wanted to see if he could pick up a few things before he sat out on his journey west. He knew he needed a good rifle and possibly a good handgun. Jake knew he was out of practice but he would make time every day along the way to stop and hone his skills with his guns. As a cavalry soldier he used a saber a lot during the war. His was quite proficient with a pistol and rifle but over the last few years his only practice was with a set of tongs and a hammer. That would soon change.

Jake climbed down from the buckskin in front of the Easterly General Store and Hardware. The store stood to itself across from a saloon and a brothel right in the middle of what was always known as the red light district of Atlanta. The men and women that occupied this part of town were the questionable type that was wanted by the law or should be. He knew that by purchasing what firearms he needed in this part of town, the transaction would be quickly forgotten about soon after the exchange of money for goods was made. The face of the building was nothing fancy and the smell of whisky and piss occupied the morning air. On the front of the building was a boardwalk about ten feet wide. The doors to the establishment were wide open and did not conceal Jake's broad shoulders and lean waist as he strolled into the store. A man about his age greeted him with a broken smile.

"Good morning! Hey aren't you Jake Powell? You served with my brother Ben during the war…Third Georgia Cavalry twas." said the man standing behind a wood counter. He wore a white cotton shirt and a red apron. His hair was pretty much gone from early balding but he had a pencil thin mustache that set off his small thin lips. As he walked around the wood counter Jake noticed a limp that made his movements very slow. "Name's Rhett, Rhett Cooper. He stuck out a hand and Jake took it and gave it a friendly shake.   "What can I do for you today?"

Jake reached into the right pocket of his pants and fingered the coins that Oliver Currie used to pay him with the day before. The cash money he received from Mr. Longhorn was kept in a leather pouch that was stowed safely away in Jake's shirt just above his belt and just to the left of the center of his belly. He looked toward the firearms on display on the wall behind the counter. There were pistols hanging on pegs stuck in the wall and rifles and shotguns leaned up against the wall all in a row. He wasn't sure what he wanted but he had to make his choice.

"I need some firearms." Jake stated still looking at the row of weapons.

Cooper's eye brows went up and he walked about around to the wall of guns to take down whatever Jake wanted to look at. He looked at Jake's face and wondered if he had plenty of cash. He took a deep breath and let it out with a slow blow. Cooper was hoping for a sale. It had been a while since he had one that made him much money.

Jake pointed his finger toward a 1860 Colt Army Revolver in .44 caliber. "How about a look at that one," Jake asked as he stepped up closer to the counter. Cooper quickly took it down and handed it to Jake.

It was a blue steel finish and stained oak grips. The pistol felt good in Jake's hand and when he extended his arm and looked down the barrel the site alignment was easy. He was confident this pistol would serve him well. He was used to carrying two…one on each side in a cross draw fashion during his time at war and that was what he was comfortable doing now.

"Do you have another just like it?" Jake asked still holding the pistol out and keeping the sites perfectly set on an ornamental ball that set above the sign across the street that read "Saloon".

Cooper's tongue tied as he spoke with anticipation of the sell. "Why yes, mah Mr. Powell I sure do." He almost dropped it as he took it from its peg on the wall.

"How much for both with two boxes of .44 shot, powder and caps and holsters as well?" Jake asked.

Cooper through a big smile said, "I can let you have all of that for forty dollars."

"I'll give you sixty dollars for all of that plus that Henry .44 rim fire leaned up there too." Jake reached for his paper money and counted out the amount for the sale. The Henry rim fire 44 caliber rifle had an overall length of forty four inches with a tubular magazine that held fifteen rounds. The brass receiver shone as new brass should.

When Jake left he had a canteen for water, a bedroll, a coffee pot and cup, a rifle scabbard for the Henry and two hundred rounds of ammo, two shirts and two pairs of pants. Cooper threw in a leather haversack, a set of spurs, and a hog hair tooth brush with a box of tooth powder. Cooper told Jake the whores across the street used it to clean their teeth. That was good enough for Jake.

Jake walked out of the Constable's Office disappointed after he found out that as of yet there were no witnesses in the murder case of Oliver Currie. Jake rode away hoping that one day he would run across the man that killed his friend.

All of Jake's wares were packed in his haversack and tied to the buckskin with his bedroll. The rifle scabbard was secured to the right side of his saddle and it was fully loaded. His two Colt pistols set in their holsters in cross draw fashion and a bowie knife he forged himself was strapped onto his belt on his right side in a sheath he made from a beaver's tail. He wore a new pair of denim trousers and a gray colored cotton button down shirt. A heavy wool jacket was inside his bedroll in case the nights got cold. Everything Jake thought he needed for his journey was either on him or the buckskin. He knew along the way there would be others things to purchase with his money which was tucked inside his shirt safe and out of view inside a leather pouch right along with the deed to the property left to he and Sarah. Land she will never see.

He saddled up and slow walked the horse around the Tunstall house for the last time. As he pointed the buckskin south to head to the road he would take out of Atlanta he saw Martha Barkley open the front door of her house and run to the street. He stopped to say his last goodbyes.

"Jake, do stay safe. I know there is nothing I can say to keep you here." Martha spoke through tears as she reached up and placed a soft hand on Jakes thigh. He reached down and touched her hand.

"Thank you for everything you've done to help me these last few years. You know I really appreciate all you've done," Jake said as he looked into in her beautiful eyes. He hated to see her cry over him. "Goodbye Martha, and thanks again."

79

Martha stepped back as Jake spurred the buckskin forward. He had one more stop to make. He knew he would never return and he had to see the graves of his family.

At the cemetery he stood before the graves of the Tunstalls, Miss Peachy, Sarah and their children. He held his gray felt hat in his hands and wept as all of the memories raced through his mind. He saw all their faces...everyone with a smile. He remembered the softness of Sarah's tender touch when she ran her sweet finger tips across his face. He heard the laughter of Jacob and Flora as if they were playing at his feet. The sounds of Miss Peachy hard at work cooking his favorite supper after a long day at the blacksmith's shop rang in his mind as he took in the words carved on her headstone. He would never forget his family. No matter how far he roamed from Georgia, he would never forget.

Jake turned the buckskin's head and gave his ribs a gouge with his spurs. The horse stepped up to a trot. He thought to himself that he would have rather stayed here with the folks he loves, safe, sound and healthy, but that was not the hand that was dealt. He remembered the dream of Sarah and the children as they strolled toward a setting sun, a brilliant sun full of wonderful warm light that was setting in a western sky that pointed toward...Texas.

Chapter 5

Jake's route to Texas took him in a southwestern direction out of Atlanta that led him toward Montgomery, Alabama. He had hoped to make it to Montgomery in a couple of days after he started out but he didn't want to push the buckskin too hard. He noticed at the end of the first day of travel the horse looked tired. Its light brown coat was darkened by the sweat that covered its neck below his long dark mane. He decided then that he had better take it easy on the buckskin. Traveling all day was a bunch different than riding the short way between the Tunstall house and the blacksmith's shop.

Along the way Jake took in the landscape. It was much like what he saw on his long walk back from South Carolina after the war. He thought of the miles he covered then, not because he wanted to walk but because the yanks relieved him of his mount and belongings before sending him back home, pretty well with nothing but the ragged old Confederate uniform he had had on for months. He knew on this journey he would stop every now and then just to bathe in a creek or river. Jake figured he would run across plenty of water to cook his meals and coffee as well as keep his self somewhat clean. He liked the taste of the tooth powder he bought before leaving Atlanta. It was different than the baking soda Miss Peachy always supplied for him. He laughed at the thought of it being the brand used by the whores across the street from the store he bought it from.

The road he traveled down cut its way through a huge forest, a stand of pine trees like Jake had not seen in a while, not since he was away from Atlanta for those war years. It's easy to take for granted these beautiful sights when you live in a city like Atlanta for a few years. Huge majestic trees like these that rose almost to heaven, was something Jake had not laid his eyes on in way too long. Both sides of the old road were covered thick in them to the point you couldn't even see through. He figured these woods would hold plenty of deer to hunt. The thought of that made his stomach groan. It seemed like forever since he had tasted some of Martha Barkley's beef stew and cornbread. Which brought his mind to something else...he would have to learn how to cook.

After all the meals he missed finished running around in his head, Jake stopped for the day. He picked a spot in a little creek bottom that was surrounded by big oak trees. In the top of one oak tree that looked hundreds of years old he saw a bunch of dried leaves all clustered together which told him a squirrel's nest was there. Jake knew he could roast a squirrel over an open fire in no time.

Jake pulled the Henry 44 caliber lever action rifle from its scabbard when he pulled the saddle off of the buckskin. He found a log nearby to sit on so he could keep an eye on the squirrel nest. He heard a few of the little furry tree rats arguing and chasing one another in another tree not too far from where the nest sat nestled between a large fork in the huge tree. Jake kept his eyes on the tops of the trees looking for one to peek around the trunk of a tree. Barking like a squirrel a few times got the arguing bunch to come closer to check out the noise. As they did, Jake saw one looking at him from behind a tree trunk about twenty feet up from the ground. He eased the rifle up and aligned the sights up with the varmints head and pulled the trigger. The shot went through the critters head and he fell to the ground.

Jake decided he was a little hungrier than he thought before and decided to wait for another to stick his head out to see what happened to their buddy. Soon one did and Jake's aim proved true again as the second squirrel hit the ground headless.

He filled his canteen from the nearby creek and made coffee to go with the two squirrels roasting on a stick over the camp fire he made. It was summer time and the night air was still warm. Jake hoped for a breeze. Before dark he saw heavy dark clouds coming from the west that told him he was looking at getting wet either during the night or sometime in the morning. He had lived through it before and he would live through it again.

Thunder announced the arrival of a new day. Just before what little sun that was going to show for the day introduced itself, Jake finished his only cup of coffee before the day's ride. The sky was dark with low moving rain clouds that brought with them the promise of a wet day. As the clouds moved east, the thunder and lightning raged and rain fell hard. The wind moved the tops of the giant pine trees and shuffled the limbs and branches of the hardwoods. Jake shook his head at his luck. He pulled his hat down over his eyes and kicked his own butt for not thinking about a rain slicker when he bought what little provisions he had acquired from Cooper. Once he got to Montgomery he would have to rethink the idea of a pack horse or mule for this trip. He wasn't too worried about the powder in his haversack since it was leather treated with oil. His bedroll was going to be a mess at the end of this day.

Jake rode as the rain kept him soaked all the way down to his long johns. He held his head down allowing the rain to run off the brim of his hat. Every now and then he would look up to make sure the buckskin wasn't about to walk off the edge of the world...he wasn't sure since he didn't recall ever being this far west in his life. He pretty well had just decided to put his stomach right out of his mind and stopping to build a fire was an idea that he pushed right over with putting food in his belly. This was going to be one miserable day.

As the miles came and went the rain never seemed to let up a bit, he knew he had passed a farm or two but didn't want to place a burden on anyone so he just kept riding. He did see an old fellow sitting on his front porch that stood up and waved at him. Jake thought how nice it would be to sit and visit a spell, at least long enough to let his clothes dry out, which might take a week. The decision was made in his mind that the next farm he came across was going to have a wet visitor.

Finally, a small wood frame house came in view. It was made of rough cut lumber from pine wood in board and batting style with what looked like cedar shingles. The porch took up the whole front side of the house that looked to be about twenty five or so feet long. There was a chimney made of what was probably local rock, maybe iron ore and smoke came from the top of it. That told Jake that there might be vittles on or at least a pot of coffee. He hoped that the occupants were welcoming. As he approached the front of the house the solid wood door came open and the barrel of a shot gun introduced itself to him.

"Whachu want?" the voice of girl holding the shotgun demanded. She stepped into Jakes site and peered at him with eyes of raw steel. She was pretty to Jake even though she held the shotgun like she was ready to load him up with buckshot.

"Ma'am, I was just hoping to get out of the rain and maybe warm up my insides with a little of your coffee. I don't mean you no harm." Jake said right after he took a hard swallow.

The woman raised the shotgun up and leveled her sights on Jake and said, "You ain't none a them carpetbaggers are ya?"

Jake dismounted the buckskin and took his hat off so she could see he was just a wet traveler trying to find a dry place to rest. He held his hat in front of his chest and with a humble voice said, "No Ma'am I ain't and I'd just soon cut my own throat as to be a carpetbagger."

After a few seconds of thought the girl lowered the shotgun. She stepped out on the porch and gave Jake another look over before she made up her mind whether she was going to welcome him into her home. A boy about ten years old stepped into the doorway behind the woman. He was about five foot tall and wore a pair of bib overalls and no shirt nor shoes on his feet. He was holding what looked to Jake to be a Hawken 50 caliber flintlock rifle. He held it with purpose and there was no doubt in Jake's mind that this youngun knew how to use it. Most youngsters raised out in the country like this knew how to shoot by the time they was ready to take off the teat.

"Ma'am, I'd be more than happy to just go to the barn until I dry out, if that's okay by you." Jake said still hoping he wasn't about to catch lead.

"Naw, you can come in while Tommy tends to your horse." The girl said lowering the shotgun and turning to the boy. "Go take care of his mount. Give him oats and hay...and don't be plunderin through his stuff either. You leave it alone...you hear me Tommy?" She commanded with a voice that told Jake that she was the boss of this outfit.

"Okay, Rachael." The boy replied rolling his eyes and shaking his head like she should know better as he leaned the old rifle against a corner behind the front door of the house. The boy ran over to Jake to take the reins of the buckskin to lead him to the barn. He stopped and held out his right hand give Jake a friendly shake, "Names Tommy, glad to meet you sir."

Jake shook Tommy's hand and gave him the reins as the water steadily ran off the brim of his hat. The buckskin took to the boy right off and gave no resistance as Tommy gently gave the horse a tug toward the barn.

"I'll wipe everything down and brush the horse too for you Mister." Tommy assured as he and the buckskin splashed through the muddy water that stood between the house and the barn. The barn, like the house was built in a board and batting style with cedar shingles. Jake figured it was all built about twenty or so years ago. He was still standing in the rain watching the boy go into the barn when his attention was jarred as the girl hollered at him through the roar of the rain.

"Mister, you gonna come in out of the rain or should I chunk you a bar of soap and a razor?" the girl said with a light laugh in her tone.

Jake turned like he was goosed. He figured he was just used to getting rained on and he hardly even noticed. He put his hat back on his head and stepped up to the front door of the wood frame cabin. The girl met him and stood there and stared up in his eyes. Their gazed locked on to one another and he finally saw just how pretty she was. Her eyes were the prettiest green he had ever seen. Her auburn hair fell straight all the way to the middle of her back. She shook her hair away from her shoulders as she took the hat off that she had put on before opening the door to greet Jake with the shotgun. Her face was slender and her lips were delicate and thin. They gently turned up just at the center of her mouth making her face naturally lovely. She stood about five feet and five inches tall and her shoulders were petite in spite of the work she was likely forced to do around the little farm. The girl looked to Jake to be about nineteen years old. She wore a white cotton dress with a pink checker pattern that was probably made by her hands from material bought at a country store. Her feet were bare but not unclean. It showed that she takes great care in keeping herself clean. Jake admired that in a woman and this young lady was as pretty as a flower in spring.

"Come on in and get those wet clothes off. You can wrap a blanket around you and set over by the stove to keep the chill off. My name's Rachael, what's yours." She said as she hurried into a small bedroom that set to one side of the cabin. There were two bedrooms, one to the front of the cabin and one to the back. The living and cooking areas were set to the opposite side of the cabin. There were two chairs in the living area and a small eating table with three chairs where Rachael and Tommy took their meals.

Jake was embarrassed at the thought of getting undressed in front of Rachael so he just took his hat off and hung it on a peg just to the right of the front door. He took of his gun belt off and re-buckled it and hung it on the peg next to his hat. He stood there looking kind of lost as she returned from what Jake figured was her bedroom with a patch work quilt in her arms. She stopped and looked at Jake and stomped a small foot against the floor.

"Are you gonna git them clothes off or just stand there and catch your death of cold?" Rachael asked like she was now being a mother to Jake.

He looked around as if he was looking for a tree to hide behind before he started peeling out of his wet pants and shirt.

He held a confused look on his face like he didn't know what direction to take.

"Go in Tommy's bedroom there, unless you want to go to mine." Rachael commanded with a smile at her suggestion to go to her bedroom.

"Yes Ma'am, thank you." Jake said like a scared boy.

Jake tiptoed into Tommy's small bedroom and closed the door. The room was very clean. He had to say that it was spotless. He wasn't sure if Rachael took care of the place here or maybe there was a Maw whom he hadn't met yet that sees to the house chores. He pretty well settled on it being Rachael who runs the whole place and probably makes sure that Tommy keeps his chores done.

He had just stepped out of his long handles when he remembered the quilt Rachael retrieved for him to wrap around him when suddenly the door to the bedroom flung open and Rachael stepped in holding the quilt. Jake almost jumped out of his skin when he saw her. His eyes saw her smile. Her eyes saw his manhood.

"Here…you forgot the quilt." Rachael said with a big smile. She turned for one last glance at Jake's nakedness. She stopped and their eyes met for a quick second. Rachael gave him a wink before she turned and walked out closing the door behind her.

The rains continued to fall on the little Alabama farmhouse as evening settled in. Rachael cooked up a nice supper of fried chicken, mashed potatoes, cream peas and cornbread with dewberry cobbler to follow for dessert. Jake and Tommy both leaned back in their chairs and rubbed their bellies as an obvious sign of enjoyment. Through the whole meal and even from the time Jake walked barefoot out of Tommy's bedroom with the handmade quilt wrapped around his naked body,

Rachael hardly took her eyes off of him. She thought to herself, 'He is just about the purdiest man I ever did see.' Through dinner she asked him questions about his plans.

"So Jake, where you headin?" Rachael asked as she pushed a lock of her beautiful hair over her right ear while giving him a smile that showed total interest his way.

Jake was in the middle of a sip of coffee when the question and look came from the lovely young woman setting to his right. He let the hot liquid go down with a bite of cobbler and then he set his cup down before he answered her question. He scratched the back of his left ear while he gave thought to the question before him. He wiped his mouth on a white cotton napkin and turned and looked Rachael in the eye.

"I'm heading to Texas. I decided to go there and make a new start. There has been a lot of things happen in my life and I just figured I'd go there and begin again." Jake told her. He sat at the little wood kitchen table next to the pot belly stove and told Rachael and Tommy his whole story. He told them about returning home from the war and finding that his sweetheart Sarah had given him a boy and girl after he left to go and join the cause for freedom from a tyrannical government. Then he told her about how Sarah's life was taken from her by evil men clothed in Union Army uniforms after they had their way with her. Rachael wept when he told her of Jacob and Flora dying the same day after their struggles with breathing and Miss Peachy soon after from a broken heart. He told her of Oliver Currie and how someone took his life and burned down the blacksmith's shop with his body still inside.

"I'm making my way to Texas to start over on the property Sarah's father had left for us. I will always miss her. I ain't seen her since I left for the war," Jake explained looking at the specks of grounds in the bottom of his empty coffee cup. He stood holding the quilt around himself and approached the coffee pot setting on the stove. He poured himself another cup and offered some to Rachael and Tommy. They both declined and he went back and took his seat and looked over at Rachael and said, "So where is y'alls folks?"

Rachael pulled the corner of her cotton apron up to her face and dabbed a tear away from the corner of her eye. It had been a long time since she had any company to the small farm ran by her and her little brother Tommy. She was used to most people not caring anything about the two of them. It touched her heart for anybody to ask of their parents. The memories began to stir around in her mind about the father and mother who had loved her and Tommy. How they had taken care of them and taught them the things they would need to know in case they were left orphaned. She was always grateful for the devotion her parents had for this small family.

"Our paw went off to war just like you did. He was part of one of the infantry companies. We really didn't know which cause we was to young to understand all that. Tommy was just a little boy back then. Momma didn't want poppa to go but he went anyhow. While he was gone momma got sick and died. There was a neighbor up the road came and buried her upon the little hill out back of the house here and a preacher came from Montgomery to talk over her about the Good Lord. After that I just felt like I needed to take care of Tommy and the farm. I been hopin that poppa would come home, but I ain't seen him. When I seen you at our door I was hopin it'd be him." Rachael dabbed her eyes again and then got up from the table and began to collect the dishes from supper to be washed.

Jake turned toward her as she worked at the tub of water that sat on the work counter where she started washing them up. Her back was to Jake but he could tell she was crying. He heard her sniff a time or two. It broke his heart that all their

91

conversation brought back such sad memories. He thought about going to her and wrapping his arms around her to comfort her but then thought better of it since he was naked under the quilt and he didn't want to put things in her head. So, he got up to check his clothes that hung on a rope near the wood stove to see if they were dry.

Rachael turned and faced Jake. She placed both her hands on the counter behind her as if to brace herself. She looked at Jake and right away he knew she had more than just the memories of her parents on her mind. She looked at Tommy and gave him a nod to go to his room. He never said a word, just got up and complied, closing the door behind him.

Jake stared at her with confusion on his face. He was not prepared for what was coming. Rachael rushed to him and wrapped her arms around his shoulders and pressed her mouth to his. Her lips were warm with the taste of dewberry cobbler and her tongue was moist and left his mouth wet as she slid her soft cheek against his stubbly face. In his ear she breathed hard as she brought her soft hand down and forced open the quilt exposing his nude body. She tried to grasp his privates but Jake forced her arms down and held them. The quilt hit the floor but he held her arms and her body away from his.

"Rachael please stop this now, it is not right and I ain't havin it." Jake said not feeling much resistance from her. There was sternness in his voice that made her yield to his demand. He released her and quickly bent down and picked up the quilt in a heap at his feet. He wrapped it around his waist and hurried back over to his clothes still hanging above the potbelly stove. He gave up on trying to put his long johns on while still clinging to the quilt so he just tossed it to the side onto a chair. In silence he pulled the under garment on and then reached for his pants. He turned and found Rachael standing before him holding his shirt. Their eyes met as he looked down toward her pretty face. Her eyes were full of tears and Jake caught one with his finger as it rolled down her soft cheek. He gave her a smile and said, "I just can't take advantage of you Rachael."

She looked deep into his eyes with understanding. She knew the man who stood looking into her soul was a good man. One who would always be true to the woman he loved. She felt bad that she let her desires control her to the point she would compromise her upbringing. Rachael placed her head against Jake's warm chest and let her tears go. He wrapped her in his arms and held her there, the softness of her hair pressed gently against him.

After a few minutes had passed Jake pulled her head up and softly kissed her forehead. He looked again into her eyes and smiled a smile that told her that he understood how life can be lonely at times. He hoped she would be swept off her feet one day by a real southern gentleman who would work hard for her and make their home a castle of true love and devotion.

Rachael and Jake pulled away from each other and turned away. The two resumed the tasks they left to briefly touch the heart of one another, with no shame. Jake being a typical man thought that one day he would regret it, but in his heart knew he made the right decision to keep Rachael pure.

After he had completely dressed he reached up to the peg sticking from the wall by the front door of the cabin and took down his gun belt. He strapped around his waist and then grabbed his hat. The warmth of his shirt and pants from the heat of the stove felt good against his skin and he thought if he hurried across the way he could get to the barn before he got completely soaked. Jake hoped that by morning the rain will have stopped and the sun would shine away all the muddy mess left behind by the storm.

Rachael quickly turned and said, "You ain't leavin are ya?" a look of concern on her angel like face.

Jake stopped as he reached for the door knob but did not face her, "I think it best that I stay in the barn, I've caused you enough grief for one night."

He opened the door and hurried to the barn his boots splashing in a muddy slush as he ran. Once inside the barn he checked on the Buckskin as it stood stalled munching hay. He approached the horse and rubbed his face with his hand and talked to him in the way he always did. Even though it was pitch black inside the barn the buckskin knew he was in the presence of his master and friend. Jake picked a spot on the floor next to the horse to make a bed. The bedroll he still tied to his saddle and all of his gear was accounted for as he gave it a quick looking over. Tommy did a good job wiping it all down. He wrapped the bedroll around his shoulders and curled up at the feet of the buckskin. Jake quickly went to sleep...the scent of Rachael still in his mind.

When morning came Jake saddled up the buckskin and, after tying down all of his gear and possibles he had, he led the horse out of the barn and up to the hitching rail in front of the cabin where Rachael and Tommy slept the night away. There was smoke from a cook fire coming out of the stove pipe on the side of the house that told Jake that Rachael was awake and may have coffee going inside.

Suddenly the front door opened and Rachael stepped out with a cup of hot coffee. She handed it to Jake before she said anything. She gave him a smile which he returned. The air was already warm from the sun and she still had on a thin sleeveless cotton night shirt that revealed her beautiful pale shoulders that were specked with freckles. Her hair was brushed back and her face glowed with radiance. She gave Jake another perfect smile and stepped down to the bottom step from the porch. Their eyes were almost level with each other and she gazed into his before reaching up and touching his face.

"I know you're on your way and I figured a cup a coffee would hit the spot." Rachael said still locked into his stare.

Jake took a long drink of the hot brew and licked his lips and said while shaking his head, "Yes Ma'am...it's just what I needed."

They stood close to each other for a few minutes not saying anything, because neither one of them knew exactly what to say. Rachael still held on to her desires she showed the night before when she threw herself at Jake. He still wondered what would have come of the situation if he had given in to her advances.

Suddenly they both embraced and held on to each other for minutes. He had to admit she felt wonderful in his arms as her firm breast pressed against his chest. The scent of her hair would be something he would never forget. He hoped she would save herself for the man of her dreams. Jake considered himself just an old dog that showed up at her door step cold, wet and hungry, yet, he enjoyed the feel of her slender body against his for another minute before pulling away. Their eyes locked in another gaze into their souls again and their lips moved slowly together. Jake enjoyed the long sweet kiss from Rachael and when they both released each other both smiled a smile that said it was good that they had met. Jake handed her the coffee cup and turned toward the buckskin. He turned just in time to see Rachael walk to the door of the house wiping her face with her soft hand. Tommy stepped up to her and hugged her neck. He waved goodbye as Jake raised his hand and turned the buckskin and rode away.

Chapter 6

Montgomery, Alabama, the capital of Alabama was a busy city of the south with a population of over ten thousand people. The cotton community was a growing city of trade and commerce. Once the capital of the Confederacy, Montgomery Alabama was still just a little too big for Jake to hang his hat in for very long. His intention was a quick trip through to get what things he needed for the rest of his journey and get out. He knew there is always opportunity around every corner to get into trouble in a town with this many people in it. From his whole life being spent around Atlanta, he knew there were people in places like this were nothing but a problem waiting to happen and problems were something he didn't need.

Jake rode the buckskin all the way through town before he settled on stopping in at the general merchandise and feed store that set on the north side of the dirt street right next to the outgoing city limits sign. It was a wood framed building painted in a light blue color. There was a façade on its front that reached as high as twenty feet and on it was a sign that read City Limit General Store. He pulled his horse up to a hitching rail and dismounted. There was an old man sitting on a wood bench in front of the store who looked to be in his nineties. His old straw hat was down over his eyes and his denim pants and gray wool shirt looked to be as old as him. A corn cob pipe hanging from his mouth was surrounded by pure white whiskers that hung down to the middle of his slender frail chest. The old man's hair was the same color and protruded from under a worn out felt hat that was covered with sweat stains from many years ago. His skinny legs were crossed and his shoe laces were untied, but he appeared to Jake to be enjoying a good nap. As Jake opened the wood framed screen door to the store the squeaking hinges never disturbed the old fellow's slumber.

Inside the store a gentleman stood behind the counter arranging canned items on a shelf that went clean to the ceiling. The ceiling looked to be about nine feet high and all the shelves looked to be full as if a new shipment of canned goods had just arrived. The gentleman looked as if he was in his late fifties smiled revealing a mouth full of cavities but Jake didn't stare. He just stepped up to the counter and asked if he could pick up supplies.

"Howdy, what can I do for you?" the man said as he ran a hand along his bald round head. His white cotton shirt was starched and ironed to a crisp neat appearance that to Jake looked uncomfortable to wear. He like most merchants wore an apron...his was red and it hung down the front of his five foot and ten inch frame to just below his waist. His waist was full and his pants hung on him by red suspenders that looked like they matched his apron.

Jake gave the man a list and stood there in front of the counter in silence while the man looked it over. After a minute the clerk took a cotton sack out from under the counter and began to place items Jake wanted in it. There was six cans of peaches, a bag of coffee, a small sack of flour and a small package of cornmeal. Jake still had it in his head to travel light. The one thing he made sure he got was a rain slicker because he had no intention to be caught in a deluge like he was caught in a day or two ago.

Jake asked, "Is there a place to camp along the way?"

The man looked up from calculating the sum of the items in Jakes order and said, "Yeah, you can go out back to my barn and sleep there for the night...I won't charge you nothing."

Jake took his hat off and wiped his brow with his sleeve. He reached into a clear glass jar on the counter and pulled out several sticks of pepper mint and told the man to add them to his tab. The man handed Jake a small paper bag that he put his candy in so his hands wouldn't get sticky. He felt foolish buying the sweet treats but he would enjoy it.

"I guess I can if you don't mind. I never like being any trouble. I appreciate it. Do you know where I can pick up a pack horse?" Jake asked twisting the sack of candy up tight and putting it in his shirt pocket.

The merchant smiled a rotten smile and said, "Yes, I have such an animal for sale. I keep a few head of stock in the barn there behind the store just for this very need. All I have is gentle and I guarantee they will not give you a problem."

"Good, I'd like to take a look at what you've got." Jake said sucking on a stick of pepper mint.

"Very well, names Jones...Melvin Jones. I own the place. I bought it after the war. The previous owner went off to fight and got himself killed." Jones said taking ten dollars from Jake for his purchase.

Before dark the old man on the front porch of the store woke up and went home and later Jones and Jake ate beef steak while sitting at a four foot square table on the back porch of the store that also had living quarters, the dwelling place of the store's owner. The night was warm and the mosquitoes buzzed about making themselves a nuisance as they flew around their faces in the darkness. Jake had already gone over the stock Jones had for sale and settled on another gelding, an eight year old paint horse. It would do for carrying supplies.

Jake made a bed for himself in the barn close to the buckskin and decided it was time to turn in for the night. He had made a spot clean to lie down on and the ground was not to awfully hard for sleeping. Jake as always thought about Sarah and the children when he closed his eyes. Miss Peachy met his thoughts as well giving him instructions on how to take care of himself. He smiled just thinking about what she would say if she saw him lying on the ground in a barn when he could be in the crisp clean sheets at the Tunstall house.

Jake woke up at the sound of a couple of horses walking slowly to the front of the store building. He heard two sets of boots touch the ground and a man drag back deep into his nasal cavities and hark up a glob of snot. He spat it somewhere Jake couldn't see but still he thought the one who was making the God awful noise was probably drunk. The man hollered loud enough to wake the dead and the other man just laughed.

"Jones...get your worthless fat ass out here and open up, I need some chew. I'm out and I want some more right now...so get up and get to movin afore I come in and drag your carcass out of there." The drunk demanded as he stumbled up on the porch of the store building.

"I ain't tellin you again Jones...now I mean it. You know me and you know I mean what I tell you." The drunk finished his demand with a mumble nobody, not even another drunk could understand.

Jake heard movement across the hardwood floor inside the dwelling part of the building. He was hoping Jones was getting a gun or a club to take care of these two drunken imbeciles who just barged in with no respect for the living. He got up and strapped his pistols around his waist and slipped on his boots and quietly walked out of the barn and onto the back porch of the store building. His steps were slow and soft so he might not be detected. Inside the store he heard Jones open the front door of the building and the commotion that followed.

"What took you so damned long you fat little bastard?" The mouthy drunk yelled as he rushed into the store.

The drunk and mouthy one stood about six feet tall and had on a smelly sweaty cotton shirt that might be red if it weren't for all of the dirt and grime that stuck to it in a fowl smelling crust. His brown hat was covered with a stinking sweat stain that covered the entire surface of the crown and brim. He had on baggy denim pants with the legs partially tucked into the tops of his black pull on boots. The liquor smell of his breath was as bad as the stench from his body.

The other man was just a follower. Probably scared of the drunk he ran with. He was dressed in a dark blue cotton shirt covered by a brown leather vest. The spots under his arm pits ran all the way to his pant line and could be seen from under the vest which was three sizes too small. He wore what once looked like dress pants but now are just filthy britches. His pants cuffs covered the tops of brown lace up work boots.

The drunk man that did all of the talking grabbed Jones by the throat and shook him violently. Jones lost his water and a big spot covered the front of his night shirt. Tears began to well up in the store owner's eyes as the drunk and smelly man continued to abuse him. Jake watched from a window at the back of the store. Rage began to build up inside of Jake as the assault escalated to blows.

The man held Jones by the collar of his night shirt and began slapping him across the face. Jones cheeks quickly turned red as the opened flat hand of the drunk struck him over and over.

Blood began trickling out of Jones nose and he wept out loud as he begged the man to stop.

The follower stood by and laughed as he watched Jones being wailed by his liquored up running buddy. Jake was fuming inside but kept his composure. He walked around to the front of the store...the door still opened and the moon light shone, in creating an eerie glow coming from outside. The man doing the slapping suddenly noticed a shadow the room. He turned and saw Jake standing just outside the double doors of the store, his hands held to his sides.

The assailant let go of the store owner and turned to face Jake. The follower did the same just as the loud drunk put his right hand inside the right pocket of his nasty pants. He could not see Jake's face from the glare of the moonlight that pressed against Jake's back. It showed through the long sandy brown hair that fell over Jakes ears and shoulders. The man spit on the floor of the store in Jake's direction as a show of no respect. He had no idea of the rage Jake was feeling inside. To watch a man abuse another man was something he just could not let go. He had no intention of doing so because it was just too brutal and disrespectful.

"What the hell do you want...piss ant"? The drunk and disorderly man asked with a chuckle in his voice.

Jake wasn't jarred a bit by the hoodlum. He kept his eyes on the man that had his hand in his pocket that did all of the talking and the slapping. He was ready to draw a pistol and go to shooting and he was ready to pull his knife and go to cutting...at this point Jake didn't care. Something needed to be done and that something was about to happen.

The man pulled his hand from his right pocket and produced a jack knife. He opened it and showed it to Jake. The man began to make a low laughing sound as if he was deranged. He hoped it would scare Jake to turn and high tail it back to where ever he come from but it didn't work. Jake reached to his right side and pulled out the hand forged Bowie knife from the beaver sheath and held it down to his side. His heart pounded not knowing what this crazed mad person was going to do.

Suddenly the man closed his knife and put it back in his pocket and Jake slid the Bowie back in its sheath. The drunken man rushed toward Jake to go hand to hand. As he rushed Jake the man extended both hands to grab Jake by the throat but Jake blocked his assault and sent a hard right fist into the man's ribs on his left side. The air rushed out of the man and he let out a grunt. Jake grabbed him by the back of the head hurled him outside with his head bent over. His head crashed into the hitching rail in front of the store and he went down in a heap.

Jake turned to the other man who was no longer laughing and grabbed him around the front of his smelly vest. The man left his feet as Jake threw him out the door onto his stinking friend. Jake rushed outside and kicked the follower in the face with a hard boot. The man's nose exploded in crimson sparks like fireworks on the fourth of July. Jake grabbed him and picked him up over his head and planted him across one of the horses that the men rode up on. Jake didn't know which man the horse belonged to and didn't care.

He then turned to the drunk that did all of the slapping around of Jones. He took two hands full of nasty smelling shirt and pulled the man to his feet. The man stood in front of Jake as Jake began to slap him across the face just like he did Jones in the store. Each time Jake slapped him across the face the man let out a grunt. After several hard slaps by a strong right hand, he decided it was time for his fist. He reached back and brought a hard right to the man's cheek just below his left eye then a back hand to the right side of his face sent the man to his knees in front of Jake.

103

The drunken man's eyes quickly swelled closed and he hung by one arm that was thrown over the hitching rail where the other horse was tied. Jake caught a bloody ear and pulled the man to his feet. He spun him around and heaved him head first over the saddle of the horse.

Jake grabbed an ear again and pulled the man's head up and asked him, "Are you awake badass?"

The man grunted as he tried to answer as bloody drool hung from his mouth compliments of the beating he just received. Jake still holding his head up by an ear told the man, "A word of advice... get off tobacco, it's bad for you."

Jake slapped the butts of both horses and they rode away carrying the drunken men

The pack horse Jake bought from the storekeeper Jones took the load of supplies that was purchased the day before like he was trained for it. A rain slicker was tied to the back of the pack saddle that was secured to the paint gelding as well as other provisions Jake might need. Texas was still a world away as for as he was concerned. Jones came outside into the morning sunlight and winced as the brightness touched his sore eyes causing him to throw a hand up in front of his bruised face. He leaned on a post in front of the store entrance and held out his hand as to give something to Jake. Jake looked up and saw Jones had money in his hand. It was obvious he was offering it to Jake.

"What's that for?" Jake asked turning back to the task of securing his gear.

"I want you to have it back for what you did last night. You could have just let them beat me even worse or even kill me."

Jones said drawing back the hand holding the money Jake spent at his general store. He extended the money toward Jake again thinking he might change his mind and take it back.

"You don't owe me anything." Jake said his voice low and gravelly. "I'd helped anybody with those two knuckleheads, so you keep that money."

The store owner slowly pulled his hand back with the money and pushed it into a pocket at the front of his apron. He was touched by the act of kindness by this stranger, Jake Powell. He knew that not very many men would have stepped in and defended him like that but this man did and for that Jones was truly thankful. He just stood there really not knowing what to say.

Jake tightened the saddle on the buckskin and mounted up. As Jake turned the horses head he touched his hat and said, "Thanks for the beef steak, it was good. Thanks for the place in the barn too, it was a descent place to sleep." He touched a spur to the animals side and the buckskin headed west with the pack horse in tow.

Jones stood and watched Jake as he rode down the dirt road leaving the City of Montgomery. When Jake was about a hundred yards away a man road rode up to Jones on a shining black horse. He wore a gun and a badge on his shirt just above the pocket. A black felt hat sat on his head and his pants were black corduroy. He wore a large mustache on his face that was as black as his horse and he had a Colt Dragoon Revolver in a holster on his right side. Long hair the color of his mustache fell from under his hat. He pulled up and stayed on his horse and leaned over the saddle horn to look at Jones with hard blue eyes.

"I heard there was some trouble here last night Mr. Jones is it?" The man said who was a Deputy Marshal for the City of

Montgomery. "Couple fellers say they were assaulted here last night by some crazy man. Do you know anything about it?"

Deputy Roscoe Ellis was an old lawman who had worked for the people of Montgomery for the last five years. He arrived back from the war and picked up where he left off as one of the towns lawmen. He had been in many a scrap and always came out on top of the situation. He was quick with the gun and fist and knew when he was being told a pack of lies.

"Deputy, I don't recall anything like that happening here last night." Jones could have told the deputy the whole story but he knew the deputy would light out after Jake and he didn't want that... so he just left it at what he just said.

"Well...I'm glad to hear it." Deputy Ellis said with a chuckle and a smile at the outcome of this bit of law enforcement work. He knew the two men that came staggering up to the City Marshals Office this morning holding their bandaged heads saying they had been assaulted as a couple of good for nothing drunks. He knew if they totted a whoopin from somebody they probably needed it.

Roscoe Ellis looked down the road at the back of a stranger riding away then turned his big black horse and rode toward town. Ever few steps Jones could hear the deputy laugh as he slowly rode away. Jones took a broom and swept the front porch of his store. He was thinking about what he might do if those two ever came back to his store looking for trouble like they did last night. He decided his only course of action would be to arm himself with his old black powder shotgun he kept in his bedroom just in case those two or others like them ever showed up at his door again. Jones decided he would order one of those repeating rifles like Jake had to give him the better edge on defense. He thought to himself how scared he was to fight back last night but with a rifle the odds would change.

106

The way from Montgomery to Selma, Alabama was not much more than a pig trail. The buckskin and the paint gelding followed an old road west toward what Jake hoped would be Selma. There was nothing along the way to tell him one way or the other as to what town or settlement he would be seeing ahead of him. He came to a river that looked low enough to cross and he spurred the buckskin on and, lucky for Jake, the paint followed like he had been walking behind the buckskin for years. Jake hoped he would continue to be the good horse he seemed to be so far.

The sun was getting low in the sky and Jake decided a camp, next to the river he just crossed might be best since he was tired of the saddle for a day and he knew the two horses could use a rest. He stripped the saddles from their backs and then used a brush he had bought on each of the horses. He wanted them to know just how much he appreciated them on this trip so he brushed them for a good half hour before starting a fire and putting on water to boil for coffee. A tater he bought from Jones would go good with a few bites of jerky. Jones assured him the jerky was from a buck that was brought to him last winter in lieu of payment on some material a feller got for his wife to make dresses for their two daughters. Jones claimed his jerky was the best in the land and that people paid him every winter to make it from the deer that was hunted and killed.

Jake ate his tater with salt and chewed on the jerky which turned out to be pretty tasty while he sat on the ground by the fire. Afterward he enjoyed a cup of coffee with a stick of peppermint before he turned in for the night. The coyotes yelped and hollered most of the night but Jake knew they wouldn't come to close to the fire. He had fed dry wood to it that he found in the forest until it put out enough light to see about forty yards around the camp. He set up under a stand of cedar trees and the smell from them in the air reminded him of those on his old home place outside of Atlanta. He crossed his ankles and touched the pouch he kept under his shirt with his spending money and land papers. He thought of all the things he wanted to do once he got settled on his land in Texas. Jake rolled around in his head the size herd he wanted as well as the size garden he would grow to sustain him through an East Texas winter. Winters in the south could be mild one year and harsh the next and Jake wanted to be prepared no matter the case.

Jake lying on his back looking up at the stars and his fire dying down, unbuckled his gun belt and laid the strap and the buckle side straight out to his sides. He knew he could quickly buckle it back if need be, knowing you never put nothing past anyone. The drunken man at Jones store last night was a prime example of the need to always be ready for trouble. He still hoped for a good night sleep even if it was with one eye open.

The noise from the coyotes continued to cut through the night. He swore he hear a voice nearby and he strapped his pistol belt back around him and laid still with his ears open to any sound that didn't belong to the darkness. Again he heard it, this time the voices were closer and coming from the trees to his left. He was facing the river and the moon was to his back as the voices got closer.

Jake rolled to his right and stood behind the cedar tree he was using to prop up his head. He checked for movement from around the tree and finally saw two fellows walking along between the river and the woods. One was carrying a lantern with what looked like a candle burning on the inside of it and the other carried a rifle. They saw the light of Jakes camp fire and stopped. They were trying to shade their eyes from the glow of the moon to see if they could see anyone by the fire. They slowly approached with rifle raised to the ready position and the lantern was held high.

"Who's there?" the one carrying the lantern asked with fear in his voice. "I know you're there and ain't no cause for hidin so just come on out so as we can see you."

Jake shook his head while leaning against the cedar tree. He remained quiet until the two approached several more steps closer. They were just about to the light of his camp fire when he spoke.

"Okay, that's close enough...what's on yalls minds?" Jake asked as he eased the .44 out of his left holster with his right hand. He could tell the rifle was an old flint lock squirrel gun with one shot but it could still be a threat.

The one holding the rifle said, "Wez coon huntin...whatchu here for?"

"Well, I was trying to sleep until you two come sashayin through like two old widow women headin to meeting." Jake said with a chuckle in his voice. Truth was he had about had all the winks he could stand and was ready to get up and stoke up the fire for coffee. "Now if you two hombres would put down that squirrel, gun I wouldn't feel so threatened."

The one holding the rifle swallowed hard and raised the rifle higher almost to his shoulder before he struggled with saying, "Well how do we know you ain't no threat to us? And what's a hombre anyhow...ain't that what chu called us?"

"Hombre, is Spanish for man." Jake said nearly laughing. "Now put that rifle down."

As he made his command he brought his pistol around the tree and pulled the hammer back. The sound of the pistol being cocked was enough to cause the one holding the rifle to drop it to the ground in front of him.

"Now you two...hombres...take a seat on the ground in the light of the fire so I can keep an eye on you."

The two young men rushed to the ground next to the fire and looked at Jake with their eyes nearly popping out of their sockets. They were both dressed in dirty bib overalls with no shirt and each wore a brown denim jacket and no shoes but had a black felt flop hat on that looked like it came out of the same box. They both looked to have hair cropped short in a burr cut probably done by each other considering the gaps in their hair that even their hats couldn't cover. Each boy looked to be about sixteen years old and frightened at the site of Jake as he came around the big cedar and into the light.

"So you boys are out here coon huntin. Don't you know with all that talking yall was doin will scare off all the coons?" Jake said as he sat down across from them. Jake reached over and took the coffee pot and a canteen of water and started the brew as the two boys looked on. "Yall got a cup in your pocket?"

Both boys shook their heads 'yes' as they reached into a pocket of their jacket and brought out a tin cup for coffee. After the drink came to a boil, Jake poured them both a cup and then one for himself. He noticed they both kept an eye on him as if they were both scared senseless. Jake figured if he suddenly hollered 'boo' right quick they both lose their water and their mud. The three sat and sipped coffee until the whole pot was empty. By then it was good daylight and time for Jake to move on down the trail.

"What is the next town west of here?" Jake asked getting up from the ground. The fire had burned itself out and the coffee was nothing but grounds and the sun peeked over the trees to the east.

"If you keep going west down that trail you'll come to Selma. It ain't far. When you come to the Alabamy you raise that flag there by the dock and the ferry will come over and get you to float you over to town," said the boy with the lantern.

Jake saddled his animals and tied on his bedroll and mounted up. He turned to the boys and touched his hat saying, "Boys, happy hunting". He spurred the buckskin and away he went. Next stop, the Alabama River.

The ride over the Alabama River went good for Jake but the two horses were rather skittish at first but he soothed them booth with a touch. The paint pack horse come to trust Jake and it didn't take long for the three to become trail pals. Both mounts bucked a little when one of the steam ships approached a landing to dock. The horn of the ship was too loud for Jakes liking, but the Captain of the ship didn't make too much fuss with it. The vessel looked to be carrying people and freight. There were folks on the dock platform waving to loved ones as they arrived back to Selma. Jake didn't intend to stay long in Selma, maybe just to feed the animals and have a bite himself.

He walked the two horses into town and settled for a livery stable next to the St. James Hotel. Jake figured he would leave the two mounts at the livery and see what kind of food the hotel had in its restaurant. It looked fancy. It was a three story building that sat on a street corner and the livery stable was behind it. There were doors all the way around the side and face of the hotel building and the second story had a balcony that ran the entire front and one side of the building with a beautiful ornate railing as well. The third story had windows that overlooked two sides of the building. Jake hoped the owners would let an old saddle bum in for a meal. He might even get a room. A good night's sleep would do him some good.

When he approached the livery stable a young black man approached him. "What can I do for you sir?"

He was about twenty years old and was dressed in a black shirt that looked like it was several sizes too big and a pair of denim pants that looked the same. In place of a belt, the fellow had a rope tied around his waist to hold his pants up. He had on old leather work boots that had holes in both toes and a dark blue bandana on his head that covered a thin dark hair. He looked to be about five and a half feet tall and his big white top teeth stuck out of his mouth when he spoke.

"Would you feed them both a good helping of oats and hay while you give them a good brushing. They would sure be your friend if you did." Jake said while he undid the saddle of the buckskin. He pulled the saddle bags off and threw them over his shoulder and slid the Henry out of its scabbard. The black livery hand went to work the supplies and pack saddle off the paint with joyful glee beaming from his dark face.

"I get right on it. I bet you'd like some grub. Dat place rat there will sho treat you right. They got good vittles. Dats where I eat eva work day" the man said leading the two horses into the livery stable.

Jake walked into the fancy St. James Hotel and was greeted by a female desk clerk behind a high counter. His boots made a loud thud sound like someone beating a drum with every step he took across the shining hardwood floor of the hotel lobby. The beautiful lady standing behind the counter watched Jake as he approached her. Immediately she noticed his manly swagger. He had all of her attention. She was wearing a pink dress with white lace that ran along the seam that framed her rather large breasts. She had blonde hair that would cause you to shade your eyes if you looked at it for too long. It hung in waves down both sides of a gorgeous round face that possessed a smile that incorporating two full lips that said 'what are you doing here?' Her blue eyes that looked deep into the eyes of the man in front her, asked the same question.

She looked Jake in the eye with her brows high. She didn't say anything only stared into his eyes. Jake leaned in toward the blonde beauty across the stained wood counter and returned the glare. He was now entertaining himself with what he figured at this point to be some arrogant female that believes this hotel is just a little too swanky for the likes of him. Their stares continued for almost a minute when she finally gave in and spoke.

"I guess you want a room here at the St. James Hotel." She asked looking Jake over.

Jake smiled under his hat and said, "If it ain't too much trouble, yes Ma'am I would."

Still smiling she returned, "Got five dollars?"

"Why yes, as a matter of fact I do. Shall I pay in advance?"

"Why yes...if you don't mind. Can you sign your name?"

"Why yes, I can." He returned, never letting go of her gaze.

Jake signed his name and reached in his pocket and pulled out paper money. Her soft hand touched his rough paw as she took it. She took several seconds pulling her hand away from Jakes all the while looking deep into his eyes. When she finally pulled her hand back he gave her a wink.

"Do you have hot water and a bath tub?" Jake asked know she could smell the trail reeking from him from across the counter.

The woman was pleased at the question. "Yes I will have it brought up to you. Is there anything else you'd like…Mr. Powell?" She asked as she looked down at her register to see his name. As she looked up she gave him a wink and shook away a lock of golden hair that fallen over her right eye brow.

Jake smiled and winked as he started toward the stairs and the third floor.

After Jake had a hot bath and a shave he walked down to the restaurant inside the hotel. As he passed the lady desk clerk their eyes again met and again they exchanged a wink. He went on to the dining room and had a beef steak with a potato, sweet peas, cherry pie and coffee. With a full belly Jake realized just how tired he was from the saddle. He hadn't covered so much ground sitting on leather since the war and he was looking forward to stretching out.

Jakes room was clean and very comfortable. The bed was big and soft with two feather pillows that felt so good to his head as he lay there wearing nothing but his pants. He figured that most folks were tucked away in their beds at home sound asleep. From an open window next to his bed came distant noises like people in a bar or saloon having a happy evening with song and drink. He just laid there looking at the ceiling wondering how many miles he would travel the next day. Suddenly a knock on his door jarred his thoughts. He got up and approached the door.

Jake thought about opening the door with a .44 in his hand but decided to just open up and see who was there so, he turned the knob and gave it a pull. Standing there was the blonde desk clerk with that mischievous or even impish grin on her face. She was playing with a lock of golden hair that hung down to her left breast and the look on her face said she had something on her mind. Without saying a word she walked into Jake's room. As she passed him she looked up and gave him a wink. Jake closed the door behind her.

Chapter 7

Before the sun rose on Selma, Alabama, Jake had risen from tangled sheets where the voluptuous blonde desk clerk still lay in blissful slumber after a night he would not soon forget. He used the hog hair tooth brush and powder before a quick spit bath with water from a white porcelain bowl and pitcher to at least make him presentable on the road ahead. He left the stubble on his face, figuring if he was going to meeting he would shave, but simply going on down the road he looked just fine. He hoped he could get out of town before the blonde woke up so he crept around on bare feet as quietly as possible. He thought a floor creaking when he snuck out of the room to use the privy, might have brought her out of her sleep, but she turned over and her rhythmic breathing picked up, moving a lock of golden hair up and down with each breath.

Jake had just buttoned up his pants around his waist when he heard footsteps outside his hotel room door. He walked over to see if he could hear anything else when suddenly the door crashed open. It came with such force that when it hit Jake it took him to the floor. A bearded man about the size of Jake rushed in with fire in his eyes. The blonde on the bed screamed as the ruckus jarred her awake and she almost lost her water at the appearance of the man. He wore a black silk vest over a white cotton shirt that looked newly pressed. His black pants were creased and his dress shoes were shined to perfection. He had coal black hair that was combed straight back on his head and his beard hung down to the first button on the silk vest.

"You harlot"! The man screamed in a voice loud enough to wake every occupant of the hotel.

The blonde screamed again as the man approached Jake. He was just getting up from the floor after being struck by the door as it came off its hinges. The man reached down with a growl and pulled Jake up by his hair. The man's right fist went back and Jake reacted by throwing his left arm up and around. He made his move just in time to block the mighty blow that was headed for Jakes face. As his block followed through Jake sent a right fist in the direction of his assailant's nose and it landed right on the tip of it bringing a splatter of blood to the bearded man's cheeks. He stumbled back but sent his left to Jake's right jaw and then his right to Jake's left jaw. This made sparks flash in Jake's head and he would have sworn he heard a bell ring. This man could swing his fist much like a mule kicks.

Jake fell to the floor on his butt. He quickly felt of his chin to see if his face was still connected to his head. The man bent down to get another grasp on Jake. When he got close enough Jake reached up and took as much of the man's beard in his hand as he could get and pulled hard. While clinging to the man's black facial hair he pulled himself up to his feet and brought around another hard right fist landing it against the man's left temple. This blow staggered the man and Jake gave him another and another. He finished the man with a hard right back hand to the nose. The man buckled and fell.

"You broke my nose!" the man cried as he dropped to both knees in front of Jake. He stepped back and gave the man plenty of room in case he wanted to make another attack. While the fight was going on, the blonde curled up in the sheets still naked, was wincing at every blow by both men. Jake walked over to the pitcher of water and poured more into the bowl setting on the large oak dresser against a wall. He wet a towel and held it to his mouth that was bleeding and then to the scratches on his knuckles. He walked over to a bed post where his gun belt hung, took it up and buckled it around his waist. He tucked in his shirt and pulled on his boots all the while the bearded man held his hands over his face crying…"You broke my nose."

Jake looked at the blonde who had wrapped the bed sheet around her and said. "A friend of yours?"

With her eyes closed and a frown on her face she replied, "I guess you could say that. He thinks he's my boyfriend, or he wants to be anyway."

Jake took up his rifle, saddle bags and hat and walked to the door of the room which laid on the floor off its hinges and turned around and said, "Well, I'll leave you two alone...so yall can get to know one another." He turned and left the room and went down the steps to the front desk and lobby. Another beautiful blonde stood behind the desk, Jake handed her his room key.

"Did you enjoy your stay at the St. James Hotel?" she asked with her lips slightly puckering as they smiled at Jake.

He returned the look and said, "Yes I did, thank you." He gave her that same little wink before turning and walking out the door leaving the St. James Hotel behind him.

A week later Jake rode the buckskin into Raleigh, Mississippi and right up to a saloon at an intersection of sixth and Hampshire streets. He was happy to finally get off the horse and stretch his legs. There was the sound of a piano playing inside and it reminded him of how thirsty he was for something other than creek water. He tied the buckskin and the pack horse to a hitching rail and stepped up to the sidewalk in front of the new red brick building. A sign painted across the front of the building over a row of second story windows read 'Hotel St. Charles'. A smaller sign at the corner entrance read 'Saloon'. That's where the music was coming from and that's where Jake walked in through a set of double doors.

A few heads turned when Jakes boots set a rhythm across the hardwood floor. He stopped at the bar and nodded at the saloon keeper as he approached wiping a shot glass with a towel. The man held his eyes on Jake and a look on his face like he was in the presence of a stranger. He walked even with Jake and spoke, still wiping the shot glass.

"What can I get you friend?" asked the bartender, medium sized man with a little mustache that looked like it was drawn on his face with a piece of charcoal. His skin was pale and his hands looked like they had never seen a hard day's work in his life. He had a fancy air about him in spite of his southern drawl when he spoke.

Jake, never one to drink the hard stuff, settled for a mug of cold beer. He paid the man with paper money from the leather pouch he kept under his shirt. The man behind the bar brought change in smaller bills and a few coins. This did not go unnoticed by two men standing at the far end of the bar from Jake. The bar was about twenty feet long so the two weren't so far away to see that the currency Jake passed was a large denomination. Unfortunately for Jake, he had used all of his coins to pay for the room he got about a week ago.

The two men looked at one another after both had noticed the leather pouch as Jake removed the money from it. The one to the right of Jake nudged the other and motioned with his head to go sit down at an empty table. The other nodded in agreement knowing his partner had a plan to relieve the stranger of his money. They moved together as they walked across the room toward a table that sat on the right side of the room and a little closer to Jake so they could get a better look at him.

The two men took seats and began to size Jake up. Both men were about the same size and stature. One wore a brown derby hat and a red shirt with the sleeves rolled up past his elbows. His face was round and he sported a five-day growth of salt and pepper beard. His dark hair with white specks and streaks hung down from under the derby hat to his shoulders and he kept the locks on the sides of his head pushed back over his ears. He wore black pants, a silver silk vest and black lace up boots. An 1851 Navy Colt hung from a leather holster on his right side.

The other man was dressed in a gray cotton work shirt, denim pants and leather pull on boots. He was clean shaven and his slick bald head was tanned and uncovered. He as well carried a Navy Colt revolver on his right side in a leather holster. They sat and whispered back and forth on how they would get this strangers money.

"When he leaves we will just follow him. I don't think he's from around here. I bet he is just passing through." the first man said in a soft tone with his head down and leaning over so his partner could hear him. The other just nodded his head in understanding.

The bald man leaned over and said, "I wonder how much he's got...that pouch looked pretty big."

Jake occasionally glanced up at the ten foot mirror that was mounted on the wall behind the bar. He noticed the two men move to the table and he saw them looking at him and whisper back and forth to each other. He mentally kicked himself for allowing someone to notice the pouch under his shirt. These two looked like they were up to no good and he was not going down easy.

Jake ordered another beer just as a young girl wearing a red dress that was pulled down so that her soft pale shoulders were noticed by any man she approached. Her dark hair was pulled up in a ponytail displaying a face with soft delicate features and emerald green eyes that sat behind long thick eye lashes. She moved close to Jake and put her left hand on his right and looked up with a come and get it grin.

"Buy me a drink stranger?"

"What are you having Ma'am?" Jake asked nodding to the bar tender to come over. He was expecting the barkeep too come over anyway seeing that the girl made her move on a customer to 'keep them drinks coming'.

The girl ordered a whisky and moved closer to Jake. He felt her hand move to his side and toward the front of his shirt. She must have seen the same thing the two men at the table saw and now she was making her play. Jake figured she would at least try to get him drunk before she put her plan into motion. He figured she wanted to get to his stash of money before anyone else did. Jake moved his right hand over her roaming fingers and pulled them away at the same time finishing the last of his beer.

Jake threw down coins enough to pay for her drink and turned toward the door to leave. The saloon girl grabbed his arm and pulled him back as he turned. She made sure to press her left breast up against him in a final effort to regain his attention but Jake didn't fall for it. He pulled away and walked out the door. The two men at the table watched as Jake left the saloon. They waited until he tightened the girths around his horses, mounted up and slowly rode away before they got up and hurried to the door of the saloon. They watched him take the street heading west. Their mounts were outside as well and they quickly mounted up and fell slowly behind him.

Just down the street on a corner across for the saloon was a general store. A man outside wearing a white apron was sweeping the wood porch of the building. Jake stopped as he came even with the store and the man, dismounted and stepped up on the porch of the store. He picked up a shovel from a wooden barrel in front of the store and exchanged it for money with the clerk. The two men following kept their distance from Jake. They watched him talking to the store clerk with wonder. After a brief conversation with the merchant, Jake stepped off the porch and back to his horses.

"What's he buying a shovel for?" asked the bald headed man as he scratched his chin. The other just shrugged.

Jake tied the shovel to the paint's pack saddle and remounted the buckskin. Out of the corner of his eyes he saw the two men from the saloon slowly riding up the dirt street trying to be as inconspicuous as possible. Jake pointed his horse west and rode toward the city limits.

He wanted to get as many miles away as he could before making camp. He figured on finding a nice secluded spot under the tall pine trees that cover the country side. He had grown accustomed to the smell of pine and he didn't mind sleeping under the stars. The only thing that he hated was trying to sleep when he thought there might be snakes around and he was convinced that he had two snakes on his trail. In his mind he wondered how he would handle the situation. This was something he never wanted to happen on his journey but he also knew in his mind that if it did...he would have to handle it and handle it he will.

Jake figured he had ridden a good twenty miles from Raleigh and he was ready to get off the buckskin for a night's sleep. He was saddle weary and he had to admit stopping at the saloon didn't do anything for him but bring him possible trouble. He found a trail off of the road, he was on and he took it north. If he could lead this possible trouble away from the road he felt like he would be better off. Jake kept his eyes open for any houses that might be close. He had no idea if the two men would just leave with a friendly suggestion or if they would require more convincing. Getting into trouble while he was trying to make it to Texas was certainly not in his plans, but neither was having the money he had for a start being stolen from him either. He wondered if they would make their move during the night or if they would rush him from behind him. As he rode he kept his ears open for riders.

Virgin pines stood tall and thick throughout the forest that pressed the trail through the woods. He thought he heard horse's hooves against dirt but wasn't sure so he left the trail and dismounted, pulling the two horses into a thick clump of brush that grew around the bottom of pine tree that had to be six feet through the middle. He placed the animals behind the brush and away from the trail. The floor of the forest was covered with pine needles and twigs. The pine needles wouldn't give him up but stepping on a twig and dried limbs would certainly tell the two men following him he was close.

Suddenly Jake heard riders coming. They were moving slowly along the trail he had just left. From around the brush he could see the two men and it was the same ones from the saloon. They stopped when they saw where Jake's horses left the trail and went into the forest to their left. The two would be thieves were about fifty yards away and close enough to hear Jake.

"All right, what do you two fellows want with me?" Jake knew but still wanted to let them know they were being watched. He kept himself concealed from their view from behind the brush. The horses were surprisingly standing still. He took the Henry out of its scabbard and quietly moved the lever to ready the rifle. The two men stopped in their tracks when they heard Jake's voice.

"I believe you know what we want." said the one with the salt and pepper beard. "Why don't you just come on over here and get this little transaction over with."

Jake grinned and shook his head and said, "I can make the little transaction from here."

The two outlaws looked at each other and the baldheaded one said, "Whatchu mean?"

Suddenly Jake appeared from behind the brush and raised the Henry and fired. The man with the salt and pepper beard caught lead between the eyes. His head snapped back as a mist of blood covered the bald one's face. The dead man turned slightly toward his partner in crime before crumbling in a heap on the ground.

The bald-headed man reached for his pistol and dove behind a large pine tree. He was breathing hard and his mouth went dry making it hard for him to speak. He pointed his pistol in what he thought was Jake's direction as he looked around the base of the big tree. He didn't see the man who just shot his partner. Jake had moved to his left behind a tree as well as was making his way closer to the man going swiftly and quietly from tree to tree. He watched for every stick of wood to step over as he made his way closer to the bad guy.

"Why don't you just let me go on from here, I won't bother you no more I promise." The man said knowing that he would later try to ambush Jake on down the road. Jake knew it too and was not going to let that happen.

Jake had made his way to the right side of where the bald man was hiding behind the big pine tree. He positioned himself far enough behind the man that he was unnoticed until he raised the rifle.

"I ain't letting you go just to have to deal with you later." Jake said as the man jumped to his knees and brought the pistol up for a shot. He already had the Henry lined up on his target. When the man flinched Jake shot him in the head.

Jake walked over to the bodies lying lifeless on the ground. He would have preferred they just left him alone but they made the wrong choice. He had come to the realization when he left Atlanta that on this trip there might be situations where it was kill or be killed. This was certainly one of those situations.

The two horses were brought over close to the two bodies. He took the saddle and bridles off of both of them and let them wonder away. He was sure they would be found in time. He had no need for them and the saddles could give them problems if he left them on them.

The paint stood still as he untied the shovel and began his work. "I knew there was a good reason to buy a shovel."

After the two graves were finished Jake tied the shovel back on the pack saddle and then tightened the girths on both mounts. He scanned the woods with his eyes for any curious wanderers and found none. He had no idea how far the sound of the shooting traveled and if anyone would come looking around if they heard it. He could only hope the shots went undetected. He knew how folks in the south could be and these two skunks could have kin all over these woods. Jake knew it was time to make tracks and make them quick. He mounted up and started down the trail he took to get to this place of death.

There was a breeze blowing through the tall pines and hardwoods that filled his ears so hearing riders would be difficult. He kept his eyes moving constantly trying to be aware of any movement around him. He kicked the buckskin up to a trot to try and make it back to the road that would take him west and away from here as quickly as possible. That feeling in his stomach that he carried around so many times during the war was pulling on his guts. He just had that gnawing in him that said someone is close and this little dilemma isn't over.

As the road came into view two riders turned onto the trail and rode slowly toward Jake. They were one hundred feet away and they were armed with single barrel shotguns. Jake knew a load from one of those smoke poles and he was done for and the pains of this trip would be for nothing. He stopped and crossed his arms over his saddle horn. With his fingers he pulled the leather loops that secured the hammers of his twin revolvers to their holsters. He spoke to the buckskin in a low voice and told him to whoa up.

"Be still boy". Jake said knowing the horse would obey.

The two riders came close and stopped about ten feet in front of Jake. They were both dirty and rough in their appearance. The two men wore black felt hats and sweat stained shirts and grimy pants. It was hard to tell which of the rider's hats had the most holes in it. Their lace up boots, were covered in dried dirt from walking around in mud. Their faces were covered in brown whiskers and their teeth were covered in scum. The one to Jakes right spoke as he raised the shotgun up and braced the butt plate against his right thigh, its barrel pointed toward the sky.

"Howdy do" the man said with a hillbilly draw in his voice and a suspicious tone.

Jake nodded his head and spoke back to the man, "Howdy."

Jakes eyes went back and forth from one man and then the other. He watched their hands that stood by to make their guns ready. Jake had already made his mind up on what action he would take if one made the wrong move.

The one on the right opened his mouth exposing his green rotten teeth and said, "We heard some shooting yonder...was that you?"

"Yep, I ran across a couple of pole cats back a ways. I can't stand pole cats." Jake said, his heart pounding out of his chest.

The talker stuck his tongue out onto the right side of his bottom lip as he looked at Jake from just under the brim of his hat. His horse stepped to his left a bit but he brought him back in and steadied him.

"A couple pole cats you say."

"That's right. I don't like pole cats." Jake replied as the feeling in his guts grew tighter and tighter. He could tell this was not going to end well.

"Well we was lookin fer a couple ah our cousins and we figured you might a seenum." The man said as his grip on the shotgun became more intense.

Jake raised his head and his eyes met the eyes of the talker and said, "Not unless they was a couple pole cats."

Suddenly the man to Jakes right reached up to the shotguns hammer with his thumb to cock it back while he yelled at the other man beside him.

"Kill him!"

Jakes reaction was like a bolt of lightning as he grabbed each pistol and drew them across in front of him. He pulled both hammers on the .44 revolvers and then both triggers sending a hot lead ball into the hearts of both of the riders. They fell over backward from the mounts as both of their horses scattered in panic in opposite directions. The pack horse took a few steps to the side but stayed in the fight. The buckskin stood like a statue.

Jake replaced the revolvers back in their holsters and secured them. He wondered how many ears heard the sound of his pistols and how many of their kin folks would be coming out of the trees to run him down for revenge. He knew how some country people were, and he knew they would be out for his blood. He quickly tied the buckskins reins together and spurred to go. He turned west and went to a trot. He was hoping the pack horse would keep up. If he had to let it go he would.

They had made almost a half of a mile when to Jake's left he saw two shacks and people scrambling around. They looked to be frantic as they grabbed up long guns and pointed them toward Jake as he approached. The shacks were nestled into the trees and there were lots of forest for rifles to be hiding behind. Jake didn't want to have to shoot his way through here but he would do what he had to do. He respected the southern people, his people, and he knew there may be some about to assault him that he may have fought with in the war. Getting into a fire fight with these people was not what Jake wanted but, so be it, as rifles began to thunder and lead balls began whistling by his head.

Jake threw his end of the lead rope that was connected to the pack horse over the pack horses back to give him a chance to run. He spurred the buckskin to bring the horse up to a gallop as he pulled both revolvers from their holsters. He leaned down over the horses mane to make him as little of a target as possible. He held his fire until he got close enough to hit his target at a hard run. He trained to hit his target and he was good at it.

He was amazed at the speed of the buckskin as the shack came into pistol range. There was a man behind a large oak tree in front of the house who was reloading his rifle for another shot at Jake. He looked just like the other men he had dealt with and figured there was a whole family of pole cats living in this area, so it didn't make him feel bad when he raised the revolver and pulled the trigger on the man. Jake's target took the ball in the face bursting the head open in the front as the round piece of lead passed through the man's gourd.

The revolver thundered again and a man firing from the corner of one of the shacks fell to the ground, blood gushing from his chest. Another filthy man nearby picked up the rifle the dead man had just finished loading with powder and shot and he raised it in Jakes direction as the buckskin passed by him. Jake turned and fired a shot that caught the man in the neck. The man pulled the trigger of the black powder rifle but a searing hot lead ball cutting through his neck caused him to pull his shot wide to the right of Jake.

Jake rode hard for what he figured was three miles or so before he pulled the reins back and let the buckskin come down to a trot and then a slow walk. He turned the horse into a creek bottom and found a path going down to the creek itself. He let the buckskin drink while he listened for riders that may be trying to catch up to him. The woods around where he hid were thick in briars and thorns and he had to be careful not to stick the horse or him. He thought it might be a good place to hide for a while until he knew no more pole cats were following.

After dismounting, he rubbed the neck of the buckskin and checked him for gunshot wounds as he thought how great it would have been if a horse of this nerve and stamina would have served with him in the war. He remembered every mount that was shot out from under him and he loved and trusted each one of them. This horse is the best he ever rode and the best he had seen in a scrape. The buckskin showed his grit and kept his nerve through every second of the fray with the pole cats. Jake thought again as he mounted up…'I don't like pole cats'.

"Let's get out of here ol' boy."

After riding along for about an hour, the sun was beginning to sink in the west. The air was cooling down and Jake began to

129

grow weary in the saddle. He figured it would be a cold camp since all of the supplies he had were strapped to the pack horse that he left behind at the pole cat shanty town he had to shoot his way through. He kept his fingers crossed that none of them were following him or trying to catch up to him. He had enough killing to last him the rest of his life. He was certainly not going to lose sleep over the lives he took today. They had all presented a threat to him and he answered that threat the only he knew and that was to fight back...kill or be killed. He knew the first two pole cats were after his money but the rest were after revenge. Still they meant him harm and dead is what they got for their trouble.

Jake stopped to survey a place to make camp. He would try to stay as far out of sight as possible. There was no telling how many more families of outlaws lived in these parts of Mississippi and he didn't want to find out. Suddenly he heard the sound of horse's hooves coming at a trot. The sun had pretty well set and he couldn't tell much about who was approaching so he ducked back off the road into the trees to get a look as the rider passed. As the rider got close Jake could see that the horse was loaded down with supplies and the rider set higher like he was riding on top of the supplies. The closer the horse approached the more it looked like his paint gelding and his provisions. He stepped out into the road and held a pistol up and pointed straight at the face of the rider. Jake grabbed the lead rope that was attached to the horse's halter when he got close and pulled the head of the horse to one side to make him stop. The rider screamed with fright.

"Who are you...let go of that rope" The voice coming from the horse was a girl voice. She began to slap at Jake with her hands and kick with both feet. She didn't stop fighting until Jake reached with his free hand and grabbed her by the shirt and pulled her down from the horse. He then had to throw her to the ground to get her to stop slapping and kicking.

"That's enough of that. Why are you on my pack horse?" Jake demanded as he looked down at the girl laid out on the ground.

The girl got up and as she brushed the dust of her baggy pants and shirt asked with a surprised look on her face. "Are you the one that killed those McDonald boys?"

Jake picked up her old slouch hat that fell off of her head when he pulled her off the pack horse. He brushed off the dust he could see in the dusk of the day and handed the hat to her. She put it back on her head of dark hair that hung just over her ears. It looked as if she had taken scissors to it herself and that she may have been in a hurry when she cut it. She was bare footed and her pants would hardly stay pulled up to her slender hips. She had to hold on to them or they would fall off of her.

"I don't know the McDonald boys. Are they who lived in those two shanty houses back a ways and how did you wind up with my pack horse?" Jake asked. He clenched her shirt in his fist and pulled her up close enough to search for a pistol or a knife.

"Hey...why are you feeling around on me like that?" she said squirming around like a small child getting her face washed. "Yur ticklin me...stop."

"I'm gonna make sure you ain't one of their friends coming after me. I done had my fill of these McDonalds, did you say, and I ain't putting up with no more of them." Jake said letting her go satisfied she had no weapons on her.

She pushed his hand back and straightened her clothes the best she could considering how much they swallowed her petite frame. She looked up at Jake in the evening glow from the sun that had just about disappeared behind the tall pine trees. She had big blue eyes and her oddly cropped hair was shining black like obsidian. Her pug nose over her bright smile would melt the heart of any man or boy.

"What is your name?" Jake asked turning toward the pack horse and taking the coffee pot and coffee from the haversack that hung from the pack saddle. "You want some coffee?"

She smiled again and approached the gelding to lead him into the forest where the buckskin waited munching on grass. The girl and Jake walked together picking up limbs that had fallen from the trees to make a fire. Jake decided to go ahead make a fire since his feelings of danger subsided with the appearance of the girl.

"I'd love some coffee. My name is Lilly Wilson. I come from west of here about two days ride. Them McDonald boys took me. I don't know none of them by name but I know they is worthless as all get out."

"Do you mean they kidnapped you?" Jake asked as he knelt down to start a fire for the coffee to be put on to boil.

"I guess you could say that. They made me cook for them and they done all kinds of nasty things to me. For the first week they had me they never let me have my clothes. I just hope I ain't carryin one of their babies. Pa would have a fit." Lilly said through tear filled eyes. "I'm sure glad you came along when you did. I seen you come through there like blue blazes with them pistols workin. I was lookin through the front window when you did it. Then I seen that pack horse come through and I ran out the house and jumped on him and held on for dear life."

When the coffee finally came to a boil Jake looked up and saw that Lilly was leaning back against a big hardwood sound asleep.

He poured himself a cup and settled back against the same tree. When the air cooled down he threw his blanket over her and let her sleep.

The stars shine bright through the Mississippi forest that covered Jake and Lilly. The usual sounds of the night begin its lullaby that sung Jake to sleep. He slept leaned up against the same tree as Lilly. Her soft breathing told Jake she was resting and that she had no fear of him. He decided he would help her get back home to her pa. He had no remorse for taking the lives of such bad men as the McDonalds after learning they had kidnapped Lilly and did awful things to her. He would sleep well when sleep came.

The next morning came with blue skies and the usual summer-time heat and sultry air that sometimes took a hot knife to cut through just to get a breath. Jake put Lilly on the buckskin behind him to give the pack horse less to carry. There was no doubt the buckskin could carry him and Lilly with no difficulty.   The two rode all day before making camp. Lilly figured another day would have them at her family's farm that set about fifty miles east of the Mississippi river and Natchez where Jake intended to cross over by ferry into Louisiana.

"There's the farm I live on, right there through them trees." Lilly said with excitement in her voice. "I hope pa ain't mad thankin I just up and runned off."

Jake straightened up in his saddle. He stood in the stirrups and stretched the best he could. It would be a relief to get out of this saddle. Lilly had assured him that it would be all right if he stayed over a night before going on toward Texas but Jake would have to be invited by Mr. Wilson before he did. Intruding on someone is something Jake would never do.

As Jake and Lilly rode closer to the cabin, a man stepped out onto the porch that covered one corner of the front of the house. The house was built of logs hewn flat and wood shingles dressed the roof of the cabin. There was a window on the front and a rock chimney on the side that faces west. The man standing on the porch was dressed in bib overalls and no shirt. His work boots were untied as if he just slipped them on to step out onto the porch to greet the riders approaching.

Lilly slid of the buckskin and ran to the arms of her pa. He held her tight and Jake could see his eyes were full of tears. Lilly kissed the cheeks of the grizzly man that stood almost as tall as the porch ceiling. He had gray hair that was all but gone and a gray mustache that hung lower than his jaw bones on each side of his face. His hands looked strong and calloused from work and from the looks of his arms this man could lift a steer over his head with no problem.

"I ain't gonna ask you where you've been. I'm just glad you're home. I've been worried sick over you. Who is this yur with?" The big Mr. Wilson asked with a soft gentle voice, setting Lilly down after holding her up off the floor of the cabin porch.

"Pa, this is Jake. He brung me home. The McDonald boys from over towards Raleigh took me right out of the garden that day I went missin pa...I swear." Lilly said tearing up too. She took her dirty shirt sleeve and wiped her father's eyes and then her own before she went on with her story.

"They took me Pa and made me do thangs to them that ain't right. They made me go naked and they cut my hair. I didn't like it, I promise." Lilly sobbed.

The rage showed on Mr. Wilsons face and his bear like fist clenched so tight his knuckles turned white. "I reckon I'm gonna go over towards Raleigh and kill them McDonald boys."

134

Lilly wiped her eyes again and said, "You ain't got to Pa, Jake here done killed every last one of them mangy critters."

Wilson looked over at Jake and gave him a nod. "I appreciate what you done and specially for bringin my Lilly home. I owe you."

"You don't owe me anything. I would like to bed my horses down for the night if that's all right with you." Jake said getting off the buckskin. He walked over and extended a hand to Mr. Wilson.

Wilson shook Jakes hand with total gratitude and said, "You can stay for as long as you like Jake".

"Just tonight is fine. Do you have a creek nearby that I can wash the dirt off of me in?" Jake asked taking off his hat and wiping the sweat off of his forehead.

Lilly took Jake by the hand and said. "I'll draw you up a bath. That would be better. I need one myself."

"You go first and I'll see to my stock." Jake said pulling the two horses to the barn with Mr. Wilson walking along side.

While Jake and Mr. Wilson saw to the buckskin and packhorse they became acquainted. Jake told Wilson about Sarah and the kids and how he lost them and Miss Peachy. Wilson spoke of his son Nathan who had went off to the war but didn't come back and how that made Lilly his only child. He told of how he had to raise them both after his wife Ruth died suddenly after she was kicked by their mule. He had tried to guard Lilly from all things bad and when he returned from a trip to Nachez found Lilly gone, he figured she just ran off because she didn't want to be on the farm any longer. He always knew she would be ready to wed one day, but it was a day he dreaded to see come.

"Thank you for letting me stay the night. I'll sleep in the barn here with the horses." Jake said giving the animals a bit of hay.

"There are plenty beds in the cabin so you can stay in there with me and Lilly. She won't have it any other way. She's a purdy good cook too. She'll whup up something here in a bit. Come on in."

Chapter 8

Jake crossed the Mississippi River at Natchez with no fuss from the horses. Both were at full strength after the oats and hay at the Wilson farm and Jake was feeling well rested and fed after enjoying some of Lilly's home cooking. He didn't want to stay to long since Lilly was taken the way she was by those McDonald boys. Her pa would hardly let her out of his sight once she returned home, thanks to Jake and his revolvers.

He stopped in Natchez on the east bank of the Big Muddy before crossing and got supplies he had run short on. The D. Moses and Sons Cheap Cash Store had everything he needed including another handful of stick candy. Jake figured it was better to gnaw on hard candy than to stuff his mouth with chew or have a cigar hanging from his lips. The candy smelled a heap better than tobacco anyway.

Jake saw numerous beautiful homes still standing in Natchez that survived the war. Cotton farms were back in full swing and the fields were speckled with white for as far as the eye could see in some spots. Black and white farm hands worked the cotton patches side by side just as it should be. Jake never saw himself a cotton farmer, especially after it being a product of such importance to allow its profits to rule the hearts of men to want to keep people bound up to work the fields. If you work a man...pay the man...is what Jake always thought. Thank God the days of slavery are over, Jake thought as an old black man lifted up his head from his labor and gave him a wave and smile that reminded him of Miss Peachy's beautiful ebony face.

Once through the town of Vidalia Louisiana Jake traveled though stands of thick forests of pines and briars that looked so thick that a rabbit would be sure to snag an ear if not careful traipsing through it. Jake was hungry for fish and while stopped in Vidalia he bought a box of fish hooks and string. He figured on making him a fishing pole if he came across the right piece of cane suitable for jerking in a catfish or two for his supper.

Just east of Jonesville along the Black River, Jake pulled up and made his camp. He used his handy shovel to dig for worms to put on a fishhook for bait. He had no trouble finding plenty bedded into the rich black dirt that was covered with moist leaves carpeting the floor of the thick forest by the river. He got a campfire going and put on his coffee to boil before throwing out his first hook with bait. The day was warm and Jake rolled up his shirt sleeves to get as comfortable as he could. A slight breeze blew from the northwest and cooled him a bit as he sat down under a big pine tree on the bank of the river. The road he traveled was just to the south of where he camped and the ferry that took travelers back and forth to and from Jonesville wasn't getting much business today. Jakes line went tight and supper was brought up to the bank...a nice fat flathead catfish.

Jake sipped coffee and picked the fish out of his teeth while leaning against a majestic southern pine while the late afternoon sounds of the forest spoke softly to him. He crooked his head to the right to listen for sounds coming from the road. His camp sat about twenty yards north from the road that lead up to the river. He thought he heard the squeaking of wagon wheels moving toward his camp. He stood as the sound got louder and louder. Finally a covered wagon being pulled by a team of mules came into view. There were two people sitting on the bench seat at the front of the wagon. They both wore old looking gray hats and work clothes. He couldn't see them well enough to tell much about the individuals until they came closer.

The squeaking stopped at the edge of the ramp that would lead onto the ferry when it docked to take on travelers. The driver of the team got off the wagon and walked over to a bell that hung out from a post to the left of the ramp. He took the leather cord that hung down from the clapper and worked it back and forth. The clanging of the bell got the attention of the ferry boat captain who waved over in agreement to cross over to load the wagon.

Jake got up from under the tree and decided to go over as well. He quickly saddled the horses and gathered his supplies. Jake kicked the fire until the flames went out and then poured water over the ashes to make sure it went out. He walked the horses over and got in line behind the wagon to load up onto the ferry.

The ferry was about thirty feet long and fifteen feet wide so there was plenty of room for the wagon and his two horses. He walked them on and stood with them to the left side of the wagon. It looked like it was loaded down with the usual household items like furniture and barrels of supplies. Its canvas cover looked brand new and the wood of the wagon had an unused appearance about it. The two riders were dressed in work clothes and hats that were pulled down over their faces. They kept quiet through the whole ride over the river. The ferry boat captain didn't say anything until they landed on the other side.

"That'll be two bits for the wagon and a nickel for the two horses" the boat captain said as he opened the front gate of the ferry to let the people move off of the boat.

The man driving the wagon tossed a quarter to the captain and proceeded to move the wagon from off of the ferry. The captain grabbed the bits of the mule closest to him and gave it a tug.

"Wait just a darn minute….you a darky so you pay four bits," the man demanded through gritted teeth. The countenance on his face full of hate and spite told Jake that this man had no manners.

"Why are you requiring me to pay double... this is preposterous." The young man who drove the wagon said, with perfect diction and the air of aristocracy in his voice.

The ferry boat captain took his gray kepi hat off of his head and scratched the temple of his head that was covered in greasy black hair. "Boy, you sure talk funny. You talk like you got smarts or something."

The captain smiled showing tobacco stained teeth and places where teeth once were before he hollered "Woowee!...we done got us a educated high yeller here... dang it all. Hell, there's two of you and thatun there is a girl."

"Sir, would you please let us pass. We wish no altercation with you so please if you will." The young man asked extending his left hand to the man in a peaceful gesture.

"Danged if you ain't got the purdiest talk of any mulatto I ain't ever done seen." He flashed a broken smile and a wink toward the young female sitting to the right of the young wagon driver. "I tell you what...I'll let you pass if I get me a little romp with the mulatto chick-a-dee here. I might even give you your two bits back if she smells purdy."

Jake rolled his eyes and nudged the buckskin with a spur. The horse walked right up to the nasty mouthed ferry boat captain and kept going. The neck of the horse pushing the man from his place as he let go of the wagon reins tied to the bits of the mule's bridle.

"Who the heck do you think you are? I'm conducting business here and you got no right to be pushing on me," the captain said stumbling back almost falling on his butt.

The man gathered his footing and approached Jake sitting in the saddle of the buckskin. He gritted what few teeth he had and showed himself mad by the spit that flew from his mouth as he threatened Jake.

"I'll kill..." came out just as Jake's right boot suddenly collided with the man's uncouth mouth. This time the man landed on his butt while his feet carried on over his head. He stopped with his knees on the ground and his face looking up at the man that just planted leather in his mouth. Dust settled on the oily hair that was stuck to the top of his head. His hat lay on the ground behind him after it rolled off of his head. The man stood up and glared at Jake who never budged.

"Not another word from you," Jake said as he tossed the ferry boat captain a nickel and then waved the wagon on. Jake fell in behind the wagon with his pack horse. He looked back at the man that still stood by the boat landing with blood coming from his mouth. Jake shook his head, "Just another pole cat."

Jake rode along with the wagon until it was dark. They stopped and made a camp in an area where three rivers came together, the Quachita, the Tensas and the Little River. It looked like an area where people had camped as they travel west and it would be a suitable place for these three weary travelers. After the camp chores were done the three gathered around the campfire and enjoyed a meal prepared by the young female who traveled with the young mulatto man. At this point none had thought to introduce themselves, they just worked to make the camp comfortable.

"That was a fine meal Ma'am," Jake said as he finally pulled his hat off and crossed his legs at the ankles and settled into sleep. The young mulatto female had not said a word to Jake all evening and it made him wondered if she might be a deaf mute or something. He just minded his own business and kept to himself. Finally the young man spoke.

"I think it would be proper if we introduce ourselves to you sir," the young man said looking over at the female who sat quietly with her hat down low casting a shadow over her face. Jake could tell that her hair was pushed up under the hat she wore. It looked a couple of sizes too big for her. It was brown felt and the brim was bent in front of her face not allowing her features to be seen very well. She wore a brown cotton shirt with sleeves buttoned, denim pants and pull on leather boots. Jake couldn't tell a whole lot about her size because her clothes were so loose on her body. The man was dressed the same way except his clothes fit him well.

"My name is Julius Broussard and this is my sister Tammy. We come…". The girl, Tammy nudged him on the side as if she didn't want him to reveal where they came from. "Tammy…it's okay. I think we are far enough away from there. Not only that, I'm certain no one is following us," Julius said turning back to Jake who was trying not to be curious about the two people he had just befriended.

"That's all right. You don't have to say anything about anything," Jake assured them as he straightened up his back against a large oak tree.

"I can assure you sir that we are not running from the authorities if that is what you are wondering." Julius said placing his right hand over his heart to stress the truth in what he just proclaimed. "Tammy and I are merely traveling to Texas to attempt to make a life for ourselves."

Jake looked at the young mulatto man with short cropped hair that looked more brown than black. His eyes were hazel and his complexion was light yet his facial features were that of a black man. Julius stood six foot tall and his voice did tell he was educated and confident. Jake figured he was about twenty

143

one years old. He hadn't seen enough of Tammy to tell much about her.

"So I think it is fair to tell you that we came up the Mississippi to Natchez from Baton Rouge. We lived there with Mr. and Mrs. Charles Broussard who obviously gave us his name. Our parents were mulatto and they were domestics for them. We were raised in the same household with their son and daughter so we learned everything as far as reading and writing, the sciences and mathematics. We both speak French and we both play two instruments...the violin and the flute."

Jake looked around, trying to keep from showing that his mind was hard at work. He had during the most of his trip gave a lot of thought about how he was going to make a cattle farm work by himself. Although he just met Julius and Tammy, he wondered if they would be two that wanted to make a start on a cattle farm. During the time it took to set up the camp, they worked together and got it done quickly and efficiently. It was like they were a team. He didn't know why but he just asked Julius.

"Can you raise cattle?" Jake asked seeing Tammy's hat brim come up giving him a glimpse of her beautiful face. His heart stopped for just a second. His mind was in a whirl and when she took the brim of her hat and pulled the hat from her head, he closed his eyes and then opened them up to make sure he wasn't dreaming.

Tammy shook her head from side to side letting her dark brown hair fall from the its bun on the top of her head. Her hair shone in the light from the camp fire. As it fell, it bounced from the waves that gave her hair its magnificent radiance. She turned her gaze toward Jake and fixed her stunning hazel eyes to his. Her face was that of an angel in Jake's mind. He had never seen a woman as beautiful. Her skin was light brown and the glow from the campfire gave it a softness that was indescribable. Her petite nose was snub and delicate and her lips looked smooth and soft. Her top lip gently turned up and each side of her mouth as it came to the center of her face just under her nose, in what would remind you of the top portion of a heart. They slightly pursed as she stared into Jakes eyes as she gave him a tender smile. Her slender face was radiant and its beauty burned an image in Jakes mind that he would never forget.

Jake had lost track of the conversation so he just settled back against the trunk of the big oak tree and pulled the brim of his hat over his face. Julius was about to answer his question about raising cattle but decided it could wait until another time. Tammy wrapped herself up in a blanket and curled up with her head on Jake's saddle. He didn't mind giving it up for what could possibly be the roughest old tree in the south.

The night was peaceful as Julius and Tammy slept. Jake kept one eye open all night thinking about the ferry boat captain who is now missing more teeth. He had come to like his two travel companions. Jake had never been one to belittle folks whose ancestors were sold into slavery and brought to this country. He knew there had been a lot of slave girls who gave birth to babies that were fathered by the plantation foremen and even plantation owners and their sons. There was no reason on earth for that ferry boat captain to treat these two people the way he did and Jake didn't, in the least, feel bad about giving the filthy man a kick in the teeth. Sometimes a man just has it coming.

Jake rose before the sun came up and took a swim in a nearby river. He knew he wouldn't stay in the water long because of gators. He went in and came right back out quickly, then dressed and cleaned his teeth. He took a bucket to get water from upstream to boil for coffee. He got plenty for Julius and Tammy to take a quick bath, if they didn't want to brave the river. He didn't know how sheltered his new friends were growing up. Just by what he has seen and heard from them they were extremely sheltered so he didn't know what the outcome would be if one of them encountered a gator or a cottonmouth. It could be bad, so Jake felt like he had to take special measures to see to it that something bad didn't happen.

When he walked back to camp Tammy was sitting up and looking around with a sleepy look on her face. Jake thought she was still as pretty as a picture even though sleep was all over her. She smiled at Jake and he smiled back. While watching him make the coffee, she thought about how grateful she was that Jake was there to put a stop to the mean ferry boat captain. She didn't know if Julius could protect her in a situation like that. Jake just had a way of putting an end to the situation that left a lasting impression with everybody involved. She felt safe with Jake and she trusted him completely. While she lay still in her blanket the night before she wondered if Jake would ever consider taking her for his wife. Tammy knew there was a gap in the ethnicity but she also knew love can bridge that gap. She knew Jake was a man that did not judge people just because they were of a different race although she is as white as she is black. He is also the prettiest man she has ever seen in her life...a thought that brought a smile to her face.

"What's so funny?" Jake asked with a grin on his face. He looked into her eyes as he squatted down by the camp fire to give the coals a stir.

Just then Julius began to roll around in his bedroll. He was making an awful groaning sound that took Jake and Tammy's attention off of each other and on to him. He jumped up like he was having a fit. He danced around or actually ran in place, trying to get loose from something. He was screaming while he moved his legs but not going anywhere.

"Ahh...it got me...I think it bit me!" Julius screamed, still running but going nowhere.

Jake and Tammy looked in amazement at the fit Julius was throwing. They could not figure out what was happening until finally a red and white striped snake fell to the ground at his feet. It came from under his shirt. Julius looked down at the little critter and sighed hard in relief. He bent down and picked up the eight-inch reptile and walked away from camp mumbling under his breath.

"You are going to have to find you another place besides inside my shirt you little rascal," Julius exclaimed. "I'm sure glad you weren't a copperhead."

Tammy laughed slightly shaking her head "He will go turn it loose. He loves snakes and such. He just doesn't like sleeping with them". She and Jake both laughed out loud.

Jake found himself watching her intently and thinking that she is even more beautiful when she giggles. It was the same sound he would hear from Flora and Sarah when they got tickled and it brought back memories of home and how he missed his family. He brought his mind back to the present and continued to stoke the camp-fire for coffee.

After placing the coffee pot close to the fire, he sat back against the oak tree that served as a place his head rested during what sleep he got the night before. Tammy got up and joined him on the ground on the opposite side of the fire from him. Sleep had left her eyes probably from using the muscles in her lovely face laughing at her brother. Jake was mesmerized by her beauty and eloquence. To see a woman as attractive and delicate as this, sleeping on the ground rolled up in a blanket

147

and then sitting Indian style by a campfire, was putting the term 'being out of place' to the extreme. She looked up and again their eyes met. They both smiled.

"Why are you going to Texas?" She asked in voice that could soothe the spirit of the savage of beast.

Jake dropped his eyes and turned his head and thought a few seconds before he answered. He didn't want Tammy to think he was running from something even though in a way he was running. Running away from memories that still haunted him at night and at the slightest crack in the shell he had tried so hard to build around his heart and mind. He turned back to the most dazzling eyes he had ever seen and told her the story of Sarah and the children and Miss Peachy. The tears in the corners of Jake's eyes did not go unnoticed by Tammy. It told her that Jake had a side that was hurting. She so wanted to move over next to him and rest her head against his chest and comfort him but couldn't make herself do it. She knew he was still in pain from the memories and she desired to quiet his soul from the misery caused by his loss.

Jake saw a tear in her eye and, when she realized he had, she turned away. She did not want him to know she was crying for him. She quickly touch the corner of her right eye with her loose shirt before she got up and took the bucket of water Jake had brought back from the river. Tammy walked to the woods behind where Jake sat against the oak tree. She returned after a couple of minutes. Jake had gotten up and fed the horses and mules. He wondered what was taking Julius so long. Jake figured he had found the river and was washing himself

Julius approached the river with respect because he knew the sort of creatures that inhabited the waters of Louisiana and he was not about to be gator food. He quickly washed himself and

148

got out of the water. He thought about catching lunch with a hook and string but he forgot to put such in the provisions that he quickly prepared once they rolled the wagon off of the river boat when they arrived in Natchez from Baton Rouge. He was more worried about putting as many miles behind them as possible. He just hoped that the two men that were searching for Tammy were way behind them and that their movement from the boat went unnoticed by everyone that got off with them.

The men were hired by Arthur Babineaux a wealthy runner of prostitutes and whorehouses in New Orleans. He had once done business with Mr. Broussard, whether it was legal or not was not known by Julius. When the man Babineaux saw Tammy he was suddenly consumed with the lustful desire to have her and to put her on the sex market. He knew that with a woman with such beauty as Tammy possessed, he would be sitting on a gold mine. He could put a price on her that only the wealthiest of gentlemen would pay for her company. Julius knew this and decided it best for Tammy to get her away from Baton Rouge. Julius knew that Mr. Broussard was too old to prevent Tammy from being taken.

After redressing Julius turned to go back to the camp when he heard a stick brake under a heavy foot. He turned toward the sound thinking Jake or Tammy came looking for him. To his surprise it was neither.

"Well, well, well look what we have here. Good morning young Broussard," came a voice of a man with a heavy French accent.

There were two men, both dressed in three piece suits that under the gleam of the rising sun to their backs looked black. They both wore black felt hats with straight brims. They were both adorned with silver hat bands. The man that addressed

Julius had short dark hair that showed from under his hat and a thick dark mustache that grew down past the corners of his mouth. His skin was dark, yet he was a white man. The other man was a dark-skinned black man that towered over the dandy that spoke to Julius. He was clean shaven and had a round face that gave away his youth. He held a derringer pistol that he had removed from his vest pocket. It was pointed at Julius.

Julius stared with fear at the derringer with large eyes. He held a hand up in a plea for the man not to shoot. He then looked around hoping Jake or Tammy was not approaching. His movement caused the first man to ask.

"Who you looking for Julius, are you expecting friends to come and meet you at the river?" the man said rubbing his right index finger against his chin.

"No...I'm not expecting anyone, especially Tammy. She stayed on the riverboat and should be headed to Memphis." Julius said with a quiver in his voice.

The man doing the talking just laughed as he stepped toward Julius. When he got within reach of Julius the man sent a hard right fist into Julius' stomach. The blow came so hard that it sent Julius to his knees, bent over in pain. The man reached down, took Julius' right ear in his hand, and pulled it until Julius got up on to his feet. The man let go of the ear and back handed Julius across his face, sending Julius back to the ground in a heap. The man holding the derringer walked over and picked Julius up and began slapping him across the face. He didn't stop until the other man spoke.

"Julius, are you ready to take us to see Tammy or are we going to beat the life out of you and force us to search the area until we find her?" The man, John-Claude Chastain said through gritted teeth.

Chastain was a hard-nosed hit man that was frequently used by the criminal element that ran the whorehouses and opium dens around New Orleans. His partner went by only Charbonneau. Their job was to hurt, mangle and kill anyone for money. They were hired by Babineaux to track down Tammy and bring her to him. He didn't care who was killed along the way, just as long as he got the prized lovely that drove his lustful desire for more wealth, so his illegal operations could grow to the point that he owned New Orleans.

Julius bleeding from his mouth and nose was trying to hang on to consciousness as the big black man held him up. He thought about just letting them kill him but he knew Jake and Tammy did not know about the two men catching up to them. He could only hope Jake would intervene and not allow them to take Tammy away.

"Look...I see your foot prints in the dirt there leading into the forest. Shall we go that way in hope that the tasty little morsel is waiting where your footprints end?" Chastain asked with an evil tone.

Charbonneau grabbed Julius and dragged him behind Chastain as he led the way into the woods toward the camp where Tammy and Jake were waiting, not knowing they were in danger. Julius hoped they would make enough noise to put Jake on alert. He hoped Jake was enough to handle these two evil men. Julius had already proved to himself that he was not.

Back at the camp Tammy had returned and prepared for the day of travelling. She had a cup of hot coffee and she and Jake were putting together the provisions to go back in the covered wagon and the pack horse when Jake heard someone approaching from the woods. He could tell by the sound from the brush being walked through that there was more than just Julius coming toward the camp. He buckled his revolvers around his waist and walked around to the side of the covered wagon away from where the sound was coming. He got Tammy's attention and told her to sit down by the camp fire.

"What's wrong?" Tammy asked with concern on her face and in her voice. She had tried to stay alert since she knew why she and Julius were running away from Baton Rouge. She also knew that Jake did not know. She chastised herself for not telling him.

"Act like nothing is wrong," Jake told her. She could hear the urgency in his tone.

She did as he told her as he stepped around to the blind side of the wagon. The sound from the woods grew louder as the seconds passed. He heard no talking from the people approaching which to him meant trouble. Suddenly Tammy screamed as the men came into the camp.

"My little turtle dove…there you are. I've been looking all over for you. You know it is time to go to New Orleans where you will be safely away from the forest here with all of its creepy little bugs and spiders," Chastain said, as if he was talking to a small child getting ready for bed.

"I'm not going anywhere with you…you monster. You're ugly and creepy and I'm not going with you to be your whore or anybody's whore." Tammy's voiced cracked as she began to sob at the thought of these men taking her away and what lay in store for her.

Chastain pulled a small frame revolver from a holster hidden under his jacket and pointed it at Julius' head and pulled the hammer back cocking the pistol. Julius wondered where Jake may have gone and if he was aware of what was transpiring in camp.

"Get up on your feet my little flower," Chastain said to Tammy in a demanding way that told her that he might shoot Julius if she did not comply.

Tammy rose to her feet with shaking knees. She was so scared for her life and the life of her brother. Tammy just knew that Jake would step out and make these men go away.

Chastain looked at Charbonneau and said, "Go and get the horses. We will take the wagon back. We will tie her up and gag her to keep her quiet."

The big black man turned and ran back through the woods. Jake let him get completely out of sight before he made his move. His plans had changed since the big black man left to get their mounts.

Chastain turned to Tammy with evil in his eyes. He re-holstered his pistol then pulled his jacket off and threw it to the ground. He smiled at Tammy and she could tell he had something on his mind that she did not care to be involved in. Her heart screamed out to Jake. She knew he was close.

"You keep your hands off of my sister you fiend," Julius yelled as he raised his hands to assault Chastain in defense of Tammy.

Chastain put his right hand in his right pants pocket and quickly pulled it out. He had retrieved a set of brass knuckles and he hit Julius hard on the left side of the head. His knees buckled and Julius fell to the ground unconscious. Chastain pulled the brass knuckles off and placed them back in his pocket. He was a medium size man and knew that Julius was stronger than him and he required the brass knuckles to get the better of the young mulatto.

"Now...back to you...you beautiful, alluring creature. I say, get those clothes off or I'm going to put lead in this worthless brother of yours," Chastain commanded her with anticipation of the pleasure he was about to experience. "I'm going to let you enjoy my big French tickler."

Jake hearing his words thought of Sarah and how evil men took her life after having their way with her. The fire inside him grew out of control. He would never stand by and allow this man to violate Tammy or anyone else. His heart spoke out in revenge for Sarah when he stepped out from around the wagon.

"No you're not," Jake said unlatched the leather hook from his left holster.

"Jake!" screamed Tammy. Her heart pounded hard with fear. She knew this man standing over her was ruthless and evil.

Chastain turned toward Jake and looked him up and down. He saw the pair of Colt revolvers hanging close to his belt buckle. He knew he had come too far to let some backwoods ruffian stop him from receiving the hefty payment that comes when Tammy is delivered to his employer in New Orleans. Fifty Thousand American dollars will buy him a lot of power where he wanted it. His pistol hung from a shoulder holster under his left arm and he taught himself to deploy it with speed and accuracy. He had a reputation around the gambling halls of New Orleans as being a stone cold killer and this man would be just one more to brag about.

"Why do you say such a thing to me and my tickler?" Chastain asked in a nonchalant way that displayed the arrogance of a French dandy.

"Why...you ask? Because I'm gonna shoot the tickler right off." Jake said just as his right hand went for his gun.

His left side revolver left the holster with such speed the Frenchman had no time to react. Chastain still bathing in his bloated swagger took the round between the legs. He felt the lead ball rip through the flesh of his privates. His knees tried to cross to comfort it but it did no good. He looked up at Jake with a contorted look on his face. The large veins in his temples bulged from the stress of being shot in his groin, the part of his body that he prided himself with thinking every man was jealous of and that every woman desired.

Jake looked down at the red faced man holding himself and said, "Dang...I bet that hurt." He raised the pistol and put another round through the man's head. The Frenchman fell to the ground, his lifeless eyes open, but seeing nothing.

Tammy ran to Jake and threw her arms around him. She held him tight not wanting to let go even though she knew she needed to see about Julius who was coming back from being knocked out from the blow of the brass knuckles. She kissed Jakes face. Her moist, warm lips pressed softly against his cheek. She quickly moved to his mouth and he began to melt. He stopped her, even though he did not want too and pushed her back yet holding her arms. He wanted to pull her close again but resisted the urge.

"Look...I've got to go take care of the other man. You stay here and take care of your brother. I will be back," Jake said almost out of breath from the passion that he just experienced from Tammy.

"Can't you just let him go?" Tammy said following Jake to his horse.

"If I do we will probably being dealing with him later and I ain't doing that. I'll take care of him now."

Jake figured the two men left their horses just off the road and the big black man would take the road instead of the woods, to get back to his partner. Jake rode about a quarter of a mile before coming back to the bridge that crossed the river that runs through the forest behind where they camped. The big black man was just leading a horse and riding another onto the road when Jake came into his view. Jake knew the big black man had never laid eyes on him so he kept riding toward him.

The black man stopped on the bridge to let Jake pass. He had a mean look on his face to try to intimidate the stranger approaching on the buckskin. He was ready to kill this white man if he had to or even chose to. He didn't mind killing, especially white men. He had already decided to kill Chastain after they got paid for bringing Tammy to New Orleans to be forced into prostitution, so killing one more would not matter none to Charbonneau.

"What chu lookin at white man?" Charbonneau asked with the meanest look he could give Jake for affect.

Jake wasn't moved. He said, "Your partner said you can go on back to New Orleans because he don't need you no more."

"Why is dat?"

Charbonneau suddenly knew why. The shots he heard must not have come from Chastain. He was more of a street fighter than one to draw pistols. Jake was not going to let this big man get his hands on him. He knew it would be more work than what Jake wanted to deal with...it being so early in the day.

Jake stared at the big black man. The look on his face told Charbonneau that the next move was his or either this white man wanted to give him a minute to reflect on his life.

"Those shots…dey was from you," Charbonneau said with defiance showing on his dark face.

"Yeah", Jake returned pulling his left side revolver and shooting Charbonneau between the eyes.

Charbonneau's horse moved left as he fell from the saddle and into the river below. The current taking him down as his lifeless body rolled with the flowing brown water.

Jake lead the two horses back to camp. He figured they might need them on the rest of the journey to Texas. Tammy had gotten Julius back on his feet and had wrapped a bandage around his head. The bleeding had stopped but he was still uneasy on his feet. Julius knew he was not to go to sleep but instead make himself stay as alert as possible.

Tammy was given a quick lesson in taking a saddle off of a horse. She enjoyed brushing them down and even decided to lay claim to the one Charbonneau was riding. She was a big black mare and Tammy had no problem taking ownership of her since the two men tried to take ownership of her. The other was a dapple gray mare. Both horses were a good fifteen and a half hands tall.

Jake picked out a spot in the woods to dig a grave to put Chastain in so the varmints wouldn't get sick off him. He took the shovel from the pack saddle where it was tied.

Julius holding his head looked up and said," Oh, you've a got a shovel."

"Yeah, I'm sure glad I bought it. I'm getting really good at using it," Jake said as he took a big scoop of dirt from the ground.

Chapter 9

Natchitoches, Louisiana, the oldest city in the state, was still beautiful in spite of the Union soldiers attempt to set it on fire during the war. Thankfully, a group of Confederate soldiers came through and ran them out and assisted the citizens in putting out the flames started by the fleeing Yankees. The old main street that ran through the town again stood graciously pristine as it did before the tyrannical invasion from the north. The boardwalks that ran along the store fronts were covered with people going to and fro making purchases in the shops and stopping for visits to discuss the happenings of the day.

The sky was clear and the temperature was hot with enough humidity to drown a snake. The thickness of the air didn't do anything to moisten the dust in the street, yet it didn't discourage the people at all. It was just another day.

Jake had asked Julius and Tammy to ride in the back of the wagon and to try as best they could to stay out of sight. He would not take a chance Tammy being seen by any more soldiers of fortune out to collect that hefty bank roll that came with finding her and turning her over to the big crime kingpin of New Orleans to be forced into a life of prostitution. Jake knew it was extremely warm in the back of the wagon under its canvass cover but he knew it was necessary for her safety. He knew in his heart that he had developed feelings for Tammy and he wanted her to be safe even if it meant giving up some comfort.

The towns Jake passed through on his trip always had a general store to stop at to re-supply the provisions the wagon carried. Julius had told him that he had used most of the money he and Tammy started out with to buy the team of mules and the wagon in Natchez after they got off of the riverboat. Jake didn't mind footing the bill for the things they needed when they stopped. Julius and Tammy were good company for him. He especially enjoyed the visits with Tammy by the campfire after Julius drifted off to sleep in the late evenings. She always asked the first question to start their conversations. She made no attempt to hide the fact that she was very attracted to Jake and that she found him to be fascinating. She had fallen in love with Jacob and Flora just from the stories that he told her about them and their antics as children. She wished she would have been there for Jake when they died to comfort him. Tammy knew his heart was broken by their passing and that he still felt the sting from losing them at such a precious age.

159

While sitting in the back of the wagon, Tammy could hardly take her eyes off of Jake as he sat with his back to her, his hands holding the reins and his mind on the journey that lay ahead. She knew he thought back on the trail he left behind and forward to the dreams that he was determined to see come true. She thought how much she would love to be a part of those dreams. In her mind she had already decorated a cabin for her and Jake and considered how many children they could have together. That is, of course if Jake ever asked her to be his wife. If her heart had fingers, they would certainly be crossed in hope of hearing him ask her one day soon.

As the wagon moved between the buildings that lined both sides of the city street Tammy moved up behind Jake on the bench seat of the wagon and whispered to him. She placed her soft hand on his back and leaned against him. The closeness made her feel safe and secure.

"Is this Natchitoches?" Her voice came so sweet to Jake.

"I guess that's what that sign said. I tried to say but gave up," Jake said with a slight laugh and a smile.

"It's Natchitoches," Tammy said slowly like she was teaching a child with his words.

Jake turned his head and looked into her beautiful hazel eyes and grinned, "Natch o chis".

"No Natchitoches" she said again trying to get Jake to hear every syllable.

Jake shook his head and shrugged and said, "I'm sure glad we ain't stayin long"

Jake pulled the wagon up in front of a general store. He tied the reins to the brake handle and jumped to the ground with ease. Jake stood for a few minutes stretching his lower back muscles to relieve the tension from sitting in the wagon for miles. He walked around the wagon and checked the supplies that were tied down to it. The horses that had been tied to lead ropes found the water trough in front of the store they stopped in front of and were drinking in the warm water that sat under the hot sun. Jake grabbed the pump handle at one end of the tough and went to work bringing a flow of cool water to refresh the horses. After they drank he led the mules around to have their share.

Jake untied a rope that held the canvass to the wagon and lifted it just enough to make eye contact with Tammy. He gave her and wink and she returned it with a sweet pretty smile. Her hair in slight disarray hung down with a few locks of dark brown over her eyes. A gentle move of her head sent the locks to one side giving Jake a full view of her lovely face. Her moist tongue slid across her soft bottom lip as the glow from her stare penetrated Jakes soul.

Jake smiled again and said, "I'll bring you back something sweet."

"You?" Tammy said amorously, her eyes never leaving his.

Jake just slowly closed the canvass cover and took a deep breath. He felt like the first time Sarah looked at him as they strolled hand in hand along a dirt road after church back home in Atlanta before the war. He didn't think he would ever feel the emotions inside of him again. This beautiful mulatto had reached him and brought back the desire to love and care for someone. He thought this feeling was forever lost in the memories of those he was forced to give up...memories that he so dearly treasured. Memories he never wanted to let go.

Jake turned and shook his head with a smile that extended from his heart to his face. He stepped onto the wood board walk that extended the length of the dust covered street in this

161

historic old town. The general store was open in the front. It had double doors that were pushed out toward the porch of the building and a thin wooden "open" sign hung from a rope in the plate glass window that covered the whole right side of the stores face. Another window covered the other side of the building. There was printing on both windows that simply stated "General Store". Jake walked in and made is way to the counter where a slender framed elderly lady stood looking though a ledger book. She had a pencil in her hand and she was obviously concentrating on the numbers on the pages of the open book. Her hair was silver rolled up in a bun and she wore wire rim glasses that sat at the end of her pale wrinkled nose. She was about five foot tall and showed to be a tad wide through the hips and bottom. Her pale skin and the bags under her eyes showed evidence of time. The black dress she wore was made of cotton and it was adorned with a print consisting of little pink flowers. She wore a silver pin on the heart side of her dress. She quickly looked up when she noticed Jake walk up to the counter.

"What can I do for you sonny?" said the old lady behind the counter as she put down her pencil and closed the ledger book.

"Yes Ma'am, can I get a sack of beans and a sack of rice? Oh, and a bag of that stick candy there in your jar." Jake asked as he reached for his money pouch under his shirt. "I reckon I better get a couple pounds of coffee too, please."

The elderly lady jumped right to it like she was still in her prime. While she worked he looked around the store at the newest tools and knives that were kept in the glass counter in the area where all the hardware items were on display. He never saw himself as a storekeeper. He was more of the outside type wanting to feel the sun on his neck and a breeze in his face. He knew he could raise a herd of cattle and a few horses too. He was looking forward to seeing the land he had waiting for him to become a home. He wanted Julius and especially Tammy to stay with him and make this new dream happen. He remembered he needed to talk with the brother and sister to see if they would be interested in such a venture.

"That comes to four dollars sonny," the elderly store clerk said jarring Jake from his thoughts.

Jake rushed to the counter and handed her four silver dollars and took the items in his arms. "Thank you Ma'am."

"You're welcome sonny," the lady answered as she turned back to her ledger book.

Jake walked out of the store and climbed back up in the wagon. He handed the bags of beans, rice and coffee to Tammy as she patiently sat on a sack of flour waiting for Jake. The same smile that Jake last saw on her face was still there making it hard for him to make the look on his face go away. He knew to people watching him that he looked like a happy clown passing through their town.

On the west side of town, Jake pulled up and stopped by an old black man who was stopped in the road. He was driving a single mule pulling a small cart loaded with firewood. He wore a straw hat that looked old and worn from work and sweat. He had on a faded pair of bibbed overalls with holes in both knees. His gray bearded face circled around a smile covered in tobacco stains yet his jolly attitude shone through in spite of the years that showed on his weathered ebony face.

"How y'all iz?" The old black said with a grin.

"We are fine as could be and how about you sir." Jake said as he pulled the reins back bringing the team to a halt. "Tell me, is there a road that goes on into Texas up ahead?"

"Yessah…up dah roed bout two days from where we iz rat now you gone come to a fauk. You wants to take dah fauk to dah leff. Tother'un take you to Mansfield but dat one'll take you to dah Sabine and rat on in tah Texas," he explained with a smile happy to be of help.

"Thank you sir and you have a happy day," Jake said nodding with his hat.

"Shonuf will and yall too." The old man said with a stained smile.

Jake slapped the reins against the horse's butts and headed westward. Tammy climbed up in the seat next to him and made it a point to sit as close as she could without it being obvious that she wanted to sit close. She was more than ready to get out from under that canvass wagon cover too. A coating of sweat covered her soft face and she leaned her head over and wiped it away on Jakes arm sleeve. He turned and looked in her eyes and gave his head a shake with a smile on his face. She just smiled back and gave his arm a hug. There was no doubt in either of their hearts that they were happy in one another's presence.

"How long will it be before we cross into Texas?" Tammy asked as she squeezed Jakes right arm and held her body close to him.

"According to that old feller we will be in Texas after we cross the Sabine river," Jake said taking in the softness of her touch as her delicate hands stayed wrapped around his muscular bicep. "I'm sure we may have to camp another night in Louisiana. I know you are ready to put it behind you."

"Oh Jake, you have no idea how I'm ready to get as far away from this place as I can. Please don't think I'm using you for a security blanket. I want to help you make your ranch in Texas a success and a home for you," Tammy said as she looked up making sure their eyes were locked together in understanding that she was telling him the truth. "I know I have to earn your trust and I will if you only let me. Please give me a chance."

Jake saw her eyes tear up. He wanted to trust her at her word but he knew trust was earned…not just hers but his as well. He thought about what she just said and he wanted to love again. He knew there was something between them. Something that yearned to be close and closer with every mile they traveled. He saw that he can be stone cold when it comes to evil men but he didn't want her to ever think he would ever raise a hand to her or anybody that didn't have it coming to them. Jake wanted Tammy to trust him and he made the commitment to himself that he would earn her trust in time and he wanted to trust her as well. He believed Julius was a good man. He proved that by getting his sister out of Baton Rouge and away from the men that wanted her just to make money serving rich clients in bed. He could have easily turned her over and probably received a reward of some kind, if he could trust the evil man that vowed to pay it. He didn't, and for that on its on merit meant something to Jake.

The fork in the road the old black man spoke of was a two days journey from where they met him. The fork was located in the little town of Many. Before entering into Many, Jake pulled up the team and the three travelers made camp along the road they had been moving down for the last couple of days. Jake handled the horses while Julius and Tammy searched for firewood for a campfire. Back up the trail Tammy put beans in a pot of water to soak for their supper. She would boil up some rice to go with the beans and a pan or cornbread as well. Jake had sure been hungry for some meat and he decided that when they stopped, it would be time for him and the Henry to go sit in the woods.

While Tammy worked on getting their supper ready, Jake took the Henry 44 caliber rifle to go and look for signs of deer. It was hot and the leather pouch with his money and land deed was sticking to his skin so he decided to take it out and place it in his saddle bags for safe keeping until he got back. He had put the saddle bags in the back of the wagon just to keep it out of sight while he was gone. He wanted to put his complete trust and faith in Julius and Tammy but that was all he had to make his start. His hope was that trust would be built between all three of them, but he knew that would take time.

He gave the brother and sister a wave as he started toward the forest. Tammy smiled that smile at him as she always does anytime their eyes met which gave Jake a spring in his step as he started out for to his hunt for meat.

It did not take him long to come upon a game trail... a path made by the different animals of the forest from rabbits to coyotes. Jake knew the path probably lead to a source of food or water. On it he saw a track made by a deer, most likely a doe, judging by the size of the track. He followed them for what seemed to be at least a mile before he saw what he was looking for. Just in view through the green foliage from the trees was a large oak tree and there several deer under it, feeding on the acorns that had fallen from the tree and covered the ground below it. The wind was in his face so he knew his position was right for him to approach without detection. He crept as silently as he could to close in on the small deer herd.

Jake saw five does and two young bucks still with spike antlers munching on the acorns. One or two deer at a time, usually the does, would look up from their eating and look about to see what else might be approaching whether it was a mature buck or a predator. Jake remained still as he could to prevent being seen by the deer's keen eye site. He was almost close enough. Jake figured about one hundred and fifty feet from the big oak tree would be in range for the Henry to take down a doe with one shot. He was quite the marksman and he knew if he got the right shot the deer would go down.

Jake raised the rifle to his cheek and picked the deer he wanted to take. He aligned the sites to a spot just below the left ear of one of the smaller does and pulled the trigger. The rifle bucked as the bullet exploded from the end of the octagon barrel sending fire and smoke trailing behind. The round hit its mark and the deer went down where it stood. The other deer scattered in different directions at the sound of the shot.

The work was about to start with hauling the deer carcass back to the camp. Jake had walked what he knew was at least two miles but he didn't mind so much after he took the guts out of her. He tied all of her legs together just above her joint in her lower legs and strapped her around him like a haversack. He decided less the guts the doe weighed about fifty pounds which would not be too much for him to carry a couple miles. He knew it would be good for him to carry the load since he hadn't done a day's work in a while.

Tammy bent over the campfire to give the beans another stir. In her heart and mind she was cooking for her man and that made her so happy she was humming a tune as she worked. Even as a young girl she dreamed of the day she would have a man in her life to cook and care for as well as give many children to. She knew society was changing and in her mind there would come a time when everyone loved one another and there would be peace and happiness for all to enjoy. Tammy rose from her work when suddenly horses rushed up to the camp and pulled up quick to a stop. There were three riders with hoods over their heads and faces on the horses and they all dismounted quickly and approached Tammy and Julius with pistols pulled.

These men all wore tan colored dusters and carried revolvers. Each horse had a lever action rifle protruding from scabbards that were attached to each saddle. The fronts of their shirts were covered with dust as was their pants as well. They approached and pointed their pistols at Tammy and Julius. Julius protested their invasion into camp and stepped up to express his displeasure.

"This is preposterous. What is the meaning of this violation?" Julius demanded as he stepped up in front of the lead man, a medium height individual with a Colt Model 1861 revolver in his right hand.

The man smelled and when he spoke Julius could smell whisky on his breath even though his face was covered by his hood. The man's eyes were that of evil pierced through the holes cut in the white canvass bag that masked his identity. He brought the back of his right hand up and struck Julius hard against his face sending him to the ground.

"Boy, I'd watch my tone with me ifn I was you. What you doin using all them high flutin words at me anyway? Now you get over by that gal and keep still." The man said through what Julius could tell by the sound to be through gritted teeth.

Tammy rushed over and clung to Julius as he sat up after falling to the ground from the outlaw's backhand. Both of them thinking how they wish Jake was here and how these men would not be so tough if he were. Tammy relied on his sence of awareness when he did approach camp after the run in with the Frenchman. Julius figured that these men were here to harass them after all of the hatred shared by blacks and whites after the war stilled brooded in some parts of the south.

"Y'all go through the wagon and see what you can find. Let me know if you find anything," the man that struck Julius demanded.

The other three men hopped to the order and jumped into the wagon and began going through all of Julius and Tammy's things. They tore through the belongings with no regard. If a garment was torn or ripped the men cared not. A hope chest with under garments the Broussards had bought for Tammy was broken and its contents thrown out of the back of the wagon. A wooden chest, full of books Julius studied and practically memorized were thrown out with no respect for the knowledge each contained. Pots and pans Tammy wasn't using were scattered all over the road by the campsite. The whole wagon and its contents were thoroughly turned into shambles. Tammy's heart was broken seeing what little possessions she had strewn about as if they were garbage.

Suddenly one of the men searching the wagon yelled out, "Johnny Boy looky what I done found."

"Bring it here," said the man holding the gun on Julius and Tammy never taking his evil eyes off of them.

The outlaw appeared and at once Tammy saw what he had found. She jumped to her feet and ran at the man with fire in her eyes. She could not let them take Jakes money. The man held the leather pouch that contained every cent Jake had and the deed to his land in Texas. She rushed him but he slapped her away causing her to fall to the side of his path.

"Little gal the next time you attack one of my boys I'm gonna put lead in you. You better understand that I mean business."

The gang leader said putting his pistol back in his holster. "Keep an eye on these two."

The other two men forced Julius and Tammy back together and made them sit down under a nearby tree. They held their guns on them even though neither put forth anymore fight. Both Julius and Tammy clung together rubbing their faces where they had been struck by these two evil men. Tammy prayed Jake would suddenly show up and make these bad men go away. She hated they had found his leather pouch with his money and land deed. She had seen the evil these men are capable of and she knew they would never hand it over and go away. She pleaded with God that she and Julius would be spared and that these awful men would just ride away. Her prayer was answered after the gang leader spoke.

"Well...a blind hog found a acorn boys." The man said as he fingered through the currency and coins contained in the leather pouch that Jake had put in his saddle bags. "High time in old town tonight," the man said as he turned to his horse, mounted up and galloped away as the other two followed.

Tammy and Julius watched the men ride away the same way they came. She thanked God the men did not kill her and Julius. She tried to convince herself that what the men took was only money and no amount is worth their lives. They sat for about an hour before they finally got up and started picking up their belongings the men scattered along the road next to their camp. They were hard at work collecting their things when Jake finally walked up carrying the deer he had killed on his hunt for meat. Tammy looked up and seeing him ran to him and fell in his arms as he dropped the dead doe to the ground.

"Jake...thank God you're back," Tammy cried as she held herself close to Jake. Julius walked up with a concerned looked on his face. This told Jake something had happened.

"What happened?" Jake asked pulling Tammy away from him so he could look into her eyes.

She began to weep uncontrollably as Jake held her by her arms. Julius stepped up closer and put his hand on his sister's shoulders. He rubbed her, trying to bring her comfort, although he knew she only found comfort in Jake.

"We were robbed while you were away on your hunt Jake. They found your leather pouch." Julius said still trying to comfort Tammy.

"How many were there?" Jake asked taking Tammy in his arms again and pressing her against him.

"There were three. They rode up from the east and they rode away in the same direction," Julius explained seeing the fire in Jakes eyes build to a raging blaze.

Jake stood there with Tammy in his arms for another minute. His thoughts were racing each other in his head trying to decide how he wanted to handle this. He had to get the leather pouch back. There was no other alternative. He was not going to the law. He would handle this himself.

"What did they look like?" Jake asked as he walked over to the horses still holding Tammy with his right arm.

"They had on hoods. We never saw their faces. They all wore those long duster type jackets and they were all covered in dust. They are mean Jake. I am surprised they didn't kill us. All I can figure is that God had His hand over us." Julius said as he picked up a bridle that was still on the ground before handing it to Jake.

Jake saddled the buckskin and filled his saddle bag with extra 44 rounds for the Henry and shot, powder and caps for his pistols. He led the horse out to the road as Tammy walked close to him. She wanted to plead with Jake to just let them go and that the money is not worth his life, but she knew it would be no use.

Jake looked at the tracks left by the horses to see if there were any flaws that could help him stay on the trail. He saw that one horse had a flawed nail. From the impression in the dirt it had a nail that had come loose and had bent itself over making a mark in the horse's track that he will be able to identify. He made a mental note of the flaw before he turned to Julius and Tammy.

"Listen...if I'm not back before daylight the two of you go ahead to Texas. I will find you." Jake said as he pulled the buckskin around to mount up.

"No Jake, please," Tammy begged as she took him in her arms. Her tears began to flow again. She was tired of the evil men coming into her life. She just wanted to get away...as far away as she could with Jake.

"Tammy, listen to me. Those men took the only means I have to make a start in Texas or anywhere. I am going after them and I will get it back from them. You have to trust me," Jake said as he looked down into her moist eyes, his heart breaking with dread, knowing there was a possibility he would not be coming to find her.

Tammy held Jake close again and suddenly pulled her face up and pressed her lips to his. Her soft lips took all of Jake's mouth as her passion for him burst forth. He embraced her and tasted the warmth of her kiss hoping this would not be the only kiss he ever received from her. He could have easily lost himself in this moment but he knew he could not. They released each other and Tammy on her tip toes moved her mouth to Jake's ear.

"Jake, I love you," Tammy whispered as she pulled away from him.

They gazed into each other's eyes for a second more before Jake kissed her forehead. He turned and mounted the buckskin and reined it in the direction of the tracks left by the outlaws.

Jake followed the tracks about twenty miles when he saw that the riders left the road and went down another road that was probably made by wood cutters working the forest harvesting trees. Jake dismounted and closely examined the tracks until he found the one made by the bent over horseshoe nail. He took his hat off and wiped his shirt sleeve across his brow then took a drink of water from his canteen before mounting up on the buckskin. This area was thick with virgin timber of both pine and hardwood. The area was lowland with marsh and creek bottoms on both sides of the road known as the El Camino Real. He knew the land he was on his way to Texas to take ownership of, was just off of this very road. He had no idea what lie ahead of him on this road that led into more thick woods. He slowed his pace and kept his eyes open for signs of shelters or any type of hiding places that might be used by the men he sought.

Jake slowly rode down the little road that passed through the heavy forest. On both sides of the road a man could hardly see into the forest itself because of the thickness of the briars and underbrush that covered the floor of the woods. If a man had to escape into the forest he would not make it very far without being cut to shreds by the thorns and bramble that made up the thicket. He kept his eyes moving trying to stay aware of anything that would be a threat. The horse's tracks were still very visible but he knew before long the sun would be down and he would not be able to see where the outlaws went. He hoped that they would stop and make camp giving him the chance to overtake them.

The forest began to thin out as Jake slowly rode onward. Suddenly he smelled wood burning. He stopped and dismounted. He thought it better to continue on foot in case he was spotted. He wanted to be able to take cover behind the many trees that made up the thick forest. He led the buckskin in the woods and tied him to a smaller tree. He took the Henry rifle and walked back to the road and continued tracking the hoof prints left by the bad men that took his future away from him.

The smell of the smoke grew stronger as he slowly crept down the road. He kept himself as low as he could, trying not to stand out. He quickly stopped in his tracks when he saw a brick chimney with smoke coming from it. The cabin it came from was concealed by the forest so Jake continued keeping a constant visual on the chimney. As he went on, the cabin came into view and he saw two men sitting on the porch that made up the whole front side of the house. There were three horses tied to hitching post in front and they were all unsaddled. One man still wore the tan duster that Julius said the robbers were wearing. The one without the duster was looking through the leather pouch that belonged to Jake Powell and this made Jake Powell's blood boil. There is one thing that he cannot tolerate and that's a thief.

Jake moved back out of sight and then left the road into the woods. The cabin sat on the right side of the road and it looked to be only one room. It was built of hand hewn logs with a roof made of sod and a thick cover of moss. He quietly moved through the woods until he came to the back of the cabin. There was a back door in the center of the house and it was standing wide open to allow a breeze to come through the house to cool it off. The outlaws were more than likely cooking a meal or boiling coffee in the fireplace.

The sticks and twigs on the ground were dry so Jake had to be extremely cautious as he made his way closer to the cabin. He went from tree to tree until he was close enough to make a move. He knew the one in the cabin was occupied with what he was cooking so it would be the two on the porch that would be his primary targets. He made it to the cabin and pressed his back against the outside wall and slowly made his way to the front corner. The cabin was not more than sixteen feet square so Jake knew he was in for a close quarter fight.

When Jake made it to the corner of the cabin he stopped and listened to the two on the porch talking. They were discussing the robbery they just committed against the two mulattos on the road.

"That little gal was sure purdy...we shoulda took her with us," one said as he cleaned his finger nails with his pocket knife. He was tall and lanky and wore his tanned duster and a black hat. His face showed several days growth of whiskers and long salt and pepper hair hung out from under his hat past his shoulders. The other man was wearing a dirty work shirt, denim pants and wore out leather pull on boots. He had a black mustache that hung down to both jaw bones and his hair was cropped short. His pale scalp showed from under the gray felt hat that sat at an angle on his head. He was counting Jake's money which told Jake it may all still be there.

"They's almost five thousand dollars in this pouch. We'll split it up here in a bit," the one holding the leather pouch said with big eyes thinking he had become rich.

Jake had his left side revolver out and he gently and quietly pulled the hammer back. Quickly he turned the corner of the house bringing the two men into view. The one with the pocket knife saw Jake first. His eyes bulged when he saw Jake's 44 level toward his face but it was too late for the man to even scream. Jake fire and a lead ball ripped through the man's left eye. The shot passed through the man's skull and hit the wall of the cabin behind the outlaw that was holding Jakes leather pouch.

The other bad man wasn't given time to go for his pistol that hung in a holster on his left side. Jake pulled the hammer of his revolver back again and shot the man through the throat. Blood flew from the wound made by the 44 caliber ball and scarlet flesh surged forth as the man fell back and landed on the floor of the porch trying to scream but instead made a dying gurgling sound.

Jake heard the man inside the cabin let out a curse just before he heard the sound of a hammer being pulled back. When the man came into sight he was firing a pistol wildly. Jake turned toward him and returned fire. Jake felt a burning pain in his side as he fell backward. He continued to fire at the man standing in the door of the cabin but Jake knew he had been hit. The pain was great but he refused to quit fighting. He had emptied his revolver and with his left hand grabbed the other on his right side and continued to fire away. The man took all six rounds in his chest. He was thick man...especially through the chest. Jake could tell by looking at him that in a hand to hand fight this man would be a hand full. The man fell to his knees and then onto his face...dead.

Jake reached to the pain in his side and felt the warmth of blood on his hand before falling to the ground. He hoped he had not been gut shot. If he had been, all was lost and his death would be agonizing. He tried to get up but kept falling with each attempt. He had no strength, it had left him. He managed to crawl to the leather pouch that was dropped when the man holding it received his just reward for stealing it. He opened it and saw that all the money was in it as well as the deed to his land. He put it back in his shirt where it should have been to start with. If he had left it there when he went hunting, he would not be going through the burning pain he was going through. He then thought how the money may have taken the minds of these dead bad men off of taking Tammy with them.

Jake kept passing in and out as he tried to make his way back to the buckskin. He was almost in sight of the horse still where the buckskin faithfully waited on his friend to return. He fell to the ground again. The pain was torturous and he needed a drink of cool water so bad. He mouth was dried but he still managed to pucker his lips and blow out a whistle to the horse. The buckskins head popped up and then jerked his head back hard enough to come untied. He walked over to his master lying injured on the ground. The horse came close and touched his nose to Jakes face taking in the scent of his human friend. Jake reached up with a hand that was not bloody and touched the buckskins nose. He softly spoke to the horse as he tried to muster the strength to get up and mount up. Then everything went black.

Chapter 10

The morning appeared at the camp where Jake had left Julius and Tammy. Both of them were up hoping to see Jake riding up at any moment but that moment never came. Tammy paced back and forth in the road and periodically stopped and looked in the direction Jake had taken when he rode away yesterday. Julius could tell the wait was working on her patience but he said nothing, figuring she would lose her temper with him if he did. He feared the worst although speculating did nothing but made ones imagination run wild. He took his last sip of coffee and hitched up the wagons and loaded the back of it never expecting Tammy to help because her mind was lost in worry over Jake. He dreaded telling her that it was time to move out.

"Tammy, it's time to go," Julius said approaching her in the road where she continued to walk and look.

She ignored him as if he never said a word. Tammy just kept pacing back and forth keeping a constant eye out for Jake. Her heart pounded with every step she made as her heart tried to make the picture in her mind of him coming into view come to be. Tammy saw herself making a mad dash in the direction he took, screaming his name, but knew that would do no good. Finally, she stopped and with tears rolling down her face she screamed.

"Jake...Jake...!" Tammy cried as her heart gave in to the brokenness it felt from the thought of Jake not coming back. Her hope was that at the sound her cry he would appear on the buckskin and ride to her and take her up and ride away.

Julius went to her and wrapped his arms around her and held her tight. He wept too.

"Tammy, listen to me. Jake is fine. You know he is going to find us just like he said," Julius said hoping his words would soothe her mind. "He told us that he would find us and I trust what he said."

Tammy always trusted her older brother. So many times he was the only one she had to bring her comfort and she was always there for him as well. This time would be no different. She relaxed in his embrace and she let her tears flow. He held her tightly and rubbed her back while the anxiety that had welled up inside of her was released. She trusted what Jake said. He will find them.

It took shear effort for Jake to open his eyes. He suddenly became aware of the pain that screamed from his right side. The last thing he recalled was going down after being shot. His hope was that he would not die from the hole in his side and it looked like someone had their hand over him. His eyes come open and he gained his focus and looked around at his surroundings. He was in a room, but where? There was a soft bed under him and it felt good considering the wound to his side. There were walls around him that were adorned with pretty wallpaper with flowers. He saw fancy furniture against each wall. Furniture that looked too fancy like the furniture in Mr. Buckhorns office back in Atlanta. He tried to move but the pain kept him from it. He knew that if the bleeding had stopped moving about to much might do damage to any fixing the

180

wound had received. He felt like just closing his eyes to see if he could wake up again and see Tammy by his side.

"Hello", a soft voice said coming from the right side of the bed he was lying on.

Jake turned and saw a lady looking down at him with a sympathetic look on her angelic face. She looked to be somewhat older than Jake, maybe in her late thirties. Her hair was a light grayish color but he could tell that at one time it was golden blonde. Her eyes were an emerald green. Her lips looked to be soft and full. The lady had a slender face that glowed with southern charm and beauty. She stood looking down at Jake as he lay there with an amazed look on his face. She was taller than most women and in spite of the white cotton dress she wore her curves were distinct and very complimentary. Jake batted his eyes a few times as he tried to determine if he was dreaming or was seeing an angel in Glory.

"Hello...". Jake said in return. "Who are you?"

The lady gently sat down on the bed and turned gracefully toward Jake and said, "Well, my name is Ann, which is short for Annabell...I don't like the name Annabell so please do not call me that."

Jake noticed a sweet fragrance coming from her which reminded him of the fancy perfume that Sarah sometimes wore. He thought he smelled a hint of it from Tammy the first time she got close to him. He tried to rise up because he was tired of laying in the position he was in and pain shot through him from his left side and he stopped. Ann got up and walked around to the other side of the bed.

"Here...let me help you. I know you are uncomfortable." Ann said as she put her hands under his arms from behind and together moved Jake into a sitting position with his back against

181

the beds headboard. "Now, I bet that's better. Are you thirsty? Maybe some water."

"Yes please, thank you." Jake said as he tried to settle in to straighten his back.

Ann walked over to a pitcher sitting on a dresser made of stained wood and poured some water in a glass there by it. She brought it back over to Jake then took a seat next to him, handing it to him. Jake noticed that she moved with grace and elegance as walked. When she spoke her voice had the sound of one from southern aristocracy and looking at the room he was in, there was no doubt the house was fancier that anything he had ever been in, including the Tunstall house.

Jake suddenly became aware of the fact that he was without his clothes. He began looking around for his shirt and pants and especially his leather pouch. Ann realized what he was looking for and smiled.

"You must be looking for your clothes. Don't worry…they are here, all cleaned and pressed. I also repaired the nasty hole in your shirt left by that lead ball that forced its way through your side." She said as if it were nothing to be concerned about.

"What about my leather pouch?" Jake said not trying to hide the suspicion on his face and in his tone.

"Don't worry its right here." Ann said almost sarcastically as she reached under the very mattress that Jake was lying on.

Jake showed relief as she pulled the pouch out and handed it to him. He wanted to count the money but didn't, in fear of insulting the lady that saved his life. He put it on the bed next to him sighed and closed his eyes.

"That ugly leather pouch must mean a lot to you." Ann said adjusting her position on the bed where she sat next to Jake.

Jake opened his eyes and looked into hers and said, "Yes Ma'am, that's all I have. The deed was left to me and the mother of my children before she was murdered. It then went to our son who died with his twin sister of a severe cough and fever. After that, I just decided to take it and get away from all the memories. So I'm heading to Texas to start over."

"I am assuming those men you killed stole it from you," Ann said wondering if he was going to admit to the killings.

"How did you know about that?" Jake asked not sure he wanted to go into detail about the incident.

"I was not far from there when all the shooting started. After it was over I snuck up and saw you crawling toward your horse. I didn't think there for a minute he was going to allow me to help you. He's one heck of a horse," She added with sincerity. She had an appreciation for horses. "I'm going to keep the other three for myself."

"One needs to be shod. It's got a flawed nail in one shoe," Jake said as he saw a confused look come over Ann's face. "That's how I was able to track them."

Ann nodded and stood up and said, "I bet you're hungry, so I made you some potato soup. It will do you good."

"Yes, thank you. I feel like I haven't eaten in a week," Jake said touching his flat belly.

"You haven't, you've been unconscious for five days," Ann said turning and looking his way.

Jake was heartbroken. The thought of Tammy and Julius rushed into his mind. He knew that by now they had given up on him. The pain in his heart showed on his face.

"What's wrong?" She asked.

"I had no idea I was out that long. I was suppose too catch up with two people I was traveling with. I know they are worried sick about me, if not given up on me all together," Jake said leaning his head back and closing his eyes.

"You'll catch up to them. You've got it in you and nothing will hold it back," Ann said having no idea how much her words meant to Jake. "Any chance her name is Tammy?"

"Yes, how did you know that?"

"You talk in your sleep or at least you did last night." Ann said relieved that he did because it gave her hope he was coming back around. "Let me get your soup."

After Jake took three bowls of Ann's delicious potato soup he started feeling like the living again. He was surprised though that he hadn't seen domestic help in the house. From what he could see the house was considerabley large. When Ann came through the bedroom door he could see a hallway and another room across the way but that was all. He decided to ask her how she keeps the place going and if she has hands or a helper that is taking care of the buckskin. After Ann gave him the last spoon full of the third bowl he finally got up the nerve to ask.

"So do you take care of this place by yourself alone? You are the only person I've seen," Jake asked having no idea what her answer was going to be.

Ann wiped his mouth with a white linen cloth and set the tray down on the floor next to the bed. She adjusted her position and pushed her long hair back away from her face. Jake could tell she was giving thought to the answer she was about to give him.

"I live here alone. The house and land was left to me by my late father and I've kept it going well enough to suit me. I don't require any domestic help since I've closed the portions of the house off that I do not use. I have this one bedroom that you and I have been sharing since I brought you here." Ann said with a mischievous smile which brought Jake to full attention.

"You mean we've been sleeping together since I've been here?" Jake asked, as the thought almost jarred him right out of the bed.

"Yes we have. I even gave you a bath last night. I must say, I enjoyed it immensely," she said with a look of fond recollection on her face. She looked at Jake through the corner of her eye to check his reaction.

Jake tried to laugh but stopped. "Please don't make me laugh. It hurts to bad."

"I wasn't trying to be funny," She said still with the same look on her face. "You are quite handsome."

"Thank you," Jake said with surrender.

Jake adjusted himself again to allow his back to straighten. He looked in the eyes of this beautiful lady who saved his life with amazement. Here she is all alone taking care of house and land with assistance of no man. He was truly impressed with such a woman. He was especially impressed how she remained so lovely knowing the hard chores that are require to maintain such a place require muscle and brawn. This woman looked as elegant as a Confederate Rose in bloom. She was stunning and still very alluring in spite of the years she had on Jake.

"Would like to get out of bed and get some sunshine? There is plenty of daylight left outside," Ann asked standing up and reaching for Jakes pants.

185

Jake smiled with enthusiasm as he started to throw the covers away from his body but stopped, remembering he was naked. She handed him his pants before she turned and walked out of the room.

"Do go slow...I don't want that wound to open up and you bleed on my rug any more than you already have," she said as she strolled to the door brushing the tail of her white cotton dress.

When Jake stood, the pain in his side was enormous. He closed his eyes tight and winced as the pain traveled to his brain and back again. He took a few steps away from the bed and stepped into his pants which brought more pain to his side. Jake looked down at the bandage wrapped around his mid-section to see if it was turning crimson. He breathed a sigh of relief to see that it was not. As he pulled his pants up to his waist the pain seemed to be letting up a bit. He hoped after taking a few steps it would completely go away, but that was only hope. He buttoned the fly of his pants and then strapped his belt around his waist without more pain. He was relieved to get his feet back under him again after realizing he had been out for those days. Jake thought how easy it is to take something so simple for granted.

Jake walked out of the bedroom with no boots on his feet. The fancy rug felt good to the bottoms of his feet as he made his way down a hallway to the dining room. There was a large crystal chandelier hanging from a cathedral ceiling that had to be sixteen feet high. The stained oak dining table sat in the middle of the room directly under the chandelier, and there were a total of twelve places anyone could set and have plenty room to feast. Two buffet tables, the same style and design as the dining table, sat against one wall and three large bay windows on the opposite side of the room allowed an abundance of light into the rather fancy eating room.

Jake made his way into the parlor off the dining room where Ann sat in a red velvet baroque throne chair. Her slender long legs were crossed and her back gently pressed against the back of the chair giving her breast more definition than Jake had first noticed. She was definitely a lady of refined elegance and charm, bred from the finest of southern blue bloods.

The parlor was furnished with taste and spoke of a grandeur that indicated wealth and importance. Three large bookshelves stood against two walls of the room. There were titles from the great masters of literature as well as books on military strategies and history. Jake felt just a tad bit out of place.

"Are you in much pain Jake?" Ann asked as he moved across the large parlor room to a matching velvet love seat.

"It's pretty tender but I'll make it. Can we go outside for a bit?" Jake asked not yet taking a seat.

"Well, of course. There are chairs outside where we can sit and visit.

Jake reached out his hand as any gentleman would do and Ann took it and stood up. She directed him toward the front door of the mansion and onto the front porch. The porch wrapped around the front of the mansion in a semicircular fashion. Tall colonnades standing thirty feet held the roof of the porch that adorned the face of the noble house that Ann had called home all of her life. The paint on its exterior was a brilliant white and looked to be fairly fresh. The roof of the two story estate was covered in clay shingles the color of clay and each window was between shutters painted in green.

Ann and Jake made their way to pair of ornate metal chairs and sat on a brick patio to the left of the porch of the house. There was a matching table between the chairs where a white porcelain vase sat. It held three long stemmed red roses that looked freshly pruned from their bush. A clear glass pitcher of lemonade sat a on a sterling silver tray with two matching glasses and cubes of sugar to sweeten. Jake held Ann's chair as she sat down.

"I hope you are thirsty Jake," Ann said as she poured a glass of the drink and offered it to him.

"Yes Ma'am I am...thank you," Jake replied as took the glass of lemonade.

"There's sugar if it's not sweet enough for you. I remember my father like his extra sweet," she said took a glass for herself.

"Tell me about your father. What was his name?" Jake asked as he sipped the sweet drink.

Ann pushed her long straight hair over her ear and smiled. Jake could tell from the look on her face that Ann had fond memories of her father. She let the cool lemonade dampen her throat before she spoke, her thoughts racing for words to describe the man she loved and admired all of her life.

"My father Richard Faulkner was a General in the Confederate Army. He never spoke of the war so I don't know any of his exploits to tell of. I can't even tell you what company he served over because he just did not talk about it after he came home. I presume losing the war had a lot to do with that and I can't say that I blame him. It is a part of our lives we want to put behind us and forget," she said then taking a sip and swishing it around inside her mouth she continued. "He took care of things very well here. Everything I have is free from any legal bindings. His fortune his tucked away in a bank in Mansfield and it provides for me a very comfortable living. We were very fortunate that the northern armies missed this house. I guess it being so secluded was the reason."

Jake poured more lemonade into his glass and turned to her and asked, "How do you keep the place by yourself? Don't you need help here?"

"Not at all," she said making a face to show how ridiculous his question was and then said, "I am quite capable of taking care of myself."

Jake leaned back and let that statement register in his mind. Here is a beautiful and refined lady of the south cleaning stalls, making meals and cleaning a large Louisiana mansion on what is more than likely large plantation. Jake was having a hard time wrapping his mind around the thought.

"Do you raise animals here or crops of some sort?" Jake asked still rather confused over the story he just heard from Ann.

"Well you might say I do. I keep a spring and fall garden which yields plenty of vegetables to carry me through the year. I've become quite the gardener since the slaves were freed," Ann said as she got up and extended her hand. "Come, let's take a walk."

As the two made their way around the grounds of the estate Jake took in the beautiful flowers and plants that decorated the outside of the old house. Everything was trimmed and manicured with care and expertise. All of the shrubs that grew along the outside of the house were neatly kept and the grass was cut so that not even a snake could cross the yard without being detected. Jake was amazed at the determination Ann shows in her day to day life.

"I guess you don't use the second floor of the house," Jake assumed as he stopped and looked up at the roof line of the mansion.

"No, I only use the bottom floor but I do go up to make sure the squirrels haven't taken up residence in the attic. I keep it dusted and swept as well, but I have no need to live in it." Ann said looking up at the home she has made for herself, an obvious look of pride showing on her face.

Jake turned and said, "I almost forgot…I've got to bury those bodies before the varmints find them if they ain't all ready."

Ann looked his way and let out a little giggle and said. "No need because I've already taken care of them."

"You buried them?" Jake asked with a shocked look on his face.

Ann let out another little giggle and said, "Right after I found you it come a big rain. I dragged them all three in the house and set it on fire. I needed to burn the place down anyway. It didn't do anything but attract the likes of those three thieves."

"What if their remains are found?" Jake asked truly curious.

"I have no idea what you're talking about," she said with a grin.

Jake and Ann sat together in the large dining room finishing their dinner with cups of hot coffee served in exquisite china cups that Jake found to be so delicate that he hated to touch them. He had never put anything as fancy as this to his mouth in his whole life and the thought of breaking one, made him so insecure he almost asked for a tin cup instead. He didn't want to insult Ann with his childish uncertainty pertaining to his clumsiness, so he took extreme caution as he drank his coffee.

"This meal was really good. You are quite the cook," Jake said meaning every compliment.

Ann bowed her head and then looked into Jakes eyes and gave him a rather mischievous smile and said, "Well, thank you, Jake."

Changing the subject, Jake asked, "Have you ever been married?"

Ann put her cup down and pressed her back against the back of her chair. She blew out a breath and then inhaled before answering Jake's question.

"No, I haven't. I was once engaged but that didn't happen. Gregory O'Connor was his name. He didn't return from the war. As a matter of fact we got word just after the war started, that he was killed when he was thrown from a horse during a training exercise. He never was much of a horseman," Ann said obviously over the strain of losing someone she was in love with. "After that I just decided not to get wrapped up in such an emotion like love."

Jake listened intently as Ann told of how she and Gregory met and how their relationship blossomed into love. The mansion and all of its acreage and stock were to be theirs, along with cotton fields and the staff to work them, but it all turned out to be like so many other dreams shattered by an unnecessary war. President Davis knew slavery needed to be abolished and the countless number of individuals caught up in the institution of slavery needed to be educated and brought into the saving knowledge of Christ. Yet, Abraham Lincoln had other plans that cost the lives of many.

Over the next three days, Jake found himself being able to move about with limited pain. He even found himself out back of the cook house chopping firewood for the stove. His mind stayed on finding Tammy and Julius and then getting back on

191

the journey to Texas. He figured surely by now they were there and had probably given up on him all together. He made his way out to the barn where the buckskin was stabled. He brushed him and talked to him in the same tone he always does making sure the horse knew his voice. He missed the trail and was eager to set out. He decided to pack up and leave now but knew it was only proper to sit and talk to Ann before he did. He wanted to express his sincere gratitude for saving his life after being shot by one of the thieves that took his money pouch.

Jake noticed that all day Ann had stayed to herself. The two had not said two words to each other since they ate breakfast together in the big dining room. Ann knew that the time for Jake to leave was approaching and she had grown so fond of him that she dreaded to hear his voice tell her good bye. She had lost herself in mending things she hadn't worn in ages. During the tasks she performed she kept asking herself why she was doing this…she knew she would never wear these things again. She only knew that as long as she stayed busy and away from Jake he could not tell her goodbye. She loved him being here with her. Ann retired herself to a hot bath hoping that a long soak would clear her mind.

Afterwards Ann was in the parlor finishing up on a dress, of all things. The hem that runs along the bottom of the garment had come loose and she was just finishing it, with a needle and thread sewing it back together. She tried to remember the last time she wore the thing, but through the clouds she had created in her mind from dwelling on thoughts of her guest, she couldn't grasp the memory. She clipped the thread and pushed the needle into her pin cushion and closed her eyes. She had been sipping from a decanter trying to ease the stress she had put on her life bringing this man into her house. She just wanted to help this man who had been shot and at the brink of death.

Ann sat quietly in her white cotton nightgown and let the warm drink soothe her mind, giving her the courage to approach Jake. She took the last swallow from her crystal goblet and set it on the table next to her chair when she heard Jake's footsteps softly echoing up the hallway and turning into the bedroom she had been sharing with him for the last two weeks. She got up and made her way to the room knowing disappointing words were about to be spoken.

Jake was standing at the dresser with his hands resting on its vanity. He was trying to bring himself to say goodbye to Ann. He felt her presence when she stepped into the door of the bedroom. He slowly turned and looked her in the eyes. She looked deep into his for just a moment and then she walked over to where he stood. He could tell the same thing was on her mind and he gave her the chance to speak but she said nothing.

"You know I must go," Jake softly said as he held her stare.

"I know you do," Ann replied still looking into his eyes.

"I really do appreciate everything you've done for me. If it were not for you I know I'd be dead." Jake saw her gently close her eyes as to stop a tear. She opened them and met his again.

Ann slowly walked up to Jake and took his hands in her hands as she closed in on his space. Her soft finger tips stroked his hands as she pressed herself against his chest. She reached up and pressed her lips to his as they both allowed their passions to grow between them. Jake tasted brandy from her mouth as her lips pushed his desire onward. He knew this wasn't right but he considered the lonely woman who desired him at this moment.

She pulled away from him slowly and reached down and untied the cotton strap that held the front of her night gown together between her firm breasts. Ann let the gown fall from her soft shoulders and onto the floor.

"In the morning..."

Jake rode the buckskin off of the ferryboat after crossing the Sabine River into an evening sun. Its brightness causing him to look under the brim of the sweat stained felt hat. He pulled it off and wiped his soaked forehead with a bandana that was tied around his neck. The whiskers on his face had all but turned into a beard and his sandy brown hair hung to his shoulders. His shirt was soaked and grimy but it was the only shirt he had. When he sat out to find the men that took his leather pouch containing his money and land deed, he had no intention of being gone three weeks. He wondered if he would be able to find Tammy and Julius in such a large state. He hoped they had not gone far from the state line and all he knew to do was travel west in hopes of running across them before he reached his destination.

A wooden sign set off the road leading off of the dock where the ferryboat landed read, 'San Augustine' with an arrow pointing westward. Jake stopped and looked at the landscape that surrounded the country side which looked pretty much like what he had been traveling through since he left Atlanta. The tall pine trees and hardwoods reminded him of home but he thought about the vastness that lay ahead of him. Jake held the determination in his heart to make the start he had been dreaming about since he left home and here it was in front of him. It was up to him to make it happen and make it happen was what he was going to do. He had read books about this place where every kind of landscape known to man can be found from coastal waters to deserts with cactus, rocks and rattlesnakes, piney woods to prairie brush could be found right here. Jake had finally made it...to Texas.

Chapter 11

It took Jake another day of steady riding before he reached San Augustine, Texas. The old town dates back to the early 1700's when Europeans began to settle this part of what would become The Republic of Texas after winning its independence from Mexico before it become the State of Texas. This town of about two hundred and fifty people set deep in history and pride was on what is known as the San Antonio Road and the El Camino Real. It is known to be the path taken by David Crockett on his way to the Alamo where he fought and died for the right to be free. In 1836 in San Augustine, Sam Houston was chosen to lead the Texas military to go forth and defeat Santa Anna at the Battle of San Jacinto. By the time of the War for Southern Independence, San Augustine was a center for shipping cotton. Its men stepped up to answer the call to fight against the northern invasion of the south.

Jake made his way down the main street that ran in front of the courthouse and jail. He considered stopping to see if the sheriff may have seen Julius and Tammy come through but he decided against it because of the lack of activity around the old building there in the center of town. He decided to stop at the San Augustine Hotel for the night and see about a bath and to have his clothes washed. In the morning he would check with the general store across from the hotel about a new pair of pants and a shirt.

The San Augustine Hotel stood two stories high and, like most of the architecture of the area, had a covered porch with a balcony above that ran the length of the front of the building. There were two large plate glass windows on either side of a double door entrance. "San Augustine Hotel" was painted on the one window and "Fine Dining" on the other. Jake had become accustomed to Ann's cooking during the time he stayed with her where he was nursed back to health from his gunshot wound. He would always look back on her with appreciation as well as fond memories. She was a fine woman.

The lobby of the hotel was clean and it looked like a place that could provide a comfortable bed and a good night's sleep. Jake noticed a Coglan parlor clock on a table behind the counter where a desk clerk stood waiting on Jake to make his request for a room. The clock indicated that it was twenty five minutes after six telling him it was supper time.

He approached the desk clerk, a middle-aged slender man wearing a white shirt buttoned to the neck and black pants that were creased and starched so well that they looked to Jake as if they could stand on their own. He had a bald head and a long-shaved face that looked as if it never received much sun. He watched Jake approach and greeted him in a kind voice.

"Good evening sir. Would you like a room?" the clerk asked with a smile that matched his voice.

"Yes sir, I'd like to stay the night and maybe get a bath and my clothes washed if possible." Jake said as he reached under his shirt for his leather pouch to pay in advance.

"That will be three dollars...sign here please," the clerk said turning a registry around for Jake to write his name in. He then turned and took a key from a peg board behind him next to the clock. "We also have a very good restaurant in the building. The food is excellent and you will find the service to be impeccable. It's right through those doors."

"Thank you sir, I think I will have a bite before turning in for the night" Jake said as he took the room from the clerk. "Can I get my clothes washed tonight?"

"Yes, when you finish your dinner just let me know and I will send up for them. They will be washed and dried by a stove and be ready for you first thing in the morning," the clerk assured Jake with a smile.

"Thank you. I hope I don't stink too bad to go into the restaurant." Jake said pulling his shirt and giving it a smell.

"No sir, you are fine. We have cowhands come in all the time," the clerk said

Jake was pleased that, to the desk clerk, he looked like a cowhand and grinned at the thought of the idea of him being a cowhand being his destiny. He was ready to put his mind back on getting his operation started and setting out on a brand new venture. Again Tammy and Julius came to mind and he wondered where they could have wound up since the last time he saw them. He remembered the promise he made Tammy that he would find them. He decided to ask someone to see if, by chance, they had seen the two traveling through.

The restaurant was decorated with flowers on each table and each table had a red and white checkered cloth over it. It looked very homey and the smells coming from the kitchen was very inviting. It made Jake's mouth water just thinking about fried chicken and mashed potatoes with gravy and biscuits. He thought he could catch a hint of apple pie in the aromas that came from the kitchen just off the dining room. A young woman dressed in a light blue dress with a red apron came over with a glass of water and set it on the table Jake had taken a seat at by the big plate glass window. Its curtains were pulled back so he could stare out the window while waiting for his food.

"What can I get for you this evening?" the waitress asked in a true Texas country girl voice. Her blonde hair was pulled back in a ponytail and her sky blue eyes sparkled as she looked into Jakes. Her smile was sincere and her soft round face made the woman look to be no older than eighteen.

"Do I smell chicken being fried?" Jake asked as he took a sip of water.

"Yes sir, the best in East Texas. Would you like that for your supper? It comes with mash taters, pinto beans, cornbread or a biscuit," the young waitress said with a sweet grin.

"Cornbread or biscuits, you say." Jake said as if he was vying for a favor.

She sweetened her smile even more and said, "For you, cornbread and biscuits."

"Thank you Ma'am."

The young blonde waitress stacked the plate and saucers from the table after Jake finished his meal. She made conversation with him about the area and its people and how the community was close to each other. It was apparent to him that she knew everybody and saw most everybody that passed through this small town. After she had taken the dishes to the kitchen, she returned and wiped the table cloth before she sat down across from Jake. She looked at him with wonder and the expression on her face showed her curiosity.

"You ain't from around here are you? I know I ain't never seen you," the girl said with a grin

Jake chuckled and said. "Nope, I'm just passing through."

She looked at him for a few seconds and said, "You look like all the other cowhands around...I figured you was just another. They come in usually after they get their pay on Saturday to fill their bellies with good grub and then let loose down at the saloon yonder at the end of the street."

"I try to stay out of them places. There are way too many pole cats that hang out in there," Jake said returning her smile. "Say, I was wondering if you may have seen a couple of friends of mine that may have passed through over the last couple of weeks."

"Don't know, what'd they look like?" the young woman asked.

"They are brother and sister and are travelling in a covered wagon. Both are mulattos from Louisiana. The female is very pretty." Jake added.

The young waitress thought for a few seconds and finally said, "Yeah I remember them. They came in and got them a meal made. She came in and made the order and I filled the basket she had with beef sandwiches. She bought four of them. I figured they was just in a hurry. We would have put them in the back room yonder on a count of they was colored, but I remember she was real purdy...had the most beautiful eyes you ever did see."

Jake perked up and leaned in closer and asked, "Did she say where they were going from here?"

The young woman thought and said, "Kind of I guess. She asked what towns were west of here. I told her Nacogdoches and then Alto. I got a aunt that lives in Alto, Aunt Trudy. I told her she might get a job in her restaurant cooking if she good at it. She said she might do that and that she was waiting on somebody. Would that be you?"

"I reckon it is," Jake said leaning back with a look of relief on his face.

"My name's Jenny by the way...I wish you could have seen the look on her face when she told me that," the waitress said.

"Why is that?" Jake inquired. "I'm Jake by the way."

"It was the look of a woman in love."

The next morning, just after daybreak, Jake rose from a night's sleep and got dressed. His clothes were hanging on the doorknob outside his room and they were clean and fresh and ready for another coat of dirt, sweat and grime from the El Camino Real. His plan was to make it to Nacogdoches by the end of the day, then Alto the next. He walked down the stairs to the lobby of the hotel and turned in his key before walking across the street to see if he could find clothes suitable for the trail. He was glad to see that not only did they have clothes to fit him, but they had the stick candy he had grown to love so well. He was set for traveling except for the lack of coffee, a pot and cup. The stick candy would have to get him by.

Jake covered the miles between San Augustine and Nacogdoches in one day. He saw how the landscape changed the further west he traveled toward his dream. There was lush pasture land suitable for raising cattle and horses that covered the country side with large stands of timber along the countryside too. He passed a crew of wood cutters taking the trees from the forest to turn them into logs to go to a mill to make lumber. Those trees were destined to become houses and furniture for the people who made up the communities he saw on his way.

Some of the pastures looked like they stretched a half of a mile or better. He saw herds of cattle as well as horses of every color. This made his dream get bigger and bigger as each mile passed. He had never believed that he would wind up in Texas. The thought felt good to Jake. He had heard many stories of the fighting men from Texas that served in the war. Every story told painted a picture of true fighters and warriors. A warrior that General Lee called on many times knowing they were tough as boots and meaner than a cottonmouth.

Jake reined up in front of a livery stable in Nacogdoches. A town where, like San Augustine, got the whole story Texas

201

started. The sign of the livery stable simply read "Livery" and when Jake dismounted the buckskin, he walked inside through two double barn doors that were standing wide open. He was met by a short man wearing a derby hat, an old brown work shirt with denim pants. It was hard to tell if the shirt the little man had on was brown or tan due to the sweat and dirt that covered it. His face was dirty and he had a big reddish mustache and a growth of stubble on his small face that looked like he last shaved about a month back. He saw Jake and walked up wiping his face with a soiled rag he pulled from his pants pocket.

"What can I do for you friend, put your horse up for the night while you go get a bath?" he said with a laugh so high pitched and wheezy it was possible his lungs were full of mud and sand paper.

Jake handed him the reins of the buckskin and thought 'you're one to talk about a bath'.

"Can you put him up for the night and give him plenty of hay and oats," Jake requested amazed by the little man's overly friendly manner.

"I'll even give him a good brushing. Why afore morning he'll be my new best friend. That'll be two dollars in advance," the man said as he held out his filthy hand and took two coins from Jake. "The hotel's yonder and the kitchen across the street serves up a good supper."

Jake tipped his hand and made his way down the street toward the hotel carrying his saddle bags with his new clothes slung over a shoulder and his Henry in his left hand. He thought how all these nights in comfortable hotel rooms were going to make him soft. He wondered where he would find a bed as comfortable as what he was used to sleeping in to go in a cabin once he gets settled. He didn't know where, but he knew he would. The thought of one day sharing it with Tammy brought a smile to his face.

The summer sun was setting in the western sky of Texas as Jake stood at the window of his hotel room. He had managed to talk the desk clerk into a coffee pot, a cup and a small bag of coffee when he checked in. A small metal stand made from two horseshoes served as a stove for the pot and a candle for a fire to boil the brew. The kitchen across the street was everything the dirty little man at the livery said it was and more.

As he watched the skyline with its purple tint fade to black, the twinkle of the stars introduced themselves to the approaching night. Jake wondered where Tammy and Julius were and if they were well. He so wanted to look into her beautiful eyes again. Each mile he traveled since he was wounded in the gunfight with the men that robbed their camp, Tammy has been on his mind and in his heart. There were times he would come awake and the scent of her skin softly pressed against his cheek would enter his thoughts as if she were there next to him. The way she held him in the road before they parted left his soul longing for her embrace. The taste of her kiss as she pressed her lips to his will forever be engraved in his thoughts. He had to find her and he knew he was getting close. Jake vowed to himself the he would leave her no more.

"Would you please just lie down and get some sleep Tammy, you are about to make yourself crazy waiting for Jake. You should know by now he is not coming," Julius said as he raised up from the bed and leaned on one elbow.

Tammy sat at a window that faced the street in front of a one room house sitting behind the restaurant owned and operated by one Trudy McQueen. Trudy gave Tammy a job cooking and Julius a job washing dishes at her eatery simply called "Trudy's". The place sat on the main street that passed through the small town of Alto along the Old San Antonio Road right where two roads crossed. One went north that connected Tyler and south would take you to Lufkin. The road heading east took you to Nacogdoches and west went to Crockett. All trade centers in the piney woods of East Texas. People travelling through from all four directions stopped to enjoy the home cooking that Trudy was so known to prepare. When Tammy showed her how well she learned, Trudy hired her on the spot since Trudy was getting up in age. She had been thinking on passing her recipes on to someone and Trudy took to Tammy like lard takes to flour. When Tammy took the job she told Trudy it might be for temporary because she was expecting Jake to come just any day. That was almost a month ago. Julius had already given upon on Jake but Tammy refused.

"I know he is close, I just know it," Tammy said with tears burning her eyes. She had sat in the evening after the restaurant closed and stared out this same window in hopes that Jake would show. Night after night she sat and watched and night after night she would cry herself to sleep disappointed and heart broken.

Late the next day as Tammy took another five loaves of homemade bread from the oven her mind remained on Jake and his returning. She refused to believe that any man or even three getting the best of him in a fight. He was cunning and ruthless when he had to be and utterly dreamy otherwise. She took the loaves and set them on a sheet pan to cool before taking a break in a small room off of the kitchen where she would have a sandwich or a bit of what was left over from the lunch special Trudy served for the working men in the area, if they were close enough to come in for a meal. Tammy sat trying to keep the tears back that came when her mind was overcome by the thoughts of Jake.

Julius was just finishing up the dishes from the lunch rush when Trudy waddled into the kitchen where he was working. She stood just slightly slumped and had her reddish gray hair was pulled up in a bun. Several straids had given up the bun and hung wildly around her wrinkled face. She wore no makeup since she gave up on attracting men a long time ago. She still liked to flirt with male customers that came in daily to enjoy her food. She wore a red dress that stretched in places that held the larger parts of her pear shaped torso. Her legs were short and weary from the years of carrying her plumpness around. She spoke with an accent that told right away she was from the south and the volume of it gave all indication that she was the boss.

"Julius, go sweep the dining room and the porch when you're done there sweetie," she said giving Julius a start.

"I'll get right on it immediately Miss Trudy." Julius answered with soap suds from his finger tips to his biceps. His shirt sleeves were rolled up as far as they would go.

Trudy trudged into the little room where Tammy sat with her thoughts. She developed a love for Tammy in the few short weeks she had known her. She could always tell when Jake was on her mind and by the way she reached up to an eye to catch a tear before it escaped down her delicate cheek, she knew Tammy felt the worst thing had happened. Trudy pulled up a chair a sat down at the table next to Tammy.

"Tammy dear, you are going to worry yourself sick thinking about Jake. He probably took a wrong turn somewhere. There are enough little towns along the roads that somebody will know how to get to Augusta and they all go right through our little town here. It's just across the Neches west of here. He will be along any day now you just hang on to your faith, you'll see." Trudy said sounding just like a sweet mother.

Tammy looked up with tears in her eyes. She made no effort to hold them back. "I just need him so much. I feel safe with him. I feel complete with him when he is by me. I tried to tell him but..." Tammy suddenly looked as Julius rushed in.

"Tammy, come quick," Julius said out of breath. "I was sweeping the porch and..."

Tammy had gotten up and ran through the dining room of the restaurant not even giving Julius a chance to tell her what he saw. She went through the door of the eatery like a flash and stopped in the middle of the street. Her eyes looked eastward and saw a rider coming on a buckskin horse. Her heart leaped with joy as she saw Jake coming up the street. She ran toward him not giving him the time to make it to her. Jake dropped the reins and dismounted as she hurried to meet him. She jumped into his arms and wrapped both her arms around his neck and both legs around his waist. She pressed his face to her breast and threw his hat off his head. Tammy began kissing Jakes head and face to the point he couldn't catch a breath. It took Jake several seconds to break loose from her passionate embrace.

"Hold it...Tammy...let go...are you trying to smother me?" Jake asked as he put his hands under her arms and lifted her up. "I'm glad to see you too."

He put her down in front of him and their eyes met. Her smile showed him the joy coming from her heart as he took her by the hands. He held them and stepped back taking a good long look at her. He was moved as well at the sight of her. She was very beautiful in his eyes and he was as glad to see her as she was to see him. They stood and gazed at each other for a long minute before they both wrapped each other in their arms. The two stood together feeling the warm passion each had for the other. Their lips met confirming their love.

"I don't ever want to be away from you again," Jake said as he pulled away. He looked her directly in the eyes and reaffirmed his statement. "I never will be away from you again."

"Oh Jake, I love you."

The Old San Antonio Road was lonely this afternoon. It hardly saw any travelers going either way. Ann Faulkner had been to the City of Mansfield on business and was driving her one horse buggy onto her road that goes passed the old burned out cabin where Jake was engaged in a shootout with three robbers. She didn't notice as she made the turn that a rider was behind her and had been for several miles. He rode a sorrel mare with four white socks on her legs. He had seen her in Mansfield and he decided to follow her.

Ann pulled the carriage into the open barn where she kept her horses stabled. She took the harness off and hung them on a peg on the wall in the tack room next to the stable where she kept one of her horses. After feeding and brushing the horse she went into her plantation style mansion from the back door. She changed her clothes into the same cotton night gown she wears daily and retired to the parlor for a brandy while she read through legal papers concerning her father's estate. After more than half of the decanter of the drink was gone, she felt herself getting drowsy. She could tell by the lack of light coming through the tall windows that provided the room with sunshine, the day was coming to a close.

Ann gathered up the papers she was reading and placed them on a solid oak desk that sat in one corner of the room next to a large book shelf. She decided to skip dinner since she was quite full of brandy and lie down in her bed. As she lay on top of the sheets she remembered the nights Jake laid next to her and how she had grown accustomed to him being here. He could have remained if he had wanted to and she would have gladly allowed it. The brandy took effect and she drifted off to sleep.

The rider of the sorrel had ridden until the large white house came into view at which time he entered the woods next to the house and stopped. He kept the house in view through the trees and waited to see if there was any more activity other than the lady. He saw no employees or hands about the place and no children or grownups moving around. The big house looked as if it was only occupied by the lady on the buggy. Patiently the man watched the front of the house waiting for the slightest movements from inside. After the darkness completely fell, he approached.

Before the man walked out of the woods he took his boots and clothes off. He calmly walked to the front door of the house and slowly turned the knob. It was unlocked and he quietly opened the door hoping it would not make a squeak. He carried nothing in his hands as he made his way into the foyer that was just inside the entrance to the mansion. To his right was a large parlor that was not occupied. There were no lights burning, yet he was able to move through the house from the light of the full moon that filled the windows. Off the foyer was a hallway that looked to be thirty feet long. There was a doorway on the right of the hall that was open.

He slowly walked to the door and looked into the room. Someone was lying on the bed facing away from the door. From the glow coming from the window on the side of the room he could tell it was a woman. The faint light showed the contour of her hips and the slimness of her waist. Her legs were long and her skin looked smooth and pale. She quietly slept. The only sound she made was the whisper of her breathing.

The man slowly walked around the bed to face her. The front of her nightgown was untied exposing her breast. His shadow crossed over her. The man then leaned down and kissed her face. Suddenly Ann Faulkner stirred and came awake. Her eyes opened wide and she found herself staring at a man completely nude looking down at her.

"What are you doing?" Ann screamed as she raised her hands to cover herself.

The man grabbed the front of her nightgown and ripped it off of her body. She tried to fight him but his strength was too much for her. His muscular arms provided more than enough strength to subdue Ann with little to no effort. She screamed but no one heard her as the man forced himself on top of her. She tried to struggle but his large frame would not move because of her lack of size and strength. He had complete control of her.

He forced her to give in and he violated her. The control over this lady, to him was exhilarating and the struggles and screams coming from her brought a heightened level of excitement as he continued in his brutal assault. Her chastity completely belonged to him and that thought drove him to intensify the act. His low moans turned to laughter as he brought his hands to her throat. He wrapped his fingers around her delicate neck and with his palms pressed hard causing her breathing to stop. Her eyes began to bulge and her face quickly turned red as her struggle grew more intense yet still not being able to escape her assailant. The muscles in his arms were like steel and his hands were like a vice that squeezed the life out of Ann Faulkner. His head went back and his eyes closed as the peak of his excitement reached its pinnacle. His body twitched as the thrust of his assault came to an end.

Ann's body lay still and lifeless as the man moved off of her. He lay alongside her body and pressed himself against her. He took her in his arms and held her as if they were lovers on their honeymoon. The man fell asleep.

When morning came, the sunlight pressed through the window of the bedroom causing the man to wake. He had held Ann's dead body all night. Rigor mortis had set in and her body was cold and stiff. He turned her over and kissed her lips.

"Good morning sweetheart," the man said in a deep voice. "I hope you slept well."

The man got up and searched around the room until he found a pair of scissors in the sewing bag Ann kept on a table by a window where she would sometime sit and sew. He held it up in front of him and with his fingers worked the blades back and forth.

"I hope you don't mind, but I just want to take a little souvenir with me...you know a little something to remember our night together." The man said as he gathered the long gray hair that was once blonde in his powerful hand. He snipped the hair off as close to her head as he could. He looked inside a chest of drawers and found a pink ribbon about eight inches long. He tied the ribbon around the center of the sixteen inch lock of hair. After tossing the scissors down on the bed next to

Ann's dead body he walked out of the room and left the house still naked.

When the man returned to his horse he removed a leather bag, much like a haversack, from his saddle. He placed the lock of Ann's hair in the bag and wrapped its strap around the saddle horn. He dressed and mounted up then found his way back to the Old San Antonio Road and headed west.

Chapter 12

The Neches River was low this time of year, yet because of the wagon, the three reunited travelers crossed at the Bodenheimer Ferry Crossing and made their way through more forest area as they got closer to their final destination. Augusta, Texas was a small community in the northeastern part of Houston County, the county named for the once President of the Republic and later Governor, Sam Houston. Before the war, Augusta served as trading center for the nearby cotton plantations. Its population was just shy of one hundred and eighty inhabitants yet had a school, a general store, a church and a cemetery. Jake knew he had to make the trip to Crockett, which was the county seat, to register his land deed with the Houston County Clerk as well as purchase the tools he and Julius would need to build a cabin and a barn. Jake figured while he was there, he would try to meet cattle owners to attempt to purchase a few head of momma cows to get his herd started.

The general store in Augusta sat in the middle of the community. There were houses built of lumber and painted as well as cabins built from the yellow pine that grew in abundance in the forests that surrounded the little village. He wanted to find the property and set up a camp and get an idea of the trees that he would cut to build a cabin for him, Tammy and Julius.

"Let's stop in the general store and see if anyone here knows how to get to the place," Jake said pulling the wagon up to the front of the building.

The general store was a wood structure built in board and batting style. It appeared be about forty feet square. It had a porch across the front that was stocked with wooden barrels holding garden tools like rakes and hoes. A sign above the roof that covered the porch said "Augusta General Store".

Jake walked in through a screen door at the front of the building and was immediately addressed by a middle aged lady dressed in a pink dress with a white collar. She had solid gray hair that was pulled into bun on the top of her round head. Her nose held a pair of wire rimmed glasses that fit snug against her motherly face. She had a very pleasant smile and when she spoke she looked at you directly through big brown eyes.

"Hello...welcome to the Augusta General Store," the lady said with a smile that told Jake she was eager to please.

"Hello." Jake said as he pulled his hat off. "My name is Jake Powell and I have come all the way from Atlanta, Georgia, to settle a piece of land that was left to me by the grandfather of my children. It is supposed to be in Augusta and I was wondering if you could tell me how to get there."

"Oh, how delightful...are your wife and children with you? They must be tired so let's get them in here and get some food in their little bellies. I'm so sorry, my name is Lydia Edge. My husband Walter and I own the store. He is gone to Crockett on business right at the moment...now where are those children?" she said as she hurried about like she was receiving royalty.

Jake stopped her, "Ma'am, there are no children. They died before I left Atlanta. While I was gone their mother and her

213

parents were killed by some of Sherman's men." Jake said as he looked down at the floor.

Lydia stopped next to Jake and placed a hand on his arm. She looked at him with sorrowful eyes that quickly moistened to tears.

"I am so sorry Jake. I hear he was a real terror, that Sherman," she said as she dabbed her eyes.

"Well, I've just come here to make a new start. The brother and sister who are with me I met along the way. I hope the community will accept them as well as me." Jake said expecting Lydia to change her feelings.

"Why wouldn't we Jake?" Lydia asked still resting a gentle hand on Jake's arm.

"They are mulattos." Jake said hoping she would have an understanding heart.

Lydia looked up at Jake and smiled. "You have nothing to fear Jake. The people in Augusta are good people and we don't judge. Character is what's important, not the color of one's skin. Why don't you bring them in and then you can tell me where your property might be...if you have your deed I might be able to tell you."

Jake took the paper from his leather pouch and handed it to Lydia and then walked out of the store and to the wagon. Tammy looked down at him with the smile she always has when their eyes meet. He held up his hands to her and she went to him and rested in his firm grasp. He gently set her down to her feet and they embraced.

"Come inside. The lady wants to meet you and Julius. Come on down Julius." Jake said as he took Tammy by the hand and led her to the door of the store. Julius quickly followed.

"Mrs. Edge, this is Tammy and her brother Julius," Jake announced as the three approached the counter where Lydia stood.

"You call me Lydia," she said as she looked up from the property deed Jake had handed her. "My gracious Tammy, you are just lovely. I don't think I've ever seen a more beautiful young lady. Do you have some dresses?"

"No Ma'am, I didn't bring any with me. We left in such a rush." Tammy said causing Lydia to look even more impressed after hearing the sweetness coming from Tammy's voice.

"Well, I've got some that I'm going to fix you up with. They will look just darling on you." Lydia said, making a fuss.

Tammy looked up at Jake and smiled. She was already feeling at home. She took Jakes arm in her hands and gave him a loving squeeze before she buried her face in his chest trying to hold back her tears.

"Dear, are you okay?" Lydia asked as she reached out to Tammy and patted her shoulder.

Tammy looked over to Lydia and then hugged her. "Yes I'm fine. I just feel so at home here, like it is where I'll be safe."

"You will be safe here." Lydia said giving her a squeeze and then turned to Jake. "Jake, the property is right down that road across the way there. It's close, less than a mile. It runs west along the San Pedro Creek, so if you cross the creek you've gone too far. It takes in a lot of bottom land suitable for just about anything you want to grow from peas to kids"

Jake's eyes perked up and he looked at Julius they both patted each other on the back. Lydia handed him back his papers and they all had a happy moment. Jake couldn't believe he had finally made it. The start he dreamed of through his whole trip was at his fingertips.

"Of course, you will need to go to Crockett, the county seat, and file your papers with the County Clerk. Travel west a few miles and you come to a crossroad. Turn south and keep going, you'll know when you get there. The County Clerk will make it official." Lydia said. "Now, is there anything you need? Just look around."

After leaving the store the three found the property. Jake couldn't wait to take a look around the place and start making plans.

"Oh Jake, this place is beautiful. I think right over there would be a great spot for a cabin and right over there a garden and maybe right there a coop for chickens and…" Tammy said with enthusiasm boiling over in her heart as she moved about pointing here and there. She was like a child on Christmas morning. She stopped and looked at Jake and Julius as they stood watching her. Their eyes looking at her and then back to each other. The looks on their faces told Tammy they were hanging on her every word…in a humorous kind of way.

Jake walked over to her and took her by the hand. "Let's go for a walk."

The two strolled through the pines and hardwoods holding hands their fingers intertwined as they slowly swung their arms back and forth with each step. The floor of the forest was covered with pine straw and twigs and every now and again an iron ore rock protruded from the sandy loam soil. The pine trees were tall and straight and would be ideal for logs to build a cabin. Soon the forest opened up and a lush green pasture stood out. Its grass was ankle high and looked to go on for a half of a mile. Jake visualized the field speckled with cattle grazing while calves suckled from their mommas. He could see horses prancing about with their tails high in the air. He saw life and a life with Tammy by his side making it all happen. He knew he needed Julius and Jake wanted him here. It could be a home to all three of them.

Jake stopped and pulled Tammy close to him. She looked up at him with her innocent smile. He placed his hands on each side of her neck. He felt her soft skin under his strong hands. His thumbs slowly stroked her delicate cheeks as they lost themselves in one another's eyes. With her dark, silky brown hair over his fingers he brought her head up and their lips met sweetly. Their hearts opened wide to receive the love they had found in one another. A bond forever sealed, with a kiss.

The two continued their walked until they came upon a creek. It was about twenty feet wide and the current moved toward the west. Its water was clear and it was easy to see fish swimming under the surface of the water. Jake noticed deer tracks on the bank in the mud. He was glad to know the area was abundant in wildlife. It would be their only meat source until the calves he intended to raise came old enough to slaughter. He knew a smokehouse would have to be built close to the cabin as well to preserve an adequate supply of meat to eat. There was so much to do and Jake was ready to get it started.

Back at the camp, Jake, Julius and Tammy made plans for the next day. Jake had killed several squirrels and Tammy busied herself frying them in a skillet over the open fire. She made a loaf of homemade bread as well.

The next day Jake and Tammy saddled up the buckskin and the big black and headed for Crockett. There was business to be taken care of at the court house. Jake wanted to ask around for ranchers that might sell him a small herd to get started on a cattle operation of his own. They passed farms and ranches along the way and seeing them drove Jakes aspirations to their peak. They saw children playing in the yards while a woman hung out clothes to dry. There was a man breaking up ground for a fall garden and a young man working a horse in a round pen. They met wagons being pulled by horses and some by mules. Some wagons carried piles of hay and others cans of milk and crates of eggs. This area was certainly a farming community.

When Jake and Tammy rode into Crockett, named for the statesman and hero of the Alamo they were amazed at the movement going on. There were wagons filled with cotton bales and numerous buggies and men on horseback making up a hustle and bustle like Jake hadn't seen since Atlanta and Tammy hadn't seen since she left Baton Rouge. The courthouse square looked to be the busiest place in town. There were seven dirt streets coming from every direction that came together at the big brick building in the center this East Texas town just like spokes on a wagon wheel. There were markets and office buildings, eateries and saloons that made up this center of trade and commerce. They rode their horses to a hitching post in front of the courthouse and dismounted.

The courthouse was built of red bricks and stood three stories high. The red brick jail set to one side of the courthouse making it easy to move prisoners back and forth on court day. Jake and Tammy walked in through one of the two entrances and looked for the office of the County Clerk.

They found the office at the end of a large hallway on the first floor and walked in. They stepped up to the wood counter that separated the business and legal area from the public entrance. A man setting at a desk behind the counter looked up and noticed the two walk in. He got up and approached the counter. He was a tall man wearing a three piece suit with a red tie. His short hair was pressed down to his head and it shone from the grease that held it down. A large nose sat upon a slender face that was cleanly shaven.

"How may I help you... a marriage license perhaps?" the man said with a slight grin.

Tammy looked up at Jake and smiled big. Suddenly butterflies began flying and soaring in her stomach. She wrapped her arms around Jake's left arm and continued to smile. Tammy knew why they were there and she knew the question struck Jake just like it did her.

"Someday we will but, today I need to file this land deed with you." Jake said as he presented the paper to the man.

The man almost looked disappointed but took the paper and said, "I see. Yes...okay let me look this up, make some entries and look at the status of the taxes. I'll be right back."

The man was busy for just a few minutes. He returned and handed the deed back to Jake and said, "It looks like everything is up to date and paid up. The taxes will be due next year in October."

"Thank you. Do you know where I might be able to buy some cattle to start a herd on my property?" Jake asked the man.

"Yes I do, as a matter of fact, and once you decide on a brand for your cattle I would encourage you to register it with this office. On your way back toward Augusta you will come across the Hollingsworth Ranch, you may have seen it. He has helped several young ranchers in the area get started. He is a very fair man and a gentleman."

"We will do that but first we have to build fences." Jake said

"Of course, you know those things will walk away if you do not." The man replied.

"Thank you for helping us." Tammy said as she and Jake turn to leave.

"You are quite welcome young lady and, hopefully the next time I see you it will be for a marriage license." He said giving her a wink.

Tammy turned and whispered, "Me too."

The "Rocking H" ranch, a fifteen hundred acre spread was located half way between Crockett and Augusta and Jake and Tammy had no trouble finding it. They both remembered passing the large cedar post entrance to the ranch. The name of the ranch was branded into a thick timber making up the cross piece that was suspended sixteen feet off of the ground between two big cedar posts. The lane leading up to the ranch house ran between two large pastures where red with white faced cattle grazed on lush thick grass. They saw calves playing in the meadow but never venturing to far from their mommas. There were several cowboys on horseback pushing several head of the beeves toward a corral. It was time to turn the bull calves into steers as well as brand them. Jake was amazed when he saw the ranch hands throwing loops from lariats around the heads of the calves, catching and throwing them as their horses kept the rope tight. He knew he had a lot to learn but he was never one to run from a challenge.

The main ranch house was a two story wood framed structure that sat upon a hill overlooking the lane coming from the road. It was painted white and had shutters at all of the windows painted in a green. There was a green picket fence around the yard and a flag pole stood in the middle of a rock garden in front of the house with the flag, The Lone Star of Texas, waving in the breeze.

"Are y'all looking for Mr. Hollingsworth?" a voice from the porch of the house called.

A lady standing behind the white railing of the porch looked down with her hand over her eye brows shading her face from the western sun. She looked to be in her early fifties and had red hair that was showing signs of gray that hanging past her shoulders. She wore a white cotton dress and a black apron with yellow flowers. She carried her slight frame down the steps off of the porch with the spryness of a teenager. The lady hurried to greet her visitors with a smile. She stopped at the gate of the picket fence.

"Mr. Hollingsworth is yonder at the barn. I'm his wife Effie. Who might you two be?" she asked with a pleasant demeanor. She smiled big at Tammy who stood close to Jake and she immediately returned her sweet smile she is known for, especially by Jake.

Jake took off his hat and held it in his hands in front of him and said, "Yes Ma'am, we would like to talk to Mr. Hollingsworth about maybe buying a few heifers to get a herd started for ourselves. Do you think he would have a minute?"

"I bet he does...there he comes now." Mrs. Hollingsworth said pointing over Jakes shoulder toward the barn.

A broad shouldered man in a light brown cotton work shirt with sweat stains on the sides walked up to Jake. He was wearing a gray felt hat with dark stains around the crown and brim. His denim pants were tucked into high top pull on boots that showed plenty of wear. His face was wide and tanned from the sun and he had a mustache that extended past the line of his jaws. The hair showing under his hat was cut short and dark

221

with lines of gray that matched his mustache. He extended a large hand to shake with Jake.

"John Hollingsworth, how are y'all." he said in a voice as rough as the ground he stood on.

"Jake Powell and this here is Tammy Broussard. We are settling on a place south of Augusta and we are looking to start a cow herd." Jake said shaking Hollingsworth's hand.

"Sounds good...let's go up on the porch and sit in the shade. I bet I can talk this ol' girl into making us some lemonade out of some cool water from the well for us to drink." Hollingsworth said looking at his wife giving her a wink.

"I sure can. Come go with me dear and I'll let you help while these two men talk." the misses said, taking Tammy by the arm and gently leading her up the walk to the house.

As the two gentlemen talked about cattle and beef prices Tammy and Mrs. Hollingsworth sat at another table on the opposite end of the porch. Tammy told her of where she came from and how Jake had rescued her from being taken to New Orleans to be forced into prostitution. Mrs. Hollingsworth's eyes began to tear as Tammy told her story. She told of Jake and how he decided to come to Texas and start a new life.

"I'm glad Jake came along when he did. You two look very happy together and I know there are a lot of happy years ahead for the two of you." Mrs. Hollingsworth said dabbing her eyes.

"Well, what do you think of Mrs. Hollingsworth?" Jake asked Tammy as they rode back toward Augusta.

"She is a very sweet lady. They have no children after their two sons died in the war. There are no grandchildren since they weren't married." Tammy said hoping they could discuss the subject.

Jake looked over at her and saw she was staring his way. "What are you thinking?" he asked as he glanced over at her and then quickly back to road ahead.

"Jake Powell, you know exactly what I am thinking."

"No, what are you thinking?" Jake asked hardly able to hold back a chuckle.

"I can't believe you asked me such a..." she said as she spurred the big black horse and rode on ahead.

"Well, I was just getting ready to ask you something," he said with a laugh.

Tammy immediately pulled the reins back and stopped in the road. She turned the horse so she could face Jake as he pulled up next to her. She looked at him with expectation gleaming from her face.

"I was just wondering if you'd like to maybe one day...ah...ah...you know" Jake said struggling with the words.

"One day what Jake Powell..." Tammy asked, her expression changing from great expectation to growing impatience.

"You know..." Jake stammered.

"No, I don't know. One day what..."

"Helping me and Julius with the stock I agreed to buy from Mr. Hollingsworth." Jake said with anticipation of what was to come.

"Oh...Jake Powell, you are...just ...just. I can't believe you," she screamed as she pulled the reins around and started up the road.

Jake laughed to himself and said, "You don't want to help? Well, would you consider being my wife?" he said almost rolling off the back of the buckskin.

Tammy turned the big black around and rushed to Jake's side. She threw herself off of the horse straight into Jake's arms. He caught her and pulled her up into the saddle with him and kissed her right there in the middle of the road. After a few seconds of affection, he hugged her up and headed toward home.

"We have a lot of plans to make and a lot of things to get done before we can do this." Jake said. "We have to build a cabin. It will have to be big enough for all three of us."

"Yes and plenty big for the passel of kids we're going to have." Tammy added.

"That too...I guess." Jake said with concern in his voice.

Tammy noticed the dread on his face and said, "Don't you want to have children Jake?"

Jake looked into her beautiful hazel eyes that were shining with tears and said, "I just don't want them to die. That is the hardest thing I've ever had to go through."

She reached up and touched his face and locked into his gaze and said, "Jake, it's okay, we will be there to take care of them. I'm willing to take the chance of having a life with you and that means taking a chance at making life. Children with you would make me so happy Jake."

He looked at her again and said "Tammy, making you happy is what I want."

They held each other as the buckskin took them onward, the big black following.

When Jake and Tammy arrived back at the camp, they found that Julius had been quite busy while they were gone. A clearing had been created by Julius cutting several trees down, all of which were suitable for logs to go into the construction of a cabin. He had begun hewing the logs making them flat for the walls of the house. They were all southern pine and were ideal for the project. He had also chopped down several smaller cedar trees that can be cut into shingles for the roof. Jake was surprised at the knowledge Julius had about the building of cabins.

"Where did you learn how to build a cabin?" Jake asked

Julius wiped sweat from his forehead with his shirt sleeve and said, "Well, I read a lot."

"Where did you come up with the axe and adze to work these logs?" Jake asked as he admired the job Julius had done while he and Tammy were gone.

"Oh I went up to town. You have a charge account at the store now. I told Mrs. Edge you would come in and make the payment on the tools." Julius said giving Jake a smile.

"Well, all right. I'll do that first thing in the morning." Jake said.

"I'm going too." Tammy said.

For the next four months the three worked diligently building a cabin, a barn, a corral, cook house, a smokehouse and an outhouse. The cabin was constructed in a dog run fashion with three separate rooms. There was a center room where they would eat their meals. Tammy decided to sleep in this middle room where they will take their meals since she and Jake were not yet married. The sections on both sides of this room were occupied by Jake and Julius. The cabin had a combination roof covered in cedar shingles. The windows were all fashioned with shutters to keep out unwanted sunlight. Jake promised Tammy glass windows would be put in place as soon they could return to Crockett to purchase them. She was quite pleased with that and insisted the front porch have a swing so she and Jake could spend time, in the cool of the evenings, making plans and deciding upon names for children.

A spot for a garden was picked out. A plow with harness and reins were purchased from the general store. Tammy was given several dresses by Lydia Edge. They fit her just right and she was excited to wear them on Sundays to the community church in Augusta. The first time she and Julius walked in to the church for meeting the people were surprised. Lydia Edge with her husband Walter quickly quelled any indications of unrighteous judgments that might show its nasty head. The community quickly realized Julius and Tammy were sweet people and deserved the respect that they were so quick to show. Jake quickly became a man of the community that the other men trusted so they often sought his opinion concerning things from wagon wheels to politics.

Jake and Julius worked hard every day but Sunday to get a split rail fence built to keep the cattle Jake would soon purchase from John Hollingsworth. He chose to fence the whole property lines and allow the cattle to roam free. They did fence off San Pedro Creek so the cattle would be less likely to cross it onto a neighbor's property as well as fall victim to a hungry gator. They were known to travel the waterway from the Neches River just a few miles away. This area was once where Indians roamed and lived. It was common for Jake to find arrowheads as well as spear heads while he plowed a garden spot. The ground was practically littered with artifacts after a heavy rain. Jake loved his home and it was full of promise and his heart was full of dreams. Dreams that he would do everything he could to make come true for Tammy.

East of San Augustine a farmhouse belonging to Samuel Clayton was being observed from a thicket across the road. Muscular hands pushed aside a clump of brush as he patiently looked upon the farm waiting for his opportunity approach. Samuel, a slender man in his fifties worked a hoe against the ground in his garden. He cultivated the soil and chopped away the weeds in his toils to beat out a living for him, his wife and daughter. Clayton, a gray headed man with a full beard, worked away totally unaware he and his farm was being watched. He wore bibbed overalls and an old straw hat that had absorbed a lot of sweat over the years. His weathered face and suntanned arms knew what a hard day's work was like and his spirit knew the importance of getting the job done.

Samuel's wife Helen worked at the clothes line that stretched from the back corner of the house to a front corner of the barn. She had been busy all day putting laundry on and taking laundry off of the clothes line making sure her family had clean clothes to wear and clean bedding to sleep on. She was a chubby woman and short in stature with red hair that now was streaked with gray. Her cheeks were rosy and her blue eyes were sharp and still sparkled for the man who chose to take her for his wife some twenty years ago. Their daughter Clarisse worked hard by her mother's side. Her full figure was one to be desired by most men, but she chose only Troy Masters who lived up the road from the farm. Her hair was red like her mothers and her eyes matched those of the lady who carried her for nine months as well. She had very large breasts yet her waist was slender. She was a beautiful young girl of nineteen years.

The day came to a close and the family retired to their bedrooms for a nights rest. The man watching the house moved to the barn where he stopped and watched to make sure the movement about the house had ceased for the night. When he was satisfied the family was asleep he removed his clothes and walked to the back door. He slowly lifted the wood latch that simply held the door closed and carefully stepped into the kitchen area. A long butcher's knife hung from a nail at the back of a kitchen counter. The man slowly removed the knife from the nail and checked its edge by touching it to his right thumb. It felt razor sharp. The kitchen had a wood stove that sat away from the back wall and cabinets covered the front and side walls of the room. There was a square table and four chairs that sat in the center of the room where the family took their meals. The door leading out of the kitchen, led into a family room   where they gathered in the evening to discuss the happenings of the day or read by candlelight. There were two doors to the left that went into two different rooms. The room farther away from the kitchen was the bedroom occupied by Samuel and his wife Helen. The man slowly looked around the edge of the doorway and watched. Both husband and wife were sound asleep on a bed that sat against the center of the wall to the man's left. He carefully approached and stood over the sleeping Samuel Clayton.

The muscular man held the long knife in his right hand. He took the knife and moved its point to the right side of Clayton's face as he lay quietly on his back in slumber. The man's grip tightened on the handle of the knife and its tip slowly moved downward and into the eye socket of Clayton and into his brain. Samuel Clayton never moved.

The man slowly pulled the knife from his victim's head and then leaned over and slowly cut the throat of the sleeping wife. He left her staring toward the ceiling into death. The murderer left the knife lying on the bed between Samuel and Helen Clayton.

He then slowly turned and walked out the Clayton's bedroom. He went to the door that went into the room of Clarisse. The young woman lay peacefully dreaming of the day she would marry Troy Masters. They had made plans to raise many children and grow large gardens to feed many. Those plans would never see themselves through. The nude muscular man slowly and quietly closed the door...the screams from Clarisse would never be heard.

Chapter 13

South east of the town of Nacogdoches sat the small
community of Chireno. There were a few houses gathered
around a local church and general store. Most of the
inhabitants of the little East Texas village worked for the cotton
gin belonging to Thaddeus Walker a miserly man who was
known for treating his employees like trash. If he could get a
week's work out of a man for a day's pay, he would celebrate
the fact he had saved himself a bit of money. He was known to
make the fact clear with those that worked for him that they
were of low status, and that he cared nothing for them and the
fact their families went hungry and without the essentials they
needed to clothe themselves. Thaddeus Walker was just a no
good scrooge of a man. One could say that Walker lived high on
the hog. He dressed simple enough in his work clothes and high
top lace up boots that made him look more like a prison boss
than a business owner. He was a short man with a pot belly and
white hair and beard. His complexion was pale and his wide

cheeks often turned red from the sun. When he was not asleep he normally had a large cud of tobacco bulging out his right cheek making his face to appear wider.

The T. Walker Cotton Company sat on the south side of the small community and ran from sunup until sundown every day of the week. Walker had no regard for Sunday being a day of rest. As far as he was concerned, if the gin wasn't ginning he wasn't making money. East Texas being a large cotton producing area meant as long as cotton was coming from the fields, the T. Walker Cotton Gin would be in operation. Some of the employees who worked every day for Walker did so with glee. They were glad to get the steady work during harvest season. Even though it was extremely hot in the cotton gin they worked and they work hard. There were those, however, who had a different outlook on the demands set by Walker and they were about to reach a boiling point.

The Frank brothers, Luther and Arch were deserters from the Union Army that stayed hidden on the battlefield at the Battle of Vicksburg. They, along with Ned Brundage, Johnny Hawthorne, who they all called Taterhead because his head looked like a potato, Bill Daily and Cletus Frank, the little brother to Luther and Arch, worked the gin together and shared a bunkhouse. Cletus made his way down the Mississippi after the war to meet up with his brothers after the death of their mother. He was a simple minded boy of 18 and his brothers did the best they could to tolerate him.. The fact was they cared nothing about him and cursed their mother for dying and causing Cletus to come looking for them. He was a large boy with broad shoulders and muscular arms. It was said many times that he didn't know his own strength. Like his brothers he had coal black hair and a lot of whiskers on his face but not much of a beard. His eyes were ice blue and cold just like his two brothers. They all stood about six feet five inches tall and

231

were all mean and rotten to the core. Luther, the oldest had a temper to match a badger and was always known to be someone you should never turn your back on. Archie was no different and was known to kill a man for the gold in his teeth.

Taterhead was a huge man standing six feet eight. He stayed quiet most of the time hardly ever saying a word. If he wanted something he simply took it never saying a word. He met Archie and Luther in Natchez after the two brothers deserted from the Union Army. Taterhead has been committing thefts in general stores since he was six years old. In his mind he stole because he needed to steal so he wouldn't go hungry. One incident he stole whiskey from a freight wagon before heading west. It didn't do anything to satisfy his belly however, the driver of the freight wagon lost his life when Taterhead crushed his windpipe with a single blow to the throat. Hawthorne was extremely strong and very muscular through the arms, chest and shoulders. He found it hard sometime to find shirts to fit him. He met a drummer that was rather large through the mid-section on a road just outside of Mansfield and relieved him of every shirt he had along with two pairs of trousers that fit him snug around the waist. The drummer found out that day that his life was worth only the price a few garments and twenty six dollars.

Ned Brundage left the Union Army with Luther and Arch in the very same way. They all three along with Bill Daily, plotted their desertion in the battle field. They knew that as many bodies and body parts lying about no one would ever know they did nothing more than desert their posts. Brundage was a tall lanky man. He had thin blonde hair that covered almost none of his head. He kept a razor in his pocket that he used to shave his face every morning. He claimed that when he tried to grow a beard it itched to bad that he chose to keep his face shaved. Green eyes sat behind a slender face that wore several scars from the many brawls he had been in. His long arms and hard fist made him a hand full for any man that went hand to hand with him. He grew up on a farm in northeastern Tennessee. He and the Frank brothers and Bill Daily were part of Grant's Army of the Tennessee that laid siege to Vicksburg. They had all grown tired of the war and together devised a plot to run and head south. Bill Daily, however, tried to talk them out of it but went along in spite of his fear of getting caught and shot.

Bill Daily was looked at by the rest as a weakling. In situations where an evil disposition was required he often gave hesitation. He always tried to talk the others into not creating attention to them fearing they would be recognized as the deserters they were. He still had the same baby face he had during the war even though he was a grown man. He stood five foot ten inches and had a fat face and a bald head that made him the subject of jokes from the rest of his associates. Like Brundage, Daily kept shaved because he didn't like the jokes about the thin stray whiskers that grew from his smooth red cheeks. He really had no business running with such a bunch. He always said they would be the death of him.

The Frank brothers, Taterhead, Brundage and Daily shared a bunk house that stood in a corner away from the cotton gin. It was a wood structure much like a lot of shacks in the area. It was built with a wood frame and had board and batting for the exterior. It had a porch across the front of the building and a wood burning stove served for warmth and cooking. It was big enough for three bunks to line two walls. A table about eight foot long made out of planks an inch thick sat in the middle of the floor where the men took their meals and played cards until they turned in for the night. For the most part they stayed there on their off time. They never went to the town of Nacogdoches because they would have to walk if they did and by the time they finished their work, there were no more hours left in the day for such a trip. This made them hate their boss worse.

"How much longer are we going to sit here in this dump and work for the scoundrel Walker?"Taterhead asked wiping the sweat from his bald pointed head.

The three Frank brothers and Brundage sat at the table playing cards and drinking coffee while Daily lay in his bunk asleep. Luther looked up from the game and gave Taterhead a glance and shook his head. These four were tired of the situation and Luther and Arch had made comments to each other about robbing the fat slob of a boss they had and cutting his throat.

"We're waiting on a friend to show up and then we will turn this thing around. How would you guys like to head toward Dallas. We hear there is quite a bit of action of all kinds up that way. I mean girls, whisky and girls." Luther said as he threw his cards down.

"What friend?" asked Taterhead. His tone was full of contempt, not being sure he could trust this friend of Luther.

"Just a guy we knew who was at Vicksburg with us. He wound up in Atlanta and stayed there after they got done with the Rebs." Arch said as he threw his cards down too. "We would write him there under the name Aunt Theresa so they wouldn't know it was us."

They all had a big laugh about them being their friend's aunt. Taterhead agreed that he didn't know everybody each of them served with in the Army. There were a lot of men there and not everone knew each other.

A steam whistle would be blowing at straight up five o' clock so they all were accustomed to going to the rack early. They walked outside and went to the back of the house and relieved themselves on the ground before going to bed. The stars shone bright and the moon hung low in the sky. Luther rolled a cigarette and put a fire to it. He found himself standing in the dark alone. He thought of the plans he had been making in his mind for his future and the future of his brothers.

Making a living the honest way was nothing Luther Frank really gave much thought to. The only reason he went into the army was to keep from going to prison and the same for his brother Arch. They were both destined for a life of crime and the two made no bones about it. They were both kicked out of the house at an early age because their father didn't want to absorb the cost of raising them any longer, after they both reached the age of fourteen. Their father didn't care for schooling and coal mine work was all he knew. Cletus was just a baby and the old man felt obligated to taking care of him at least until he reached the age of his older brothers. Luther and Arch were just a year apart in age so they both were made to leave together.

So, on their own Luther and Arch went to stealing to get food and clothes. They both swore they would never set foot in their father's house again. They considered sneaking in one night and cutting his throat for making them leave but, after the whisky wore off, they thought better. They made the mistake of writing their mother. All it did was cause their little brother to show up in their lives claiming their mother had passed and she had given them the task of taking care of him. Luther despised Cletus and decided to either lose him in their travels or put a lead shot through his head. He never could figure out why he went this long having him around. When his friend Sal Maselli showed up they were going to set out and make their way to Dallas for some fun times and he didn't want Cletus around.

The five o'clock whistle blew bringing the workers of the cotton gin awake and ready to report to their work stations when the gin started up at five thirty sharp. Walker would not tolerate his workers being late. If he had to dock a man for being two minutes late, he would dock him for the whole hour. This made the men quick to rise and quick to get set for the day. At the time, jobs were hard to come by so if you had a job at the Walker gin you did everything you could to keep it.

The men often swapped duties during the day to break the monotony of the job. One would run the press making the bales of cotton and one would wrap the bales for transport. It was hard work and done in the hottest part of the year.

Things got hotter when Thaddeus Walker showed up at the gin just before quitting time. He walked in, dressed his usual with his gray work pants tucked into the tops of knee high lace up boots. His jaw was bulged out with its usual wad of tobacco. He stood in the big entrance going into the gin with both sets of knuckles resting on his hips. He bent over slightly to spit a stream of brown tobacco juice from his mouth. His hard eyes peered from under the brim of his straw hat and his eyes brows curled downward above his nose that indicated he was not happy.

"I want every bit of this cotton baled by the time the sun goes down or I will dock every single man in this place a day's pay. So that means you better get to moving and work faster." Walker screamed at the top of his lungs. His face had turned red before he was finished with his demand.

Arch and Luther were both feeding the press when Walker roared his command. They looked at each other and they both gritted their teeth in anger. They both had all they could take from this bag of wind. If one of them would have had a rifle handy, they would fought over it for the honor to take a shot at the crusty old man.

Thaddeus Walker lived in a large two story mansion that sat on a hill overlooking the cotton gin. It had a large front porch that circled around half of the house. A balcony extended over the porch in the center of the second story that made a good look out for the boss when he wanted to see what was going on in the direction of the gin. Luther often saw Walker standing on the balcony looking toward his workers as they labored in the heat of his operation. So many times he saw himself with a Union issue rifle sending a fifty caliber lead ball into his large chest. The thought of the cheapskate falling from the balcony with his heart blown out put a smile on Luther's face.

The crew was glad to hear the steam whistle blow alerting them to end the work day and turn the gin off. Twelve hours in a hot house such as this will quickly take a toll on a man. Every man walked out of the gin wiping sweat from their heads and faces. All of the men who worked at the gin lived in shacks belonging to Walker. He often reminded them that living in one of his houses as he called them, was worth at least ten dollars per month rent. The houses were nothing more that run down shanties in need of repairs but Walker would never admit it.

When the brothers with Bill Daily, Brundage and Taterhead arrived at the shack a man was there leaned against the post that held the roof over the front door of the bunk house. He was tall and muscular and held a hand rolled cigarette in his lips. His hair was black and he wore a black hat on his head. A sorrel mare stood tied to the same post he was leaning on. There was a leather bag hanging from the saddle horn and a Henry rifle stood in a scabbard on the left side of the saddle in front of where the rider's left leg would be. The man looked at the men as they walked up. He sized up each one of them. He quickly made up his mind that he would be the leader of this bunch. He

237

saw nothing here that looked like they could get the best of him. He knew Luther and Arch, but the other men he did not know but could tell just by looking at them for a brief second he was their better.

"Sal...Sal Maselli, it's good to see you." Luther said as he walked up to the man. Luther extended his hand for a shake but the man ignored him. Arch didn't bother.

Sal walked over to his horse and removed the leather bag, his bedroll, saddle and rifle. He turned not saying a word and went inside the shack and laid the saddle in the first corner to the right of the door and put his bag and bedroll on the bunk where Daily slept. Bill just put his head down and never said a word.

Sal sat down on the bunk and said with a low deep voice that was hardly a whisper, "What you have to eat?"

"Ah...Sal we have some rabbit stew. It's real good. Do you want some?" Arch asked moving toward the wood stove to make a small cook fire.

"Yeah...I want some. Make some coffee too." Sal demanded.

Sal had looked over each man and he quickly knew they all feared him. His size and mystique had them baffled. They each saw the large knife he kept strapped to the wide black leather belt that was cinched around his waist. A 44 revolver hung from a cross draw holster opposite the knife. The men looked at Sal Maselli as a ruthless man full of evil that was capable of any kind of violence. He looked at them as being a group of men that he could lead into any crime whatsoever and they would follow him. He cared nothing for them except to take a fall if circumstances required it. There was not a one that he would not slice wide open and let their guts fall to his feet if he wanted to hear him scream.

"So Sal...what do you have planned?" Luther asked trying to give him a tone that would make Sal think he could hold his own.

Sal glanced at Luther and then stood and took his gun and knife belt off and dropped it onto the bunk once occupied by Bill Daily. He took off his long duster and hung it on a peg next to the bunk. He rolled the sleeves of his tan cotton shirt up to his elbows and walked over to a tub that sat on a counter under the only window that showed a view of the gin. He filled the tub with water and washed his hands.

"You...get me a towel." He ordered Taterhead who got right up from the table and went to a shelf and removed a hand towel that was folded and stacked on others. He gingerly handed it to Sal as if the man might bite him and then turned and took his seat back at the table.

Luther, the strongest of the three brothers, and the oldest, didn't like the tone that Sal was using with him and his friends and brothers. He wasn't accustomed to men talking to him as if he was a dog or dirt under their boots. He decided to open up the conversation about what they had in mind to do with their future.

"Sal, we plan on going to Dallas. We've had all of working in this hell hole we are going to take. I've really been giving thought to going into the big house yonder on the hill and cutting Walker's fat throat and seeing if he is hiding any loot in the house. I'm sure there is a safe in there somewhere that he stores his money in. We just have to go in and take it." Luther explained as the others shook their heads in the affirmative. Sal just looked at him like he was nothing.

Sal stepped over to where Luther sat at the table and bent down in his face. His breath smelled of whiskey and wickedness. He found Luther's eyes for a second before Luther turned away. It was just the response Sal wanted. He just made himself the leader of this little gang of misfits. He would use them to his pleasure.

"Have you ever cut a man's throat Luther?" Sal asked in his low voice.

Luther struggled to get the words to come out of his mouth but he finally managed to answer. "No...Sal I haven't."

Sal looked into Luther's eyes and said. "Until you do, shut your mouth about it."

Luther was stunned at what he had just heard from Sal. He thought at one time, while they were on the battlefield that Sal was his friend, or at least another man with a mutual respect. Now however, he saw none coming from Sal. He saw the evil in the man's eyes and he could tell that Sal had changed into something Luther had never seen. What Luther did not know was that Sal had turned into a stone cold killer.

"We will take the big house and we will do it my way. Do you guys understand what I'm saying?" Sal asked as he checked the eyes of each of the guys except Bill Daily. He had curled up by the wall by the door of the cabin. He watched and listened intently but did so in silence.

"Can we do this tonight?" Luther asked, still hanging on to his pride, at least by a thread. "I'm tired of the cotton gin and know these guys are too."

"Yeah...we can do it tonight. I will tell you how after I eat some food. Now get it in front of me." Sal said with all disrespect.

Arch walked over to the pot of rabbit stew and pulled up two big ladles full of the rabbit meat potatoes and carrots and put it in a bowl that was somewhat clean. He poured a cup of hot black coffee as well and brought them to Sal. Sal ate in silence as the other men watched patiently waiting to hear the plan to take the big house away from Thaddeus Walker.

After Sal finished his meal, he stood and walked over to the window of the shack and peered through it toward the house on the big hill overlooking the cotton gin and the other shacks occupied by the men and families that worked for Thaddeus Walker. He saw a light in the bottom part of the house through a window. There was a light in second story window as well that Sal figured as being a bedroom. He guessed in his mind the bottom room was a study occupied by the boss of the house and his wife could be found in the bedroom. Once the lights went out, he and these other men would approach the house and make entry.

It was after midnight before the house went dark. Sal and the other men walked out of the shack and up the hill to the house occupied by Thaddeus Walker and his wife Claudia. Luther and Arch thought about the valuables that waited inside. They both knew how to get rid of things they would find like silver candlesticks and fancy tea pitchers, silverware and old coins. They both got good at stealing from the homes and plantations during the war. They made away with quite a lot of booty from the southern people during the four year invasion of the Confederacy by the Union forces. It was common for Yankee troops to take jewelry and dresses and send them home to their sweethearts as gifts when those items were nothing more than stolen property. The Frank brothers made their living committing burglaries and robbing stores as they travelled the back roads to get to this humble community in East Texas.

The gang silently made their way to the back of the big house. The back door proved to be unlocked just as Sal

241

expected it to be. He turned and quietly gave the others quick instructions.

"Luther...you and Arch are going in. Look for guns and money, nothing else. Do I make myself clear?" Sal whispered in his low-toned voice. "The rest of you stay out here. The more that go in the more likely there will be a problem and we don't want to wake up the country side. Before we go in take off your boots. We want to be as quiet as we can. Here Chubby, hold my rifle until I get back." Sal ordered Daily.

All the men shook their heads in agreement. Bill Daily was scared and he wasn't keen on burglary as a way of making a living. He simply went along because he always just went along. He watched on as Luther, Arch and Sal made their way into the house. Ned Brundage, Cletus and Taterhead stood by as well. They backed into the shadows hoping they would not be seen by anyone. The chance of that happening was slim since it was somewhere past midnight and most folks were in bed asleep.

The three men slipped inside the back door of the house. They went into a room that Mrs. Walker used to wash clothes. Thaddeus was too cheap to hire domestic help so Mrs. Walker was left to do the household chores herself. From there they went into a hallway that passed all the way through the house to the front door. No doubt the hall served as breezeway on hot summer days. There was a kitchen to the right that connected the dining room. To the left was a pantry and further down the hall was a parlor room where the Walkers entertained clients, family and friends. There was a large fireplace against the far wall that was at least ten feet across. The end of the hall came to two rooms on each side. The stairs going up was directly to the left and past it was a formal sitting area and, across from it to the right of the stairs, was a study where a large desk sat against the far wall in front of a tall window. There were pictures on the walls. Paintings of outdoor scenes decorated the study along with several deer mounts that were trophies from hunts Thaddeus Walker had gone on in the western part of the state.

Sal and the two Frank brothers could see each other in the dim light coming from the large windows that were in the front and sides of the house. In front of the windows opposite the entrance to the study sat a large desk made of solid oak. It was stained a dark rich tint and three drawers sat down each pedestal. Each drawer had brass pull handles. The floor of the study was covered in a dark multi-colored rug that matched the curtains that hung along the sides of the tall windows.

Luther attempted to pull one of the drawers open but it would not move. He looked up at Arch and Sal with a determination on his face that showed in the faint glow of the moon coming through the windows. He pulled harder and finally the drawer came forth with a sound that surely alerted the occupants of the house. They froze and waited to hear movement from upstairs. Sal stepped over to one of the tall curtains and concealed himself behind it. Neither Luther nor Arch noticed him hide. Luther was so occupied by what he saw in the drawer he was not paying attention to what was going on around him. Arch stepped up and peered down into the open drawer at a stack of money. It was made up of large denominations and had to be at least several thousand dollars in all. Luther split it in half and handed Arch one and he kept the other. They each folded it and placed them in a front pocket of their pants. Suddenly a sound from the bottom of the stairs caught their attention.

"Who the hell are you and what in hell are you doing," thundered the voice of Thaddeus Walker. He stood at the entrance to his study holding a Colt revolver and it was pointed at Luther and Arch.

Suddenly Mrs. Walker stepped off of the stairs behind him. "Thaddeus, what's going on...who is this in our house?" asked the pear shaped woman dressed in a large white nightgown. Her gray hair was pinned up tight to her head and she wore no shoes on her feet. Her face was contorted in complete shock of having her home invaded.

"What is the meaning of this invasion, you ruthless wretches? How dare you come in here like you own the place, this is my house." Thaddeus Walker roared. "I'll have both of you arrested and charged with robbery."

Walker pulled the hammer back on the revolver he held but before he could raise it any further a shot rang out from behind the curtain where Sal hid himself. Black powder smoke filled the air and sparks flew from his revolver as a hot lead ball struck Thaddeus Walker in the left temple. Blood and brain matter exploded through the exit hole and splattered Mrs. Walkers face. She screamed and fell backward onto the stairs she had just walked down from her bedroom.

Sal came from behind the curtain and approached the hysterical woman. He pointed his pistol directly at her face, cocked the hammer back and pulled the trigger. His shot hit the poor woman between the eyes sending her head back and instantly killing her.

Sal quickly turned to Luther and his brother after picking up Walker's pistol, "Look around for guns and more powder and shot."

The two began searching through cabinets and drawers until finally Arch called out. "Here's some of both and a bag to put it in." Arch grabbed it up and started his search again when Luther called out.

"Hey...here's a Sharps rifle and a Henry lever action. The Sharps is in a 52 caliber and the Henry is a 44." Luther said as he pulled them both from a cabinet in the corner of the study. There were ten boxes of cartridges for the Sharps and eight for the Henry.

"This will get us started. We need to get moving because someone bound to had heard those shots." Sal said as he slid his revolver back in its holster.

Arch and Luther approached Sal with weapons. Sal looked at both of them and held out his hand. With his soft low voice Sal said, "Hand it over."

Both men were shocked at the demand made by Sal. They gave each other quick glances with confused looks on the faces. They had never in their lives had that much money at one time and the thought of having to hand it over to Sal buried itself under their craw. Luther considered trying for a head shot but knew Sal was quick and heartless. He would kill him and his brother at the drop of a hat and he wasn't going to take a chance. Besides, there might be an opportunity later to take care of Sal.

Luther and Arch both reached into their pants pockets and brought the money out and handed it to Sal. Regret showed on their faces as Sal took it and placed the bills into the inside pocket of his duster. He gave them both a shake of his head.

"If that happens again, I'm going to kill the both of you." Sal said as he walked toward the back door of the house. "We split it among us all."

"That's fine." Luther said, still disappointed they had been seen with the money.

When the three walked out of the big house they met back up with four that stayed outside in the dark. Bill Daily shook with fear but didn't say a word. He cursed himself for getting involved with these men. He knew they be would be the death of him but he followed them none the less. They started west through the woods behind the big house. They tried to keep the road that led to Nacogdoches in their sight to give them a bearing on where they were as they walked.

"Sal, we need some horses." Luther said as they followed him through the trees and brush.

"I know that...mine is lame and no good to me and I have no intention of carrying my rifle and bag all the way to Dallas."

"I'll carry your bag." Ned said as reached over to Sal's shoulder and grabbed the strap.

Suddenly Sal hit Ned with a hard right fist that sent Ned to the ground in a heap. The tall lanky man looked up in the dark at a face he could hardly see with a shocked and dazed look on his face.

"What did you go and do that for. I was just wantin to help." Ned said rubbing his left jaw where Sal planted a right hook to his face.

"You don't touch my bag...you got that. None of you ever touch my bag. If you do...you die." Sal said as he pointed to each of the men that stood in awe of what just happened. "Now where are we going to find horses?"

The men looked at one another as if they each were waiting on one to say something. The moon was full so they could each see the looks on the other one's face. Suddenly Cletus, the youngest raised his hand as if he was asking permission from his school teacher to speak.

246

"Ah...ah...I know something." Cletus said almost jumping up and down in place.

"Cletus, be quiet while we think," said Arch knowing his little brother was going to come up with some childlike plan that would get them nothing but sore feet and hard candy.

"No...no...Arch, I...I...know something." Cletus insisted.

Luther gave a big sigh and said, "Okay, Cletus what is it."

"When...when...I...I...went to town one day for the boss...I mean Mr. Walker...I seen some real pretty horses and a bunch of em too." Cletus said stuttering his words like a young kid.

The men looked at each other and then back to Cletus. Luther and Arch tried to remember when Walker sent Cletus to town but they both shrugged their shoulders and dropped the thought. They would just have to trust what Cletus said.

As they started in the direction Cletus told them to go, Sal turned to the other two brothers and whispered to them both.

"If your simpleton brother leads us on a wild goose chase...I'm going to put a lead ball through his hollow head. Do you both understand what I'm saying?" Sal said through gritted teeth.

"Yeah, we understand Sal." Luther said thinking to himself that he didn't care if Sal did carry out his threat or not. He cared not one grain out of a cow patty about Cletus.

Cletus lead the gang of outlaws through the woods to the road that leads to Nacogdoches and headed west. After they walked down the lonely road about ten miles they came to a ranch on the north side of the road. A lane led up to a white framed house that was completely dark. There were no lights shining through the windows and the place looked peaceful. In the meadows that surrounded the house horses were grazing on grass while some stood still in place more than likely asleep. The yelps of coyotes could be heard passing through the woods that framed the house and pastures of the ranch. Two owls hooted back and forth as the band of men slowly walked through a stand of trees along the east side of the house. There was a barn with stables that stood between them and the house and the plan was to make their way to it and see what horses might be kept there.

When the men left the woods and started toward the barn, a dog began to bark and slowly make its way toward the men. The dog could see them with its keen eyesight and it knew these were intruders that slowly made their way toward his territory. It continued to approach them as they made their way to the barn. Inside the barn there were horses stabled that looked to be that of fine stock. They all had shining black coats and stood seventeen hands tall. The dog kept coming closer and closer still barking and now giving the intruders a low growl.

The men went inside a tack room and left the door open, hoping the dog would follow them inside. Luther found a rope and tied it to the door to make a trap for the barking dog. He hoped the dog barking was common, knowing they do when critters come around the house at night. The dog took the bait and entered the threshold of the tack room door. Luther pulled the rope forcing the dog inside. Arch used another rope and looped it around the dog's neck and gave it a hard tug. The dog began to struggle and Sal took his knife from his belt and quickly stabbed the dog in the neck. It quickly bled to death. They all breathed a sigh of relief when the dog fell quiet. They stayed in the darkness of the tack room until they were satisfied no one in the house was coming to see what all of the barking was about. Sal and Luther peered through a space between the siding of the barn toward the house. After twenty minutes they saw no movement. Sal was satisfied that the dog did not wake anyone in the house.

Sal took off his boots and then his clothes.

Chapter 14

The moon was high in the night sky as Sal made his way to the back door of the house. The house was a one story wood framed home painted in white like so many other houses that covered the East Texas landscape. It belonged to Matthew and Nancy Wright who have been breeding horse stock since they were married in the spring before the beginning of the war. They had no children so they consider the horses as their family. Neither blamed the other for not being able to make children, they just accepted the fact and lived their lives quietly on their farm. Their horses were known as some of the best in Texas.

Matthew Wright was a thirty five year old who served in the Confederate Army as a cavalryman in a unit that mustered out of Nacogdoches County. He made it through the war with few scars and was noted to be quit the horseman. He was a short stocky man with reddish brown hair and a thick mustache that stretched almost to both of his ears. His hands and arms stayed strong from serving as his own farrier for fifty three head of horses.

Nancy Wright, the wife to Matthew was a petite lady with golden blonde hair that hung like silk down to the middle of her back. Her blues eyes sparkled for her husband who everyone in the area knew was the love of her life. She was ten years younger than him and had known him all of her life since she grew up on the farm just west of where she now lives. The beautiful Mrs. Wright was lying asleep in her bed next to her husband lost in peaceful dreams, not knowing evil had just silently made its way through the back door of her house.

Sal had ordered the others to quietly round up horses while he went inside the house. He threatened death to any of them that defied his orders. They each set out into the meadows that surrounded the Wright's house to round up as many of the horses that would follow them back to the corral that sat adjacent to the barn and stables. Sal took his leather bag and weapons to the house and silently set them on the floor just inside the back door.

Bare feet made no sound as Sal crept in the house. The back door offered no creak as it slowly opened into the room where Nancy Wright made the meals for her and her husband. Sal held his knife in his right hand as he made his way through the house. He looked through room after room as he, like a snake made his way to the bedroom where the sleeping couple lay in slumber, completely oblivious of his wicked presence. He stood in the door of the room and watched their chests rise and fall as they breathed. Mr. Wright lay on his back with his right arm resting on his forehead. The man's chest kept a constant rhythm as he took in air and then exhaled yet making no sound.

Mrs. Wright lay on her side facing Mr. Wright, her slight curves illuminated by the glow of the moon coming from a window to the right of Mr. Wright. Its soft curtains were pulled back allowing the light from outside to fill the bedroom. The bedroom sat on the front of the house away from the barn which may have kept the couple from coming awake as the dog barked at the invaders outside. Mrs. Wright wore a white silk night gown that went just above her knees. It was snug to her skin which displayed her slender body. She slept on the outside of the bed closest to the door that leads into the hallway of the house.

Sal slowly walked around the bed to the side closest to the window where the light from the moon shined. He stood over Matthew Wright and continued to watch him breath. After several seconds Sal tightened his grip on his knife and grabbed the hair of Mr. Wright and brought his head up and sliced his throat open. Sal dragged him to the side of the bed and dropped him onto the floor as the man gurgled and struggled to breathe though a windpipe that had been cut open along with the big artery in his neck. He was quickly bleeding out.

Nancy Wright woke to the sound of her husband losing his life's blood. She raised her head up and screamed at the sight of Sal Maselli standing over her bed holding a bloody knife. She screamed louder as she saw the blood of her husband dripping from its blade. Sal threw the knife down and its point stuck in the floor next to the bed. He sent the back of his hand into the face of Nancy Wright causing her to tumble back on the bed.

Sal reached and grabbed her night gown and ripped it from her body. The blow to her face had silenced her, but when she felt the cool night air touch her naked skin, she began to scream again. Sal took her silky blonde hair in his fist and pulled her up to him. The excitement thrilled him. He turned her around pressing her delicate back against him. He moved his hands to her neck and forced her to bend forward. There he viciously violated her. She tried to fight but the force against her efforts would not allow her to escape. Her screams grew weaker as Sal's grasp around her throat tightened. His fingers pressed harder and harder as his attack grew more sinister. As minutes went by her struggles began to tire and she finally went limp. His face was contorted to that of a demonic monster. He gritted his teeth together and threw his head back as his evil seed burst forward into Nancy Wright's lifeless body. Still holding her by the throat, Sal picked her up and tossed her against the headboard of the bed. She landed hard and rolled over onto her face.

Peeking around the corner of the window outside of the house was the bulging eyes of Cletus. He watched the whole assault take place and was scared at what he saw. His child-like mind could not comprehend what he just witnessed. He slowly backed up, his mouth wide open in shock, and stumbled back to where the others were. They had caught several horses and had brought them back to the corral. Cletus covered his eyes as he walked and mumbled to himself..."I didn't see it...I didn't see it."

Sal picked up the silk night gown worn by Mrs. Wright and brought it to his face. He pressed it against his mouth and nose then took in a long breath of air. He savored the scent from Mrs. Wright's body that came from the garment. He folded it up and took it with him. He searched the house for money and found three hundred dollars in currency and a leather bag with at least fifty silver dollars. The money was in a desk drawer in the room Mr. Wright used for an office when doing his horse business. He found five matching Winchesters in an oak gun cabinet. They were all 1866 models and chambered in rim fire .44 Henry. There were six boxes of cartridges to go with the rifles. Sal smiled at the fact that they were so well armed. The rifles will work much better if a posse gets on their trail. He is a specialist at laying and waiting on an adversary.

When Sal made his way back to the barn there were enough horses caught and saddled for each of them to make an escape. Luther and Arch found a saddle in the tack room for all of them as well as four rifle scabbards. They all looked brand new. Sal handed each of them a rifle.

"Load the rifles...we may need them." Sal ordered as he picked a mount to ride.

The horses all looked the same. They were bay colored with black manes and tails. They all looked big enough to carry them anywhere they wanted with plenty of stamina and endurance. When the horses were all saddled and the guns loaded they set out toward Nacogdoches. They slow walked the horses to keep from making any undue noise. Attention was one thing Sal did not want.

Cletus kept his distance from Sal. His facial expressions he showed were concealed by the darkness of the night. Cletus was shaken by what he had seen. He struggled in his mind if he wanted to tell Luther and Arch what he saw at the Wright Ranch. He was scared Sal would shoot him if he made a fuss over it so he tried to put it out of his thoughts. In a few hours the sun would be coming up and Cletus hoped it would clear away the image in his mind of the defenseless woman.

Sal and his gang traveled through the forests that lay between Chireno and Nacogdoches until the sun came up. They stopped and dismounted to rest the horses and give the day a chance to fully come forth. There was no doubt, the bodies of Mr. and Mrs. Wright would be discovered eventually and they wanted to be in Nacogdoches when that happened. They wanted to blend into the day to day movement in the city to draw less attention as possible.

"Once we get to the town we will look at taking the bank. They are bound to have plenty of money in it from all of the cotton gins in the area. It will make a nice chunk in our pockets. Don't you think so Sal?" Luther said hoping to get an agreement.

Sal cut his eyes at Luther as they both sat under a couple of hardwood trees. The sun was coming up and Luther could see the look of annoyance of Sal's face. The man had changed since he saw him last in Vicksburg. Sal had turned evil, more so than Luther had ever seen before. He knew Sal had a special hatred for the people of the south. He remembered Sal telling him that he wanted to inflict as much pain to these people as he could. Luther figured Sal was still full of hate for these southerners. Luther didn't care much for them either but he saw no reason to get himself in a bunch of trouble that would lead him to the end of a rope.

"I've got plenty of money to make it to Dallas." Sal said with a smirk that told Luther he was his own man. He also gathered that what he thought meant nothing to Sal.

Luther was surprised by what he had just heard from the man he thought was a friend. He looked over at Sal and held his eyes on him. Luther felt himself boiling over inside and he wanted to lash out and take a chance on whether he was

254

stronger than Sal, but he also had the feeling in his guts that Sal would kill him if he did.

"I thought we were going to split that up." Luther said trying to stay calm.

Sal turned and looked Luther in the eyes and said, "I'm the boss here and, if you don't like it, you can try and take that away from me. I don't mind seeing you take your last breath. It won't affect me a bit."

Luther stared at Sal in silence. There was a rage inside of him that wanted to explode in an assault on Sal but fear stopped him.

Sal had it in his mind that if or when the gang went down, it would be the men who followed him that would take the fall. It would not just be a fall in the hands of the law, he would kill each one of them if he had to and escape leaving them to be blamed for all of their crimes. He decided they needed to make their way to Nacogdoches but it needed to be done through the woods that ran along the Old San Antonio Road toward that town. They would stay deep enough to see any movement going up and down the road but still stay out sight of any travelers.

They mounted up and slowly made their way west. As they rode Luther sided up with Sal to try and make a plan to take the bank in the town.

"Sal, we need to make a plan if we are intending on taking the bank." Luther said looking straight ahead as they made their way through the trees and brush still east of the town.

"Why are you so worried about taking the bank?" Sal asked, giving Luther hope that he would finally engage him without threatening him.

"We need money Sal." Luther answered.

"You need money? Here, take this money. I'm tired of hearing you squawk about it." Sal said as he took a stack of bills taken from the Walker house and handed it to Luther forcefully hitting him in the chest with back of his hand that held the bills.

Luther took the cash and folded it before stuffing it into his shirt pocket. The look of surprise on Luther's face said he wasn't expecting Sal to give it over.

"I still want to take the bank and I want you to help us do it Sal." Luther said still looking in the eyes of evil.

Sal nudged his horse and rode on ahead through the thick cover of the forest. Luther watched him ride on, not sure of what to do once they got into Nacogdoches. He knew he needed Sal behind him when they took the bank. Luther thought in his mind how he could turn on Sal if it came to it. He knew Sal well enough to know that he would turn on them because he had already proved it. The others didn't know what they were dealing with when it came to Sal Maselli.

Once the men made it to the outskirts of the town, they held back in the forest and made a cold camp. Sal told Ned, Bill, Cletus and Taterhead to be at the back of the bank, after the bank opens in the morning. Sal, Luther and Arch rode into town as the sun went down...Sal first and then the brothers.

Sal figured the bodies of the people that had been killed the previous night had not been found. He was counting on the commotion of the murders to occupy the law enforcement in the area while their plot with the bank was carried out. People tend to go about minding their own business which gave Sal and this gang of outlaws a chance to get into town in what he would certainly call...a night of pleasure.

The town of Nacogdoches was alive after the sun went down with cowboys and night owls visiting the local watering hole. There was plenty of traffic moving through the dirt streets of the town. Sal, Luther and Arch watched the horses and wagons travel through what is believed to be the oldest town in Texas. They began to ride into to town one at a time so that no unwanted attention would be brought to them. Sal rode in first and went straight to the Broken Bucket Saloon that set on the main street that went west through the city. It was a typical storefront building with batwing doors that swung into a night life that Sal enjoyed especially if there were girls working. There was a piano playing in the corner to the right of the entrance. The player was a short man with fingers so short one would wonder how he could make the chords he played. Sal walked to bar and leaned against it as the bartender approached.

"What'll it be for you?" The man asked. He was dressed in a crisp cotton long sleeve shirt with thin red and white stripes. His dark hair was greased back and his moustache was pencil thin. A white apron was tied around his waist and he busied himself wiping the inside of a shot glass that held in his hand.

"Whiskey and leave the bottle." Sal said as he threw down two bits. The bartender complied and walked away.

The hard liquor burned Sal's throat as it went down and the feeling satisfied him for the moment. A blonde saloon girl walked over to make company with him as he drank. She was thick through the bosom and stood about five feet and five inches tall. Her lips were painted bright red and her cheeks were pink with powder. To Sal she smelled sweet and even more, she looked very desirable. He allowed her to get close to him as she played her game. He knew that her only objective was to make him spend as much of his money as she could entice him too but, little did she know that in his evil heart, he made plans for her.

Luther and Arch came in together and took two seats at a table at the back of the saloon in a corner against the stairs that went up to the second story of the building. There were men with saloon girls walking up and down the stairs arm and arm. Satisfied customers spending their week's pay on the girls that work the floor of the bar plying their trade in a loose and sinful world.

Cletus was made to stay in the woods with Ned, Taterhead and Bill. The truth was Luther and Arch wanted to enjoy some hard drinking before the others came into town the next morning. Then they would take the bank when it opened up. Their camp was cold but, it being the hottest part of the year all they had to worry about the occasional copperhead. The four stayed and kept their heads down and waited for the sun to come up.

Luther and Arch had taken a room and a saloon girl each. Both girls were able to stomach their experience with the Frank brothers after each received ten dollars in folding money. The redheads both lay sound asleep in the beds they each shared with the two outlaws as they themselves quietly walked down the back stairs into an alley between the saloon and boarding house. Wash pots lined the wall on the alley along both buildings. They both walked around and took a seat in front of the saloon to watch the town as it came to life.

Upstairs Sal Maselli casually dressed and quietly walked out of the room he shared the night before with the blond that talked him out of ten dollars worth of drinks and then a promised night of ecstasy. When he quietly closed the door to the room, he walked to the back stairs and left the same way as the brothers. The saloon girl hung nude and lifeless from the headboard of the bed, her wrists tied to each post. Her mouth was gagged and her throat was cut.

The four that stayed with their horses in the woods outside of town slowly wandered in and met Luther and Arch in front of the saloon.

"Go through that alley behind the street and go left through the alley that runs along the backs of those buildings to the back door of the bank and wait there." Luther ordered. The men and horses moved in single file as they were told.

Up the street about hundred yards was the First Bank of Nacogdoches. A man in a three piece suit was walking up to the front door where he unlocked a large single door and swung it open. There was a set of double doors with glass windows in them that displayed the name of the bank painted on the glass. He unlocked the right side door and went inside. The left side door stayed secured by a bolt on both the top and bottom that inserted into a steel ring attached to the thick timbers above the door and inside the floor. The man in the three piece suit is the bank president, Rand Golden.

Golden moved to the town of Nacogdoches from Houston and took the job as the banks President after his wife took ill and died. He was a tall slender man that believed in taking care of himself daily. His whole life was regimented and balanced in every way. He kept his waving brown hair neatly comb and his leather shoes always shone from the polishing they received every day. His suit was starched and pressed and he was cleaned shaven and he enjoyed wearing fancy cologne. He enjoyed hearing the ladies say how good he smelled to them. He opened his office and went inside and sat down at his oak desk just as his teller arrived for the day.

Joey Dents was a kind lad who was born and raised in Nacogdoches. He was always quick with numbers which was the skill that landed him the job as a teller for Mr. Golden. He had plans to attend Baylor University in Waco after he earned enough money for the tuition and then move back home and be ready to take the office of Mr. Golden upon his retirement. Golden took pride in Joey's plans and always encouraged him to follow through with them.

Joey was a small framed young man with short blonde hair. His face stayed free of whiskers and he always stayed neat and clean, just like his boss, something else that made Golden overflow with pride. He considered Joey an intern of sorts and he shared Joey's dream with extreme enthusiasm. They often talked about the world of finance after business hours were over. Golden was always impressed with Joey's knowledge on the subject. Joey Dent had just opened the window of the bank, when through the front door he heard excitement coming from the street.

"Sheriff...get the Sheriff. There's been a murder." screamed a man on a wagon pulled by a team of horses. He drove into town from the east and went by the bank stirring dust in the street as he drove through. "Sheriff..."!

From the top floor window of the saloon a woman screamed. Luther and Arch looked at each other with curiosity. Sal and the two brothers had just walked down the street toward the bank after they were met by Cletus, Ned, Taterhead and Bill. The four led the horses through the alley way behind the buildings on the same side of the street just as Luther had told them. Sal walked up next to the brothers and then looked around at all of the commotion.

"It's time to go to the bank." Sal said as he led the way.

Sheriff Beau Jamison was sitting at his desk looking over a new batch of civil papers from the courthouse when suddenly the door to his office flew open. Rusty Pike a ranch hand on the Wright's Horse Ranch ran in out of breath. Dust from the street came in the office behind him as he rushed through the door. He was pointing east and trying to describe what he had seen.

"Sheriff...there's been a murder out at the horse ranch." Pike said gasping for air as he spoke.

"What...settle down Rusty and tell me what you saw." Sheriff Jamison said as he got up from behind his desk.

"I had just got to the ranch for the day and noticed some of the horses were missing. I walked into the back door of the house just like I always do expecting to smell coffee boiling. I called for Mr. and Mrs. Wright and I got no answer. They wudn't at the barn cause I done went in there and harnessed the team to come in for feed. I went on through the house and I found them in their bedroom. Mr. Wright's throat had been cut and Mrs. Wright was laying there naked and they was both dead." Rusty Pike was about to turn blue talking so hard and fast. "I don't don't know how long they been that way since I was off yesterday."

"Okay, let me get saddled up and I'll ride out there. You take the Justice of the Peace with you. Go get Judge Nichols up while I get my horse ready to ride. You can take him out on your wagon." The Sheriff said as he strapped on his Colt revolver. He took a lever action rifle from the rack nailed to the wall and grabbed a bandolier with rounds for the long gun and placed it around his shoulder and started to the door.

Joey Dent addressed the two men who had just appeared inside the bank. They were dressed in dirty clothes and didn't look like they had much business at the bank. He cleared his throat to get their attention as they looked through the window at what was going on down the street.

"May I help you two gentlemen?" Joey asked in a pleasant and accommodating voice.

Sal stepped up to the window and handed the teller a one hundred dollar bill. "Can you change this into smaller bills, please?" Sal said as he looked at the man from under his the brim of his black hat.

"Yes I think I can do that for you."

Sheriff Beau Jamison, a veteran of the Confederate Military and Terry's Texas Rangers returned from the war with more than his share of battle scars. His six foot five frame carried the marks of the awful time in our country's history that he would just soon forget. He proudly served Texas and later was asked to become a Texas Ranger and ride for the state he dearly loved but chose to serve his community when the people of Nacogdoches County asked him to run for Sheriff. He was elected in a virtual landslide. He has held the office for the last five years. A confederate gray felt hat sat upon a head of wavy brown hair that hung to his shoulders. A thick wide mustache connected both jaw bones that were solid as steel. His lean body was as strong as two men and he was known to punch like a mule kicks, with either fist. He had made a reputation for clearing his Colt revolver as quick as a man could blink his eyes while punching out a gnat's eye with all six shots and was as good with a long gun in any caliber or action.

Deputy Danny Martin ran up to the front porch of the saloon where Sheriff had stopped on his way out of town to the Wright's Ranch. He was a twenty two year old hometown boy that longed to be a lawman for his county since he was just a kid. He was a muscular six footer who helped the Sheriff in calls for help as well as in the jail when needed. He always has a smile for those he met on the street and all the girls like his freckles and red hair. He tried to grow a beard but just never could, so he gave up to keeping his face shaved and clean. He wore his revolver cross draw because it was the way Sheriff Jamison wore his. He tried to imitate every move he saw from the Sheriff.

"Danny, I need you to look into this while I go out and check the Wright Ranch. Rusty rode up saying they have been murdered. I'll be back as soon as I can." The Sheriff said as he pulled the reins and headed east.

"Sure thing Sheriff." Danny said as he went inside the saloon.

Danny was not prepared for what he saw once inside the room where the young blonde saloon girl hung bound by her wrist to the bed posts in one of the upstairs rooms. He quickly felt sick to his stomach as he looked into the lifeless eyes of the girl everyone called Kitten.

"Is the bank president here?" I'd like to talk to him about a loan to start up a business." Sal told the teller as he counted through the smaller bills he had just received from the teller.

"Yes, Mr. Golden is here. May I give him your name?" Joey asked, as he walked over to open the steel gate that led into an office area behind the teller window.

"Yes, my name is Maselli." Sal said as the gate came open.

Sal walked into Mr. Golden's office behind Joey as he pulled his pistol from the holster on his belt. He pointed it at both of them. Both men froze in shock as the man stood before them armed and looking very dangerous. Inside the bank Luther and Arch had used this opportunity to close the front doors of the bank and secure them from inside. The sign saying "Open" was turned around to say "Closed". All of the blinds were pulled down so no one could look inside the windows of the bank.

"All right...we can do this one of two ways. You can cooperate or you can not cooperate." Sal said with a sneer in his voice. Mr. Golden and Joey both looked frightened which brought a smile to Sal's face. He always enjoyed striking fear into the hearts of those he chose to victimize. His mind quickly raced back to the previous night and how the saloon girl begged for her life as his knife sliced open her soft neck.

Sal grabbed Golden by the lapel of his suit jacket and pulled him up to his face. The heinous stench of whiskey coming from his breath hit the banker in the face like rotten guts from a dead rat. Sal wanted to bring pain to the man so he holstered his pistol and pulled his knife. He placed the point of the knife inside the left nostril of Mr. Golden and sliced his flesh as the man stood on his tiptoes. The blade made its way through his nose while the man screamed.

"Now, are you ready to open that vault?" Sal asked as he placed the point of his blade inside the other nostril.

"Yes...yes...yes...I will...I will now. Please don't cut me anymore." Golden said begging for the mercy of a mad man.

Joey stood by watching as the front of his brown suit pants developed a spot at the fly that grew larger as his water ran down his leg and onto the green rug that covered the floor under the large oak desk.

"Look Sal...you scared the boy so that he peed himself." Luther said as he gave Joey a disgusted look.

"Tie him up." Sal ordered, then drug Mr. Golden to the vault. "Now open it."

The other men had made their way around the bank to the back door. Arch opened it up and saw them there before he turned back to the interior of the bank. He signaled them to be quiet and to keep the horses still.

Mr. Golden managed to open the vault door in spite of the pain coming from his face. Blood covered the front of his suit and his eyes watered so bad he could hardly see anything. Sal ordered him to fill up a canvas bag with all of the money stored in the vault while Luther and Arch helped. The drawer at the teller window had already been emptied of all the paper money before the vault was opened. The total amount taken was thirty seven thousand in cash and coins. This was more than enough to get the gang to Dallas where they could blend into the city with not much problem.

"All right...that's it." Sal said as he pulled Golden away from the vault and back into his office where Joey Dent was tied to a chair.

He placed Golden in his big leather office chair and tied him up so he couldn't move. Sal told Luther and Arch to get mounted up. When they left the office Sal stepped up to the front of Mr. Golden. He bent down in his face again the same evil coming from his breath.

"Thank you for your cooperation and I appreciate your business." Sal said as he pushed the point of his knife deep into Rand Golden's chest. His eyes widened as the blade sunk into his heart. Blood quickly covered the front of his shirt and pants when Sal slowly pulled it out from the man's body.

Sal stood and walked around to where Joey Dent was tied and he faced him just as he did Mr. Golden.

He looked down at the young man with wet pants and then he chuckled. He leaned down into the face of Joey Dent and said in his low deep voice, "You're such a little girl to piss yourself like that. I just regret I don't have enough time to show you just how much of a little girl you really are...but I don't" Then Sal pushed the point of his knife through the innocent heart of Joey Dent.

At the back of the bank the horses were mounted except for Bill Daily who had dismounted to stand in front of Sal's horse steady him. No one outside wanted the task in fear of having to come in close contact with Sal when he rushed out of the bank. Ned even had thoughts of leaving him afoot hoping he would get captured by the Sheriff. Bill Daily held the reins with trepidation. He really wished he was somewhere other than in the company of these men.

Suddenly Sal rushed out of the back door of the bank. Bill handed him his reins but when did he dropped his own. The horse spooked and dodged Bill's grasp for the reins. It ran east along the buildings next to the bank with its tail high in the air. Bill's heart dropped as the horse ran out of sight.

"Can I ride double?" Bill asked with shock on his baby face as he looked toward each of the men for help.

"Looks like you're done." Sal said as he raised his revolver and shot Bill in the chest. A spot of red appeared on his white shirt and blood sprayed across his belly as he fell back on the ground. He looked up as the men who he thought were his friends rode away.

The people on the morning streets of Nacogdoches were in hysterics. There had been murders reported on the east side of the county as well as a murder in a room of the saloon's second floor. People were running toward the saloon to get a look at what girl had been killed during the night. Some gathering around the front of the building murmured that 'that's all a place like this good for and that girl leading the life she led was doing nothing more than asking to be killed'. Danny was trying to hold down the panic that had been escalating ever since Rusty rode in with the news of the Wrights being found killed. He was trying to keep his wits about him and stay calm. He hoped that everything he did was as Sheriff Jamison would want it.

Upstairs Danny looked up from viewing the body of the Saloon girl, Kitten, when he heard a gunshot. He was the Sheriff's only deputy and he knew that as long as the Sheriff was gone he had the town to take care of. The County Judge came to declare Kitten dead since Judge Nichols the Justice of the Peace, was with the Sheriff at the Wright Ranch.

Judge Hiram Patton strolled into the room where Kitten still hung to the headboard of the bed where she died by the hands of a ruthless murderer. He was dressed in a tailored suit that fit his rotund shape as best it could. His thin gray hair was neatly plastered to his head and his large gray beard hung to the middle of his barrel chest.

"Yes...I would say she is dead...Poor girl. Do we know who did it?" Judge Patton asked as he bent down while holding onto the lapel of his suit jacket.

No one said anything. Danny had left chasing down the sound of the gunshot.

The deputy ran toward the bank after someone yelled out that the shot sounded like it came from that direction. He made the run in a quick pace and met with a man standing at the corner of the bank and the alley next to it.

"Danny...he's back here. He's been shot but he is still alive." said Lester Stamps. He had just come into town for a load of hay to feed his milk cows when he heard the shot ring out. The old farmer walked around to the back of the bank with Danny.

Danny walked over to the man and knelt down next to him. The man's shirt was covered in blood but his chest moved showing he was still breathing. Danny slapped the man's face to get him to come back from an unconscious state.

"Hey mister, can you hear me?" Danny asked.

The man opened his eyes and looked up at the deputy. He batted them to gain focus on the man that was looking down at him. He tried to get up but was stopped by the deputy and the severe pain in his chest.

"Hold it right there and try not move. We'll get you some help. Lester, go get the doc and bring a wagon around to put him it." Danny told the old farmer.

"I'll do it." Lester said as he jumped to the request.

Danny looked down again at the man and asked, "What's your name mister?"

"Name's Bill Daily, I ain't...from around here." Bill said his breathing very labored and wheezy.

Danny thought for a second, trying to remember if he had ever seen this man before. He could not recollect. His mind searched through the dodgers the Sheriff gets from time to time wondering if Daily might be wanted but didn't remember the name or likeness.

"Bill, do you know who shot you?" Danny asked figuring the man knew the answer to the question.

"Yes...his name...is Sal...Maselli. He is a very...bad man." Bill said in a whisper.

"Do you know where he went?" Danny asked hoping Bill would hold on to life.

Bill coughed up blood. It ran down the side of his mouth onto the ground under his head. Danny propped up Bills head and rested it on his thigh after positioning himself closer to the dying man.

"They want to get...to...Dallas. They think they can blend...into all...the people...there...where nobody...will...find ...them." Bill said in pain. "I know...I...shouldn't...been...with...them. I just...didn't have...no... where...to go. They robbed...the bank."

Danny looked up and saw Lester had brought his wagon around the building. They picked Bill up and loaded him into the bed of it. Lester then drove Bill Daily to the office of Doc Simpson.

Slowly Danny walked into the back door of the bank that had been left open. He made his way into the business part of the bank and into the office of the bank president where he found the dead bodies of Joey Dent and Mr. Golden. Right away he recognized the cause of death. Danny went to the front doors and yelled down the street for Judge Patton to come to the bank for two more inquests. The deputy knew he had to do something now. He had to put together a posse and go after these men.

Chapter 15

Deputy Danny Martin rushed into the Sheriff's Office and hollered for the Jailer Elijah Harris. Harris was hired to keep any occupants of the jail safe and secure whenever there were occupants to secure. The old gray cement building wasn't always the home for outlaws and drunks, but on occasion there would be that lone cowboy that got a little too much hooch in his belly and raised a little cane down at the Empty Bucket.

Harris was a big strapping young man that grew up in Oklahoma but migrated down to East Texas with his folks after their farm went bust. He grew up fighting a mule over a plow and was known to whip three men and not even break a sweat. He stood six foot two and had shoulders so broad his momma had to make his shirts. He kept his face shaved and his sandy brown hair cut high and tight.

Pat McCoy was the only inmate Harris had to keep secure. He was a small slender cowpoke that got arrested for breaking the eight foot mirror that once hung on the wall behind the bar of the Empty Bucket. He had no money to pay for it since he drank it all up getting in the mind to break the thing in the first place so he decided to lay it out in jail. McCoy was a small man about five feet seven inches tall. He dressed like most cowboys in denim pants, a cotton work shirt that once was white but now took on more of a tan color from the dirt. His boots were knee high with spurs that jangled with each step. He was awake when he heard Danny holler for Elijah.

"You need something Danny?" Elijah asked as he finished sweeping the floor of the jail.

Danny was loading his pockets with 56-56 cartridges for a Spencer repeating rifle he pulled from the Sheriff's stock of long guns on a stand up rack mounted to the wall. He dumped a whole box of fifty rounds in one pocket and then another box in the other pocket of his denim pants. He began to load the rifle as Harris walked into the office.

"Elijah, we have to put together a posse. The bank has been robbed and there have been murders right here in town as well as out in the county. Sheriff Jamison is gone on those in the county and we have to go after the bank robbers. They killed Joey and Mr. Golden."

Elijah dropped the broom he was using and said, "I'm going. Let me run to the livery and I'll get our horses saddled."

"While you're there, tell Isaiah we need him too and anybody else you run across that is capable." Danny said as he finished loading the third rifle.

He grabbed up a leather bag for powder, shot and caps for his revolver and slung it on his shoulder. Danny then took the keys and opened the jail and walked to the cell occupied by Pat McCoy. He opened the door and held it open.

"McCoy, you can leave. Your fine is served." Danny said as he turned and walked back to the Sheriff's Office.

"You mean I can go...just like that?" McCoy asked with confusion on his face.

"That's right. I need Elijah and there is nobody else to watch you so you can leave. Here's your things McCoy...stay out of trouble" Danny said as he took a belt, holster and pistol from a desk drawer and pitched it to the cowboy.

"Did I hear you say you need a posse?" McCoy asked.

"Yep...I do." Danny said back to the man. He had put away what he thought would be enough ammo and grabbed up three canteens and filled them from a wood barrel of fresh water the Sheriff kept for drinking and coffee.

"Can you shoot that thing?" Danny asked looking at the pistol and belt McCoy was in process of strapping around him.

"I can...and I can track too. I can track a dead buck back to his grandma." McCoy proclaimed.

"Okay you can go. Take one of these rifles and let's get saddled up." Danny said as he started toward the door of the Jail.

Just then Judge Patton walked up. "Danny, are you going after those bank robbers? I bet they are the ones that did all of these killings as well. We have got to find them."

"Judge I'll do everything I can to catch up to them. Tell the Sheriff where we went. The tracks behind the bank headed west." Danny said as he mounted his bay gelding and slid his Spencer down in its rifle scabbard.

"I'm going to saddle my horse at the livery." McCoy said as he took off running down the street.

McCoy, Elijah and Isaiah rode up ready to go. Danny handed them all a rifle and cartridges and they turned their horses and headed to the back of the bank. McCoy looked down at the tracks left by the outlaws and headed west along the back of the buildings that line the north side of Main Street with the other three riders behind him. The tracks turned back through an alley and came out on the Old San Antonio Road and headed west, out of town.

Sheriff Jamison had gotten to the Wright Ranch and found the couple dead. There was no doubt to him that the death they suffered was from the hand of a violent and evil man. He had never been required to deal with such a gruesome case as this since he had taken the job of Sheriff in this quiet community in East Texas. The Sheriff made a note of what he saw in the bedroom where the two people had lost their lives. The house itself did not appear to be disturbed in any way.

There was nothing broken so he concluded the motive of the killing was just out of sheer meanness. Mrs. Wright being nude told him that she had been brutally assaulted by the man that invaded her home. The blood that had flowed from between her legs was evident that she suffered greatly at the hands of her killer.

He stretched her out and wrapped her small body up in the bed sheet she died on. A blanket was found in the cedar chest that sat at the foot of their bed. Mr. Wright was bundled in it and both bodies were loaded into the wagon Rusty had used from the ranch to bring out Judge Nichols to declare the Wrights dead.

With the wagon loaded, Sheriff Jamison and Rusty Pike with Judge Nichols started down the lane leading back to the road to Nacogdoches when they were approached by a man on foot. He was yelling to get the Sheriff's attention as he ran toward them. He ran up panting for air and having a hard time conveying the message he was sent to deliver.

"What's wrong?" Judge Nichols asked. "You look like you are all out of sorts."

"They's been a killin out at the gin...the big house. Somebody's...done shot the Walkers." The man said as he wiped sweat from his face and head. He sat down on the ground in the middle of the road trying to catch his breath. " It's terrible...just terrible."

By the time Sheriff Jamison and Judge Nichols were done at the Walker house it was getting late in the afternoon. Jamison was at loss for words as he thought of the crimes that had been committed in his jurisdiction. Murders like this just don't happen in this part of the country. This is a quiet area, full of honest hardworking people, not cold blooded killers. He searched his mind for a possible motive for the Wrights killing and decided it was for the horses since there were several missing according to Rusty Pike who was their only ranch hand. After searching the home with Pike, it was discovered that rifles were taken as well as ammunition meaning now the suspects were armed, and armed well.

Sheriff Jamison concluded that at the Walker house, robbery was the motive. Some of the gin workers said the only hands that were missing were the Frank brothers along with three others that shared a bunkhouse with them. Their absence made it easy to suspect them of the killing. One of Walker's employees did mention seeing a strange man that showed up a couple of evenings ago. The man had abandoned a sorrel horse that was lame but they had no other information about him.

It was not uncommon for the hired hands of Walker's gin to not see him since they kept their distance from him. When the morning bell didn't ring for the second morning in a row one decided to walk up and chance a scolding from Walker just to see if everything was fine. When no one came to the door the house was entered and the grisly scene was discovered.

Sheriff Jamison had ridden ahead of the wagon that carried the bodies of the Wrights and the Walkers. Judge Nichols and Rusty Pike traveled together on the wagon that brought the gruesome remains to Nacogdoches to be turned over to the local undertaker.

When the Sheriff arrived back to town, he met with the County Judge Hiram Patton as he stood in front of the jail waiting for his arrival.

"Sheriff, this has been a terrible day for our town." Judge Patton said as he wiped a tear from his eye.

"Yes your honor it has. We lost some of our citizens. The Walkers at the cotton gin have been murdered as well." The Sheriff said as he dismounted and tied his horse to the hitching post in front of his office.

Judge Patton shook his head and said, "That's not all Sheriff...the bank was robbed and Golden and Dent have been murdered as well not, to mention young Kitten at the saloon."

Sheriff Jamison stopped in his tracks and closed his eyes. He was wishing he could just wake up and find that he was having a bad dream. He let out a breath and then stepped up on the porch of the jail.

"Where is Danny?" Jamison asked.

"He made a posse and took out after the bank robbers. They went west. I would have gone along but I'm too old to keep up Sheriff." Judge Patton said with true regret.

"I understand Judge. Who went on this posse?" Sheriff Jamison asked as he went inside to fill his canteen so he could head west to try to catch up with Danny and his posse.

"Danny took Elijah, Isaiah and Pat McCoy, that cowboy who was doing time for breaking up the saloon and that's all. McCoy claimed he could track." Judge Patton explained.

"Listen Judge...I'm going to see if I can catch up to them. How long have they been gone?" The Sheriff asked.

Judge Patton took off his fedora and scratched his head as he thought. "I'd say since about nine thirty this morning."

"Dang...they are way out ahead of me." Buck Jamison said wrapping the strap of his canteen around his saddle horn. "Do we know how many men we are looking for or what they look like?"

"Sheriff, I'm afraid not. There was so much going on that nobody other than Golden and Dent probably saw their faces and they're dead."

"Okay, I'm going to see if I can get on their trail. I'll be back as soon as I can." Sheriff Jamison said as he mounted up.

Judge Patton stepped up to the side of the Sheriff's horse and looked up at him. "Is there anything I can do while you are gone?"

Sheriff Beau Jamison took off his sweat stained gray hat and wiped a sleeve across his forehead. He took a deep breath still trying to take in all that happened today. He set his hat back on his head and looked down at the Judge.

"You need to gather a group of men to watch the town while I'm gone. Use your own judgment on who you get. You know these people." Sheriff Jamison said looking west. "I'll be back as soon as I can."

Sheriff Beau Jamison rode west hoping Danny and his posse were safe. He considered the lad and how he believed he would act with caution if he happened upon whoever they were chasing. Not having a clue as to the identity of these men sent a dread through Jamison that made him very concerned for the safety of the posse. Danny, Elijah and Isaiah he knew and loved. He saw them every day and the thought of one of them getting hurt, or worse, sent the Sheriff's heart into a rage of anger for these men who brought their evil to the community he was responsible for keeping safe.

"Lord, be with Danny and them boys."

Danny rode behind Pat McCoy who kept the tracks in sight made by Sal and the others. They stayed on the Old San

278

Antonio Road but leaving it from time to time. McCoy figured anytime they met a rider or a wagon they hit the woods and stayed until it was clear to pass without being seen. The forest that covered the area west of Nacogdoches was thick with brush and foliage which made it impossible to detect someone hiding. Each time the tracks left the main road going west the posse stayed with it. They all kept their eyes peeled for anyone who might be staging an ambush. Danny thought about how important it was for him to not muddle this up since Sheriff Jamison put his faith in him enough to make him his Deputy.

"McCoy, are you still able to see their tracks in all of this pine straw?" Danny asked as they pulled up to let the horses rest.

"Yeah, I'm still seeing them in the sand. Sometimes it's hard when the pine straw is thicker but then the ground turns to sand again and they are plain to see." McCoy said after he dismounted.

They all gave the horses a few minutes to blow while they took in water and relieved themselves. They each thought how nice it would have been to grab a bit of bacon and a few biscuits before they lit out. Then Isaiah pulled a canvas bag off of his saddle and passed around beef jerky. It would have to do. After a few minutes rest they were back on the trail.

"All right pull up and let's give these horses a rest. We've been pushing them pretty hard. If there is a posse out there we are way ahead of them." Sal said as he climbed down from the big bay mare.

The others did the same with the same in mind. They all looked at each other and wondered when Sal was going to give them all their share of the money from the bank. It was apparent that Sal was the boss of this little gang but he could

279

still show some respect for the rest of them. None of them wanted to say anything to him in fear of causing their own demise. Luther on the other hand held a little more grit in his teeth and wanted to know when the money would be split up.

"Sal, there is a chance a posse is behind us so don't you think we should split up that money?" Luther asked feeling unconcerned with Sal's position and ferocious demeanor.

Sal looked hard at Luther under the brim of his black hat. Luther looked right into the evil eyes that glared into him. Luther didn't budge…he wanted his share of the money and he had had all of Sal and his crazy way of treating him and the rest of the gang.

"Let's do it tonight when we make camp. First we are going to have to take care of the posse that is for certain following us. We have torn that community a new one and you can rest assured they are angry and want revenge." Sal said as he turned to mount back up.

Sal considered in his mind how much he required the others right now. He knew if they all jumped him it would be bad for him. His wit and cunning would have to keep everything smooth between them. He saw the looks of their faces and realized he could not take them all on. With a posse possibly on their heels, he needed them to at least take lead for him.

The others looked around at each other and shook their heads in agreement. Luther again spoke up looking straight into the eyes of Sal.

"Okay…we will do that…tonight in camp." Luther said shaking his head still looking at Sal.

"Good…let's go." Sal said turning his horse and touching his spurs to its side.

"McCoy, do you think they will stop and make camp for the night?" Danny asked as they rode their horses back onto the Old San Antonio Road. The tracks were all very visible and stood out in the sandy road that was packed hard from travelers.

"You'd think so unless they stay on the road. If they do they can go west all the way to Laredo." Pat McCoy said as he rolled a cigarette from paper and pouch.

"Have you ever been all the way to Laredo, McCoy?" Elijah asked. He had never been out of Nacogdoches County since he and his family moved there from Oklahoma.

"Yep...I worked a cow ranch out there below San Antonio. Comanche got so bad I got out and came east." McCoy said.

"Did you ever have to fight the Comanche?" Isaiah asked his interest perked up hearing their new companion had been where the tribe roamed. He was a young man full of life and promise yet he had never ventured outside of the Pineywoods.

McCoy took a drag off the cigarette and blew the smoke out of his nose. "Yeah...they raided the ranch I worked on a time or two looking for horses and steers. They was always stealing horses from us. The steers they stole was always butchered and ate by their own people. If we caught'em at it, we would always take shots at'em. Sometimes we'd hit one but mosta the time they was movin too fast."

"Dang...I bet that was something." Isaiah said with his mouth open in amazement.

"There's times we lost a ranch hand cause of the Comanche." Pat McCoy said as he knocked the fire off of the end of his smoke and dropped it in the dirt road.

Elijah and Isaiah looked at each other with shock on their faces. Their young imaginations were running wild from what McCoy had just told them. They both leaned in the saddle toward McCoy on edge waiting to hear the rest of the story about what happened to the ranch hands.

"What happened to 'em." Elijah asked.

"Well they was out ridin herd when the Comanche would sneak up and put an arrow through 'em. They is mean like that. They didn't want us around. They said we destroyed the land and made their people sick." McCoy explained.

"That ain't no cause to be killin fokes though." Elijah said shaking his head at the thought.

"Well...they would and even take scalps off the guys too. I heard they like to hang them from their spears and decorate themselves with them." McCoy added seeing the others were still on the edge of their seats.

"Well I'm glad they ain't none around here." Danny said as he rode up next to McCoy. "Let's get a move on...these horses have cooled down enough."

"Look, this drops down in what looks like a river bottom. See that row of trees down there? I'd say there is a river on the other side of that tree line, and if we are going to wait on a posse that'd be good a place as any." Luther said turning to face the others. Sal never said a word. He just rode on pass Luther.

"Luther are we gonna ambush them when they come down into this bottom?" Ned asked as he swallowed hard at the thought of gun play.

"That's the plan. If we can get that posse that is sure to be following out of our hair, we should have no problem from here." Luther answered.

The men rode down into the river bottom that stretched what looked to be three-quarters of a mile. The land in the bottom was cleared and good farm land, more likely for cotton. It was wide open and would be the perfect place to pick off the posse as it approached the river. The tree line along the river would be an ideal spot for cover from any return fire the posse may give. The land was cleared and the dirt was right for cotton. The soil was dry and cracked from the lack of rain and as the gang rode toward the tree line their tracks stood out for the posse to follow.

When Sal and the others reached the river they found the water level to be low. In the hottest part of the summer when there was not much rain, the river got low of water and had little flow. There were gravel beds that ran across the river which made crossing easy for the horses. They rode across and went up the opposite bank before they dismounted.

"We can hide the horses over here behind these trees and then cross back over on foot and make our stand." Luther said as the horses made it across. The water was so low very little splash was made from their hooves.

Once across, the riders climbed the opposite bank and concealed their horses behind the trees that ran along the bank of the river. Large hardwood trees stood on both sides of the river and they supplied plenty of concealment for the gang to make their ambush of the unsuspecting posse. When they crossed back over the river, Luther gave orders to the men.

"Yall spread out along the bank. If you keep yourselves low, they shouldn't be able to see you until they get right upon us and then it will be too late." Luther said as he hurried up the

283

river bank with a rifle in his hand. "You all have plenty of bullets so feel free to shoot them all dead."

The gang spread out along the bank over a space of about three hundred feet. The bank was clear of brush in that area so their heads could only be seen after the posse got within rifle range. The perfect ambush was staged and the wait had commenced.

"I was hoping we would catch them before they got to the Angelina River but it don't look like we did. The river bottom drops off right up here." Danny said as they approached the decline in the landscape.

"Yeah...you can tell they are at a fair trot as the tracks head down. They were moving at a quick pace. I was hoping those horses would give out by now." McCoy said as he leaned over in the saddle to look at the trail left by the bank robbers.

"That's the county line ain't it Danny?" Isaiah asked.

"Yeah that crosses into Cherokee County, but we are going on...I don't want to lose their trail." Danny said thinking Sheriff Jamison would do the same thing. He knew the Sheriff of Cherokee County would have it no other way.

"It's gonna be getting dark before long. You think we ought to camp along the river tonight and see if we can pick the trail back up in the morning." McCoy asked.

Danny took off his hat and hung it over his saddle horn. He pulled a bandana out of his back pocket and wiped the sweat from his face. He didn't want to give up the trail. He knew that if he gave it up all together, it would be at the orders of Sheriff Jamison. He found himself wishing the Sheriff was here and in control of this posse.

284

"After all these men have done to our town, we have to stay after them if it means riding clean to California. We can't quit." Danny said with determination in his voice. "Let's go."

The posse headed down into the Angelina River bottom with McCoy and Danny in the lead. The tracks left by the band of outlaws were easily seen in the dirt that a few weeks earlier were covered in cotton. The last crop had been picked and sent to nearby cotton gins. In the distance, deer ran across the field toward the wood line that marked the route of the river. There were does with fawns trying to keep up as well as young bucks in velvet mixed into the small herd.

The posse covered the three quarters of a mile in several minutes. They did not push the horses knowing that a wrong step on the uneven ground could be disastrous for a horse as well as the rider. They were approaching the river bank about fifty yards away when gun shots rang out. McCoy was hit in the center of his chest. His body fell backward off of his horse and lay on his back on the ground. Blood gushed from the wound in his chest with every beat of his heart. His body lay still. The young cowboy was dead.

The same instant other shots rang out and the other three riders fell dead on the ground. Their horses turned and ran east in a panic. All four members of the posse were fatally hit by bullets from the long guns of the bank robbers that hid themselves just beyond the bank of the river.

The gunman waited a few minutes to make sure the men of the posse did not move. They all emerged and approached the men as they lay dead or dying. Sal Maselli walked up with a triumphant smile across his evil face. The three brothers, Luther, Arch and Cletus relieved that their chance of escape had just been solidified. Ned Brundage and Taterhead breathed a

285

sigh of relief knowing now that they would have safe passage to their destination.

Ned Brundage ran over to Isaiah's body and grabbed one of his boots and pulled it from his right foot. Ned then held it to the bottom of his right boot to compare the size. It looked the same so he pulled his wore out boot off and put the dead man's boot on his foot. He then pulled the other one off of Isaiah's other foot and put it on as well. He stood and admired the fit before he went through the young man's pockets taking two silver dollars he had made that morning at the blacksmith's shop. Ned shoved them in his pocket and started toward Elijah before Taterhead stopped him and shook his head.

"This here dead man is mine so you just go on your way." Taterhead demanded.

Taterhead sat down on the ground next to Elijah and tried his boots on. They fit fine to him and he walked off pleased...other than the fact Elijah was penniless.

All of the dead posse members were stripped of their guns and ammo and anything the bank robbers thought might be of any value. Their bodies were left where they lay.

"We'll leave the coyotes their supper." Sal said as he tore the badge off Danny's shirt and put it in his leather bag. He had made it a point to put the bullet in the young lawman's chest as he rode to his death. The badge would serve as a nice memento of their brief encounter. The pistol Danny carried was tucked behind Sal's belt. His powder shot and caps were placed in Sal's saddle bags.

"Let's cross back over and put some miles behind us before dark. The sound of gun shots can be heard for miles." Arch said as the outlaws headed back toward the river.

They crossed back over and retrieved their horses and headed west for several miles. They came upon a farm house that had no movement around it. The riders were looking at the back side of the house. It looked like it sat off of the Old San Antonio Road by looking at the lane that leads away from the front of the house. The lane had a split rail fence along both side of it and inside the fenced pasture were several black and white milk cows. They were grazing in the pasture as the night approached. The western sun was almost behind the tree line that ran along a large pasture.

The band of men stopped in the trees and kept an eye on the farm house to see if anyone was there. There was one light shining from a window on the east side of the house but it soon went dark after the sun was completely set.

"Whoever lives there will be moving early in the morning to milk those cows." Arch whispered leaning over to Luther.

"We go in tonight." Sal said. "When we get up to the back door I'll go in. You guys stay out until I give the go ahead."

Luther and Arch looked at each and Luther said, "Sure Sal whatever you say."

When the moon was high the men removed a section of split rails from the fence that bordered the pasture in back of the farmhouse. They led their horses across to a barn with milking stalls in it. They tied the horses as Sal approached the back door of the house. It was a simple wood framed house with board and batting for siding. It was small and had two windows on each side the house. The front of the house had a porch that ran the width of the house.

Sal pulled his boots off as he always does before entering a house where the occupants are sleeping inside. He quietly made his way in the back room and was able to go from room

287

to room by the moon light that shone through the windows that had the curtains pulled open. He found that one woman was asleep on a bed in the only bedroom of the house. She was a large woman and snored as she slumbered.

The floor creaked when Sal stepped into the bedroom. The sound brought the woman from sleep and she quickly raised her head up. She was about to cry out in alarm when Sal clubbed her across the face with his pistol. She immediately fell back to the bed unconscious. A large knot quickly developed on her forehead and blood ran from her nose. Sal rolled her onto the floor between her bed and the window and hit her several more times in the head killing her. The lady's head had been split open so severe her brains were exposed. Her eyes were open but saw nothing. There was no one else in the house so Sal walked out the back door and back to the barn where the others waited.

"What did you see?" Luther asked as Sal walked back into the barn.

"We can unsaddle the horses and feed them. The house is a good place to camp for the night. There was an old woman in there but she don't care if we stay the night." Sal said with a chuckle.

Luther knew right away Sal had killed the old woman. He did consider looking through the house for valuables. There was no sense in going so far as to kill the owner of the house and not make it worth their while.

"We move at first light." Sal said as he pulled his boots on and started back to the farmhouse. "Let's split this money up."

Chapter 16

Sheriff Beau Jamison rode most of the night to try to catch up with the posse until his eyes would no longer remain open. He stopped and made a cold camp under a big oak tree on the side of the Old San Antonio road. From the light of the moon Sheriff Jamison looked at the hands of his pocket watch that read ten minutes after three. He closed his eyes until the east sun peeked through the forest bringing him awake. He drank water and saddled his horse. Before the hour reached eight o'clock he had made it to the Angelina River bottom.

Before making the descent into the flat, the Sheriff heard a rustle in the brush to his right. He turned and saw a horse with its saddle slid down to its side. There were three others grazing in the grass along the slope that drops down into the river bottom. They were all saddled, which told the Sheriff that all was not well. He caught each one and tied their reins to separate low limbs on trees nearby and secured their saddles. His heart was heavy, knowing that Danny and the others knew better than to leave their mounts like this.

He rode on toward the Angelina River after seeing the horses came from that direction. As he got closer to the river he saw the bodies of the posse laid out on the ground where they had been shot off of their horses. He went straight to Danny and fell to the ground next to his body.

"Danny...Danny." The Sheriff said through anguish boiling over in his heart.

The gray tint and the coldness of Danny's skin told him that the young Deputy was dead and had been for several hours. Blood had dried on the front of Danny's shirt where a bullet from an evil man's rifle had ended the life of this young man. A young man that Beau Jamison believed would go on to be a Texas Lawman of the highest integrity. The others were good boys too, and he was sure that the rowdy cowboy Pat McCoy was a decent young man as well.

The Sheriff ended his search for the bank robbers to go and gather the horses he had left tied. He fought tears as he lifted each young man and placed him over the saddle of a horse. He felt the terrible feeling in his gut of the hurt the community would feel and, telling their friends and loved ones of their death weighed on his mind as he tied the bodies to their saddles for the trip back to Nacogdoches. Still he knew he had a job to do and he was determined to get it done. He would bring those men to justice whether it was from a court or from the barrel of a gun.

The sun was sinking as Sheriff Beau Jamison slowly rode into the town of Nacogdoches. The day had been one he hoped he would never have to live through again. As he slowly approached the front porch of the jail the door came open and Judge Nichols stepped out. He bowed his head when he saw the bodies of the four young men that made up the posse that went after the men who robbed their bank and murdered their fellow citizens. He stepped off the porch and into the street and walked over to the horse that carried the body of Isaiah. He softly placed his hand on the young dead man's shoulder and closed his eyes and prayed. As he prayed, he went to each one of the men who gave their lives and prayed over them that their spirits were in Heaven and at eternal peace.

"Beau, what are we going to do?" Judge Nichols asked as he wiped his eyes with a handkerchief he pulled from his back pocket.

The Sheriff was so tired and it showed as he slid down from his saddle. He stepped up on the porch and sat down on a wood bench that was smooth from years of occupants sitting on it swapping tales and lies. He took off his hat and let it hit the wood floor of the porch and buried his face in his hands. After a minute he raised his head.

"I need a night's rest and then I'm after those men." Beau Jamison said.

"Do you intend on going alone?" Judge Nichols asked, as he walked over and sat down next to the Sheriff.

"Yes...I'm going alone and I'm not arguing with you about either." The Sheriff said in a voice that drew a conclusion to the issue.

"I understand." Judge Nichols replied knowing any discussion would be useless. "I just wish Danny would have taken more men with him."

Beau shook his head and said. "No...that would mean I would have brought back more bodies. They were ambushed at the Angelina River. They never saw it coming."

The Sheriff stood up and reached for the reins tied to the hitching post. The Judge quickly took them from him and started down the street.

"Get you some rest Beau. I'll take these down to the undertaker." The Judge said as he started up the street. "I'll drop off the horses at the livery when I'm done."

Sal and his gang of thieves and killers made their way into Alto. They found the only saloon in town and made their home at a table in the back of the establishment. The night life wasn't much and they were the only customers in the place. The bartender sat on a stool behind the bar and saw to their request which was one bottle of whiskey after another. The building was nothing more than a wood frame structure with one story. It sat on the edge of town on the Old San Antonio Road and served the locals that got a thirst for a beer or something harder. A local corn farmer provided home cooked mash that the outlaws preferred. They all agreed that it packed a little more punch than the factory made spirits.

"Why don't you go on home barkeep. We'll close up for you." Arch said as he raised a glass half full of homemade corn whiskey.

The bar owner looked over and shook his head. "I can't do that. Why don't you pay your tab and go on about your business. It's getting late and yall have had enough." The burly round bartender said as he ran his right hand over the stock of the black powder shotgun under the bar.

"Well, why do you make such a request mister bartender?" Arch asked as he got up from his chair.

"Sit down Arch." Sal said. He was sitting in at straight back chair sipping the whisky from a glass.

"Say Sal...why don't we pack up and go." Luther said in a low voice.

Sal looked over at Luther and then to Arch. He didn't want a commotion in this saloon. The less attention to them would be best. He just wanted to move on through and not be noticed by too many people if it was possible. He stood up and the rest did the same. Arch had locked eyes with the bartender and it took a shove from Luther to make him relent.

"What do we owe bartender?" Sal asked

"Yall drank up about ten bucks worth I'd say." The bartender said, still caressing the shotgun under the counter.

Sal laid down a stack of silver dollars on the bar as he walked by. Luther was prompting Arch toward the door and the rest followed. The bar owner took notice of each one of the men. They were strangers and he wasn't used to strangers patronizing his saloon. He also saw something in the bunch that gave him reason to observe them close. He knew they were evil men. As he closed the front door to the saloon he watched the riders fade into the darkness riding west.

Early the next morning Sheriff Beau Jamison was up with the sun. He went to the livery stable where he kept several horses reserved for his use in the job of traveling the far corners of his county to check on its residents and picked him a good one with hard thick muscling. The mounts he kept were big and strong and had the endurance to travel long distances. He picked a red roan mare that had carried him on long trips before. She was tall and stout enough to carry him for days.

He went over the provisions for several days that he packed along with a bedroll and slicker. The restaurant down the street brought over sliced ham that had been fried and sandwiched between homemade bread. He also had jerky and could make tortilla if he needed to. He would boil his coffee in a cup and pour it into another. They took up less room than a coffee pot and he wanted to travel as light as possible. He had ground to cover and he was ready to get started. Before the sun peeked over the tops of the tall East Texas pine trees, Sheriff Beau Jamison was headed west.

Late that afternoon, Beau made it back to the place where the posse was ambushed. He spurred the roan to make the ride to the river quicker. The thoughts of the rifles going off and the lead flying through the air taking the lives of Danny and the others brought rage to his heart. He wanted vengeance and he wanted it to be harsh. The murders the men committed require punishment unthinkable and he was in the mind to dish it out to them.

The tracks made by the horses stolen from the Wright Ranch were still visible in the soft dirt that made up the bank of the Angelina River. He followed a deer trail up the bank and into an open field. He stayed on the trail left by the bad men which led him to a split rail fence where a young man made repairs.

"I'm Beau Jamison, the Sheriff of Nacogdoches County. I'm on the trail of some bank robbers that killed people in my county." Beau said as he rode up to the man.

The man stopped what he was doing and addressed the Sheriff. He was a young man wearing bib overalls and wearing a straw hat that was stained from days of hard work. He looked up at the Sheriff and held his hand up and shaded his eyes from the western sun.

"I'm Pete...I just put up the widow Parks' milk cows that got out. She was kilt last night we reckon. I found her dead in the house this morning when I brought her milk cans back." Pete said still shading his eyes.

"What happened to the lady, Pete?" The Sheriff asked.

Pete opened the fence to allow Beau Jamison to ride his horse through. The rails went right back in place after the roan cleared the spot between the two upright posts.

"The deputy from Rusk is up at the house with the Justice of the Peace now declaring her dead. I didn't want to see her like that so I come out to make myself busy getn her cows back in. The widow English ran a small dairy" Pete said as he started walking toward the farmhouse next to the Sheriff on the roan mare.

As the two reached the house a man in a white shirt and black vest and hat walked out of the front door. He was medium height and wore a revolver on his right side in a leather holster. He had a large mustache that was the color of coal and a badge hung from his vest that read 'Deputy Sheriff'.

The other man was somewhat older and much thinner. He wore a tan jacket and pants with a white shirt and a gray hat. His thick mustache hung below his top lip and completely covered his mouth. The skin on his face was weathered and gave the man a look of one who works under the sun from sun up until dark. They stopped on the front porch of the house when Beau rode around the corner with Pete still at his side.

"Gentleman...I'm Beau Jamison Sheriff of Nacogdoches County. Pete here says the lady of the house was killed." Beau said as dismounted his horse.

"Yes...I'm afraid so. I'm Judge Pearson the Justice of the Peace for this area of Cherokee County and this is Earl Sweeney the Deputy for Sheriff for James Hogg over at Rusk." Pearson said as he extended his hand to Beau.

Sweeney did the same and said, "Sheriff, how are you?"

"I've seen better days and I know you have too." Beau said as he took a canteen from his saddle horn.

"I never did like to have to look into a murder but it looks like that's what I've got here.

"How was the lady killed?" Beau asked.

"Her brains were beat clean out of her head. Whoever did this is pure evil." Deputy Sweeney said.

"I had several murders over in Nacogdoches just in the last couple of days and I'm thinking this one was done by the same bunch." Beau explained. "They're bad men and they like killing."

The Deputy and Judge Pearson stepped down and they all took a seat on the edge of the porch. Beau took another swallow of water and told them what had transpired in his county.

"I think this all started over at Thaddeus Walker's Cotton Gin...the best I can see. The Walkers were shot and there were a few guns stolen from their house. I believe the killers may have worked for them. Then those guys went to the Wright Horse Ranch where they stole several horses and killed Mr. Wright and assaulted and murdered Mrs. Wright in an awful way." Beau said seeing the look on Judge Pearson's face turn grim.

"Oh my Lord...poor woman," the Judge said.

Sheriff Jamison agreed and continued. "Then they rode into Nacogdoches and murdered a saloon girl and robbed the bank, killing the Bank President and his teller. They made off with over thirty thousand in cash."

"That's a shame. Y'all have a really nice town over there." Deputy Sweeney said as he stood and waited for the wagon that was coming up the lane in front of the farmhouse.

"We have to take poor Mrs. English to Rusk since there ain't no undertaker in Alto. I will try and get on their trail as soon as I can." Deputy Sweeney said as he stepped back inside the house to help the wagon driver with the dead body of Mrs. English.

Beau Jamison returned to his saddle and turned to go down the lane away from the house. He thought about these men that have done all the killings in the last few days. He knew they had to be brought back to receive justice. Hopefully a rope was what they had to look forward to. There are some men that hard labor, for the rest of their lives, is just not enough to pay for the things they've done. Sometimes a man deserves to be put to death and that's just what these men deserve.

Sheriff Jamison turned west and started toward Alto. He hoped that someone in town may have seen these men come through. Beau decided that he was not going to quit until he caught up with them. He did not care how far their trail took him. He was determined to stay on it.

"Sal don't you think we should ride a little harder?" Luther asked as they rode past a large mound of dirt.

"What's them big mounds for Archie?" Cletus asked as he gave them a hard look.

"I don't know boy. I reckon it's where Injuns that lived around here buried their kin." Arch answered not really sure what to say.

"Well they sure is big. You figure they's still Injuns around, Archie?" Cletus continued to wonder. "I don't want to wind up losing my hair."

"They ain't no more Injuns around here Cletus, now be quiet." Arch said losing his patience. He was determined not to be stuck with answering all of Cletus' questions.

"I was just wonderin." Cletus said, still looking hard at the large mounds of dirt.

The gang of outlaws had made it to the Neches River. They had no idea the mounds Cletus was so interested in were left there by the Caddoan tribe of Indians that once lived in this part of East Texas.

"Still they just give me the heebie-jeebies." Cletus continued in spite of Archie's patience running thin.

"Cletus, I said be quiet. Now shut up." Arch demanded. His hate for his little brother was beginning to come out.

The youngest of the brothers ducked his head just like a scolded child. Tears welled up in his eyes, his heart broken by the brother he admired. His simple mind could not think like a man, especially like the men he rode with. They were evil, but in his way of thinking they were not, especially his brother Archie. He knew not of the feelings Luther and Archie had for him in their black hearts, so he would stay true to them not knowing they hated him.

"This looks like another river to cross. Once we get over to the other side we will make camp for the night." Sal said as he and the other riders descended the slope to the river bottom below.

When Beau Jamison rode into Alto his belly was 'cuttin a rusty'. He had not stopped for a meal during this whole ordeal and he was feeling it. He saw the little restaurant called "Trudy's" and decided it was time to fill his belly with some grub. He dismounted and walked into the place. It was about time for most folk's supper and the air was filled with smells of delicious food. He sat down at a table that was just big enough for two people.

A large woman walked over to take his order.. He could not help but give her a smile. She just brought it out in people. She carried a glass of water and had a white rag draped over one shoulder. There were specks of sweat on her face that gave away the fact that she was the cook.

"What can I get for you mister, or shall I say Sheriff from the star on your chest. My name is Trudy and I own the place." She said waiting to hear back from her guest.

299

"Evening Trudy, I'm Beau Jamison from Nacogdoches. I'm looking for a group of men that may have ridden through your town." Jamison said.

She looked through him with sharp eyes and said, "Don't recall seeing anybody like that. When do you suppose they come through?"

Beau took a long sip of water and then smacked his lips and answered, "Maybe late yesterday."

"I close at eight. I guess it could have been later." Trudy thought.

"Is there a place that would cater more to the more shady type of characters"? Beau asked hoping to get a possibility.

Trudy gave him foul look and said, "Oh heavens yes...there's a place down the street on the left. That place will stay open as long as there is a nickel to be made and a thirst to quench."

"I think I'll go by there and ask, after I satisfy this monster in my belly." Beau said with a smile.

"How about I get you my supper special...beef steak and beans with corn bread." Trudy said giving him a touch on the shoulder. "On the house, Sheriff...I just love lawmen."

"That will be fine Ma'am, thank you."

After Beau finished his supper he rode down to the saloon on the edge of town. There were a couple of horses tied to the porch and a light shone through the door from the inside. There was not much noise, if any, coming from the place. Before Beau walked in he stopped at the door and surveyed the patrons.

Inside there was a table with two men playing a game of checkers and drinking beer. The bartender stood behind a bar that was empty of drinking customers. Beau Walked in and straight to the bar.

"What can I get you…Sheriff?" The bartender asked after he gave a good look at the star on Beau's chest.

"All I want is information." Beau returned still looking around the room.

"We don't serve information, Sheriff." The barkeep said with a frown.

Like a bolt of lightning Beau grabbed the man by the collar of his dirty shirt and pulled his face down to meet the barrel of his revolver. The man grunted when the end of the barrel pressed against his nose.

"If I wanted a wise crack, I would slap one out of you. Now I'm looking for some men that have come through here maybe yesterday or last night." Beau said through gritted teeth.

"I think there could have been…you're killin my face mister." The bartender screeched.

"That just means you understand me now. Now, how many were there?" Beau Jamison asked as he pressed the barrel harder against the man's nose.

"Ahh….Ahhhh…maybe a half a dozen…I didn't count them. Mister please let go." The bartender begged. "It was a little past midnight…last night."

"Not yet…one more thing…which way did they go when they left your, wonderful dump?" Beau asked, looking around at the filthy night spot.

West…they went west." The man said in pain.

"Thank you. See that was easy now wasn't it." Beau said as he released the man from his iron grip.

The man straightened up and rubbed is nose where Beau tried to insert his forty-four. The man's eyes watered from the pain Beau had inflicted on him. The Sheriff didn't have time for the likes of a bartender like this after what he had gone through. Losing good friends to evil men will make a man lose his patience.

Beau stepped backward while keeping his eyes on the bartender as he made his way to the door out of the saloon. He saddled up and rode west out of town. He figured the men were still a day ahead of him. He stayed on the Old San Antonio Road and kept the horse at a trot.

"I know I'm tired of sleeping on the ground. There's one thing I can't stand and that's an old cottonmouth." Luther said as he turned over in his blanket under a large pine tree.

The men had made camp on the west bank of the Neches River, just inside Houston County. They planned on riding at first light and making a turn north.

"Sal, we could travel with the river to maybe hide our trail." Luther suggested as he looked up at a black sky.

"There are bound to be roads going north that would make traveling a lot faster. We need to split up too. We've been seen together and we need to change up." Sal said, as he stretched out on his bedroll.

"When we get to Dallas do you want to get a job Luther?" Arch asked rolling over to remove a pine cone from under his blanket.

"I don't know until we get there. I think you and me can stick together and them others can do whatever they want." Luther said wishing Cletus was smart enough to catch on.

"What about me Archie?" Cletus asked feeling his brothers were going to abandon him.

Arch did not want to think about having to take care of Cletus in a city like Dallas. He rolled over in his mind the possible ways of getting rid of his younger brother. He hoped that Luther had a plan to do it and make it permanent. Once they got there it would be easier. Maybe a home for the mentally ill would be a place to dump him off. The solution that would get him out of their lives for good would be more appropriate.

After a time all three men were snoring except for Sal. His eyes were fully open and his mind was at work. The thoughts about roaming a city like Dallas intrigued him greatly and he looked forward to being loose in such a place. There would be whorehouses in abundance filled with interesting ladies of all shapes and sizes that he could enjoy. It will be a pleasure to make their acquaintance.

Sheriff Beau Jamison sat by a small fire and sipped his second cup of coffee. He stopped about a quarter of mile east of the Neches River at the mounds of the Caddoans. He held a respect for the culture of the Native Americans. On this sight once stood a thriving community where the tribe carved out a life breaking soil and harvesting their crops. The woods were filled with wild meat to feed their families as well as the nearby Neches River and its abundant fish.

His horse munched on the last of the oats he brought and then grazed in clumps of green grass that grew in the field next to the Old San Antonio Road. Tomorrow Beau needed the horse to be ready to travel hard. In his heart he believed he would catch up to them.

In his mind he saw the faces of Danny, Elijah, Isaiah and McCoy…young men whose lives were taken by the evil men he hunted. He wanted to catch them and bring them swift justice, but he had sworn to uphold the law and that meant to bring them back bound to their saddles or thrown over it, one way or the other.

Beau settled into his blanket and closed his eyes. He knew by morning the fire would have died out and he had no intention of brewing anymore coffee. He intended to get on the trail again at first light if not earlier.

"Jake Powell, why aren't you in your bunk?" Tammy asked as she sat in the glow of the moon on the front porch of the log cabin occupied by her, her brother and Jake.

"Well I might just ask you the same thing. Why aren't you in your bunk ma'am?" Jake asked as he walked over to where Tammy sat.

"I just love looking at the night sky. It's so peaceful here. I'm so looking forward to making a life with you Jake." Tammy said with a deep sigh and a bat of her eyes toward the man she fell in love with.

"Well, I've been thinking." Jake said

"You better not back out on me Jake Powell. That would just break my heart." She said with a pooched lip.

Jake sat down on the porch next to the chair Julius built for Tammy and laughed out loud. "I wouldn't dare. I know how much it means to you to marry me and I feel the same way."

"Oh Jake, I do love you with all of me." Tammy said as she ran her fingers through his long brown hair.

Jake took in the feel of her soft hand and he submitted to her sweet affection. He was in love with Tammy and he was going to make a life for her and all the children she wants to have. He lay many nights dreaming about and planning all of the things he wanted to do on the ranch. He had purchased twenty five heifer cows and had them in his pasture. It took him and Julius many hard days working to get the ranch fenced off using split rails from hardwood trees, but through determination they got the job done.

Tomorrow, he has planned to ride to John Hollingsworth's cattle ranch and purchase a herd bull and bring him back to turn him in with the heifers. He is expecting that in a couple of years there will be steers ready to take to market. Then he would buy Tammy some pretty dresses and Julius a new suit. Thankfully Mrs. Edge, down at the general store, fixed Tammy up with a wedding dress that fits her perfectly. Jake, of course, will not be allowed to see her in it until the wedding day. Julius will have the honor of giving her away and Jake will be more than honored to take her.

He still thinks of Sarah and the children but Tammy has brought him through those hard times and given him a new outlook on his future and hers. He loves to see the look on Tammy's face as she plans and dreams of a life with him. His heart jumps every time she looks at him and then gives him that smile that she is known for that will make him do whatever she wants, but he doesn't mind at all.

"What are you thinking about Jake Powell?" Tammy asked as she stroked the side of his face.

Jake smiled and looked down at his feet like a school boy with a crush on the prettiest girl in the class. "I'm thinking about how happy I am that you came along in my life."

"That's so sweet Jake. I'm glad too. I never knew a man could make me feel the way you make me feel. I will be even happier when I am your wife." She said. Tammy leaned her head down and rested it on his.

"You don't have too much longer to wait. Two weeks is all."

"Yes, I know and I'm counting down every minute." She said as she got up.

Jake got up as well and Tammy leaned into him. He embraced her and their lips met for a long deep kiss. They stood there together in the moonlight holding each other while their hearts raced with a passion that most young lovers search for and never find. As they pulled away they held each other's hands and looked into each other's eyes taking in a moment that both wished would never end.

"Good night Jake. I love you."

"I love you Tammy. Good night."

Chapter 17

In the French Quarter of New Orleans, mist filled the air and rage overflowed in the bedroom of Arthur Babineaux. This millionaire Frenchman controlled most of the real estate and all of the crime in the southern Louisiana city including the gambling and prostitution. He had awakened another day only to find out the two hoods he hired to find Tammy had not returned with his prize. His plan was not coming together as he had planned. The beautiful Tammy Broussard was to be his gold mine, in the flesh for sale business, and he would go to great lengths to see that she be brought here to be forced into his employment. Her beauty is beyond compare and his wealthy clientele will pay dearly for her company. Every day that goes by is another day that money is not jingling in his pockets. The fifty thousand dollars he put up to have her brought to him, is a sizable sum for any soldier of fortune on the market for such of an assignment. He had put his trust in John Claude Chastain and Charbonneau to find her and bring her to him after her brother Julius was eliminated. He knew Julius would not pose a threat to his two henchmen, so there was no worry about any effective resistance. Another day of waking with no Tammy sent Babineauz into a fit of rage.

Arthur Babineaux sat back down at the side of his bed. There was a young tanned-skin creole girl, no more than seventeen years of age, lying sleeping on a feather stuffed mattress covered with the finest silk sheets. He sat wearing a black silk robe and nothing else as he pondered on what to do to find the one beauty he desired most for his harem of young ladies. His long black hair in disarray on his head fell around a slender face that was tan and shaved clean. His slender six foot frame slumped over as he sat with his mind racing in search of a solution. He turned to the girl and threw the covers off of her soft naked body waking her up with a start. She lifted her torso up revealing her firm breasts and a beautiful face complete with a swollen jaw and black eye.

"Get up and get out." Babineaux ordered as he slapped her butt.

"Yes Mr. Babineaux. " The girl said, as she quickly jumped from the bed and hurried out of the bedroom, not taking time to dress.

Babineaux stood and walked to a table full of decanters and glasses. He poured himself a glass of bourbon and then retired to a high back chair covered with red velvet cushioning. He took a long drink of the spirits and then reached for a cigar. He loved the imported ones from Cuba with a stout glass of bourbon for breakfast even though it was one o'clock in the afternoon. He also loved the night life.

"Carter, get in here." Babineaux screamed at the top of his lungs.

The door to the large bedroom opened and a man stepped in. He was dressed in a black suit with a gray vest and tie. His shoes were shined to perfection and his stance was very erect with a professional manner. He had a head of gray hear that was combed straight back and his goatee was trimmed with precision. He had been employed by Babineaux for the past twenty five years and his trust and loyalty were unquestionable.

"Yes sir...what may I do for you?" Carter said, as he stood with his hands behind his back showing complete obedience to his employer.

"Have you received any word from Chastain or Charbonneau?" Babineaux asked, as he touched the flame from a match to the end of his cigar.

"No sir, I have not, other than the letter from Chastain that you received several months ago." Carter replied.

Babineaux took in a long toke from the smoke and leaned his head back and closed his eyes as he savored the taste that filled his lungs. He let it out and then reached for the glass of bourbon on the table next to his chair.

"This may be harder than I expected but, none the less, it will be done. I am willing to up the ante if I must, and it looks as if I must." Babineaux said after a long pull from his glass. "Get me Gordon Landry. He will be found in the same little hole in the wall dive you found Chastain. Do you know who I am talking about Carter?"

"Yes sir, indeed I do. I will leave immediately." Carter said. "Will there be anything else before I embark on my search sir?"

"Tell him to meet me over dinner here, and run me a bath."

Deep in the lower parts of New Orleans, close to the shore of the Gulf of Mexico, where the sailors and sea rats dined up when they were not at sail, the local cutthroat's hang out was a small, out of the way pub, called "The Bloody Knife". The mist from the ocean hung heavy in the afternoon heat, after a rain blew through from the gulf and the sun brought the humidity up. The small building sat against a boardwalk that faced the water. It's wood facing was gray from the weather, and the stain of blood from the weary patrons that had fallen victim to the many low life regulars that frequently came to enjoy the flowing beverages of the establishment. Not too many days and nights went by that a soul was cut or stabbed after walking out with money hanging out of a pocket. Here one could find those who for a buck would cut the throat of a preacher in church during service. The men that occupied this out of the way tavern, were the lowest of the low, and it is here Carter knew he would find one Gordon Landry.

Carter came dressed in a gray shirt that fit loose to his body and old denim work pants with rough out boots in place of his shiny dress shoes. A felt hat was pulled down low on his face. He stepped into the Bloody Knife stopping just inside the door to look over the men inside. He found the man he was in search for standing at the end of the bar. The man wore a red shirt with its sleeves rolled up to his elbows showing large hairy arms. His pants were held up by suspenders and a leather belt was wrapped around his waist. The belt held a 44 caliber revolver in a holster and a long knife in a leather scabbard. Black hair hung to his shoulders from under a brown felt hat and his face was covered with a large black beard. He looked up and made eye contact with Carter who motioned him to meet him at a table to the left of the door, in a far corner of the not so large room. The large six foot four man nodded and came over.

"Mr. Landry..." Carter started to speak, but was hushed by the bearded cutthroat.

"Don't tell me, Babineux needs something dastardly done. Am I right or have you decided to come and hang out with the lower crust?" Landry said with a chuckle.

"Actually he would like to have the, ah...pleasure of your company for dinner this evening." Carter said.

Landry sat down in a straight back wood chair that creaked under his weight. He leaned back and laughed hard and loud. The amusement from what he had just heard was overwhelming in a sick kind of way.

"Well I am honored, probably for the first time in my life, Carter. Tell me what does the dapper bag of gold coinage have on his mind?" Landry said as he stopped laughing.

"He has an interest in a certain female that somehow got away from his control and he wants her back, unharmed." Carter said, in just over a whisper.

"Oh he does, does he? How much is he willing to pay to, shall I say, regain his control over her?" Landry asked.

"That is something that you and Mr. Babineaux will have to discuss. I'm sure that if your meeting goes favorably there will be some rather beautiful entertainment provided for you in one of his suites." Carter said knowing that's how his employer did business. A little added incentive in the cost of doing business never hurts. There are plenty of girls in Babineaux's bank of females that will take care of Landry with a little extra in their pay.

"Tell the old devil I will be there at 8 o'clock with bells on." Landry said as he stood up and walked back to the bar without another word.

The cobblestones, making up the streets that ran along the large side by side mansions in the French Quarters, amplified the sounds made by the shod horse Landry rode as he slowly made his way to the Babineaux house. He dismounted and walked up to the large double wooden doors just a few feet from the street. A steel door knocker hung on the face of the entrance to the mansion. He used it to pound the message that he had arrived. One of the doors opened inward and Carter appeared and with the motion of his hand directed Landry to enter.

The entrance to the home of Arthur Babineaux opened up into a large foyer with marble floors decorated in numerous colors and designs. The walls were all covered with stained hardwood and the furnishings were all built especially for Mr. Babineaux.

Carter led Landry down a hallway from the foyer into a large dining room. The walls there were lined with paintings from the great masters of the art world. The long hardwood table was stained and polished to a shine in that Landry could see his reflection. He took a seat to the right of the head of the table. Babineaux had not yet entered the room, still Carter filled a glass with water for the man and another with red wine.

"Tonight I will be serving Lamb with potatoes and carrots then cherry pie and cream sauce for dessert. I hope it is to your liking Mr. Landry." Carter said as he finished filling the wine glass for the second time.

"Yeah, that sounds right tasty. Where's Babineaux?" Landry asked as he turned up the glass of wine and poured it into his mouth. Drops of it rolled down the sides of his mouth and through his beard. He wiped it away with the back of his sleeve.

"He will be down momentarily."

Landry answered with a loud belch.

When Babineaux appeared, he wore the same silk robe from this morning. He had slippers on his feet lined with the same black silk. He held a glass of bourbon in his hand and a cigar in the other. His stride brought him quickly to the head of the long dining table where he sat down. He looked at Carter and nodded his head indicating it was time to serve dinner. Carter immediately turned and left the room.

"Landry, as you know I have a small little issue that requires someone of your quality, if you will, to deal with it. I am willing to pay quite a large sum of money at the completion of this task. Are you willing to listen to my issue?" Babineaux asked and then poured the last of his drink past his lips.

"Well, that just depends on the task you are requiring and how much is at risk for me." Landry said as he filled a crystal wine glass to its brim.

Babineaux leaned back in his chair and took a long drag from his cigar. He then laid it in a crystal ash tray that sat on the table to his right. The smoke from his lungs billowed high as he blew it out of his mouth. He stood and walked to a table holding several bottles of bourbon and brandy. He took a bottle from the table and returned to his seat. He sat after he filled his glass to the top.

"Is Bourbon more to your taste Landry?" Babineaux asked.

"Yep, fill her up." Landry said, pushing the wine glass toward his host after he downed the last gulp.

"I'm willing to pay you one hundred thousand dollars for the safe delivery of a beautiful lady. Do you think you can do that?" Babineaux asked. "I do mean safe delivery. No cuts, no bruises, no nothing...I mean completely intact in every way. Do you understand Mr. Landry?"

"Yes, I understand perfectly. She is to be brought to you completely intact with no bruises and no cuts and not assaulted in any way. I'm sure you are talking about her chastity. It is to be kept as innocent as the day she was born." Landry said reaching for the bottle of bourbon.

"That is exactly what I'm talking about. When you see her, you will know she is the one I am speaking of. Her name is Tammy Broussard and she is a mulatto with shining brown hair and hazel eyes that you will find so alluring that you might consider having a taste of this lovely creature. Yet, if you violate her in any way I can assure you that for the rest of your life, you will find it a requirement to always look over your shoulder at all times. Do I make myself clear Mr. Landry?" Badineaux said as he leaned forward and looked straight into the eyes of the man Landry.

"Is this who you hired Chastain and Charbonneau to find? They were bragging about being hired to do some high paying job months ago." Landry said.

"Yes, that Chastain is just a little too high on himself. I'm afraid he has either given up or found her and ran away to make his own fortune." Babineaux said, filling his plate from the platter of meat and vegetables Carter had brought in and set before the two men.

"He was always full of hot air." Landry said as he took a turn at the food.

"I received a letter from him some months back that said Tammy and her brother Julius got off of a steamboat in Natchez, Mississippi, and then crossed the river into Vadalia, Louisiana, and from there went west by way of mules and a wagon." Babineaux said before taking a bite of lamb.

"This Julius fellow, is he anything to worry about?" Landry asked.

"Not at all, he is not to be worried about, he is not a fighter. They were both raised in the home of a business acquaintance of mine in Baton Rouge. That is where I first saw her and decided then and there that I must have her." Babineaux said remembering back to that time and smiling at the thought of his future with Tammy in his flock of beauties.

Landry leaned back in his chair and rubbed the hair on his chin, giving the assignment thought. He knew Babineaux has deep pockets and he wanted as much of what is contained in those pockets as possible. He cut his eyes to the man that needs his services and looked through him with greedy eyes.

"Babineaux, I'm going to require riders to go with me. The more eyes there are looking for this girl the better. I really think a hundred and fifty thousand would buy the manpower that I will need." Landry said testing the waters of Babineaux's overflowing desires.

"One hundred and fifty thousand dollars is what you are telling me that you require?" The man asked trying to hold back the rage he found suddenly brewing inside of him.

"Look, it's going to take men...at least five good men to help track these people down from a trail that no longer exists." Landry said seeing Babineaux's blood boiling.

Babineaux got up and walked back to the table where more bottles of bourbon sat. He picked one and filled his glass again. Instead of going back to the table and sitting down he remained standing until the glass was empty. He filled it again and then returned to the table.

"Okay, I'll make it one hundred and fifty thousand dollars. You had better deliver or you get nothing." Arthur Babineaux said still fuming from Landry's demand.

"It's a deal. When I return with the little flower you pay me and then I will pay my men. I will expect cold hard cash." Landry said smacking his lips. "Now I'm ready for dessert. I mean the warm and soft kind of dessert." Landry said wiping his mouth with his sleeve.

"Sure thing Landry...go up the stairs to the first room on the left. I hope you like them hefty." Babineaux said with a sordid smile.

Judge Nichols made his way up the steps to the office of Doctor Micah Roundtree a frontier sawbones that drifted down from Missouri after the war. He had served as surgeon in an infantry regiment that mustered out of Springfield in late 1862. Before that he attended medical school in St. Louis. He felt like the southern air was better for his breathing. The move also came well requested if not demanded by a jilted lover that bore the same last name as the state's governor. One story claimed it was his oldest daughter.

"Oh, Judge, come on in. I was just going over the patient and I believe he will pull through just fine," the doctor said, looking over his wire rimmed glasses. His blonde hair was in the process of turning gray and it had begun to thin as well. He stood about five feet ten inches tall but was broad through the shoulders and still carried himself with plenty of spry agility. A black vest covered a white cotton shirt with the sleeves rolled up and his black pants were clean but wrinkled somewhat from sleeping in them all night watching over Bill Daily, his only patient.

"I'm glad to hear it. I just hope we don't have a mob form to come and haul the man away and lynch him" Judge Nichols said, as he walked over and stuck his head in the door of a room set up for patients.

"Yes...well I was able to get the ball out of him and stop the bleeding. He has been unconscious ever since he was brought in but he is breathing fine but very shallow and he has a good heartbeat. He will pull through." The doc added.

Judge Nichols sat down in a straight back chair next to Doc Roundtree's desk. The doctor took a seat at the desk and immediately pulled open a bottom drawer and removed a bottle and two glasses. He filled them both half way and handed one to the Judge.

"With Beau gone after those other gang members I feel a need to question the patient once he comes awake, if it's all

317

right with you." Judge Nichols said, as he sipped the whiskey from his glass.

"I don't see why not. I think we should try and find out as much about this gang of men as we can. You were once the Sheriff here, so you know how to get the truth out of people." The doctor said as he looked over his glasses at the Judge.

"Doc..." came a voice from the patient's room.

Doctor Roundtree and Judge Nichols both stood up and walked into the room. There Bill Daily was trying to sit up in the bed. His face contorted from the pain in his chest.

"Here I am son. You sit still and just lay back and relax." The Doc said as he fluffed the pillow for his patient.

"I just want to talk to somebody about all of this that has happened." Bill said as he laid his head back.

"We want to hear what you've got to say but you have to stay still. We don't want your wound to open back up and cause you to bleed to death." The doctor said as he filled a glass with water. "Here drink this because you need to get as much fluid in you as possible."

"Do you feel like talking now, son?" Judge Nichols asked.

Bill took a swallow or two of water and shook his head yes. "I would like to if I can."

Judge Nichols pulled a chair up to the side of the bed and sat down next to the patient. "What is your name?"

"My name is Bill Daily. I worked at the cotton gin with those other men except the one called Sal Maselli. We served in the Union Army during the war. We deserted at Vicksburg and came here and went to work for Mr. Walker."

"Who killed the Walkers, Bill?" The Judge asked hoping he would tell him the truth.

"I believe Sal is doing all of the killing. He is a very mean man. He went into the Walker's house with Luther and Archie Frank. There was two shots fired and he was the only one with a pistol when they went inside. They come out with a few guns." Bill said as he took another sip of water.

"What about at the Wright's horse farm?"

"Sal went in the house alone. That was after he took off all of his clothes." Bill said.

The doctor and the judge looked up at each other. It was said that Mrs. Wright was brutalized in the worst way and that she was nude when her body was found. Doctor Roundtree pulled his glasses off and went outside to take another drink of whiskey.

"What about the other men. Can you tell me who they are?" The judge asked.

"There's Luther, Archie and Cletus who are all brothers. I don't think Luther and Archie like Cletus to much because he is simple minded. Then there is Ned Brundage and a guy we all call Taterhead. You'll know him if you ever see him. His head is shaped like a potato." Bill said as he held his chest where the round ball from Sals pistol hit him. "That Sal though, is a mean one."

"It sounds like it." Judge Nichols stated as he received a glass of whiskey from the Doc as he came back to the room.

"Yeah...after we all left the Walker's house he hauled off and hit Ned Brundage just because he reached over and grabbed a leather bag Sal carries with him. He was trying to help carry things after we left the big house. Sal told us all that if any of us

319

touched his bag, he would kill us." Bill said with fear in his eyes. "I believe he meant it too."

"I think you're right Bill. What about the bank?" Judge Nichols asked.

"I didn't go in the bank. Luther, Archie and Sal did. Sal came out last. Did someone get hurt, Judge?" Bill asked, knowing in his mind that if Sal was involved someone very likely did.

"Yes...two men were stabbed and killed," the Judge answered.

"Sal was the only one that went inside that carries a knife on his belt." Bill said with tears for the victims rolling down the side of his face. "Judge, I shouldn't had been with those men. I had been telling myself that ever since Sal Maselli showed up. I am so sorry Judge, please believe me."

Judge Nichols leaned up and rested his forearms on his thighs. "Bill, I believe you. Get you some rest. We may talk again after you gained some of your strength back."

Judge Nichols stood up and he and the doctor started to the door. Bill reached his hand out to the judge and stopped him.

"Judge Nichols, are they going to lynch me? Bill asked his voice shaking with sorrow.

"We're not going to let them do that Bill."

The judge and the doctor walked back into the examining room and sat back down at the same desk and the same bottle of whiskey. Both men were without words after hearing all that Bill Daily had just told them. The judge pulled a letter out of his jacket pocket and unfolded it.

"The Sheriff received this bulletin this morning concerning an incident over by San Augustine. It says here that a farm was attacked by an unknown individual or individuals a few days ago and the whole family was murdered. The person responsible used a knife in two of the killings and the third victim had bruises on and around the throat." Judge Nichols explained as he held the letter.

"Do you think it's this man Sal Maselli?"Doc Roundtree asked.

"It probably is, but it's always best to make sure concerning these things. I'll have a note sent over to San Augustine and let them know what has happened here and a possible suspect might be this Maselli character." Judge Nichols said as he got up and started to the door of the Doc's office.

"I'll let you know if Bill says anything additional about the case. I would like for him to get as much rest as possible." Doc said as he opened the door.

The doctor watched Judge Nichols walk down the steps from the balcony outside his office. A man dressed in dirty work clothes approached the Judge quickly with a sour look on his face. The doctor stood and watched as the man came up to the Judge.

"Judge, are we going set back and let that bank robber up there lay up on the county's dollar. I say we drag him out here and string him up." said Hank Neely, a local loud mouth that thinks because he is big and loud that everybody should stop and get out of his way. He was wearing clothes covered in dirt from the fields that he farms just south of town. Truth is, Hank is a hard working man that raises a large amount of peas and corn that he sells locally to a lot of the people in town. He towering form stood a good foot above Judge Nichols and his large hands were rough and his fists were hard, still Judge Nichols looked him in the eyes.

"We're not stringing up anybody in this county until there is a fair trial. Now shut your yap and get out of my face." Judge Nichols said with the confidence of a young man.

"You ain't the Sheriff no more…" Hank said with his finger in the judge's face.

Suddenly a hard right fist from Judge Nichols landed on the left side of Hank Neely's face. The big farmer fell backward and landed flat on his back. Dust flew up from the street he landed on that caused the man to cough and spit. He got up in a huff.

"What do you mean hitting me?" asked Hank Neely while rubbing the side of his face.

"There will not be a lynching in this town and the first man that brings out a rope is going to get a load of buckshot. I better have made myself clear on that. I hope I said it loud enough for every person in this town to hear me." Judge Nichols said in a strong voice that echoed through the buildings and alleys of the city.

"That ain't right what you did to me Judge. Hell, I voted for you when you got elected to be County Judge." Hank Neely cried while he still held his face.

"I was the only one that ran for the office you lunkhead…now git." Judge Nichols said as Neely staggered away rubbing his face.

"I guess you better come up and let me take a look at that hand." Doc Roundtree said still standing at the top of his stairs.

"Yeah, I may have just broken it." Judge Nichols said shaking his head.

Chapter 18

Jake Powell rose early and found that Tammy was up making breakfast for him before he saddled up and rode to the Hollingsworth ranch to buy a bull for the cow herd. She was as pretty as a spring morning in the yellow dress with little red flowers Mrs. Edge at the general store gave her. The dress fit her perfectly as did all of the dresses Mrs. Edge gave her. She had become the daughter Mrs. Edge had never had, but wanted. Tammy was amazed at how uplifting it was to go visit her at the store just up the road from the ranch. She had planned to ride the black up there some time this morning to go over final plans for the wedding that was fast approaching, as well take a few lessons in sewing.

The door to the dining and cooking room of the dog run cabin was open letting the heat from the stove out as Tammy prepared eggs, bacon and biscuits for her, Jake and Julius who was up and had gathered the eggs. Jake fed the horses and looked over the garden for vegetables that were ripe for picking. After the morning meal, it was off for the Hollingsworth Ranch for the bull for Jake's herd.

"Everything tastes really good Tammy. You sure are a good cook. I'm afraid after we get married I'm liable to get fat off this cooking you do." Jake said, as he downed the last of the coffee in his cup and wiped his mouth.

"Oh I will make sure you don't get fat with all of the farm work you will be doing." Tammy said, as she collected the dishes from the table and placed them in a bucket with soapy water to wash them. She always kept the cabin spotless which gave her even more incentive to decorate it.

"That sounds good to me Ma'am." Jake said as he stood and walked over to where Tammy was washing the dishes.

He walked up behind her and wrapped his arms around her slender waist and pressed the side of his face to hers. They just stood there together saying nothing for a few minutes before Jake turn her loose. She turned and faced him, followed by a long passionate kiss. When she pulled away she fanned her face to cool the heat of the moment.

"I better get going. I told John I would be there before ten o'clock and I don't like being late". Jake said. "I'll take the short cut through the woods and along the creek to get over there. I'll probably come back that way." Jake said as he grabbed the Henry 44 rifle and started out the door. He had promised Tammy he would put his pistols away in a trunk at the foot of his bed and not wear them again. His Henry from then on was his constant companion in the saddle. He had already saddled the buckskin and left him tied in front of the house. He saddled up and rode away as Tammy stood on the porch of the cabin and waved and smiling her sweet smile that she always has for the man she loves.

As Jake rode through his place toward a gate he and Julius placed in the split rail fence, he thought more of the things he wanted to do on his ranch. He thought about how thankful he was that Mr. Tunstall, Sarah's father, acquired the property. He never knew how he acquired it and, really, at this point in his life, it didn't matter. Still, there was not a day go by that he didn't think about Sarah and the children. He knew Tammy was aware of his thoughts, yet Tammy understood. She told him she knew he would miss them and that, as time went by, it would be easier on his heart. She had also told him that she would never expect Jake to completely forget about the first love in his life. The memory of the children would always dwell in his mind even after he and Tammy had children of their own.

Jake reached the gate that left his ranch and he rode along San Pedro Creek to get to the road that turned south. After an hour's ride, he should be at the Hollingsworth Ranch. He enjoyed the ride through the wooded area. He always saw plenty of deer and squirrels that still made up most of the meat for his table. He knew that when the weather turned cold it would be time to harvest a few for their meat supply. The smokehouse he and Julius had built was a dandy and it held plenty of meat. He traded eggs and vegetables from the garden to a local hog farmer for a pig to butcher and smoke. He was thankful for the wonderful neighbors he found.

Jake rode up the lane toward the Hollingsworth house where he was greeted by Mrs. Hollingsworth who always had cool lemonade to drink. She stood on the porch and greeted him with a wave of the hand. Mr. Hollingsworth was there waiting as well. He had grown attached to Jake and Tammy. Both he and his wife looked to them as their adopted children since he and his wife lost both of their sons in the war.

"Jake my boy, come on up and get something to cool for your throat. We are glad to see you as always." Hollingsworth said, as he extended his bear paw like hand for a shake.

"How's that sweet Tammy?" Mrs. Hollingsworth asked as she embraced Jake and gave him a squeeze.

"She is as sweet as ever. She is counting the minutes until the wedding. I have to admit, I am too." Jake said.

"We are looking forward as well. I just love a wedding and we are going to make it a beautiful one too. You just wait and see." Mrs. Hollingsworth said as she handed Jake a glass of lemonade. You two talk while I go in and get some things done about the house."

"It's always good to see you Ma'am." Jake said as he tipped his hat.

"Sit down Jake and let me tell you about the bull I've picked out for you. Oh, and by the way, it is a gift to you and Tammy from me and Mrs. Hollingsworth." John said as he took a seat. "He is a dandy and he is wearing his working britches too. Let's go look at him. I know you are hankering to get an eye on him."

After Jake left the ranch Tammy went to the barn and saddled the black to ride to the store in Augusta. There she had planned to look at a batch of new material and patterns Mrs. Edge had just received from Dallas. She was excited to learn how to make her own clothes and shirts for Jake and Julius. She was especially excited about making baby clothes. Her intention was to make a lot of baby clothes for little boys and little girls.

"Where you headed Sis'?" Julius asked as he walked into the barn with an axe in his hand.

"Up to the store…is there anything you need while I'm gone?" she asked before she took the reins and led the big horse out of the barn.

"I don't guess…thank you so much for asking. I'm going to split and stack all the firewood I cut yesterday. We should have plenty for the winter with all I have piled up." Julius said as he sat down at a grinding wheel to put an edge on the axe.

"I hope to be back by the time Jake gets home." Tammy said as she rode away.

"Sal, it's time we turn north. If we keep going, there ain't no telling where we will wind up." Luther said as the bunch rode along the El Camino Real also known as the Old San Antonio Road.

Sal looked over at Luther with a look that told Luther Sal was not amused with his input. Still Sal intended on bailing out on this bunch at first trouble. They were nothing more than a scapegoat if the law ever caught up to them. He had no intention of going down if he can put all of the blame for all he had done on Luther and his brothers. Sal saw his way of thinking as self-interest. He had no feelings for any of these men, nor anyone else for that matter. Sal cared only for himself and nothing more.

"Okay here is a road that turns north. Hopefully it will take us toward Dallas and not dead end." Sal said as they approached an intersection. "What does that sign say up ahead?" Sal asked not wanting to admit he didn't know how to read. He wasn't sure if any in the bunch did.

"I can't make it out." Ned said.

"Me neither." said Archie acting like he was squinting in effort to see the sign.

"It says Augusta." Luther said, as he rode past and made the turn north. The others looked around at one another in amazement.

Beau Jamison was moving at the crack of dawn trying to catch up to the bank robbers. He crossed the Neches River and was glad to see the tracks he had been following were still visible in the dirt road he traveled. There was not much travel over this road, maybe a few wagons, so the path the gang of outlaws took was easily tracked. He hoped there would be no other innocent souls cross the paths of these men. He knew if there were, there was a possibility another murder would be committed.

Sheriff Jamison kept the tracks in sight as he made his way west. He felt in his guts that he was getting closer and closer to the gang. He didn't believe he would be able to take them down by himself but he had nobody else he could call on to help that he knew. He knew the Sheriff of Houston County was a long way away in Crockett, which is another day's ride away. He hoped to catch up to the outlaws just before they reached that town.

"Thank you so much for showing me these fabrics and patterns Mrs. Edge. I just can't wait to start making clothes for Jake and all of the babies we will have." Tammy said as she took her last sip of tea from the fancy tea cup Mr. Edge loved to serve with. She hardly ever got the chance before Tammy and Jake moved to her tiny East Texas community.

"Oh dear, you are so welcome. I am looking forward to teaching you everything I know about making clothes and quilts and canning and all the other things a wife needs to know." Mrs. Edge said before she took a bite from a tea cake she had made to have with the tea. They were from her recipe and she promised to share them all with Tammy.

"I want to learn everything I can from you. Nothing would please me more than to make Jake the happiest man in the world." Tammy said as she placed her hand over her heart and closed her eyes picturing in her mind the man she so dearly loves.

"Well you come back anytime and I will show you anything you want to see. I'm supposed to get a bushel of figs and I'm going to make preserves if you'd like to help me. You will learn it quickly. You are a very smart girl." Mrs. Edge said as she put her arm around Tammy giving her a squeeze.

"I will, I just know Jake would like your fig preserves." Tammy said as she turned to the door of the store to walk out.

"This looks like a quiet little place, too small to have a bank to rob." Arch said as the bunch rode into Augusta. "There is a livery stable with a trough to water."

The livery stable sat across the dirt street from the general store. It was where the locals could find the blacksmith Horace Luker. He was a salty old chap that lived in this area all of his life. His family was one of the first to settle this part of East Texas. He learned blacksmithing from his father who lived to be ninety nine years old. Horace was in his middle sixties and still put in a day's work. He walked out of his shop when the gang of outlaws rode up to his horse trough and dismounted.

"Howdy fellers," Luker said as he walked out of this blacksmith shop and livery. He held a cup of coffee in his hand. "That is the coolest water in these parts that comes up out of the ground at that well head. Just hit that pump a lick or two and you'll see." His head was covered with gray hair streaked with strains of black and his beard looked the same. He wore a pair of bib overalls without a shirt and his shoulders were a dark tan from the sun. "Where y'all headed?"

Sal and Luther gave each other a quick glance and then gave the old man a fake smile. They did not want to draw any unwanted attention to themselves so they put on the best smiles they could conjure up. The others just looked down at the ground hoping nobody paid them much mind or no mind at all.

Across the street Tammy walked out of the general store and turned to give Mrs. Edge one last hug. Sal looked across and saw her and quickly his mind decided he had to have her. She was the most beautiful woman he had ever seen in his life and right then and there his evil heart took control of his mind. He stood next to his horse and looked over the saddle toward this lovely girl that he had now chose to be his next innocent sufferer of his twisted game of pleasure. He watched her as she stepped from the porch of the store and climbed on her horse. She rode down the street and then turned and rode south.

"What are you studying Sal?" Luther asked as he looked over the back of his horse and tightening the girt of his saddle.

"Luther, why don't you mind your own business for once?" Sal said never taking his eyes away from Tammy's direction. "I'm going that way."

"Okay Sal." Luther said with a loud sigh. "We're right behind you."

Tammy rode up to the ranch and found Julius hard at work chopping wood. He had a large stack of hardwood neatly standing against the back wall of the three-room dog run cabin. The wood was under the covering of the porch which wrapped completely around the house. The wood should be enough to keep them warm and cook their meals next winter and the covered porch will keep it dry. Julius returned the axe to the tool room of the barn and returned to the house and met with Tammy.

"So what all did you and Mrs. Edge do?" Julius asked as he wiped the sweat from his face with a bandana.

"We had a very enjoyable morning. She showed me all of the new fabrics she just got in at the store and several patterns for shirts I intend on making for you and Jake. We had tea and tea cakes which were delicious. I must make some for you and Jake." Tammy said as she smiled when she said the name of the man she loves.

"I believe the wood I chopped will be sufficient for the winter." Julius said as he looked up and saw several riders coming up toward the ranch. "Now who is this I wonder?"

"I don't know. I wish Jake was here." Tammy said with concern. Any stranger gives her a reason to be concerned.

They watched the men ride up to them. There were six in all and they all looked like they could use a bath. One kept his eyes on Tammy as they all dismounted. The one that kept looking at Tammy walked straight up to her and looked down at her. She gave him a defiant look.

"What do you want?" Tammy said with a voice that showed her displeasure with the sudden intrusion.

Sal smiled and pushed his hat back away from his eyes. He gave Julius a glance and then turned his eyes back to Tammy. He looked her up and down and in his mind he imagined the tender soft flesh that lay just below the yellow cotton dress she wore.

"Well, you see that's a very easy question to answer, Ma'am." Sal said. "You see what I want I always get. When I saw you coming out of that little hick store back there in that little hick town, I decided I wanted you."

Suddenly Julius took a stance to defend his sister and without warning Sal drew his pistol and shot Julius between the eyes. Skull fragments, blood and brain matter exploded from the back of Julius' head as his body wilted and fell to the ground motionless.

Tammy screamed and tried to run to her brother's side but she was grabbed by the big man who stood in front of her. He forced her hands together and he used a leather strap he kept on his saddle to tie her hands together. She tried to fight him off but he was too strong for her. A bandana was used to tie around her head and pulled tight between her lips to keep her from making much sound. The man grabbed her beautiful long brown hair and pulled her up toward his saddle. She relented to the pain and went to her tip toes. Sal mounted his horse while holding her by the hair and then he lifted her up and put her on the saddle in front of him. Tears burned her eyes as she tried to scream. She tried to turn to see the body of Julius lying on the ground in front the cabin but when she did Sal forced her head down as he spurred the horse and the gang of outlaws followed him. They headed north toward Augusta.

Cletus looked on with a hurt frown on his face as the image of what he saw at the horse ranch filled his mind. He looked at this beautiful young woman as a little doll not to be treated roughly and with ill regard. He was afraid for her. Afraid Sal would treat her the way he did that poor woman he watched this mean man kill.

The riders with Tammy road back into Augusta to find the road that would take them north. Luther had no way of

333

knowing what Sal had planned for this pretty young woman they just kidnapped. Maybe for a ransom or maybe to use the girl as a shield in case the law got after them.

It only took a few minutes to get back to town. As they rode to the intersecting road in the middle of town they saw the store lady sweeping the front porch of the store. The riders spurred their mounts and went to a gallop as they passed her by. They saw the woman look up and with a shocked look saw the young girl Sal was clinging to.

"Oh my Lord, that's Tammy on that horse with those men. Walter...Walter." Mrs. Edge shouted as she hurried back into the store.

"What is it dear...you sound like there's trouble." Mr. Edge said, as he walked from the storage room of the store.

"Those men that rode through in such a hurry had Tammy. One was holding her and it looked like she was tied up and her mouth gagged." Mrs. Edge exclaimed as she turned and went back outside.

She looked down the street toward the livery stable and blacksmith shop and saw Jeremiah Gray standing in front talking to Horace Luker. They were both looking up the street and saw the riders come through. She took a deep breath and yelled for him.

"Jeremiah...oh Jeremiah, come quick I need you." Mrs. Edge yelled.

The young man heard and darted across the way to the front of the general store. He was a seventeen year old nephew of Horace who was training him to take over the livery and blacksmith shop. Jeremiah's lanky body covered the distance quickly and he came to a stop in front of Mrs. Edge.

"Yes Ma'am, what's the matter." Jeremiah asked not at all out of breath.

"I need you to saddle up and ride to the Hollingsworth Ranch and fetch Jake. Somebody took Tammy. Tell him they went north on the road out of town." Mrs. Edge instructed.

"Yes Ma'am, I'll do it." Jeremiah said as he turned and ran back to the livery and blacksmith shop.

Jeremiah was known for having the fastest horse in this part of the county and he was saddled up and had his sorrel mare stretched out in a hard run in no time.

The outlaw gang slowed their pace after riding hard for a good ten miles out of Augusta. Their horses cooled off as the men slowed to a canter. The prisoner started squirming after the horse that carried her went to a walk. The man that took her grabbed her hair again and viciously pulled her face up to meet his. His voice had a low evil growl when he spoke.

"Little gal, I will cut your throat and leave layin in the dirt of this road if you give me anymore problem. Do I make myself clear?" Sal threatened.

Tammy shook her head to let him know she understood. She knew all she had to do is stay calm and alive. Once Jake saw Julius shot dead and horse tracks left by these men he will be on their trail and he will get her back. She trusted him and she trusted his ability to protect her.

"That's better...you and me are going to get along just fine." Sal said in a sordid voice. "Tonight you and me are going to acquaint ourselves with each other. I might just make you my little toy. You are quite lovely and I love little beauties like you."

She wanted to throw up the tea cakes she had just had with Mrs. Edge. Tammy hoped that when they rode through town, her sweet friend saw her and knew she had been taken against her will. She got a good enough look at Mrs. Edge as she looked up from her sweeping to see the shocked and confused look on her face. All she could do is wait on Jake to find her.

Beau Jamison kept the tracks of the horses he was trailing in his sights as he made his way west. He came upon the intersecting road that was marked with a sign that read Augusta and an arrow pointing north. He studied the horse tracks that went in the direction of the little town. He had to take a chance and follow the tracks. He knew it was a long shot since there had been horse travel on this road and he was at a point that a chance was all he had. He turned his horse north.

"What did you see?" Walter Edge asked his wife.

"These riders come through from the south road and they had Tammy with them. They were riding like the law was after them." Mrs. Edge said as she paced back and forth on the front porch of the general store.

"Oh goodness Julius, I better go check on him" Mr. Edge said with a start. "I'll ride out to the ranch and see if he is okay. I'll be back."

Mr. Edge hurried to the livery stable to saddle up his mule to make the ride to Jake's ranch to see if Julius knew about Tammy being taken. He could still climb aboard the trusty animal even at his older age. He used her to coon hunt in the Neches River bottoms at night with some of his friends in the area that owned hunting dogs. He contributed this activity as keeping him healthy and spry.

As Walter Edge rode up to Jake's cabin he saw the grizzly sight left by the men that took Tammy. He got off of the mule and sat down on the porch of the cabin wiping his face from the sweat the stress of seeing such a sight produced. He was too old to go to fight against the north so seeing such carnage from violence was something he had never been exposed to. He thought what to do now but all he could come up with is to wait on Jake to come home.

Jake took the trail off of the road to take the short cut back to his ranch. The bull in tow didn't give any resistance since he was raised from a calf like a pet. He knew when he was being led to just cooperate because good feed and hay was always waiting at the end of the walk. He had no idea that at the end of this walk was a pasture of lush green grass and a herd of yearling heifers that were approaching their breeding age.

The trail along the creek was easy for the buckskin and the bull to navigate since Jake had been using it enough to beat down the weeds and briars. San Pedro Creek ran east and west and always had a flow to it. Jake, Tammy and Julius had enjoyed the abundant catfish from the creek ever since they arrived to the area. The creek runs off of the Neches River and keeps them in a goodly supply of table fare. Jake had been seeing a few gator skids along a more secluded part of the creek between the ranch and the river. Julius and Tammy both had assured him that the tail off of one of those big monsters was sure good to pass a palate.

Jake saw his gate come into view after a one hour ride down the back trail. He anticipated the bull's reaction to being put in the pasture with the herd and he hoped he was right in his feelings. When he went through the gate he brought the bull around and the heifers came into view. Jake closed the gate and then took the halter off of the bull's big white head. He was red with a white face just like the heifers and promised to produce a lot of calves. The bull raised his head and took in the scent of the females and let out a deep bellow before he headed their way. The introduction into the herd will soon begin. Jake smiled and shook his head.

"Mr. Hollingsworth said you were wearing your working britches. I guess he was right."

Jake mounted back up and headed to the cabin looking forward to seeing the woman he loves. He always surveyed the pastures as he rode through them. He took notice of any dead trees that might need to come down and chopped up for firewood. It was just something he became accustomed to doing since he acquired the land. It was his responsibility and he was going to live up to it. As he approached the cabin he saw the mule and Mr. Edge sitting on the front porch. He also saw the dead body of his friend Julius.

"What happened? Where is Tammy?" Jake asked as he jumped down from the buckskin.

"Tammy was taken by some men Jake. They must have killed Julius. Mrs. Edge said they rode north on the road out of town." Mr. Edge reported.

Jake looked down at his friend and then looked up toward the cabin and hurried to the door of his room. He went straight to the foot locker that sat at the foot of his bed and quickly opened it up. There were his gun belt and the twin Colt 44 revolvers along with his hand forged Bowie knife with a leather pouch that held powder, shot and caps. He snatched up the belt and strapped it around him and walked back outside. He slung the pouch around his shoulder. Mr. Edge was looking around

338

the ground at the tracks left by the riders that killed Julius and took Tammy.

"Jake you can tell there are several of them, so be careful." Mr. Edge said as he grabbed the reins of his mule. "I'll come back with the Justice of the Peace after the Sheriff can be located and they all make the trip out here."

"Okay...I'll be back with Tammy as soon as I can. How long ago do you think they rode off with her?" Jake asked as he mounted up.

"I'm figuring better than two hours." Mr. Edge said scratching his head in thought.

Jake shook his head in disgust and said, "They are way out ahead of me and I know they are riding hard."

You might stop at the store and ask Mrs. Edge what she saw." Mr. Edge said as he reined the mule around. "We will get Julius taken care of too. I'm right behind you."

In a few minutes Jake rode hard up to the front of the general store where Mrs. Edge was back to pacing on the front porch. She had already made two canteens for Jake because she knew he should be riding up and she knew finding Tammy might take longer than she hoped.

"Did Jeremiah catch you Jake? Those awful men took Tammy." Mrs. Edge said in tears.

Jake took the two canteens and hung them on his saddle horn. He pulled the Henry from his saddle scabbard and checked to see that it was loaded to the maximum. A rider approached as Jake got off the buckskin to tighten up the saddle girt. He glanced up but after a quick view he went back to his task at hand.

"Mr. Edge said that they had about two hours on me or more." Jake said as he mounted up.

"I'd say or longer." Mrs. Edge said. "Please bring my girl back Jake. Those men looked mean and desparate."

"I'll be back with Tammy as soon as I can." Jake said as he turned the buckskin and headed to the north rode.

Mr. Edge was also riding up as Jake left in a rush. The other rider rode up to the general store and pulled off his hat. A silver star hung from his shirt.

"How are y'all, I'm Sheriff Jamison from Nacogdoches." Beau said as he looked at each of the people in front of him.

"Walter when Jeremiah gets back, send him to get our Sheriff." Mrs. Edge said.

'I'll do it, looks like Jeremiah is coming now." Mr. Edge said, seeing Jeremiah

"I'm looking for a gang of men that might be in the area." Beau Jamison said trying to get anybody's attention.

Jake headed north on the north road. He didn't have time to talk. His attention was on finding these men and Tammy. He pushed the buckskin, leaving the rest still looking at each other at the general store.

Jeremiah rode up and jumped off his horse and leaped to the porch where Mr. and Mrs. Edge stood. Mrs. Edge was telling Sheriff Jamison what she had seen and what direction they were headed.

"This bunch of men come riding through Sheriff Jamison and they had Tammy with them and I know she didn't go on her own. She would never do that. She's about to be married to Jake, the man that just took out after them."

 Beau Jamison reined his horse around and took out after Jake. He was determined to not let these men get away, and he was not going to let the man in pursuit of them as well have to deal with them alone.

"Jeremiah, go to Crockett and get the Sheriff. Tell him what has happened and to bring a wagon" Mr. Edge ordered.

"I sure will Mr. Edge. I know I'm getting my riding in today, but Mr. Edge, why the wagon?" Jeremiah asked as he climbed back into the saddle.

Mr. Edge knew Jake loved Tammy so much that when he caught up to those men that took her that their day of reckoning will have arrived. "For the bodies Jeremiah," Walter Edge said as looked at the young man.

Jeremiah stared back at Walter Edge trying to absorb what the older man had just said. He looked up to Jake Powell and knew he was a good man and a good example for him. He never looked at him as a killer, but sometimes those around us keep things locked away from everyone that not everybody knows about. The boy shook his head showing his understanding and rode away.

Walter Edge turned to his wife and said. "I know where you are headed."

"You sure do...I'm going to my prayer room and I do not want to be disturbed." Mrs. Edge said. "I'm about to pray down Heaven."

Chapter 19

Beau Jamison pushed his horse hard to catch up to Jake but had to back off when the horse began to lather up under the Texas sun. The best Beau could remember, it was still August which is the hottest month of the year. He didn't want to kill his horse so he reined him back and let him walk a bit to allow the horse to cool down. The feeling he had that he was getting closer to the bank robbing murderers grew stronger in his heart. He was concerned for the man ahead of him. He didn't want to see any more victims fall at the hands of these violent men he chased. He used the last of the water in a canteen to give the horse a bit too wet its mouth. After a few minutes of rest, he mounted up and trotted along while keeping an eye on the tracks left by the horses in front of him.

He hoped the man giving chase would slow down as well so he could meet up and tell him why he was after these men. It might give him cause to hold back, knowing how desperate they are but after rethinking the conversation with the man back at the store in Augusta he figured the lone rider ahead of him would keep going until he found them. He just hoped they didn't set up an ambush like they are known to do.

The thought crossed his mind to go ahead and administer judgment on the men when he finds them but his duty requires they be brought before a court of law and receive a fair trial. A fair trial to Beau Jamison was something these men did not deserve. Still the man in front of him in this chase weighed heavy on his mind. He didn't know what the man was capable of or if he had ever been in any situations that may involve gun play. He could only hope the man didn't get to close to these desperate men before he was able to catch up to him. He spurred the horse to a faster trot to try and catch up.

Jake and the buckskin kept a steady pace hoping to close in on the men that had Tammy. The horse was showing the endurance he always proved to have in every situation he was forced into. He slowed for a time to let the buckskin cool and then Jake spurred him back up to a run. The men he chased had stayed to the road going north. Jake noticed the tracks and how they changed telling him they slowed down to a trot and then to a walk. He hoped he was closing the distance between him and Tammy so he slowed as well keeping his eyes out for any threat. Along both sides of the road was thick forest of pine and hardwood that looked to go for miles and miles. It presented an abundant means of hiding from any passersby that happened along on this road. It was used by the few people who lived in this corner of the county. There were several small farms scattered about through the woods but not close enough to the road to notice riders that come through.

It was getting late in the day and Jake knew that he would have a hard time following the tracks left by the fleeing gang in the dark. He knew in his heart that he would not stop until he caught up to them. Making camp and starting back on the trail after the sun came back up was not an option for him. Through a break in the trees he could see storm clouds forming in the eastern sky which could be another obstacle in this chase. Yet Jake pressed on keeping his eyes on the trail left by these men that took Tammy.

He heard a rider coming up behind him. The horse was coming fast and wasn't slowing until he reached Jake. The rider was a tall man with a star on his chest.

"I'm Beau Jamison and I'm chasing those men that took your girl. I'm from Nacogdoches County where I'm the Sheriff." Beau said as came along side Jake.

"Jake Powell," He said as he extended his right hand.

"Jake, these men I'm chasing have committed several murders and are very cold blooded. I understand you and the girl are engaged to be married and I don't want to see anything happen to either of you so you might let me approach them when we catch up to them." Beau said trying to convince Jake to back up and let him handle these desperate men.

"What did you say your name was?" Jake asked trying not to sound like he was dismissing the Sheriff.

"I'm Beau Jamison, the Sheriff of Nacogdoches County. These men are dangerous so please let me handle them." Beau said still trying to stress how violent the outlaws are.

Jake sighed and looked down at the ground at the tracks they were following. He took one of the canteens and took a pull from the cool water it contained. He handed it to the Sheriff to let him drink before he spoke again. Beau took a swallow or two and gave it back to Jake before he hung it back on his saddle horn.

"You say these men are dangerous?" Jake said as he pulled the buckskin to a stop.

"Yes Jake, they are very dangerous…very violent. They have murdered several of my citizens and I don't want to see them kill you and the woman you love." Beau said as he leaned over his saddle horn and turning to make eye contact with Jake.

Jake shook his head and reined the buckskin off of the road down a lane that was used by loggers that cut the trees in the Neches River bottom. Beau watched Jake ride away without saying a word. He looked down at the dirt road and saw the tracks they were following had turned and headed toward the Neches River.

"Luther we need to think about making camp." Arch said as they walked their horses along a road that went parallel with the river. They had traveled along for about five miles and the woods they passed through began to grow dark from the sun getting low to the west.

"I think you're right. There ain't nobody after us. That little hick town back there where Sal took the girl didn't look like it had any able bodied men that would bother coming after us. Besides these people could care less about this young mulatto filly." Luther said as he pulled up to dismount.

Tammy heard what the dirty looking man said yet she kept her thoughts to herself. She knew Jake would come for her. He should be on her trail by now she thought, so she refrained from saying anything to the men.

Cletus could not keep his eyes off of her. He hoped that Sal would not do anything to hurt her. Cletus was smitten by her beauty and girlish figure and could not remember ever seeing a girl as pretty as this one. He thought it would be nice to be her friend and not let anything happen to her. If he protected her she might like him is how Cletus thought in his mind. He did not like her being in the company of Sal. He is mean and he might do to her what he did to the lady at the horse ranch. Cletus decided he was not going to allow that to happen.

"Sal, let's camp here. We need to let these horses rest, besides there should not be anybody behind us that would be a threat." Luther said as he unstrapped the saddle of the stolen horse he had been riding.

Sal dismounted but kept a hold of Tammy by the strap he bound her wrists together with so she wouldn't run away. He took the reins and led the horse and Tammy further down the river road to find a spot for them to camp. He had already decided he wanted to keep Luther, his brothers and the rest of them between him and any posse that might be on their trail. When any shooting started they would be his shield from any flying lead. He also wanted to have a nice quiet place away from them so he could do to Tammy whatever his flesh desired in private.

"You guys stay there and camp. The little lady and I are going to be on down the road. We may just have us a little moonlight rendezvous. Ain't that right my little plum?" Sal said in his deep evil voice.

Tammy tried to grit her teeth but the bandana that was tied tight around her head would not allow it. She looked straight ahead and kept her eyes down to the ground. She thought this big ugly man might take it as a sign of weakness but in her heart she knew that at the first chance she had, she would flee into the woods until Jake showed up. If it came down to it and she had to give her life for Jake she would with no hesitation. Tammy knew Jake would do the same for her. After this man killed Julius in cold blood, her heart desired a special kind of revenge. She also knew the man she loves is more than capable of dishing out, in this case, a lot of necessary violence.

"Mr. Edge, how long has this man Jake been gone in pursuit of these men?" Sheriff Doyle Sadler asked from the back of his white gelding. He was an average sized man who had been the Sheriff in the county for more than twenty years. He was a widower that poured himself into his job and spent many hours keeping the people of Crockett and the surrounding countryside safe. He was wore a palm leaf fedora hat with a wide brim cocked to one side of his head. His hair was gray and he stayed clean shaven and well dressed. He wore a gray coat and pants with a white shirt. His five pointed star hung from the lapel of his suit coat. A 32 caliber revolver hung from his left side and the butt of a lever action rifle showed from a scabbard on his saddle. There were four men that he had deputized riding with him that were well armed. Another man drove the wagon Mr. Edge had suggested the Sheriff bring with him.

"It's been several hours. There is no telling how far those men got before Jake was able to take off after them." Walter Edge said from the porch of his store.

"Jeremiah said your wife saw the girl they had with them." Sadler said as he took a bite from a twist of chewing tobacco.

347

"Yes, she was out here sweeping when they rode through. Tammy was being held by one of the men and it looked as if she was tied up." Walter said.

"Is your wife here?" Sadler asked.

"Yes, she is Sheriff." Walter answered.

"I need to talk to her if I may." The Sheriff requested.

"You can't do that right now. She is talking to someone with a little more authority than you, no disrespect." Walter Edge said.

"Is that right? Well there is nobody in my county got more authority than me...except God Himself." Sadler said as he worked his chaw in his mouth.

"Well Sheriff, that's who she is talking to as a matter of fact," Edge said with a crooked eyebrow.

"I guess we better leave her alone then." Sadler said as he pulled back the reins of his horse. "We will be heading north to see what we can find. Looks like a storms a comin.'"

Jake and Beau stopped as the sun set bringing darkness to the trail. They stopped and dismounted to give the horses a break from their burden. Nightfall came and the air was filled with sounds this portion of the day bought. Jake was hoping for complete quiet but the crickets and bugs that lived in the forests of East Texas kept a constant buzz that filled the forest along the Neches. Both men stayed quiet with their ears on high alert hoping for a sound that would give away the presence of the bad men and Tammy.

Beau kept his head constantly moving trying to catch the slightest sound from the men they sought. After several minutes he broke the silence with a whisper. "Do you know how far this road goes along the river?"

"No, I've never been this far north from Augusta. I'm not even sure what county we're in. To be honest with you Sheriff, I don't care." Jake said as he took in the night sounds.

In the dark Jake could not see Beau's face. If he could he would have known that he understood how he felt and that finding his sweetheart was the most important thing on Jake's mind. Beau Jamison still felt the sting of losing the posse that went after these murderous men and he aimed to see those bad men got was coming to them.

"Let's lead the horses and make our way up the river. Those men are bound to be close. As hard as we rode we had to have gotten within a few miles of them." Jake said as he took the reins of the buckskin and began walking up river along the road at the top of the bank.

Beau stayed close as the two men searched the darkness for any sign of a camp fire. He hoped the men were so sure that nobody had followed them that they gotten careless and decided to make a camp fire for the night. The threat of gators and cottonmouths will cause a man to not want to move around or even lay still at night in these river bottom woods but when desperate and hiding from the law, you will do some crazy things.

The two made another mile before they stopped to listen for sounds of men talking. There was no sound from people coming from the night so they kept moving at a slow pace trying to be as silent as possible.

"You know you are a very beautiful woman. What is your name?" Sal asked Tammy as she sat under a large pine tree. Her ankles were tied together and her wrists were still bound. The bandana in her mouth began to taste like sweat and man odor. She looked at Sal with a look that said 'You're stupid I'm gagged and can't talk.'

Sal got up from the seat he had made against another large tree and walked over to Tammy. He stood over her to show his dominance over her life. She never looked up at him. Tammy kept him in the corner of her eye and was aware of his every move. Suddenly Sal reached down and took her hair in his hand and pulled her to her feet. She wanted to scream but she was determined to not show this man she was in any pain. He pushed her against the tree she had been leaning against and his hands began to explore her body. His breath hit her in the face and it caused her to not exhale but just hold it because the smell of it was of pour evil. She thought of Jake and pleaded with God in a silent prayer to bring him quickly. Sal touched her in places and ways that Jake had never touched her and she hated it. In the distance she heard the sound of thunder and she hoped that it was the sound of retribution coming to take the life of this sordid man who took her away from the life she loved.

In the eastern skies a storm was brewing and it was moving west. The sky lit up as lightening flashed over the tops of the trees miles away. The wind began to move and the coolness of the wind felt good to Tammy. She turned away from the thoughts of what this awful man was about to do to her and concentrated on the wind that was caressing her skin. From it she felt a comfort that all was going to be fine.

Sal moved his hand down to the end of her dress and started pulling it upward. His sinister chuckle was not heard by Tammy because she had lost herself in her own spirit, a place Sal could not touch her.

"Luther, I don't like Sal being down there with that girl. He might hurt her." Cletus said as he looked north toward the campfire Sal had built for his camp.

Luther was sitting against a hardwood tree trying to go to sleep when Cletus spoke bringing him awake. Taterhead and Ned Brundage each had them a tree to prop their heads against and Arch was sharing the tree with Luther. All of which were trying to rest up to get back on the trail for Dallas at first light.

"Cletus, you need to go find you a tree to get under and not worry about what Sal is doing to that girl." Luther said as he turned over on his side and closed his eyes.

Their campfire was providing plenty of light to keep the gators and snakes away. Cletus walked back and forth ringing his hands in worry for the girl as his simple mind played the scene he saw at the Wright's horse ranch. The terrified look on the woman's face and the cruel deed performed against her by Sal. He walked toward Sal's camp and stopped and turned around. His mind again went back to the horse ranch and what he saw Sal do to the lady in her bedroom. He kept mumbled to himself as he paced back and forth.

"It ain't right what Sal did...It ain't right...It just ain't right." Cletus said over and over.

"Cletus what are you saying?" Arch asked. He could understand what Cletus was saying about a woman but didn't know why he was saying it.

"He did it to her Arch...Sal did it. It was a nasty thing he did to that woman and he might do it to that pretty little doll

351

yonder." Cletus said. This time Arch raised his head up and Luther did as well.

"What are you saying about a woman Cletus?" Arch asked.

Cletus still pacing back and forth said, "At the ranch...where we got horses...he did it. He did a nasty thing to that woman in her bedroom."

"What, Cletus are you talking about he did to that woman at the horse ranch?" Arch asked as he got up and approached his younger brother.

Cletus stopped in front of Arch and looked him in his eyes. Arch saw tears rolling down his brother's cheeks and into his beard. He had never seen Cletus act this way which in his mind he really didn't care, he just wanted him to be quiet.

"He ain't hurtin her Arch. He ain't hurtin that purdy little dolly. I ain't letting him" Cletus said as he turned and ran toward Sal's camp.

Sal pushed Tammy back to the ground as his hands explored her petite body. The expression on his face was that of a deranged deviant full of a demonic spirit of lust. He knelt down next to her and took the bandana out of her mouth and then pulled it from her head. Her long brown hair was in disarray and she shook her head to get it out of her eyes. She gave Sal a hard look as he took his knife from his belt. She could see the edge of it shine from the light of the campfire. He moved the knife to her throat and forced head back exposing the soft skin of her neck. He touched the edge to her silky flesh just below her jaw. He smiled at the thought of her blood pouring down her tender body. He then moved the knife to her ankles and cut the rope that had them bound together. He cut the laces off of

Tammy's boots. Mrs. Edge had just given them to her and the thought of this ugly smelling man damaging them sent a rage through her.

"I have to cut these off if I'm going to get to where I have thought about going ever since I saw you in that little hick town back there. When I saw you I knew I had to have you. I knew I wanted you to feel what every woman wants." Sal said as he took the boots from Tammy's feet. He moved his hand up her leg and onto her inner thigh as he chuckled low and demented. Overhead the skies lit up as the lightning flashed and the thunder rumbled.

"You are one evil man and there will never be a moment of what you do to me that I want nor will I enjoy." Tammy said through gritted teeth. The rage in her grew the further up her leg this evil man's hand touched her.

Suddenly Sal heard the sound of footsteps running up behind him. He turned just as Cletus approached with his hands extended in front of him. He grabbed Sal by the shirt and pulled him to his feet. Sal dropped his knife from the jar he received from the furious strength Cletus unleashed on him. There was rage in Cletus' face as he screamed at Sal.

"You ain't hurtin her. You ain't hurtin her like you did that woman at the horse ranch." Cletus screamed as he sent a hammer like fist toward Sal's face. The blow hit Sal in the face knocking him to the ground.

Cletus dove toward him and landed on him with his knees on his chest. Sal felt the wind leave his lungs and he struggled to get it back. Tammy took this opportunity to get up and run. She ran as hard and fast as she could into the darkness. Her wrists were still tied but she didn't care. She just had to get away from these men.

353

Sal got his breath back and hit Cletus in the side of the face with a hard right fist. Cletus fell off of Sal but quickly got up. Sal followed up with another right to Cletus' face causing his knees buckled but he managed to stay up. Sal tried to hit him with the same fist but Cletus lifted up his steel like left arm and blocked Sal's blow. Cletus followed with a punch to Sal's face that sent him to the ground on his back.

"You ain't hurtin her, I ain't letting you." Cletus screamed as he started for Sal again. He bent down to grab Sal by the shirt to lift him up but Sal brought both feet up and planted them in Cletus' stomach forcing him back and onto the ground behind him. Sal was up on his feet like a cat and attacked Cletus in a rage. Sal pinned his shoulders down to the ground with his knees then hit Cletus over and over in the face. His nose was broken and his eyes began to water as his own blood covered his face. Cletus lifted his right fist and planted it in Sal's temple. It stunned him and Cletus gave him another. He fell away from Cletus and lay on the ground next to him.

The others come running through the woods into Sal's camp. Cletus got up and was about to pick up a large tree limb that was nearby on the ground. His intentions were to finish off Sal for the evil he had done.

"Cletus leave it alone." Luther said as he raised his hands toward his younger brother in a pleading gesture.

Cletus picked up the stick of wood and turned to walk over to Sal when a loud report came from the pistol in Sal's hand. He had pulled it from the belt holster that was on the ground nearby. The round hit Cletus in the middle of the chest but didn't take him down.

"Cletus no..." Arch screamed as Cletus staggered toward Sal with the large chunk of wood in both hands raised over his head.

354

Another shot rang out and a 44 caliber ball hit Cletus in the face just below his right eye. The ball came out the side of his head and lodged in an oak tree. Cletus fell straight back like an axe-fell pine tree. Dust flew up as his large framed body landed on the dirt dead.

Sal began to look around for the girl but she was gone. The sky flashed and rumbled as the clouds ahead closed in over the camps.

"Those shots were close." Beau said as he looked into the darkness in the direction of the two gunshots.

Jake never said a word. He mounted the buckskin and spurred it forward. He trusted the horse to see in the dark where he could not. He just hoped for no snakes and gopher holes.

In the eastern sky, the storm flashed it's lightning as it grew and settled over the Neches River. The wind picked up as it got closer and closer. Thunder clapped and the clouds moving overhead rolled with rage and anger. Jake tied his reins together as a campfire came into view. It looked to be out of rifle range so he moved closer. When the buckskin brought him within range Jake pulled up on the reins and threw his left leg over and dismounted allowing the buckskin to run on into the stormy night.

Beau stopped as he saw Jake dismount. He tried to get Jake's attention but Jake paid him no mind. He didn't want Jake to rush in and get shot. He tried to catch up to him as he moved through the brush and trees that covered the floor of the forest. He dodged them the best he could. The flashes of lightening gave off enough light for his mind to take a picture of his surroundings. Ahead he could see Jake moving swiftly toward the camp ahead. He was too close to call out in fear of being heard. He could not believe this farmer was going to walk into camp and get shot. When they could hang back and pick them off or rush them and make them give up.

As Jake got closer to the light of the camp he saw men standing around and it appear as if they were arguing. He heard screaming and yelling back and forth coming from two of the men.

"I want that girl found do you hear me?" Sal screamed. "It's because of your stupid simpleton brother she got away."

"Look Sal just let her go." Luther said. "She was going to slow us down anyway."

"I'm going out there and find her." Sal screamed before he turned and walked hurriedly into the woods.

The others stood around looking at each other not knowing what to do. The thunder and lightning moved over them and they became concerned with the wind that was getting more intense as the clouds above them moved in. The flashes illuminated the wooded forest as the light show grew and grew.

Suddenly the thunder roared above them and the lightning streaked across the East Texas sky. They each saw the man standing not twenty feet from them. He faced them and the two pistols worn cross draw caught their eyes. The light went away and then returned showing the man was not there. The men begin to panic. They looked at each other in the light of the storm. They scrambled for their guns as concern showed on each of their faces. Luther and Arch filled their hands with iron and waited for the man to reappear. Thunder blasted in the sky and a bolt traveled across clouds once again bringing the vision of the man who had invaded their camp. When the light went dark shots rang out like the sound of thunder from the Heavens. Four shots were fired. Four men lay on the ground.

Beau Jamison felt his way through the brush and trees trying to find where the shots had come from. He saw Jake's position and continued on taking advantage of the lightning flashes and the illumination it presented. He saw Jake advance to where the men lay on the ground. He approached as Jake went to each man to see if they were any left alive. The streaks of light filled the sky and the thunder continued to roar with rage. Beau looked at the face of Jake Powell as the angry storm flashed in the night. He saw the face of a man that had no hesitation to kill if the need presented itself. Jake holstered his revolvers and walked into the darkness not saying a word. He walked to the other camp and saw Tammy's new boots lying on the ground. The laces had been cut before they were removed from her feet. He also saw in the glow of the campfire prints made by small bare feet that looked like they she made them running away. He followed Tammy's tracks into the darkness.

Beau knelt down by each one of the men in the camp. There were four men with holes in their chest left by the 44 caliber lead ball from Jake's revolvers. He was amazed at the accuracy of the man's shooting. He searched the pockets of the men and the saddle bags that he found nearby. A good amount of the money from the bank robbery was there. Thankfully they had not made it to a bigger town with girls and saloons to spend it on.

Beau walked through the woods to where the other campfire had been made. There was another saddle bag containing more of the money from the bank. Just a quick count of the money showed to be more than thirty thousand in cash. Another bag lay nearby as well. Beau opened it up and immediately found a white cotton nightgown. It appeared to have torn and he concluded with no doubt that it belonged to Mrs. Wright. He stopped his search through the leather bag when a thought shot through his mind. He saw the pair of ladies boots on the ground and figured they belonged to girl the men had taken. Another campfire meant another man. Another man in the darkness and the absence of the girl Tammy meant trouble was still brewing. The thunder grew louder and the lightening flash intensified as the storm lingered overhead.

Tammy had run as far as she could through the thick brush. Her feet felt like they were bleeding after she stepped on a limb that had a branch of it broken off leaving a blunt point. It was pointed enough to break the skin of her delicate foot. She stopped and crawled under a clump of brush. She had to use the light from flashes lightning above to see. The bright bolts streaked across the sky in different directions and it provided her with enough light from it to make her way but the pain in her foot would not let her go any further. She heard the reports of gunfire that sounded like there may have been trouble at the camp. She kept her eyes on alert to catch any movement from any of the men who kidnapped her.

The sky lit up and Tammy saw the man who had taken her from her home and killed Julius. She wasn't sure what she was seeing but it looked like the man was naked. Another flash from the sky lit up her surroundings and there he was again. This time he was closer and he was looking at her. His eyes met hers as the streaks of light traveled the heavens above them. His face was that of pure evil. As she looked into his eyes it was like peering into a demonic soul. As the lightning grew more illuminating she saw him approaching her as she sat on the ground under the brush. It was as if the devil himself was leading him to his victim. In the brightness from the flashes a glimmer came from something is his right hand. He had his knife and he was closing in on Tammy.

The sky lit up again and powerful thunder roared above them. Sal was inching closer to Tammy. He had made the decision to use his knife on her while he carried out his sordid assault on her beautiful body. The thought of her smooth young skin under his power took his desires to extreme as he slowly walked her way. Her screams brought an even more heightened level of excitement as he approached her. He quickly stopped when he heard a voice behind him. He turned to face the man who spoke.

"Hey you, naked man," Jake said, standing twenty feet behind Sal.

Sal stopped and turned around to face the one who is now in the way of his devilish work. Neither men spoke as they slowly approached one another. Jake unbuckled the gun belt around his waist and as he tossed the belt away he held the bowie knife in his right hand. The razor sharp edge flashed from the bursts of light from the sky. Sal held his knife out away from his body and took cat steps in the direction of Jake. Above the thunder rolled and the light streamed across the firmament as the two men squared off to do battle.

Tammy remained huddled under the brush where she had been hiding. In the flashes of light she saw Jake and her heart jumped. She wanted to run to him but could see that the naked man had turned to face him. She curled up and watched the two men, her hopes that Jake would survive and take her home traveled through her heart.

Slowly the men crept in circles as one anticipated the other to attack. Sal could wait not longer and charged Jake swinging his knife as he advanced. The blade made contact with Jake's side as Sal passed by in his attack. Quickly Jake felt the warmth of blood at it slowly seeped down his left side. Tammy screamed as she witnessed the blade make the cut in his shirt. Her heart sank when she saw in the flash of light the dark stain on Jake's shirt.

Sal again attacked wildly swinging the knife to make contact with Jake's body. This time Sal missed and then caught a hard left fist to the side of the face as Jake swung just as the blade made its way by his side. Sal was stunned but quickly recovered. He tried to stab the point of his knife into the stomach of his adversary but missed as Jake dodged the blade. As Sal passed by, Jake slammed his right fist that held the bowie knife into Sal's left side. The wind left Sal's lungs as two of his ribs cracked from the blow but his desperation kept him from falling to the ground.

Jake moved in to finish Sal off with a hard blow to the back of his head but Sal moved and Jake's blow missed leaving him open. Sal turned and caught Jake in the jaw with a huge right fist. Jake saw more lights flash as the blow made contact. He stumbled as Sal swung again with a left hook catching Jake in the face under his right eye. Jake fell to the ground...Tammy screamed.

Sal approached to finish Jake but it was the sound of Tammy's scream that jarred Jake's senses and caused him to get up and get up fast. He bolted to his feet as Sal closed in on him swinging the blade of his knife. Jake moved his knife and the blade met the muscle of Sal's right forearm. The razor sharp blade of the Bowie knife cut deep into Sal's arm causing him to drop his knife. It fell to the ground next to Sal's boot. Jake brought his blade around again and sliced Sal's midsection. The muscle was completely cut through and Sal's guts fell out. He caught them with his right hand and held them in pain. He stood and met Jake's eyes as the lightning above flashed bring illumination to Jake's face.

"I know you," Sal said as he moved his left hand over to help hold up his intestines that were protruding from the slash in his gut. "What's your name?"

Jake looked into Sal's evil eyes and saw wickedness defeated. The grip on the handle of his Bowie knife tightened as he stepped in close to the devilish face before him.

"Reb"

Sal's eyes widened in recognition for the man standing in front of him as Jake swung the Bowie knife in a backhand motion. The blade made contact with Sal's throat and traveled deep into his flesh to his spine and through his backbone. The strength Jake sent with the strike took Sal's head completely off. It tumbled to the ground as Sal's body wilted and dropped motionless.

Jake stood taking in deep breaths of air. He looked up and watched the clouds begin to move and the thunder and lightning stopped. A cool breeze blew across his body and face. As he watched the clouds moving, the morning sunlight peeked through the trees in the east. He dropped his bowie knife to the ground and raised his face to Heaven.

"Thank you." Jake whispered. "Thank you."

"Jake..." the voice of Tammy echoed through the trees. She ran to him and threw her arms around him and kissed his face ignoring the pain in her foot. He held his hands out from her because they were covered in the blood of the man that meant to do her harm. She forced her way into his embrace not caring about the blood.

"Are you okay?" He asked as she kissed his cheeks and then his forehead and then his cheeks again. She finally got to his lips where she stayed. Her long passionate kiss brought him completely back to life. "I guess you are then."

"Yes…yes…I am. Jake are you all right?" she asked as she held on to him in the early morning sunrise.

"Yeah, I want to get this blood off of me. He got me on the side so I need to wrap something around me." Jake said as he looked down at the blood on his shirt.

"Oh my…" Tammy said in shock as she reached down and tore the bottom of her dress. "Believe me Mrs. Edge won't mind a bit."

"Probably not," Jake said as he let Tammy look at the cut on his side. "Let's go down to the river and clean it some."

Beau Jamison walked up leading his horse. He had recovered all of the money that was taken in the bank robbery and took the weapons that were taken in both the Walker house and the Wright house. The cases were solved as well as the case in the adjoining county at the small dairy farm.

"I couldn't find your horse. I hope he's fine." Beau said as he approached Jake and Tammy.

Jake stopped and looked around. The sun was bringing sufficient light to see and the air was clean and moist. He puckered his lips and whistled and after a few seconds the buckskin appeared loping toward his master. Tammy reached out to him and rubbed his head between his eyes as the gelding took in samples of her scent. He knew it was Tammy and that she was now safe.

After Jake had washed up at the river and Tammy had doctored his side and the best she could they found a large hardwood tree to sit under where Jake wrapped part of Tammy's dress around her cut foot. Beau Jamison had rode to the main north road to wait for the people Mr. Edge had sent for, giving Jake and Tammy a chance to visit and to talk about the things that had happened earlier in the morning. Mostly they sat and looked at each other like they had been apart for months. He held her hand and savored the softness of her skin. He treasured her and her love for him. Her eyes seldom left him as they sat quietly in the shade of the trees.

"I am so sorry about Julius and I'm sorry this happened to you. Did these men harm you in any way?" Jake asked pulling her close to him and holding her with his gentle strength.

"Don't be sorry Jake...it wasn't your fault. These men came riding up and before I knew it one had shot Julius and grabbed me. We didn't know something like this was going to happen." Tammy said as she rested her head against Jake's chest and wept for her dead brother. Jake let her cry as long as she needed. He held her and tried to bring comfort as she grieved.

The serenity of the morning was interrupted by the sound of a wagon and riders approaching. Sheriff Sadler rode up with other men and Jeremiah. They all dismounted and walked up to Jake and Tammy. Sheriff Beau Jamison was also with them. Sadler surveyed the surroundings and noted the dead men that were lying about. He stopped making notes and turned and faced Jake.

"Sheriff Jamison here tells me you faced all of these and killed them." Sadler said with his knuckles resting against his hips.

Jake looked him dead in the eyes and said, "They had it coming."

Sadler looked over at Tammy. He walked up to her and took her hands in his. "So, you must be the pretty young lady that these men took."

"Yes sir." Tammy said, her sweet voice melting the heart of the Sheriff.

"Did they hurt you in any way?" Sadler asked with the voice of a father speaking to his daughter.

"No sir. Jake came and stopped them." She said with tears in her eyes.

Sadler dropped Tammy's soft hands and stepped up to Jake. He extended his right hand and said, "Good job," as Jake reached out and shook the Sheriff's hand.

"Well, it looks like we are in Anderson County which doesn't matter. I'll write the Sheriff over at the county seat and tell him what happened. He won't mind a bit that we cleaned up the mess." Sandler said as he turned to the men that rode with him. "Men, get this garbage picked up and we'll take them back to Crockett and dig them a hole."

Jake and Tammy rode alongside Beau Jamison as they headed back toward Augusta. They assured Beau that they could provide him a meal and a room for the night so he could get him a good night's rest for the ride back to Nacogdoches the next morning. He agreed to stay out at the ranch with Jake and Tammy. Little did they know, Mrs. Edge was going to fix a huge meal in celebration when she saw that Tammy had returned safe and unharmed. Mr. Edge and Horace Luker had already placed Julius under the sod after the Justice of the Peace had arrived to pronounce him deceased. A memorial service will be held graveside for Julius after church the next Sunday.

"I'm just so ready to be home again. I never want to stay away from there except the night before the wedding." Tammy said as she rode sitting across the front of Jake's saddle with her arms around his neck.

"Are you sure you don't want to wait a few more weeks to give yourself time to recover from losing Julius?" Jake asked as he looked down into her lovely hazel eyes.

Tammy held his gaze and said, "No, Julius would not want that."

He took in the beauty of her smile as he considered what she had just said. "You're right, that is what he would want for us. I just want to make you happy and keep you safe."

"You will and we will both miss Julius. Time will heal." Tammy said as she touched her hand to his face. She gave him a quick kiss on the lips and rested her head on his chest as they rode toward home.

"Sheriff, looks like them clouds may be coming back." Jeremiah said as the last body of the bank robbers was loaded onto the wagon. "I think that's the last one. I just want to put that one's head to where it won't roll off."

"Yeah, it looks like it's lodged in there good. Here we'll stick it up under his arm." Sadler said as he grabbed Sal's hair and shoved his bodiless head under the dead man's right arm pit.

"The saddle bags with the stolen money went with Sheriff Jamison. What do want me to do with this leather bag, Sheriff?" It ain't got no money in it?" Jeremiah asked.

Sadler looked at the leather haversack and spit tobacco juice on the ground. "Pitch it up there with them dead men. I'll go

365

through it when we get back to Crockett. We better get a move on, the wind is picking back up."

The wagon carrying the bodies of Luther, Archie and Cletus Frank along with Ned Brundage, the one they called Taterhead and Sal Maselli and his head moved along the river road headed back to Augusta and then on to Crockett. The wind began to blow harder and the driver of the wagon slapped the lines against the horse's rumps to pick up the pace. The wagon was jarred by the bumpy road and the movement jolted the bodies carried in the back of the wagon. The leather haversack owned and prized by Sal Maselli fell over and the flap that kept the bags contents inside came open. There were articles from inside that fell out and landed on the ground of the river road.

A leather bound book came to rest in the dirt alongside a gold watch. The pocket watch was engraved with two letters, "O C" in cursive. The leather bound book fell face down.

The sky began to once again fill with dark clouds. Thunder rolled and lightning pealed across the sky as the wind gained strength. The blades of grass that lined the sides of the road started bending and waving as the invisible current traveled through the river bottom. The tops of the trees danced as the eastern air traveled through their tops adding to the awesomeness of what was taking place. A gust caught the back flap of the leather book and it opened. Its pages begin to turn as if the Hand of God moved them. Lightning flashed and thunder boomed as the atmosphere announced the presence of its Creator. The pages stopped turning as bolts of powerful energy flashed in the Heavens. The lightning flashed bright on the pages of the book and onto a passage that read,

"To me belongeth vengeance, and recompence; their foot shall slide in due time: for the day of   their calamity is at hand, and the things that shall come upon them make haste."

Once again the wind moved the pages to the front cover of the book where once more it stopped. From under a flap in the cover of the book was a cardboard print, a picture. On the image, a beautiful young lady with two small babies, one on each arm sat for the photographer. She held them with love that glowed from the smile on her lovely face that must have provided the light for the picture. Her light colored hair hung down over her delicate shoulders.

There were words written on the opening page of the Bible. There in beautiful handwriting were these words, "Presented to our loving daughter Sarah, on the day her two precious children, Jacob and Flora were born...Much Love, Your Mother and Father."

The storm above suddenly stopped and the sun's light burst through the clouds. The wind granted the morning one more gust and the book closed.